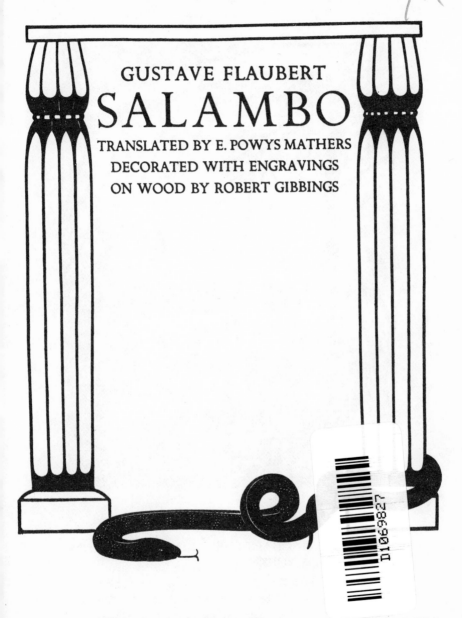

GUSTAVE FLAUBERT
SALAMBO
TRANSLATED BY E. POWYS MATHERS
DECORATED WITH ENGRAVINGS
ON WOOD BY ROBERT GIBBINGS

HART PUBLISHING COMPANY, INC. NEW YORK CITY

ISBN NO. 08055-0247-5
LIBRARY OF CONGRESS CATALOG CARD NO. 75-31406
MANUFACTURED IN THE UNITED STATES OF AMERICA

CONTENTS

PREFACE

In 1849, at the age of 28, Gustave Flaubert left his native France for the first time, embarking on a mission to the East for the French Chamber of Commerce. His itinerary called for him to tour Egypt, Nubia, Palestine, Syria, and Rhodes, and then return home through Asia Minor, Turkey, and Greece.

Flaubert greeted most of this journey with boredom and indifference. In Greece, however, he became fascinated by the historic settings he had previously only read about. He began to contemplate writing a novel depicting the ancient East, using actual historical figures as his characters. Thirteen years later, this novel, *Salambo,* appeared.

Flaubert has been called the creator of the principle of realism in modern French literature. He preached the pure objectivity of literature, its duty to hold a mirror up to nature, without judgment or comment by the author. Balzac had experimented with this concept earlier, but Flaubert brought to realism an unparalleled maturity and clarity of vision.

To Flaubert, the two great creative principles were Truth and Art. In his search for the first, no investigative reporter of today could equal his energy and resourcefulness. His researches were long, arduous, and incredibly meticulous; he would spend hours researching the data to be conveyed in a single phrase.

The perfection of his art, however, was to Flaubert even more important than his devotion to truth. In his own words, "What is said is nothing; the manner in which it is said is everything." For such a perfectionist, writing could only be a painstaking process: each of his novels took between five and eight years to complete, and each underwent many revisions before Flaubert would allow it to be published.

Following the publication of *Madame Bovary* in 1857, Flaubert journeyed to the ruins of ancient Carthage to begin his researches for the writing of *Salambo*. *Salambo* is a historical romance, set in the period of 240-238 B.C., just after the first Punic war between Carthage and Rome. It details the course of the Mercenary Revolt against Carthage which began when the resources of Carthage were exhausted and that city-state was unable to pay its mercenaries what it had promised them.

Salambo is considered by many to be Flaubert's masterpiece. It is not only the book in which his prodigious researches are displayed in their greatest depth; in it, he also gave his imagination its freest rein. Flaubert himself was partial to this novel—so much so that he would be offended when people referred to him as "the author of *Madame Bovary*."

One of Flaubert's achievements in *Salambo* is that, in spite of the enormous amount of intricate description of clothing, food, religious rites, and military strategies, he never flattens the personalities of his characters. Each is a vital, passionate, sympathetic human being, the better understood because the world in which the character exists is presented to us with such clarity and authenticity.

This product of Flaubert's ideal—the combination of truth and art—forces us to identify with even those actions which horrify us. The pain we feel as we read *Salambo* is the pain caused by the recognition of terrible truths, and it is this pain that is the measure of Flaubert's mastery.

N. S. G.

THE REVOLT OF THE MERCENARIES

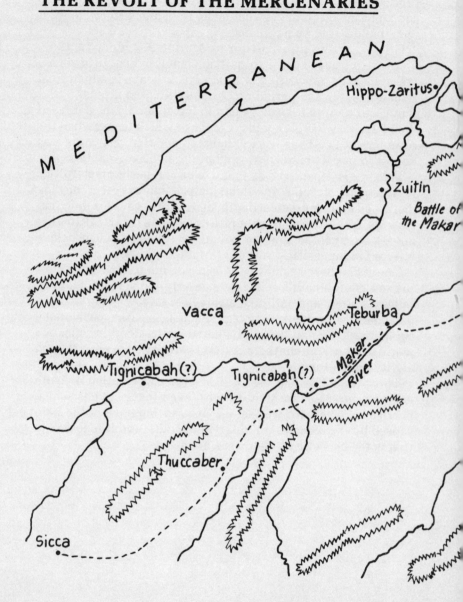

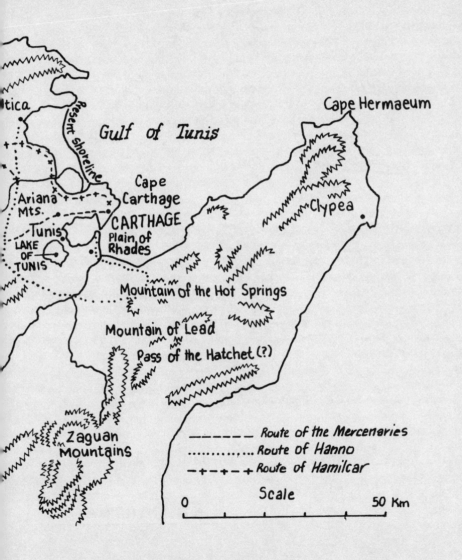

S E A

Utica

Present shoreline

Gulf of Tunis

Cape Hermaeum

Ariana Mts.

Cape Carthage

CARTHAGE

Clypea

Tunis

Plain of Rhades

LAKE OF TUNIS

Mountain of the Hot Springs

Mountain of Lead

Pass of the Hatchet (?)

Zaguan Mountains

————— Route of the Mercenaries
.... Route of Hanno
—+—+—+ Route of Hamilcar

Scale

0   50 Km

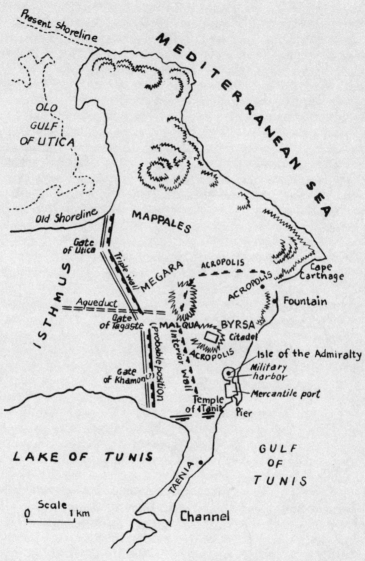

PUNIC CARTHAGE

THE FEAST

CHAPTER I

IT WAS IN THE GARDENS OF HAMILCAR AT ME-
GARA, AN OUTSKIRT OF CARTHAGE.

The soldiers he had commanded in Sicily were giving
themselves a great feast to celebrate the anniversary of
the battle of Eryx, and, as their master was away and they
were many, were eating and drinking to their heart's content.

The captains, who wore brazen buskins, had taken their
places in the middle way, under a purple, gold-fringed awning, which reached from the wall of the stables to the first of
the palace terraces; the private soldiers were scattered beneath the
trees, among which numerous flat-topped buildings were visible,
wine-presses and cellars, stores, bakehouses, and arsenals, and also
a courtyard for the elephants, pits for wild beasts, and a prison for
the slaves.

9

There were fig-trees round the kitchens; a wood of sycamores stretched away to immensities of green, where pomegranates glowed among the white tufts of the cotton-trees; vines, heavy with grapes, climbed into the branches of the pines; a field of roses blossomed under the plane-trees; lilies waved here and there upon the lawns; black sand, mixed with powdered coral, was spread on the pathways, & the cypress avenue made a double colonnade, as of green-foiled obelisks, from one end to the other, in the midst of all.

Far in the background the palace, built of yellow-veined Numidian marble, lifted its four terraced stories upon broad courses. With its immense straight ebony staircase, holding the prow of some conquered galley at the side of each step, its red doors each quartered with a black cross, its brass gratings protecting it below from scorpions, and its grills of gilded rods to close it above, it seemed to the soldiers as solemn and impenetrable in its savage opulence as Hamilcar's own face.

The Council had assigned them his house for the holding of this feast; the convalescents, who lay in the temple of Eshmun, had set forth at daybreak and dragged themselves thither on crutches; and others came each minute. They poured in ceaselessly by every path, as torrents into a lake; the kitchen slaves could be seen running, terrified and half-naked, through the trees; gazelles fled bleating over the lawns; the sun was setting, and the scent of the citrons deepened the exhalation from the sweating crowd.

Men of all nations were there, Ligurians and Lusitanians, Balearic Islanders, Negroes, and fugitives from Rome. Side by side with the heavy Dorian dialect one could hear loud Celtic syllables clanging like war chariots; Ionian endings fought with desert consonants, as harsh as a jackal's crying. The Greek was proclaimed by his slim body, the Egyptian by his high shoulders, and the Cantabrian by his mighty calves. Carians proudly nodded their helmet plumes, Cappadocian archers showed great flowers painted upon their bodies, and a few Lydians dined in women's dresses, with slippers and earrings. Others, who were smeared proudly all over with vermilion, looked like coral statues.

They lay upon cushions; they squatted around huge trays, and so ate; others, lying upon their bellies, reached out for lumps of meat

& gorged themselves, leaning on their elbows in the placid posture of lions dismembering their prey. Late-comers, leaning against the trees, watched the low tables half hidden under their scarlet coverings, and awaited their turn.

Since Hamilcar's kitchens were inadequate, the Council had provided slaves, dishes and couches. Oxen were roasting at great clear fires in the middle of the garden, which thus looked like a battlefield when the dead are being burned. Loaves dusted with aniseed vied with huge cheeses heavier than disks, and great bowls of wine with mighty water tankards, set close to gold filigree baskets full of flowers. Their eyes gleamed wide in delight at being at last free to gorge to their hearts' content; and here and there they were beginning to sing.

First they were served with birds in green sauce upon plates of red clay, decorated in black relief; then with every kind of shell-fish that is found on the Punic coasts, with broths thickened with wheat, beans and barley, and with cumin-spiced snails upon yellow amber dishes.

After this the tables were loaded with meats: antelopes still with their horns, peacocks still with their feathers, whole sheep cooked in sweet wine, camels' & buffaloes' haunches, hedgehogs in garum sauce, fried grasshoppers, and pickled dormice. Great pieces of fat were floating amid saffron in bowls of Tamrapanni wood. Everywhere was a lavish abundance of pickles, truffles, and asafoetida. There were pyramids of fruit tumbling upon honeycombs; and they had not forgotten to serve some of those silky-coated, red, fat-paunched little dogs, fattened on olive lees: a Carthaginian dish which was an abomination to other peoples. Their stomachs' greed was titillated by the excitement and wonder of such novel fare. The Gauls, with their long hair coiled upon the top of their heads, snatched at water-melons and lemons, and crunched them peel and all. Negroes who had never seen a crawfish, tore their faces on its red spines. The Greeks, who were smooth-shaven and whiter than marble, threw the leavings of their plates behind them; while herdsmen from Brutium, clad in wolf-skins, ate in silence, their faces buried in their plates.

Night fell. The awning over the cypress avenue was drawn back.

Oil lamps were burning in porphyry sconces, and their flickering frightened the sacred apes of the Moon, as they crouched in the tops of the cedars. Their screams made the soldiers laugh.

Brazen cuirasses grew alive with long wavering flames: gem-incrusted dishes leaped and sparkled in kaleidoscopic coruscation. In the mirrored convex sides of the wine bowls all was magnified and multiplied; the soldiers crowded about these, gazing with amazement at their own reflections, and bursting into laughter at the faces they made. They began to throw ivory stools and golden spattles at each other across the tables. They poured down their open throats all the Greek wines from the wine-skins, and the Campanian wines from amphoras, and the Cantabrian wines from the casks; and also jujube, cinnamon and lotus wines. They slithered in pools of spilled wine. The smoke from the meats twined with the reek of their breath as it rose into the leafage above them. The munching of jaws, the din of speech and song, the clashing of cups and the crash of Campanian vases shivering into a thousand pieces, or the limpid ring of a large silver dish, made one confusion of sound.

In their advancing drunkenness they gave vent more and more freely to their grievances against Carthage.

Being exhausted by the war, the Republic had allowed all the returning troops to swarm into the city. Gisco, their general, had been prudent enough, however, to send them back severally in detachments, so as to lighten the task of paying them off; and the Council had believed that they would in the end agree to some reduction: but for the present, since there were no funds available for their payment, the troops were an embarrassment. Also the public confused this debt with the 3200 Euboic talents exacted by Lutatius and consequently the army was considered Carthage's enemy no less than Rome. The Mercenaries understood this, and their indignation broke out in threats & rioting. At last they asked leave to meet together in celebration of one of their victories, and this the peace party granted; for thus they could seize an opportunity for revenging themselves on Hamilcar, who had been so largely responsible for the prolongation of the war. It had been in spite of all his efforts that it had come to an end; and, despairing of Carthage, he had resigned the command of the Mercenaries in favour of Gisco. The Council had decided to entertain the soldiers at Hamilcar's palace, since this would involve him to a certain extent in the hatred felt towards themselves. Moreover, the expense would be very heavy, & nearly the whole of it would fall on him.

Proud of having proved their power over the Republic, the Mercenaries thought that now at last they would return to their homes with the price of their blood safe in the hoods of their cloaks. But their hardships loomed behind them through the mists of drunkenness as something prodigious and but poorly rewarded. They showed one another their wounds, and spoke of their battles and marches, and of hunting at home. They imitated the cries and bounding of wild animals. They made bestial wagers, burying their heads in the amphoras and drinking so without cease, like thirsty dromedaries. A giant Lusitanian, carrying a man at each arm's length, ran about the tables, belching fire through his nostrils. Some Lacedaemonians, still wearing their cuirasses, leaped up and down heavily. Some walked about like women, making obscene gestures; others stripped naked and wrestled like gladiators among the drinking cups; & a band of Greeks danced round a vase painted with nymphs, while a Negro pounded upon a brazen buckler with an ox's bone.

Suddenly they heard a plaintive chant, a chant both loud and sweet, rising and falling upon the air like the wing-beats of a wounded bird.

It was the slaves singing in the slave prison. Some of the soldiers jumped up and ran off to set them free.

These came back shouting through the dust and driving some twenty men before them, who were conspicuous by reason of their greater paleness. Their shaven heads were covered by little conical caps of black felt; they all wore wooden sandals, which yet rang out the metallic clang of rolling chariots.

When they reached the cypress avenue, they were lost amid a crowd of questioners. But one of them stood apart from the rest. The long slashed weals on his shoulders could be seen through the rents in his tunic. Drooping his chin, and with his eyes half closed against the dazzling torch-light, he looked mistrustingly about him; but, seeing that none of these armed men meant him any harm, he heaved a great sigh; he stammered, grimacing through the bright tears that bathed his face; then he seized a brimming wine-cup by its ringed handles, raised it straight up in the air to the length of his manacled arms and, so holding it and looking to heaven, said:

'Hail first to thee, Baal-Eshmun, the deliverer, whom the men of my country call Aesculapius! And to you, Spirits of the fountains, of light, and of the woods! And to you, O gods hidden beneath mountains and in caves of the earth! And to you, strong men in gleaming armour who have set me free!'

Then he lowered the cup & told his story. His name was Spendius, and the Carthaginians had taken him in the battle of the Aegates: and once more he thanked the Mercenaries, speaking in Greek, Ligurian and Punic; he kissed their hands; finally he congratulated them on the banquet, but expressed surprise at not seeing the cups of the Sacred Legion there. These cups, which bore a vine of emeralds set in each of their six golden faces, belonged to a regiment composed exclusively of the tallest young patricians. They were a privilege, almost a sacrament; and nothing, therefore, in the treasury of the Republic was so coveted by the Mercenaries. They detested the Legion on account of these cups, and some of them had been known to risk their lives for the incalculable pleasure of drinking out of them.

So they sent for the cups to be brought to them. They were in the keeping of the merchant fraternities of the Syssitia, who shared a communal table; and the slaves came back to report that at that hour all the members of the Syssitia were asleep.

'Let them be wakened!' answered the Mercenaries.

The slaves returned from this second errand to explain that the cups were locked up in a temple.

'Let it be opened!' they replied.

And when the slaves tremblingly confessed that Gisco, the general, had charge of them, they cried:

'Let him bring them!'

Presently Gisco appeared at the far end of the garden with a bodyguard of the Sacred Legion. His full black cloak, which was fastened over his head to a golden mitre starred with precious stones, & hung all about him down to his horse's hooves, seemed from afar to be one in colour with the night. Only his white beard, his glittering head-dress, and the triple necklace of wide blue plaques jangling against his breast, could at all be seen.

The soldiers greeted him with loud shouts on his appearance, all crying together:

'The cups! The cups!'

He began by declaring that, in view of their bravery, they were worthy of them. The crowd howled joyful applause.

This he well knew, he who had been their general out there and had returned with the last cohort on the last galley!

'True! It is true!' they said.

But, continued Gisco, they should reflect that the Republic had respected their various nationalities, customs and religions, and that they enjoyed absolute freedom in Carthage! As for the cups of the Sacred Legion, they were private property.

Suddenly, from beside Spendius, a Gaul hurled himself over the tables and ran straight up to Gisco, threatening him with two whirling naked swords.

Without exerting himself, the general struck him on the head with his heavy ivory staff; & the Barbarian fell. The Gauls howled, and their fury, spreading to all the rest, might well have made short work of the legionaries. Gisco shrugged his shoulders, seeing the latter grow pale: his courage would not avail him against these frenzied animals. It would be better to avenge himself later by some trick; he signed to his escort and slowly moved away. Then, facing the Mercenaries from under the gateway, he cried that they would regret their behaviour.

They returned to their feasting. But Gisco might come again, and, by investing the suburb which lay against the outer fortifications of the city, crush them against the walls. This thought made them feel lonely in spite of their numbers; and they grew afraid of the great town sleeping beneath them in the darkness, with its bewildering flights of steps, its tall black houses, and its mysterious gods who were more implacable even than its people. Lights were

creeping far apart across the distant harbour, and there were lights
in the temple of Khamon. They thought of Hamilcar. Where was
he? Why had he forsaken them the moment peace was declared?
His quarrel with the Council was nothing, surely, but a trick devised for their destruction. They let their unassuaged hatred loose
upon him, cursing him, and working one another into a frenzy of
their own anger against him. It was at this point that there came a
stampede towards a certain spot under the plane-trees. A Negro
lay writhing and beating the ground with his limbs, his eyes in a
fixed stare, his neck screwed round, & foam upon his lips. Someone shouted that he was poisoned. Then they all thought that
they had been poisoned. They fell upon the slaves; a dizziness of
destruction rushed like a whirlwind among the drunken army.
They struck about them at random, fracturing and killing; some
hurled torches into the leafage; others, leaning over the balustrade
round their pit, shot the lions to death with arrows; others, more
venturesome, ran towards the elephants, to mutilate their trunks
and squander their ivory.

Meanwhile some Balearic slingers who had rounded the corner of
the palace to pillage at greater ease, were checked by a high barrier
of malacca cane. They cut the binding thongs with their daggers
and broke through, to find themselves at the foot of the facade that
fronted upon Carthage, in another garden filled with carefully
tended plants. Lines of white flowers, sweeping in harmonious
parabolas, showed as rockets of stars upon the azure earth. Shadow-
filled bushes breathed out warm honey scent, and the tree-stems
smeared with cinnabar looked like pillars oozing blood. In the
middle were twelve pedestals, each bearing a great hollow ball of
glass filled with a vague reddish glow, like gigantic eyes still flickering with life. The soldiers lighted their way with torches, as they
stumbled down the deeply cultivated slope.

They saw a little lake, divided by blue stone partitions into a number of basins. The water was so clear that the torch flames quivered
to the very bottom, showing a bed of white pebbles & dust of gold.
There came a bubbling, and floating spangles of light, and then
great fish with gems about their mouths rose towards the surface.

Laughing boisterously, the soldiers slipped their fingers into the gills of these and carried them back to the tables.

They were the fish of the House of Barca, and each was descended from those primordial lotes which had hatched the mystic egg that hid the Goddess. The idea of committing sacrilege gave a new zest to the Mercenaries' greed; they quickly lit fires under brazen bowls and gleefully watched these splendid fish struggling in the water as it came to the boil

The soldiers surged and jostled together. They had lost all fear, and now started to drink again. Great wet gouts of perfume dripped from their foreheads on to their torn tunics; they planted their fists upon the tables, which seemed to be rocking like ships at sea beneath them, and rolled great drunken eyes to devour what they could no longer grasp with their hands. Some trampled among the dishes on the purple table covers, kicking ivory stools & phials of Tyrian glass to pieces. Their songs were interspersed with the death-rattle of slaves in their last throe among the broken cups. They called for wine, for meat, for gold. They bleated for women. They raved in a hundred tongues. Some of them imagined themselves at the baths because of the fume and reek about them, or, because they could see green leaves, thought they were hunting and ran upon their fellows as upon wild beasts. One after another all the trees caught fire, and the long white whorls rising from their tall greenery made them seem like volcanoes on the point of eruption. The uproar redoubled: the wounded lions were roaring in the darkness.

The palace was lit to its topmost terrace in a single flash, the central door opened, and a woman, Hamilcar's daughter, appeared on the threshold, robed in black. She descended the first flight of steps, slanting down across the first story, then the second, and then the third, and halted on the last terrace at the head of the galley-flanked stairway. She stood motionless with lowered head, looking down at the soldiers.

On each side behind her stood a long line of pale men in white, red-bordered robes which fell straight to their feet. They were bald, & had no eyebrows. In their ring-spangled hands they bore huge lyres, and were all shrilly singing a hymn to the Divinity of Carthage. These were the eunuch priests of the Temple of Tanit, whom Salambo often summoned to her house.

At last she came down the steps between the galleys, the priests following her. She went into the cypress avenue, walking slowly between the tables set apart for the captains, who drew back a little as they watched her pass.

Her hair, violet powdered and gathered into a tower in the manner of Canaanitish maids, added to her stature. Chains of pearls fell from her temples to the corners of the half-open rose pomegranate which was her mouth. Upon her breast was a cluster of glowing stones, iridescent as murry scales. Her diamonded arms issued bare from her sleeveless tunic, which was of a deep black starred with red flowers. Between her ankles she wore a golden chainlet to regulate her steps, and her great dark purple mantle, made from an unknown fabric, trailed behind her, shaping itself to a wide wave billowing upon each of her footsteps.

From time to time the priests thrummed an almost muted chord upon their lyres; and between the notes of this music the faint sound of the little golden chain was heard, and the regular fall of her paper-reed sandals.

No one as yet had knowledge of her. It was only known that she lived in a seclusion of pious practices. Soldiers had seen her at night on the roof of her palace kneeling before the stars, wrapped about with fragrant clouds of incense. It was the moon that had made her so pale, & there was something of the gods shrouding her in a subtle haze. Her eyes seemed to look afar, beyond all earthly spaces. She walked with bowed head, holding a little ebony lyre in her right hand.

They heard her murmuring:

'Dead! All dead! No more will you come to the call of my voice as when, sitting by the lake, I threw water-melon seeds into your mouths! The mystery of Tanit turned in the depths of your eyes; they were clearer than crystal river-drops.'

And she called them by their names, which were the names of the months: 'Siv, Sivan, Tammuz, Elul, Tishri, Shebar! Ah! Goddess, have pity on me!'

The soldiers, without understanding what she said, crowded round her in open-mouthed wonder at her raiment. She turned a long look of dismay upon them, and then, sinking her head between her shoulders and flinging out her arms, she said again and again:

'What have you done? What have you done? You had bread and meats and oil for your pleasuring, and all the malabathrum of the store-houses! I had oxen brought from Hecatompylos; I sent hunters into the desert for you!'

Her voice rose; her cheeks flushed purple; and she went on:

'Where think you that you are? In a conquered town, or in your Lord's palace. And who is that Lord? My father Hamilcar, the Suffete, the servant of the Baalim! He it was who refused to lay down before Lutatius those arms of yours, which are now red with the blood of his slaves! Have you in your own lands any more skilful battle leader? See! Our palace steps are laden with the spoils of our victories! Finish your work! Burn it! I shall take the spirit of my House away with me, my black serpent who sleeps up yonder upon a bed of lotus leaves! I shall whistle and he will follow me; and if I take sea upon a galley he will speed in the wake of my ship over the foaming waters.'

Her fine nostrils quivered: she crushed her nails against the jewels upon her breast: her eyes grew tender, and again she spoke:

'Alas, poor Carthage! Woeful city! No longer have you for your defence the mighty men of old who quested across great oceans and built temples upon their shores. About you was centred the labour of every nation, and your harvests were cradled upon the plains of the sea, furrowed by your oars.'

Then sne began to sing the gests of Melkarth, the god of the Sidonians, her family's first father.

She told how he climbed the mountains of Ersiphonia, of his journey from Tartessus, and of his war with Masisabal to avenge the Queen of the serpents:

'He hunted the she-monster into the forest, and her tail wound over the dead leaves like a rivulet of silver. He came to a clearing where women, who were dragons from the buttocks down, stood upright upon their tails about a great fire. The moon was a shining disc of blood rimmed with a pale circle: the forked harpoons of their scarlet tongues curled out to the very edge of the flames.'

Without pausing, Salambo told how Melkarth, after vanquishing Masisabal, nailed her severed head to the prow of his ship.

'At each onslaught of the waves it was dashed beneath the foam; but the sun embalmed it; it grew harder than gold; yet its eyes did not cease from weeping, and ever its tears kept falling into the water.'

All this she sang in an old Canaanitish idiom, not understood by the Barbarians. They wondered what she could be saying to them, and what words she pointed with those terrifying gestures; climbing about her upon tables, couches and sycamore boughs, open-mouthed and with craning necks, they tried to grasp the mystery of these legends which hovered before their minds like cloud phantoms, veiled in the misty obscurity of the Birth of the Gods.

Only the beardless priests understood Salambo. Their wrinkled hands were poised trembling over their lyre strings, from which they now and again drew a wailing cadence of music: being frailer than old women, they shivered as much with mystic ecstasy as from their fear of the soldiers. The Barbarians took no heed of them: they were engrossed in the maiden's singing.

None gazed at her so ardently as a young Numidian chief, who sat at one of the captains' tables among his fellow countrymen. His belt so bristled with throwing-knives that it made a lump under his wide cloak, which hung by a leather thong from his temples. The stuff fell in two great folds about his shoulders, screening his face in a shadow, so that only the flashing fire from his two eyes could be seen at all. It was chance that had brought him to the feast, for his father had placed him in the Barca house, following the usual practice of kings to send their children into noble families with a view to some future alliance. During his six months' residence, Narr'Havas had never seen Salambo; and now, squatting on his heels, with his beard brushing the hilts of his javelins, he watched her with distended nostrils like a leopard crouching in the bamboo canes.

Across the tables sat a gigantic Libyian with short crisped black hair. He had stripped to his soldier's jerkin, and its brazen plates were tearing the purple upholstery of the couch. A necklet of silver moons was tangled in the hairs on his chest. His face was mottled with splashes of blood; he was leaning on his left elbow with his great mouth agape, smiling.

Salambo was no longer at her sacred singing. With womanly delicacy she addressed the Barbarians each in his own vernacular, hoping to calm their fury. To the Greeks she spoke Greek, turning from them to the Ligurians, the Campanians and the Negroes; and each of these recaptured in her voice the soothing sweetness of his native land. She was rapt away by thoughts of Carthage, and now she sang of historic battles against Rome; and the men applauded. She was fired by the glint of the naked swords; she threw out her arms and cried aloud. She dropped her lyre, and was silent; pressing her two hands to her heart, she stood for some minutes with closed eyes, sensing the seething emotions of all these men.

Matho, the Libyan, leaned towards her. Mechanically she went up to him and, understanding his pride and hoping thus to conciliate the army, poured a long stream of wine into a golden cup for him.

'Drink!' she said.

He took the cup and was carrying it to his lips, when a Gaul, the same whom Gisco had struck down, slapped him across the shoulder, uttering boisterous jests in his native tongue. Spendius was near at hand, and offered to interpret them.

'Speak!' said Matho.

'May the gods protect you; you shall be rich. When will the marriage be?'

'What marriage?'

'Yours! For with us,' said the Gaul, 'when a woman gives a soldier drink, it is an invitation to her bed.'

The words were scarcely spoken before Narr'Havas leaped up, drew a javelin from his belt and, resting his right foot against the edge of the table, hurled it at Matho.

It sang between the cups and, piercing the Libyan's arm, pinned it to the table with such force that the shaft stood quivering in air.

Matho quickly snatched it forth; but he was naked and unarmed: finally he raised the over-laden table in both arms and flung it towards Narr'Havas, right into the middle of the crowd that rushed between them. Numidians and others pressed so closely together that they could not draw their swords. Matho battered his way through them with his head; but when he raised it, Narr'Havas had disappeared. He glared round for him. Salambo too had gone.

Then turning his eyes towards the palace he saw the red door with the black cross closing on high, and bounded towards it.

He was seen running between the prows of the galleys, and again came in sight as he rushed up the three stairways to the red door and dashed his whole weight against it. Gasping for breath, he leaned against the wall to keep from falling.

A man had followed him, and through the darkness (for the lights of the feast were cut off by an angle of the palace) he recognised Spendius.

'Begone!' he said.

Without answering, the slave began to tear his tunic with his teeth; then kneeling beside Matho he tenderly took his arm, and felt in the dark for the wound.

A ray of moonlight, escaping from between the clouds, showed Spendius a gaping hole half-way up the arm. He bandaged it; but the other said irritably:

'Leave me! Leave me!'

'No!' answered the slave. 'You freed me from the slave prison. I am yours! You are my master! Command me!'

Matho walked all round the terrace, keeping close to the wall. He strained his ears at every step, & thrust searching glances through the gilded rush curtains into the silent rooms. At last he stopped with a despairing look.

'Listen!' said the slave. 'Oh, do not despise me because I am weak! I have lived in the palace. I can creep like a viper through the cracks in its walls. Come! There is an ingot of gold under every flag-stone in the Chamber of the Ancestors; there is an underground passage to their tombs.'

'What of it?' asked Matho.

Spendius was silent.

They were on the terrace. Before them stretched a mighty mass of darkness that seemed to hold vague hummocks, like the waves of a black and petrified ocean.

But a ribbon of light came up from the East. Far down to the left, the canals of Megara began to streak the green of the gardens with their white meanderings. The cone-shaped roofs of heptagonal temples, and the stairways, terraces and ramparts were slowly being etched against the paleness of the dawn; the peninsula of Carthage was girdled about with surging white foam, while the emerald sea seemed frozen in the morning freshness. As the rose in the sky grew larger, tall houses, poised upon the hill-side, stood out together like a herd of black goats coming down from the mountain. The empty streets stretched out to lengthening distance; there was no movement in the palms that here and there topped the walls; the brimming cisterns were as silver shields left lying in the courts; the beacon on the promontory of Hermaeum began to pale. In the cypress wood on the summit of the Acropolis the horses of Eshmun thrilled to the growing light and, with their hooves pawing the marble parapet, neighed towards the sun.

It rose; and Spendius uttered a cry and lifted his arms. Everything was suffused with a quickening red glow, for it was as if the god had riven his very body, and were pouring the golden rain of his blood upon Carthage in full showers of light. Galley beaks glittered, the roof of Khamon seemed a-flame, and, through their opening doors, glimmers of light could be seen in the far recesses of the temples. Heavy carts from the country went lumbering over the stone streets; & dromedaries came stepping down the gradients under their bales. Money-changers opened up the tilts of their shops in the market squares. Storks took wing, and there was a fluttering of white sails. The tambourines of the sacred courtesans sounded from the grove of Tanit, and smoke was beginning to rise from the furnaces on the Point of Mappales where clay coffins were baked.

Spendius leaned over the terrace; his teeth chattered, and he said again and again:

'Ah, yes! Yes, Master! I see now why you scorned to loot the house just now.'

The sibilant hissing of his voice seemed to arouse Matho; but he did not appear to understand. Spendius continued:

'Ah, what riches! And their owners have not a single blade with which to defend them!'

Then, pointing with his right hand to some people creeping about the sand outside the mole looking for grains of gold:

'See!' he said. 'Even as each of those poor wretches so is the Republic: she sinks her greedy arms into every shore, crouching upon the sea fronts, and the roar of the waves so fills her ear that she cannot hear the approaching tread of a conqueror behind her.'

Spendius understood that an infinite unrest possessed him, and dared say no more.

The trees behind them were still smoking, & from their blackened boughs the half-burned bodies of apes dropped among the dishes from time to time. Drunken soldiers were snoring open-mouthed by the side of dead bodies, & those who were not asleep were bowing their heads, being dazzled by the glare of day. The trampled ground was awash with red pools, and the elephants swung their bleeding trunks between the palings of their pens. In the open granaries sacks of spilled wheat could be seen, and below the gate there was a dense barrier of cars piled up there by the Barbarians; the peacocks, perched in the cedars, spred their tails and were beginning to screech.

Matho kept so utterly still that Spendius was amazed. He had grown even paler than before, and followed something on the horizon with a fixed gaze, resting his two hands upon the skirting of the terrace. Bending forward, Spendius at last discovered the thing he stared at: a golden speck was spinning in the dust far off on the road to Utica; the nave of a chariot drawn by two mules; a slave ran at the head of the pole, holding the bridle. Two women were seated in the chariot. The manes of the beasts were puffed out between their ears in the Persian manner, under a network of blue pearls. Spendius recognised them, and strangled a cry.

A great veil floated in the wind behind.

He drew Matho along to the other end of the terrace and showed him the garden, where the soldiers' swords hanging on the trees glanced in the sun:

'But here are strong men goaded to hatred, and nothing, neither family ties, nor allegiance, nor their gods bind them to Carthage.'

Matho still leaned against the wall: Spendius came nearer and went on in a lowered voice:

'Do you understand me, soldier? We should go clad in purple like satraps. We should bathe in perfumes; and I also, even I, should hold slaves! Are you not tired of sleeping on the hard ground, of drinking the camp vinegar, and of everlasting trumpet calls? In a little while, surely, you will find rest: when they pull off your cuirass and throw your body to the vultures! Or, maybe, you will hobble on a stick from door to door, blind, lame and broken, telling stories of your youth to little children and brine-pickle sellers. Remember all the injustices of your chiefs, camps in the snow, forced marches in the sun, tyrannies of discipline, and the ever present threat of crucifixion! And, after all these hardships, they have rewarded you with a necklet of honour, just as they put a collar of bells upon an ass to distract it as it plods along, and to make it forget its weariness. A man like you, braver than Pyrrhus! And yet, if you but would! Ah, how happy you will be in great cool halls, soothed by the music of lyres and couched upon flowers, and having jesters and women! Do not tell me that all this is impossible. Have not the Mercenaries already taken hold of Rhegium and other fortified places in Italy? Who can hinder you? Hamilcar is away; and the people hold the rich in execration; Gisco is encompassed by cowards, and can do nothing. But you are brave! They will obey you. Lead them! Carthage is ours; let us fall upon her!'

'No!' said Matho. 'The curse of Moloch is heavy upon me. I felt it in her eyes; & but now I saw a black ram start back in a temple.'

Looking about him, he then said:

'Where is she?'

AT SICCA

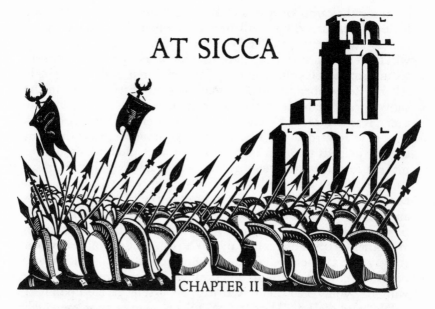

CHAPTER II

TWO DAYS LATER THE MERCENARIES LEFT CARTHAGE.
They had each been given a piece of gold, on the understanding
that they should go into camp at Sicca; and had been told in terms
of the most ingratiating flattery:
'You are the saviours of Carthage! But if you stayed in the city
you would bring starvation upon it and drain it dry. Go, therefore! Be gracious in this matter, and the Republic will prove
grateful. We are about to levy immediate taxes; you shall be paid
in full, and we will equip galleys to take you back to your native
lands.'
They could find no answer to such arguments. These men were
used to war, and grew weary of the city: it was not hard to per-
suade them; and the people stood upon the walls to watch them
go away.
They straggled pell-mell through the street of Khamon and the
Cirta Gate, archers side by side with hoplites, captains with private
soldiers, Lusitanians with Greeks. They marched with a bold step,
making their heavy buskins ring on the flag-stones. Their armour

was dinted with catapult shots, and their faces were tanned and darkened by the heat of battles. They shouted hoarsely through their thick beards; their torn coats of mail jangled against their sword hilts, & through gaps in their bronze their naked limbs could be seen, as terrible as war engines. Macedonian lances, battle-axes, spears, felt caps and brazen helmets swung all together in one wave of motion. They pressed so thickly into the street that it seemed as if its walls must crack; a mighty river of armed soldiers poured between the high, six-storied, bitumen-covered houses. From behind their iron or reed gratings, women with veiled heads silently watched the Barbarians pass.

Terraces, battlements and walls were hidden by the swarm of black-garbed Carthaginians; and the sailors' tunics were as splashes of blood against this sombre mass. Nearly naked children, clinging to creeper-clad columns, or astride palm-branches, pointed and made signs to one another. Some of the Elders of the city stood at intervals upon the galleries of the towers; the sight of a man with a long beard standing here and there as if in a dream struck all as strange: he looked, in the distance, dim as a phantom, still as stone.

The same anxiety weighed upon everyone; it was feared that the Barbarians might realise their strength and take it into their heads to stay. But they were leaving with such good faith that the Carthaginians gained confidence and mingled with the soldiers, overwhelming them with embraces & vows of friendship. They threw them perfumes, flowers, and silver pieces. They gave them amulets against sickness; but they had spat three times upon them first to bring death, or had put jackal's hair in them to sap the courage of their wearers' hearts. Aloud they called down the blessing of Melkarth upon them, and, under their breath, his curse.

Following the army in a mob came the baggage, the beasts of burden and the stragglers.

The sick were groaning upon dromedaries, or hobbling along with the stumps of spears. The drunkards were carrying skins of wine away with them; the gluttons had quarters of meat, cakes and fruits, butter wrapped in fig leaves, & snow in canvas bags. Some had sunshades in their hands or parrots on their shoulders. Some were leading dogs, gazelles, or panthers. Libyan women mounted upon asses were shouting insults at those negresses who had left the brothels of Malqua to follow the soldiers: many of them were suckling their children, who were strapped to their breasts by leather thongs. The mules, pricked on at the sword point, bent their backs under their load of tents; and there were numbers of servants and water-carriers, hollow-cheeked, jaundiced with fever and filthy with vermin, the scum of Carthage, who had thrown in their lot with the Barbarians.

When they had passed, the gates were shut behind them; but the people did not come down from the walls. The army quickly filled the whole width of the isthmus.

It split into irregular clusters. Soon the lances looked like tall blades of grass, and finally vanished in a train of dust. When the soldiers looked back towards Carthage they could see nothing but its long walls with their naked crenelles outlined against the low sky.

The Barbarians heard a great shout. They thought that some of their fellows (for they did not know their own number) had remained in the town and were amusing themselves by looting a temple. This made them laugh aloud; and then they continued on their way.

They were glad to be marching all together in the open country once again; and some Greeks were singing the old song of the Mamertines:

'With my lance and my sword I plough and I reap; it is I who am master of the house! The weaponless man falls at my knees and calls me Lord and Mighty King.'

They leaped and shouted, and the merriest of them began to tell stories: their time of hardship was over. When they reached Tunis, some of them noticed that a troop of Balearic slingers was missing. But no doubt it was not far off, & they thought no more about it.

Some found lodging in the houses, others camped at the foot of the walls; and the townspeople came out to talk with them.

All through the night fires were seen burning on the skyline towards Carthage, and the flames stretched like giant torches across the motionless lake. No one in the army knew what festival was being celebrated.

Next day the Barbarians passed through country in full cultivation. Their route was bordered by a succession of patricians' farms; irrigating trenches meandered through the palm woods; there were long green lines of olive-trees; rose-coloured mists hovered in the gorges of the hills; blue mountains towered in the background. A warm wind was blowing. Chameleons crawled over the broad cactus leaves.

The Barbarians went more slowly.

They marched on in isolated groups, or lagged behind one another at great intervals. They ate the grapes from the vines as they passed them. They lay on the grass, and gazed in wonder at the great, artificially twisted horns of the oxen; at sheep which were clothed in skins to protect their wool; at the furrows intersecting each other in lozenges; at ploughshares like ships' anchors; & at pomegranate trees sprayed with the juice of silphium. Such fertility and such cunning contrivances much amazed them.

In the evening they lay down upon their tents without unfolding them; and, as they fell asleep with their faces turned to the stars, yearned again for the feast of Hamilcar.

At noon on the following day they halted on the bank of a river, among oleander bushes, and quickly threw aside their spears and bucklers and belts. They shouted as they splashed the water over themselves; they drank from their helmets, or lapped lying on their stomachs among the baggage animals, whose packs were slipping from their backs.

Spendius, seated on a dromedary stolen from Hamilcar's parks, saw Matho at a distance, with his arm slung across his breast, bareheaded and with lowered face, watering his mule and watching the river flow. At once he ran through the crowd, calling to him: 'Master! Master!'

Matho barely troubled to return his greeting; but Spendius was undisturbed by this, and attended behind him as he walked; ever and again he turned anxious eyes back towards Carthage.

He was the son of a Greek rhetorician and a Campanian prostitute. He had first grown rich by trafficking in women; then, being ruined by a shipwreck, he had joined the Samnite shepherds in their war against Rome. He had been taken prisoner, and had escaped; he had been re-taken, had worked in the quarries, had panted in the vapour baths, had shrieked under torture, had passed through the hands of many masters, and known all the faces of fury. One day, in despair, he had flung himself into the sea from the top of the trireme in which he was rowing. Some sailors had picked him up half dead and taken him to the slave prison of Megara at Carthage. Since the Romans had stipulated for the return of their fugitives, he had taken advantage of all the confusion to escape with the soldiers.

During the whole of the march he stayed by Matho: he brought him food, he helped him to dismount, he spread a rug for his head in the evening. Matho was at last touched by these attentions, and gradually unsealed his lips.

He had been born by the gulf of Syrtis. His father had taken him on a pilgrimage to the temple of Ammon. Later he had hunted elephants in the Garamantian forests. Then he had entered the service of Carthage, and had been made tetrarch at the capture of Drepanum. The Republic owed him four horses, twenty-three Greek bushels of wheat, and a winter's pay. He feared the gods, and wished to die in his native land.

Spendius told him of his travels, and of the peoples and temples he had visited. He could do many things: he could make sandals, and boar-spears, and nets; he could tame wild beasts, and cook fish.

At times he would break off to utter a hoarse guttural cry, at which Matho's mule would quicken its pace: the others hastened to keep up with it, and then Spendius would begin again, but a prey all the time to his anxiety. This was appeased by the evening of the fourth day.

They were walking side by side to the right of the army on the flank of a hill; and below them stretched the plain, to be lost at last in the night mists. The stream of soldiers, as they looked down upon it, seemed like a curling wave in the twilight. From time to time it rose upon moonlit hillocks; then the spear-heads became twinkling stars and the helmets gleamed for an instant; these vanished, to be followed continually by others. Distant flocks were roused from their sleep and bleated, and something of infinite peace seemed to fall upon the earth.

Spendius, his head thrown back and with eyes half-closed, drank the fresh of the wind in great gasps; he spread out his arms, moving his fingers the better to feel its caress as it lapped his body. He was carried away by renewed hopes of vengeance, and pressed his hand upon his mouth to check his sobs; half swooning with intoxication, he let fall the halter of his dromedary, which went forward with long regular strides. Matho had again fallen into his brooding; his legs hung down to the ground, and the grass made a continuous rustling against his buskins.

The road wound interminably along. After each plain they crossed they came inevitably to a round plateau; then down again into a valley, and ever the horizon was blocked by mountains which seemed to glide away from them, keeping pace with their advance. From time to time the green of the tamarisks was cleft by a river, which would then lose itself round the bend of a hill. Here and there a great rock towered like the prow of a ship or the plinth of some vanished colossus.

At regular intervals they met with little square temples, built for pilgrims on their way to Sicca. These were close shut like tombs. The Libyans thundered upon the doors for admission; but no one answered from inside.

Later the country became more sparsely cultivated. They came suddenly upon strips of sand bristling with thorny thickets. Flocks of sheep were browsing among the stones, and a woman with a blue fleece about her hips was tending them: at first sight of the soldiers' spear-heads among the rocks, she fled screaming.

They were marching through a sort of great passage bordered by two chains of reddish hillocks, when their nostrils were assaulted by a nauseous stench, and they became aware of a strange object in the top of a carob tree. From above the leaves stood out a lion's head.

They ran forward: a lion was nailed by his four limbs to a cross, like a criminal. His great muzzle drooped upon his breast, and his two fore-legs, half hidden by the abundance of his mane, were spread wide like the wings of a bird. His ribs stood out severally under his taut skin; his hind legs, pierced by one nail, were drawn up a little; and black blood had trickled through his hair to form stalactites at the end of his tail, which hung straight down the upright of the cross. The soldiers made sport round him; they called him Consul, and Roman Citizen, and threw pebbles at his eyes to drive away the gnats.

A hundred paces further on they saw two more; then there came suddenly into view a long line of crosses with lions upon them. Some had been so long dead that nothing was left upon the wood but fragments of their skeletons; the jaws of others, being half decomposed, were twisted into horrible grimaces; some of them were enormous, and the trees upon which they were crucified bowed under their weight; they swayed in the wind, while flights of crows kept up an incessant wheeling in the air about their heads. This was how the Carthaginian peasants took vengeance upon any wild beast they captured, hoping to scare away others by such an example. The Barbarians no longer laughed, but fell into an enduring astonishment. 'What manner of people is this,' they thought, 'which amuses itself by crucifying lions!'

They were, moreover, & especially those from the North, vaguely uneasy, troubled, and already ailing. The aloe thorns scratched their hands; great mosquitoes kept humming about their ears, and dysentry had broken out in the army. They were weary because Sicca was not yet in sight, and were afraid of losing themselves and wandering into the desert, the country of sand and terror. Many were even for going no further; and some started back towards Carthage.

At last on the seventh day, after long skirting of the foot of a mountain, they turned sharply to the right and saw a line of walls, built upon white rocks and merging into them. Suddenly the whole town rose in view. Blue, yellow and white veils fluttered upon the walls in the crimson blush of evening, as the priestesses of Tanit ran out to receive the men. They stood ranged upon the ramparts, beating tambourines, plucking lyres, and shaking cymbals; and the rays of the sun, setting behind them in the mountains of Numidia, shot between their lyre strings as they poised their bare arms over them. At intervals these instruments were abruptly hushed, & there burst forth a strident cry, an impetuous, frenzied, drawn out kind of barking, made by a rapid vibration of their tongues against the two corners of their mouths. Others rested upon their elbows, chin in hand, stiller than any Sphynx, darting their great black eyes upon the army as it climbed up to them.

Although Sicca was a sacred town, it could not accommodate such a multitude; for half of it was occupied by the temple and the buildings appertaining to it. Therefore the Barbarians encamped at their ease on the plain, the disciplined keeping to their regular companies, and the rest sorting themselves with those of their own race, or however they pleased.

The Greeks pitched their hide tents in parallel lines; the Iberians placed their canvas pavilions in a circle; the Gauls made themselves plank huts, and the Libyans cabins of unmortared stone; while the Negroes scooped trenches in the sand with their nails to sleep in. Many, not knowing where to go, wandered about among the baggage, and lay down at night on the ground in their ragged cloaks. Round them the plain lay, ringed about with mountains. Here and there a palm-tree slanted up from a sand hill, and the escarpments were studded with firs and oaks. Sometimes a rain cloud hung stormily from the sky like a long scarf, while the country all about was bathed in an azure serenity: then came a warm wind whipping up eddies of dust; and a stream fell in cascades from the heights of Sicca where, with its roofing of gold set upon brazen columns, rose the temple of the Carthaginian Venus, mistress of the land. She seemed to inform it with her soul. All these convulsions of the earth, these rapid changes from heat to cold, these vagaries of light, were manifestations of her extravagant might and the beauty of her eternal smile. The mountain tops were crescent shaped, or like the bust of a woman offering swelling breasts; and the Barbarians felt their weariness smothered by a languor full of delights.

Spendius had sold his dromedary & bought a slave with the money. All day long he lay stretched out asleep before Matho's tent. Often he woke from a dream in which he heard the whistling of the lash; he would pass his hands over the scars chafed upon his legs by the fetters he had worn so long, and fall asleep again.

Matho accepted his companionship. Spendius would escort him like a lictor with a long sword on his thigh; or Matho would even rest his arm carelessly on his shoulder: for Spendius was a little man.

One evening, as they were walking together through the camp

ways, they saw men robed in white cloaks, and among them was Narr'Havas, the Numidian prince. Matho quivered.

'Your sword!' he cried. 'I want to kill him!'

'Not yet!' said Spendius, holding him back.

Narr'Havas was already coming towards them.

He kissed his two thumbs in token of friendship, pleading his drunkenness as an excuse for his angry outburst at the feast. Then he spoke at length against Carthage, but did not say what brought him among the Barbarians.

'Is it these, or the Republic, he would betray?' Spendius asked himself and, as he expected to profit by any and every disorder, felt grateful to Narr'Havas for the treacheries he suspected him of contemplating.

The Numidian chieftain remained with the Barbarians, & seemed eager to gain Matho's good will. He sent him fat goats, gold dust, and ostrich plumes, and the Libyan, amazed at such favours, was in doubt whether to respond to or resent them. But Spendius pacified him, and Matho let himself be ruled by the slave, for he never could make up his mind, & was sunk in an unconquerable torpor, like a man who has taken some draught of which he must slowly die.

One morning when they all three went lion hunting, Narr'Havas hid a dagger in his cloak. Spendius kept at his heels all day, and they returned without the dagger having been drawn.

Another time Narr'Havas took them a long way from the camp, as far as the boundaries of his own kingdom. They came to a narrow gorge, and Narr'Havas smilingly declared that he no longer knew the way. Spendius found it again.

But most often Matho went forth as soon as the sun rose, as sombre as an augur, and wandered about the country. He would stretch himself out on the sand and stay there until evening without stirring.

One after the other, he consulted all the soothsayers in the army, those who observed the movements of serpents, those who read the stars, and those who blew upon the ashes of the dead. He swallowed galban, hartwort, and heart-freezing viper's venom. Negro women, chanting barbarous words in the moonlight, pricked the skin of his forehead with golden stylets; he loaded himself with

necklaces and charms; he invoked Baal-Khamon, Moloch, the seven Kabiri, Tanit, and the Venus of the Greeks in turn. He scratched a name upon a plate of copper, and buried it in the sand at the entrance of his tent. Spendius used to hear him groaning and talking to himself.
One night he went in to him.
Matho was lying flat on his stomach upon a lion's skin, naked as a corpse, with his face between his hands: a hanging lamp lit up his armour, which was hooked on the tent pole.
'You are suffering?' the slave asked him. 'What is the matter with you? Tell me!'
And he shook him by the shoulder, calling him ever and again: 'Master! Master!'
At last Matho lifted great troubled eyes towards him.
'Listen!' he said in a low voice, putting his finger to his lips. 'It is an anger from the gods! Hamilcar's daughter haunts me! I am afraid of her, Spendius!'
He nestled close against the other's breast, like a child frightened by a phantom.
'Speak to me! I am sick! I want to be healed! I have tried everything! But you, perhaps you know of more potent gods, or some all-compelling invocation?'
'For what purpose?' asked Spendius.
Beating his head with his fists, he answered:
'To rid me of her!'
Then, speaking as to himself, and with long pauses, he said:
'I am surely the victim of some holocaust she has vowed to the gods?... She holds me by a chain which none can see. If I walk, she goes with me; when I stop, she also stops! Her eyes burn me, and I hear her voice. She is all about me, and within me. I think that she has become my soul! And yet it is as if the invisible waves of a boundless ocean rolled between us! She is far, far beyond my reach! The splendour of her beauty makes a cloud of light about her; and there are moments when I think that I have never seen her ... that she does not exist ... and that all this is a dream!'
So Matho wept in the darkness, while the Barbarians slept. Spendius, as he looked at him, thought of the young men who used once to entreat him and coax him with offers of golden vases, when

he paraded his troupe of courtesans through the towns. He was moved with pity, and said:

'Be strong, my Master! Exert your will, and beseech the gods no more, for they are not turned by the cries of men! You weep like a coward! Are you not ashamed to let a woman make you suffer so?'

'Am I a child?' said Matho. 'Do you think I can still weaken for their faces & their singing? We kept them to sweep out our stables at Drepanum. I have had them during assaults, under crumbling roofs, while the catapult was yet vibrating!... But she, Spendius, she...!'

The slave interrupted him:

'If she were not Hamilcar's daughter...'

'No!' cried Matho. 'She is like no other daughter of man! Did you see her great eyes beneath great brows, two suns below triumphal arches? Ah, think: the torches all went pale when she appeared. Her naked breast was brighter than the diamonds at her neck it glowed between; the incense of a temple rose in her train, and something that was softer than wine, more terrible than death, flowed up from her. Yet I saw her walk; and then she was still.'

His mouth stayed open, and he hung his head in a fixed stare.

'But I want her! I must have her! She is killing me! The thought of crushing her in my arms is a frenzy of joy to me; and yet, Spendius, I hate her! I should like to beat her! What can I do? I would gladly sell myself and become her slave! That is what you have been! You could get sight of her; tell me of her! Every night she goes up on to her palace terrace, does she not? Ah! the stones must tremble under her sandals, and the stars crane down to see her!'

He fell back in a sheer paroxysm, rattling in his throat like a wounded bull.

Then Matho sang:

'He hunted the she-monster into the forest, and her tail wound over the dead leaves like a rivulet of silver.'

And he imitated the lingering notes of Salambo's voice, spreading out his hands as if poising them lightly over the strings of a lyre.

To all the consolations offered by Spendius he replied in the same manner; and in such groans and exhortations they passed each night.

Matho thought to find oblivion in wine, but his drunkenness left him in even heavier gloom. He tried to distract himself by gaming with the bones, and lost the gold plates of his necklace one by one. He let himself be taken to the hand-maids of the Goddess; but he came down the hill sobbing, as from a funeral.

Spendius, on the contrary, became more daring & animated. He was to be seen talking to groups of soldiers in the leaf-thatched taverns. He mended old cuirasses. He juggled with daggers. He went into the fields and gathered herbs for the sick. He was witty, dexterous, full of ideas and a ready talker. The Barbarians grew used to his services; and he won their love.

Meanwhile they were expecting an envoy from Carthage to come to them with baskets of gold laden upon mules; and they kept doing the same sum over and over again, tracing the figures of it in the sand with their fingers. Each was planning his future life: some would have concubines, slaves, and lands; others would bury their treasure, or adventure it upon a ship. But the effect of this waiting was to exacerbate their tempers; and there was constant wrangling between horse-soldiers and foot-soldiers, Barbarians and Greeks; and, always and through all, the deafening din of women's shrill voices.

There was a daily influx of nearly naked men, wearing grass on their heads to protect them from the sun. These were the debtors of rich Carthaginians, who had run away from the farms where they had been forced to work. Libyans, peasants ruined by the taxes, outlaws & malefactors, all came pouring in. The merchants, the wine and the oil vendors, were in a fury because they had not been paid, and laid the blame for it at the door of the Republic. Spendius fanned the fires of resentment against her. Soon the provisions ran low. There was talk of a massed advanced upon Carthage, and of calling in the Romans.

One evening at supper time they heard a dull and heavy clanking sound, and saw something red far off coming towards them over the waves of sand.

It was a large purple litter, decorated at each corner with ostrich plumes. Crystal chains and garlands of pearl swung against its close-drawn hangings. Behind it came camels sounding the great bells at their breasts, and surrounded by horsemen armed from shoulder to heel in harness of golden mail.

These halted three hundred paces from the camp to take their round shields, broad swords, and Boeotian helmets from the cases they carried behind their saddles. Some remained with the camels, while the rest resumed their advance. Finally they displayed the ensigns of the Republic, blue wooden poles bearing a horse's head or a pine-cone. The Barbarians all rose with a cheer; and the women rushed upon the Guards of the Legion and kissed their feet.

The litter was borne forward on the shoulders of twelve Negroes, who walked in step with little quick paces, threading their way to right and left through such obstacles as tent-ropes, stray animals, and tripods holding cooking pots. At times the hangings would be parted by a fat, ring-laden hand, and a harsh voice could be heard cursing: then the bearers would stop, and start on another way through the camp.

The purple curtains were raised, discovering an unruffled, bloated human head resting upon a great pillow. The eyebrows were arches of ebony with bases meeting in the middle; there was a glint of gold dust in the crisped hair, and the face was so dead white that it might have been powdered with marble filings. The rest of the body was hidden under the fleeces which filled the litter.

In the man so reclining, the soldiers recognised the Suffete Hanno, whose slackness had been a factor in the loss of the battle of the Aegates; in his victory at Hecatompylos over the Libyans, it was only (thought the Barbarians) because of his greed that he had shown mercy; he had sold all the captives for his own profit, and reported their deaths to the Republic.

After considering for some time whence he could best harangue the soldiers, he made a sign: the litter stopped, and Hanno, leaning upon two slaves, put staggering feet to the ground.

He wore boots of black felt set with silver moons. His legs were swathed in linen bands like a mummy's, and the flesh bulged forth between the crossings; his belly stood out from the scarlet jerkin which covered his thighs, and the folds of his neck drooped down upon his breast like the dewlaps of an ox; his flower-painted tunic was bursting at the arm-pits; he wore a scarf, a girdle, and a wide black cloak with laced double sleeves. The wealth of his robes, his great necklace of blue stones, his golden clasps and heavy ear-rings did but enhance the hideousness of his deformity. He might have been some grotesque idol rough-hewn from a block of stone; for a pale leprosy covered all his body and gave him a semblance of some lifeless thing. His nose, however, which was hooked like a vulture's beak, dilated energetically as he breathed the air; and his little eyes, with their gummed lashes, shone in a hard metallic glitter. He held an aloe-wood spattle in his hand, with which to scratch his skin.

At length two heralds sounded their silver horns; the tumult died away, and Hanno began to speak.

He began by praising the Gods and the Republic. The Barbarians ought to count themselves happy in having served her. But they must show themselves more reasonable; the times were hard,— 'and if a master has only three olives, is it not just that he keep two for himself?'

Thus the old Suffete larded his speech with proverbs & apologues, nodding his head the while to encourage some least expression of approval.

He used the Punic tongue, and those who were about him (the most alert, who had hurried up without their weapons) were Campanians, Gauls and Greeks; so that no one in the crowd un-derstood what he was saying. Perceiving this, Hanno fell silent, and swayed heavily from one leg to the other, as he reflected.

He decided to call the captains together; and his heralds pro-claimed this order in Greek, the language which had been used for words of command in the Carthaginian armies since the time of Xanthippus.

The Guards struck out with their whips to disperse the mob of soldiers; and the captains of Spartan phalanxes and chiefs of Bar-barian cohorts soon arrived with the insignia of their rank, and in their national armour. Night had fallen, and the whole plain was alive with rumours: fires were burning here and there, and the soldiers kept going from one to another, asking: 'What is the matter?' And why did not the Suffete distribute their money?

He was telling the captains of the colossal obligations with which the Republic was faced. Her treasury was empty.

'We do not know what to do! Carthage is much to be pitied!'
From time to time he scratched his limbs with his aloe-wood
spattle, or broke off to drink, from a silver cup held out to him by
a slave, a decoction of the ashes of a weasel and asparagus boiled in
vinegar; then he wiped his lips with a scarlet napkin, & continued:
    'What used to be worth a sicle of silver is now worth three
shekels of gold, and the farms which were abandoned during the
war are yielding nothing! Our murex fisheries are nearly lost, and
even pearls are becoming exorbitantly scarce. Our supply of unguents is hardly enough for the service of the gods! As for things
for the table, I cannot bring myself to speak of them; it is a
calamity! For want of galleys we are without spices, and we have
the greatest difficulty in getting silphium on account of the rebel-
lions on the Cyrenian frontier. Sicily, where so many slaves were
to be had, is now closed to us! Only yesterday I gave more money
for a bath-man and four scullions than I used to give for a pair of
elephants!'
He unrolled a long papyrus and, without passing over a single
figure, read the whole list of the government's expenses: so much
for repairing the temples; for paving the streets; for ship building;
for the coral fisheries; for the enlargement of the Syssitia; and so
much for engines in the Cantabrian mines.
But the captains understood Punic no better than the soldiers,
although the Mercenaries greeted each other in that language.
Ordinarily a number of Carthaginian officers were appointed to
act as interpreters in the Barbarian armies; but after the war these
had hidden themselves, being fearful of vengeance; and Hanno had
not thought to bring any with him. Moreover, he spoke too low,
and his voice was lost in the wind.
The Greeks, girthed in their iron sword-belts, strained their ears
to catch what he said; while the hillmen, bear-like in their furs,
looked at him with distrust, or yawned as they leaned on their
brass-studded clubs. The Gauls showed no interest, and grinned
as they shook out their high-standing hair; the men of the desert
listened motionless, all hooded in their garments of grey wool.
Others pressed on from behind; the Guards were jostled by the
mob & reeled on their horses; the Negroes held blazing fir branches
at their arm's length. And the fat Carthaginian, standing on a

grassy hummock, went on with his speech.

The Barbarians began to grow impatient; murmurs arose; and each hurled some remark at him. Hanno gesticulated with his spattle; and those who wished the others to be quiet added to the din by trying to out-shout them.

Suddenly a man of lowly appearance sprang up to Hanno's feet, snatched a trumpet from a herald, and sounded a blast upon it; Spendius (for it was he) announced that he had something of importance to say. At this declaration, rapidly uttered in five different languages, in Greek, Latin, Gallic, Libyan and Balearic, the captains, half laughing and half surprised, made answer:

'Speak! Speak!'

Spendius hesitated, trembling, and at last, addressing the Libyans as the most numerous, cried out:

'You have all heard this man's horrible threats!'

Since Hanno uttered no remonstrance, it was clear that he did not understand Libyan; and, to carry the experiment further, Spendius repeated the same sentence in the other Barbarian tongues.

They looked at one another in astonishment: then, as by tacit agreement, and believing perhaps that they had understood, they all bent their heads in sign of assent.

Then Spendius began again in a ringing voice:

'First he said that all the gods of other nations were nothing but dreams beside the gods of Carthage! He called you cowards, thieves, liars, dogs, and the sons of bitches! But for you (he said this!) the Republic would not be forced to pay tribute to Rome! And through your excesses you have drained her of perfumes, aromatics, slaves, and silphium; for you are in league with the Nomads on the Cyrenian frontier! But the guilty are to be punished! He read out a detailed list of their punishments: they will be set to work paving the streets, fitting up war-ships, or decorating the Hall of the Syssitia, while others will be sent to scratch earth in the mines of Cantabria.'

Spendius repeated all this to the Gauls, Greeks, Campanians and Balearic Islanders. The Mercenaries recognised several of the proper names, and were convinced that he was giving an accurate interpretation of the Suffete's speech. A few cried out to him:

'You lie!'

Their voices were lost in the general uproar; & Spendius went on: 'Did you not see that he has left a reserve of his mounted troops outside the camp? At a given signal they will charge in to cut all your throats.'

The Barbarians turned in that direction and, as the crowd drew apart, there appeared in the midst of them, moving slowly as a phantom, a human being, bent, gaunt, completely naked, and covered down to his flanks with long hair that bristled with dried leaves and dust and thorns. About his loins and his knees were wisps of straw and shreds of linen; flabby, earth-coloured skin hung from his emaciated limbs like rags upon dead branches; his hands trembled and shook unceasingly, and he walked leaning upon an olive-wood staff.

As he came up to the Negro torch-bearers, he bared his pale gums in a sort of idiot grin; and his great frightened eyes gazed upon the crowd of Barbarians about him.

Then with a cry of terror he rushed behind the protection of their bodies, and stammered out:

'There! There they are!' pointing to the Guards of the Suffete, motionless in their glittering armour.

Their horses were pawing the ground, dazed by the glare of the torches which spluttered in the darkness: and the human spectre writhed and howled:

'They have killed them!'

At these words, which he screamed in Balearic, some of the Islanders came up and recognised him. Without heeding their enquiries, he repeated:

'Yes; all, all killed! Crushed like grapes! The glory of the young manhood! The slingers! My comrades and yours!'

They gave him wine to drink, and he wept. Then he burst into a spate of words.

Spendius could scarcely contain his joy, as he explained to the Greeks and Libyans the horrors recounted by Zarxas: he could not believe, so apt was the news of them. The Balearic soldiers grew pale on learning how their comrades had perished.

A troop of three hundred slingers had disembarked on the eve of the departure from Carthage, and had slept too long the next morning. When they reached the square of Khamon the Barbarians had gone, and they found themselves defenceless, their clay bullets being packed with the rest of the baggage on the camels. They were allowed to wander into the Street of Satheb, as far as the brass-plated oaken gate; then the people with a single rush had fallen upon them.

Indeed the soldiers remembered hearing a great shout. Spendius, fleeing at the head of the column, had not heard it.

Their bodies had then been placed in the arms of the Pataec Gods which stood round the temple of Khamon. All the crimes of all the Mercenaries were imputed to them; their gluttony, their thefts, their impiety, their insults, and the murder of the fishes in Salambo's garden. Their bodies were infamously mutilated; the priests burned their hair that their spirits might also be tortured; they hung up pieces of them in the meat shops; some even buried their teeth in them; and in the evening, to finish with them, they lit pyres in the public places.

These were the flames which had gleamed from afar upon the lake. On the fire spreading to some houses, the remaining corpses, or any that were yet in their death agony, were quickly thrown over the walls. Zarxas had hidden among the reeds on the edge of the lake until the following day; then he had wandered about the country, trying to trace the army by their foot-prints in the dust. In the morning he hid in caves; in the evening he went on his way with his bleeding wounds, famished and sick, living on roots and carrion. At last one day he saw lances on the skyline, and had followed them. His wits were unbalanced by terror and anguish.

The soldiers' indignation, held in check while he was speaking, burst into a storm; and they made to massacre the Guards and the Suffete with them. They were restrained by certain who said that they ought to hear him and know at least whether they should be paid. Then they all cried:

'Our money!'

Hanno answered that he had brought it.

There was a rush to the outposts, and the Suffete's baggage was hurried by the Barbarians into the middle of the camp. Without waiting for the slaves, they unfastened the baskets; and in them found hyacinth robes and sponges, and scratchers, brushes and perfumes and antimony pencils for painting the eyes. All these belonged to the Guards, who were rich men and accustomed to such luxuries. Then they found a great bronze tub on a camel: this had been used by the Suffete for baths during his journey; for he had taken all manner of precautions, having even brought cages of weasels from Hecatompylos, which were burned alive to make his decoction. Since his malady gave him an enormous appetite, there was also great store of food and wines, of pickle and meats, and fishes preserved in honey, with little pots from Commagene containing melted goose-fat packed in snow and chopped straw. The supply was considerable; the more baskets they opened, the more they brought to light; and their laughter rose like a clashing of waves.

As for the Mercenaries' pay, it nearly filled two esparto-grass baskets; and in one of these, even, could be seen some of the round leather tokens which were used by the Republic to economise its specie. As the Barbarians appeared surprised, Hanno told them that their accounts were very complicated, and that the Elders had not had leisure to examine them: meanwhile they sent them this.

Then everything was scattered and overset: mules and serving-men, litter and provisions, and all the baggage. The soldiers seized on the money bags & would have stoned Hanno with them; but he managed painfully to mount an ass. Clinging to its coat, he fled, howling, weeping, shaken and bruised, and calling down upon the army the curse of all the gods. His wide collar of precious stones kept jumping up against his ears. He held up his over-long cloak with his teeth, as it trailed behind him; and from afar the Barbarians shouted after him:

'Away, coward, away! O Pig, O sink of Moloch! Sweat out your gold and your plague! Faster! Faster!

The routed escort galloped beside him.

The Barbarians' rage was not appeased. They remembered that several of their number who had set out for Carthage had not returned; no doubt these had been killed. So great an injustice maddened them, and they began to pull up the tent pegs, to roll their cloaks, and to bridle their horses; every man took his helmet and sword, & in instant all was ready. Those who had no arms rushed into the woods to cut them cudgels.

Day dawned, and the wakened people of Sicca were stirring in the streets. 'They are going to Carthage,' some said, and this rumour soon spread throughout the country.

Men sprang up from every ravine and path, and shepherds were seen running down the mountains.

When the Barbarians had departed, Spendius made a tour of the plain, riding upon a Punic stallion and attended by his slave, who led a third horse also.

There remained a single tent, and Spendius entered it.

'Up, Master! Arise! We go!'

'Where are you going?' asked Matho.

'To Carthage!' cried Spendius.

Matho leaped upon the horse which the slave held at the door.

SALAMBO

CHAPTER III

THE MOON WAS JUST SHOWING ABOVE THE WAVES, and over the town, still draped in shadow, points of light and whiteness began to glitter: a chariot pole in a court yard, a dangling tatter of rag, the angle of a wall, a golden necklet on the breast of a god. Glass balls on temple roofs sparkled like great diamonds here and there; but the dim ruins, the heaps of black earth, and the gardens made masses of deeper shadow in the darkness: and at the foot of Malqua, fishermen's nets were spread from house to house like giant bats' wings. No longer could the creaking of the water wheels be heard, forcing up water to the highest stories of the palaces; and, lying like ostriches on their bellies, the camels were resting peacefully in the midst of the terraces. Porters were asleep against door-steps in the streets: the shadows of colossi lay across deserted squares: at times in the distance the smoke of a still-burning sacrifice wound out through tiles of bronze, and, along with its scent of aromatics, the heavy breeze carried sea-smells and the exhalation from sun-heated walls. Still waters made a lustre about Carthage; for the moon spread her equal light upon the mountain-fringed gulf and the lake of Tunis where, among the sand banks, stood long rose-coloured lines of flamingoes; further, below the catacombs, the vast salt lagoon shimmered like a piece of silver. The rim of the blue dome of heaven sank into the dust of the plains on one side, and on the other into the mists of the sea; upon the summit of the Acropolis the pyramid cypress trees about the temple of Eshmun swayed and murmured like the slow

46

regular beat of the waves along the mole beneath the ramparts.
Salambo came up to the terrace of her palace, attended by a woman
slave bearing an iron dish filled with live coals.

In the middle of the terrace stood a little ivory bed covered with
lynx skins and cushions stuffed with parrot feathers (for this was a
prophetic bird, consecrated to the gods) and four tall perfume
braziers filled with nard and incense, cinnamon and myrrh, stood
at· its four corners. The slave put fire to these scents, and Salambo
gazed at the pole-star; slowly she bowed to the four quarters of
heaven, & knelt upon the ground in an azure dust which was sown
with golden stars to imitate the sky. Then with her elbows pressed
to her sides, her fore-arms held straight out and her hands open, she
threw back her head under the rays of the moon, and said:
'O Rabbet! . . . Baalet! . . . Tanit!'
Her voice dragged plaintively as if calling someone.
'Anaitis! Astarte! Derceto! Astoreth! Mylitta! Athara! Elissa!
Tiratha! . . . By the hidden symbols, . . . by the resounding sistra,
. . . by the furrows of earth, . . . by the eternal silence, the unending
fruitfulness, . . . mistress of the shadowy sea & of the azure shores,
Queen of each watery thing, Oh, greeting!'
Her whole body swayed two or three times, and then she cast her-
self face downwards in the dust with out-stretched arms.

The slave raised her nimbly; for the rites demanded that someone
must catch the suppliant at the moment of her prostration: this
was a sign that the gods accepted her, and Salambo's nurse had
never failed in the pious duty.

This woman had been brought to Carthage when still quite small
by some merchants from Darytian Gaetulia, and after her emancipation had not wished to forsake her former masters. This fact was
shown by the large hole pierced in her right ear. A striped skirt of
many colours clung closely to her hips and fell to her ankles, where
two pewter anklets clinked together. Her face was rather flat, and
yellow like her tunic. An arc of long silver pins rose like a sun at
the back of her head. She wore a coral stud in her nose; she stood
beside the bed more upright than a Hermes, and with her eyes
cast down.

Salambo moved to the edge of the terrace: her eyes swept the
horizon for an instant, and then rested upon the sleeping city; and

the sigh she heaved sent a wave of motion, by raising her breasts, down the whole length of the long white simar that hung about her without clasp or girdle. Her pointed, up-turned sandals were smothered in a multitude of emeralds, & her wild hair was caught in a net of purple thread.

She raised her head to gaze upon the moon and, mingling fragments of hymns with her speech, she murmured:

'How lightly thou turnest, held by impalpable ether! It brightens about thee; the motion of thy swimming sends forth the winds and the fertile dews. As thou dost wax and wane, so lengthen or shorten the eyes of cats & the spots of leopards. Women shout thy name in the agonies of childbirth! Thou swellest the sea-shells, thou fermentest the wine! Thou makest the dead to crumble! Thou formest pearls upon the bed of the sea!

'And every germ, O Goddess! quickens in the dark deeps of thy moisture.

'When thou appearest, there rests a quietness over the earth; flowers close, and waves are lulled, and weary men lie down with their breasts toward thee; the world with its oceans and mountains sees itself in thy face as in a mirror. Thou art white and gentle and lustrous; thou art immaculate, succouring; thou art purifying and serene.'

The crescent then hung above the mountain of the Hot Springs, in the opening between its two peaks, on the other side of the gulf. There was a little star below it, and a pale circle all round it. Salambo went on:

'But, Mistress, thou art terrible! ... From thee monsters are born, and terrible phantoms, and lying dreams: thine eyes devour the stones of buildings; and when thou growest young again, the apes fall sick. 'Whither goest thou? Why dost thou for ever change thy shapes? Now, slender and curved, thou glidest through space like a mastless galley; or, with the stars about thee, thou art like a shepherd keeping his flock. Or, shining and round, thou brushest the mountain tops like a chariot wheel.

'O Tanit! Dost thou not love me? I have looked so much upon thee! But no! Thou runnest thy course through thine azure, and I ... I remain on the moveless earth.

'Taanach, take your nable and play very softly upon the silver cord;
for my heart is sad!'
The slave took up a sort of harp of ebony wood, taller than herself,
and with three sides like a delta: she set its point in a crystal globe,
and began to play with both hands.
The notes followed upon each other, hurried & deep as the buzzing
of bees, & in growing volume floated away into the night with the
plaint of the waves and the soughing of the great trees on the height
of the Acropolis.
'Be silent!' cried Salambo.
'What ails you, mistress? A breath of wind, a passing cloud, every-
thing disturbs you!'
'I do not know,' she said.
'You weary yourself in too long prayers!'
'Ah, would I could dissolve within them as a flower in wine!'
'Perhaps it is the smoke of your perfumes?'
'No!' said Salambo. 'Such fragrant odours hold the spirit of the gods.'
The slave then spoke to her of her father. It was thought he had
gone towards the amber country, beyond the pillars of Melkarth.

'But if he does not return,' she said, 'you must choose a husband
from the sons of the Elders, since it was his wish; your sorrow will
vanish in the arms of a man.'
'Why?' asked the young girl.
All the men she had seen had horrified her with their wild, bestial
laughter and their coarse limbs.
'Sometimes, O Taanach, gusts of heat seem to rise from the depths
of my being, heavier than the fumes of a volcano. Voices call me,
and a ball of fire rolls and rises in my breast; it stifles me, and I feel
that I am dying; and then, something that is sweet flows from my
brow to my feet, & passes through my flesh ... It is a caress folding
about me; and I feel crushed, as if a god were stretching himself
upon me. Oh! that I could lose myself in the night mists, in the
fountain waters, in the sap of the trees; that I could leave my body
and be but a breath, a ray, and then float up to thee, O Mother!'
She raised her arms to their full length, bending her body back,
pale and light as the moon in its white robe. Then she fell panting
on the ivory couch: but Taanach placed an amber necklace with

dolphin's teeth about her neck, to drive away terrors; and Salambo said in an almost stifled voice:

'Go, and bring Shahabarim to me.'

Her father had not wished her to enter the college of priestesses, nor even to learn anything of the popular Tanit. He was reserving her for some alliance that might serve his political ends: and so Salambo lived alone in this palace. Her mother had long been dead.

She had grown up in abstinence, in fastings and purifications, always surrounded by exquisite & solemn things, her body saturated with perfumes, and her soul filled with prayers. She had never tasted wine, nor eaten meat, nor touched an unclean animal, nor set her foot in the house of a corpse.

Of obscene symbols she knew nothing: for as each god manifested himself in different forms, the same principle was often recognized in quite contradictory cults; and Salambo worshipped the Goddess in her sidereal aspect. An influence from the moon had fallen upon the maiden; and when it was waning, Salambo grew weak. Throughout the day she would languish, and revive at evening. During an eclipse, she had all but died.

But Rabbet jealously avenged herself on this virginity which was withheld from her sacrifices; she tormented Salambo with obsessions, all the stronger for being vague, which permeated her belief and were excited by it.

Hamilcar's daughter was for ever troubling herself over Tanit. She had learned her adventures, her travels, and all her names; and these she would repeat without their having any distinct significance for her. To probe the depths of her dogma, she longed to have knowledge of the ancient idol in the most secret part of the temple, who wore that magnificent mantle whereon the destinies of Carthage hung: for the idea of a god was not clearly distinguished from his manifestation; and to hold or even see his image was to take some part of his virtue away from him and, in a measure, to become his master.

Salambo turned round. She had recognised the sound of the golden bells which Shahabarim wore at the hem of his garment.

He came up the stairways: then, at the threshold of the terrace, he paused and folded his arms.

His sunken eyes shone like tomb lights; his long thin body seemed less solid than its linen robe, which was weighted about his heels by the bells and by balls of emerald. His limbs were frail, his skull was set aslant upon his neck, and his chin was pointed; his skin looked cold to the touch, and his yellow face, deeply furrowed with wrinkles, was as if shrunken by desire and everlasting sorrow.

He was the high priest of Tanit, and had educated Salambo.

'Speak!' he said. 'What do you wish?'

'I hoped . . . You had almost promised me . . .'

She stammered in confusion: then said suddenly:

'Why do you treat me with contempt? Have I been neglectful of the rites in any way? You are my master, and you have told me that no one was so skilled as I in the things pertaining to the Goddess: but there are mysteries of which you will not speak. Is this true, O father?'

Shahabarim remembered Hamilcar's orders, and answered:

'No, I have nothing more to teach you!'

'It is a Spirit,' she went on, 'that drives me to this love of mine. I have climbed the steps of Eshmun, god of the planets and intelligences; I have slept under the golden olive of Melkarth, protector of the Tyrian colonies; I have pushed open the doors of Baal-Khamon, enlightener and fertilizer; I have sacrificed to the Kabiri who live below the earth, to the gods of the woods and winds, of the rivers and mountains. But they are all too far away, too high, too insensible, if you understand me; while She . . . I feel her as part of my life; she fills my soul, and I thrill to inward transports, as if she were leaping to escape. I seem about to hear her voice and see her face; a radiance dazzles me, and I fall back into darkness.'

Shahabarim was silent. She turned a beseeching look upon him.

At last he made a sign of dismissal to the slave, who was not of Canaanitish race. Taanach withdrew, and Shahabarim, raising one arm, began:

'Before the gods, darkness was alone, and there hovered a breath, heavy and formless as man's perception in a dream. It contracted, creating Desire and Cloud; and from Desire and Cloud was born the first Matter. This was a muddy, black water, icy and deep. It held insentient monsters, the uncohering parts of creatures yet to be born, such as are painted on the sanctuary walls.

'Then Matter condensed into an egg, and burst. One half formed the earth and the other half the firmament. The sun and moon, the winds and clouds appeared; and the crash of thunder brought life to sentient creatures. Then Eshmun spread himself upon the starry sphere; Khamon blazed in the sun, and Melkarth thrust him down behind Gades with his arms; the Kabiri burrowed under the volcanoes; and Rabbet bent like a nurse over the world, poured out the milk of her light, and spread forth her night like a mantle.'

'And then?' she asked.

He had told her the mystery of origins, to turn her thoughts to a loftier perspective; but the maiden's desire re-kindled at his last words, and Shahabarim, half yielding, continued:

'She inspires and governs the loves of men.'

'The loves of men!' Salambo echoed dreamily.

'She is the soul of Carthage,' continued the priest, 'and although her presence is spread over all things, it is here that she dwells beneath the sacred veil.'

'O father!' cried Salambo. 'I shall see her, shall I not? You will take me to her! I have long held back; I am devoured with eagerness to see her body. Have pity! Help me! Let us go!'

Roughly he repulsed her, with a gesture full of pride.

'Never! Do you not know that it is death? The hermaphrodite Baalim are unveiled only to us, who are men in understanding and women in our weakness. Your desire is a sacrilege: be content with the knowledge that you have!'

She fell upon her knees, placing two fingers to her ears in sign of repentance: and, crushed by the priest's words, and choking with anger against him and also with terror and humiliation, she broke into sobbing. Shahabarim remained erect & unmoved. He looked down at her as she trembled at his feet, and felt a kind of joy in seeing her suffer for his Divinity, whom he himself could no more embrace than she. The birds were already singing, a cold wind blew, and little clouds were drifting across the paling sky.

Suddenly he saw a sort of light mist trailing along the ground on the skyline behind Tunis: it became a great curtain of grey dust rising perpendicularly, and then, in the eddies of this moving mass, you could see dromedaries' heads and spears and shields. It was the Barbarian army advancing upon Carthage.

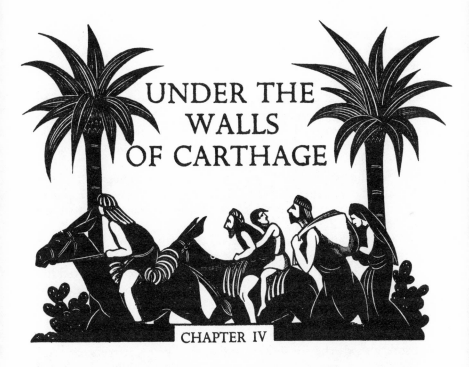

UNDER THE WALLS OF CARTHAGE

CHAPTER IV

SOME PEASANTS RIDING ON ASSES OR RUNNING ON foot, pale, breathless and mad with fear, came into the town, flying before the army. It had marched from Sicca in three days, to fall upon Carthage and wholly exterminate her.

The gates were shut, and almost at once the Barbarians appeared; but they halted in the middle of the isthmus on the shore of the lake.

At first they showed no sign of hostility. Several came forward with palm branches in their hands; but these were driven back with arrows, so great was the terror in the city.

In the morning and at nightfall some of them would prowl along the walls, & especially noticeable was a little man carefully wrapped in a cloak, and with his face hidden by a very low visor. He would stand for hours gazing at the aqueduct so persistently that surely he wished to mislead the Carthaginians as to his real design. Another man, a giant who walked bareheaded, used to accompany him.

The defences of Carthage stretched right across the isthmus: first there was a trench, then a rampart of turf, and lastly a two-storied wall thirty cubits high, built of hewn stones. This contained stables for three hundred elephants with storehouses for their caparisons, shackles and food; other stables for four thousand horses, with supplies of barley and harness; and barracks to hold twenty thousand soldiers with all their armour and materials for war. Battlemented towers rose from the second story, with bronze bucklers hung outside them upon cramp-irons.

This first line of fortifications gave immediate shelter to Malqua, the sailors' and dyers' quarter. Here there were masts with purple sails drying upon them; and, on the highest terraces, clay furnaces for boiling pickle.

Behind, the high square houses of the city rose in tiers like an amphitheatre. They were built of stone and planks and shingle, of reeds and shells and beaten earth. The temple groves showed like green lakes in this mountain of divers-coloured blocks. The public squares made levels in it at irregular intervals, and it was cut from top to bottom by a countless criss-cross of lanes. The boundaries of the three ancient quarters, which are now lost, could then be distinguished: they rose here and there like great reefs, or were spread out in enormous spans half-covered with flowers, blackened and widely streaked by cast-out filth; streets passed through their yawning gaps, like rivers under bridges.

The hill of the Acropolis, in the centre of Byrsa, was covered by a medley of monuments. There were temples with spiral columns bearing bronze capitals and metal chains, there were cones of unmortared stones banded with azure, copper cupolas, marble architraves, Babylonian buttresses, and obelisks poised on their points like inverted torches. Peristyles reached up to pediments, & there were colonnades showing scrolls of volutes; tiled partitions were supported upon granite walls; and all these things were piled one upon the other, and half hidden, in a most incomprehensible and amazing way. The whole was instinct with the succession of age to age, and with memories of forgotten nations.

Through the red lands behind the Acropolis the tomb-flanked Mappales road ran in a straight line from the shore to the catacombs; then, at intervals, there were large houses standing in gardens; and this third quarter, the new town of Megara, reached as far as the edge of the cliff, where stood a giant pharos that shone forth every night,

So lay Carthage before the eyes of the soldiers encamped on the plain.

From afar they picked out the markets and crossways, and argued about the positions of the temples. That of Khamon, fronting the Syssitia, had golden tiles: Melkarth, to the left of Eshmun, had branches of coral on its roofing: yonder, Tanit's copper dome bulged among the palm trees: black Moloch was below the cisterns, towards the pharos. At the angles of the pediments, on the tops of walls, at the corners of the squares, they could see gods with hideous heads, either huge or squat, with enormous or immoderately hollowed bellies, opening their jaws, spreading forth their arms, and holding forks or chains or javelins; and the blue of the sea lay below the streets, which in perspective took on an even greater steepness.

These were filled from morning till evening with a tumultuous crowd: young boys rang little bells and shouted before the bath-house doors; the shops for hot drinks were a-steam; the air echoed with the clangour of anvils; the sacred white cocks of the Sun crowed on the terraces; oxen bellowed in the temples as they were slain; slaves ran about with baskets on their heads; & in the depths of the porticoes a priest could every now and again be seen, draped in a sombre cloak, bare-footed, and wearing a pointed hat.

Carthage, seen thus, exasperated the Barbarians. They wondered at it, and they cursed it: they would have liked at the same time to annihilate it, and to live in it. But what was behind the triple wall that defended the Military Harbour? And again, beyond the town, in the heart of Megara, & higher than the Acropolis, stood Hamilcar's palace.

Matho's eyes were continually drawn towards it. He climbed into olive trees and bent forward, shading his eyes with his hand. The gardens were empty, and the red door with the black cross was always shut.

More than twenty times he walked round the ramparts, looking for some breach by which to enter. One night he dived into the gulf and swam for three hours without pausing for breath. He reached the foot of the Mappales quarter and tried to climb up the face of the cliff: but he bloodied his knees, broke his nails, fell back into the water, and then returned.

His helplessness maddened him. He was as jealous of this Carthage which shut Salambo away from him as he might have been of a man who had possessed her. His lethargy fell from him, and was succeeded by a mad and continual frenzy of action. With cheeks a-flame, with angrily flashing eyes, and uttering hoarse sounds, he would stride rapidly through the camp; or else he would sit on the shore and scour his great sword with sand. He shot arrows at the vultures as they flew by. His heart welled up in a fury of words.

'Give rein to your wrath, let it go like a runaway chariot,' said Spendius. 'Shout and blaspheme, ravage and slay. Sorrow is appeased by blood; and, since you cannot gratify your love, now gorge your hatred: that will sustain you.'

Matho once more took charge of his soldiers, and drilled them pitilessly. They respected him for his courage, and especially for his strength. Moreover, he was regarded with a kind of mystic awe; for they believed that he talked with spirits by night. The other captains were roused by his example, & soon the army was disciplined. From their houses the Carthaginians could hear the bugle-calls regulating its drill. At last the Barbarians marched forward.

To crush them in the isthmus would have required two armies attacking simultaneously in the rear, one landing at the head of the gulf of Utica, and the second by the mountain of the Hot Springs. But what could be done with only the Sacred Legion, which was six thousand strong at most? If the enemy turned eastward they would join the Nomads, cut off all communication with Cyrene and intercept supplies from the desert. If they fell back to the west, Numidia would rise. Finally, lack of provision would sooner or later force them to devastate the surrounding country like locusts: and the Rich trembled for their fine country houses, their vineyards and their farms.

Hanno made the most atrocious and impracticable proposals, as that they should promise a large sum of money for every Barbarian's head, or that ships and engines should be used to set fire to their camp. His colleague Gisco, on the other hand, was in favour of paying them: but the Elders hated him because of his popularity; for they looked with suspicion upon a masterful man, and in their fear of a monarchy made every effort to weaken any influence which might work for its re-establishment.

Outside the fortifications there were men of another race and of unknown origin, all porcupine hunters who lived upon molluscs and serpents. They would go into caves and catch hyenas alive, and amused themselves in the evening by making these race on the sands of Megara between the steles of the tombs. Their mud and sea-weed huts hung like swallows' nests on the cliff, and here they lived, with no government and no gods, pell-mell, completely naked, weak and yet fierce, and execrated by the people on account of their unclean foods. One morning the sentries noticed that they were all gone.

At last some members of the Great Council came to a decision. They went out to the camp in neighbourly fashion, without necklaces or girdles, and in open sandals. They walked at an easy pace, waved greetings to the captains, and even stopped to speak to the soldiers, saying that all their troubles were ended and that their claims were to receive justice.

Many of them were seeing a Mercenaries' camp for the first time. Instead of the confusion which they had pictured to themselves, all was order and terrifying silence. The army was walled about by a high turf rampart, proof against catapult bombardment. The paths were sprinkled with fresh water. Through holes in the tents they could see fierce eyes gleaming in the shadows. The mounds of pikes and hanging armour dazzled them like mirrors. They talked together in low tones; and were afraid of upsetting things with their long robes.

The soldiers demanded provisions, undertaking to pay out of the money due to them.

They sent them oxen, sheep and guinea-fowl, dried fruits and lupins, & those excellent smoked mackerel which Carthage shipped to every port. But the men walked scornfully round the magnificent cattle and, disparaging all they most coveted, offered the worth of a pigeon for a ram, or the price of a pomegranate for three goats. The Eaters-of-unclean-things, constituting themselves arbiters, declared that they were being duped. Then they drew their swords and threatened slaughter.

Commissaries of the Great Council wrote down the number of years' pay due to each soldier: but it was no longer possible to know how many Mercenaries had been engaged, and the Elders were appalled at the exorbitant sum which they must pay. They would have to sell the reserve of silphium, and levy a tax on the trading towns: the Mercenaries would grow impatient; & Tunis was already in sympathy with them. The Rich, stunned by Hanno's rages and his colleague's reproaches, urged any citizen who might know a Barbarian to go to see him at once, to win back his friendship, and to speak him fair. Such a show of confidence would calm them.

Merchants, scribes, arsenal workers, and whole families went out to visit the Barbarians.

The soldiers allowed all these Carthaginians into their camp, but by a single passage so narrow that four men could not walk abreast without jostling each other. Spendius, standing against the barrier, had them carefully searched; & Matho, facing him, scrutinised the crowd as it passed, trying to recognize someone whom he might have seen at Salambo's palace.

The camp was like a town, so full was it of people and of movement. Two distinct bodies of folk mingled without blending, one dressed in linen or wool, with felt caps like fir-cones, and the other clad in iron and wearing helmets. Among the servants and itinerant vendors wandered women of all nations, brown as ripe dates, green as olives, yellow as oranges, who had been sold by sailors, picked out of pot-houses, stolen from caravans, or taken in the sacking of towns—women who were laboured with love so long as they were young, and belaboured with blows when they were old; who, in the confusion of a defeat, would die by the roadside among the baggage and the abandoned beasts of burden. The Nomads' wives wore square tawny garments of dromedary-hair, which swung about their heels: Cyrenaic musicians in violet veils and with painted eyebrows squatted on mats and sang: old Negresses with sagging breasts gathered animals' dung to dry in the sun for fire kindling: the Syracusan women had gold plaques in their hair; the Lusitanians had shell necklaces; the Gauls wore wolf skins upon their white bosoms; and sturdy children, covered with vermin, naked and uncircumcised, butted the passers-by in the belly with their heads, or stole behind them like young tigers and bit their hands.

The Carthaginians walked through the camp, amazed to find it so full of such a variety of things. The more despondent of them looked gloomy, but the others disguised their feelings of anxiety. The soldiers slapped them on the shoulder, bidding them be gay. Whenever they saw anyone of note, they invited him to join in their pastimes. If they were throwing the discus they would contrive to drop it on his foot; or, if they were boxing, to break his jaw in the very first rally. The slingers delighted to terrify the Carthaginians with their slings, the snake-charming Psylli with their vipers, the horsemen with their horses; and the victims, who were men of peaceful occupation, bent their heads & forced themselves to smile. Some, in order to prove themselves brave, made signs that they would like to become soldiers. These were set to split wood and curry the mules; or were buckled up in armour and rolled like casks through the streets of the camp. And when their visitors started to go away, the Mercenaries tore their hair in grotesque contortions of grief.

Many, whether from foolishness or prepossession, ingenuously imagined all Carthaginians to be very rich, and dogged their footsteps, begging them to give them something. They asked for anything which struck them as beautiful, a ring, a girdle, sandals, or the fringe of a garment; and when the despoiled Carthaginian cried:
'But I have nothing left. What do you want?'
They answered: 'Your wife!'
And others cried: 'Your life!'

The military accounts were handed to the captains, read to the soldiers, and finally approved. Then they asked for tents; and these were given them. Then the Greek polemarchs demanded some of the splendid suits of armour which were forged at Carthage; & the Great Council voted money for their purchase. Then the cavalry claimed that, in justice, the Republic should indemnify them for their horses: one averred that he had lost three at such a siege;

another, five during such a march; another, fourteen which had fallen over precipices. They were offered stallions from Hecatompylos; but preferred money.

Next they demanded to be paid in money (not in leather tokens, but in silver pieces) for all the corn that was owing to them, and at the highest price it had fetched during the war; so that they exacted four hundred times as much for a measure of flour as they had given for a sack of wheat. Such injustice was maddening; yet it was impossible not to submit to it.

Then the representatives of the soldiers and of the Great Council sealed their reconciliation, swearing by the Spirit of Carthage and by the gods of the Barbarians; and exchanged excuse and flattery with all the demonstrative verbiage of the East. The soldiers then demanded, as a proof of friendship, that the traitors who had alienated them from the Republic should be punished.

When the Council pretended not to understand what they meant, they explained quite simply that they must have Hanno's head,

Several times a day they left camp and walked along the foot of the walls, shouting for the Suffete's head to be thrown to them, and holding out their robes to catch it.

The Great Council would perhaps have weakened but for a last insolence more outrageous than all the others. The Barbarians demanded maidens, chosen from noble families, in marriage for their chiefs. This idea was inspired by Spendius, and many of them thought it quite simple and practicable. But their presumption in wishing to mingle their blood with Punic blood roused popular indignation; and they were bluntly told to expect no more. Then they cried out that they had been deceived, and that if their pay did not arrive within three days they would themselves enter Carthage and take it.

The Mercenaries were not acting in such complete bad faith as their enemies supposed. Hamilcar had made them extravagant promises which, however vague, were yet solemn and oft repeated. They could be excused for believing that, when they disembarked at Carthage, the town would be given up to them, and that they would have treasures to share among them; & when they saw that it was doubtful whether they would even receive their pay, their disillusionment was as great a blow to their pride as to their greed.

Had they not the example of marvellous fortunes acquired by Dionysius, Pyrrhus, Agathocles, & Alexander's generals? The horizon of every army was bright with the ideal of Hercules, whom the Canaanites confounded with the sun. They knew that simple soldiers had worn diadems, and the echoes of crumbling empires brought dreams to the Gaul in his oak forest, & to the Ethiopian in his sand. And here had been a nation ever ready to turn courage to account: the robber driven from his tribe, the murderer skulking along the roads, the sacrilegist fleeing before the gods, all who were starving or in despair, had ever striven to reach the port where the Carthaginian agent recruited soldiers. Usually the Republic kept her promises: this time, however, a too great avarice had brought her into perilous disgrace. The Numidians, the Libyans, the whole of Africa was threatening to fall upon Carthage. Only the sea was open to her, and there she would meet the Romans; like a man attacked by murderers, she felt death all round her.

She had inevitably fallen back upon Gisco; and the Barbarians accepted his intervention. One morning they saw the chains of the harbour lowered, and three flat-bottomed barges, passing through the Taenia canal, entered the lake.

Gisco could be seen at the prow of the foremost, and behind him rose an enormous chest, higher than a catafalque, and furnished with rings like hanging crowns. Then came the legion of Interpreters, their hair dressed sphinx-fashion, & with parrots tattooed upon their breasts. These, again, were followed by friends and slaves, in such number that they pressed shoulder to shoulder. The three long barges, loaded to the point of sinking, advanced amid the cheers of the attentive army.

As soon as Gisco disembarked the soldiers ran to meet him. He caused a sort of rostrum to be built up with sacks, and declared that he would not go away before he had paid them all in full.

There was a burst of cheering, and it was a long time before he was able to speak.

Then he denounced the wrongs done both to the Republic and to the Barbarians, saying that the fault lay with a few mutineers who had alarmed Carthage by their violence. The best proof of the Republic's good intention was that it was he, the undying foe of the Suffete Hanno, who had been sent among them. They must not think that the people were such fools as wantonly to provoke brave men, or so ungrateful as not to recognize their services. And Gisco began to pay the army, starting with the Libyans. As they had declared that the lists were falsified, he dispensed with these.

They filed before him by nations, spreading out their fingers to show the number of their years of service: each man in turn was marked with green paint on the left arm; the scribes dipped into the yawning coffer, while others pricked holes with a style on a sheet of lead.

A man passed, walking heavily like an ox.

'Come up here by me,' said the Suffete, suspecting some fraud. 'How many years have you served?'

'Twelve,' answered the Libyan.

Gisco felt under his chin with his fingers; for the chin-piece of the helmet would in time cause two patches of hard skin to grow there. These were called carobs; and 'to have carobs' was a colloquialism meaning, to be a veteran.

'Thief!' exclaimed the Suffete. 'There is certainly that on your shoulders which is lacking on your face!'

And, tearing off his tunic, he laid bare his back, which was covered with bleeding scabs. He was a labourer from Hippo-Zaritus. The soldiers hooted, and he was beheaded.

As soon as it was night Spendius went and roused the Libyans, and said to them:

'When the Ligurians and Greeks, the Balearic Islanders and the men of Italy are paid, they will return to their homes. You on the contrary will remain in Africa, scattered among your tribes and defenceless! It is then that the Republic will revenge herself! Beware of that journey homeward! Are you ready to believe everything that is said to you? The two Suffetes are working together, and this one dupes you! Remember the Isle of Bones, and Xanthippus whom they sent back to Sparta in a rotten galley!'

'What ought we to do?' they asked.

'Keep your wits about you!' said Spendius.

The two following days were spent in paying the men of Magdala, Leptis, and Hecatompylos. Spendius went about among the Gauls.

'They are paying off the Libyans, and then they will discharge the Greeks, the Balearic Islanders, the Asiatics and all the rest. But you, who are but few, will be given nothing! You will never see your native land again! You will have no ships! They will kill you, to save your food!'

The Gauls went and found the Suffete. Autharitus, the man whom he had wounded at Hamilcar's palace, began to question him; he was thrust back by the slaves and came away, but not without swearing that he would be avenged.

There was an ever-growing stream of protests and complaints. The more insistent forced their way into the Suffete's tent: they tried to move him to pity by taking his hands and making him feel their toothless mouths, their wasted arms, and the scars of all their wounds. Those who had not been paid were growing angry; those who had had their money asked for more for their horses; & vagabonds and outlaws armed themselves as soldiers and declared that they were being forgotten. Fresh eddies of men kept surging up each minute; the tents cracked under the strain and fell; the multitude packed between the ramparts of the camp swayed & shouted from gates to centre. When the tumult grew too loud, Gisco would rest one elbow on his ivory staff and stand motionless looking at the sea, his fingers twined in his beard.

Matho often went aside to speak with Spendius; then he would station himself again in front of the Suffete, and Gisco could feel his eyes like two fire-darts eternally hurled against him. Several times they shouted insults over the heads of the crowd; but neither understood the other.

Meanwhile the work of paying out went on; and the Suffete found means to overcome each obstacle as it arose.

The Greeks tried to quibble over differences in currency: but he explained matters in such a way that they retired without a murmur. The Negroes demanded their pay in the white shells used for trade in the interior of Africa: he offered to send to Carthage for them, and then they accepted silver like the rest.

The Balearic Islanders had been promised something better, namely women. The Suffete replied that they were expecting a whole caravan of virgins for them; but the journey was long and would yet occupy six moons. When they were fat & well rubbed with benzoin, they would be sent in ships to the Balearic ports.

Suddenly Zarxas, who was now well-looking and vigorous, leaped

like a mountebank upon the shoulders of his friends, and cried:
'Have you kept any of them for the corpses?'

At the same time he pointed to the gate of Khamon in Carthage.
The rays of the setting sun were flashing from the brazen plates
which covered it from top to bottom; and it seemed to the Barbarians that they could see traces of blood upon it. Every time that
Gisco tried to speak their shouts broke out afresh. At last he gravely
stepped down, and shut himself in his tent.

When he left it at sunrise his interpreters, who had been sleeping
outside, did not stir: they lay on their backs with staring eyes, their
tongues between their teeth, and blue in the face. White mucous
froth oozed from their nostrils, and their limbs were stiff, as if they
had all been frozen by the cold of the night. Each had a little noose
of rushes round his neck.

Thenceforward there was no checking the rebellion. The reminder
by Zarxas of the murder of the Balearic soldiers had served to
strengthen the suspicions fanned by Spendius. They imagined
that the Republic had never any object but to deceive them. There
must be an end to this! They would do without interpreters!
Zarxas, with a sling about his head, sang war songs: Autharitus
brandished his great sword: Spendius whispered in this man's ear,
or gave this other man a dagger. The boldest tried to seize their pay
for themselves, while the cooler-headed asked that the distribution
be continued. No one laid down his arms; and the fury of all combined against Gisco in one tumult of hatred.

Some of them climbed up beside him. So long as they loaded him
with abuse they were listened to with patience; but if they tried
to say one word in his favour they were immediately stoned, or
beheaded by a sabre-stroke from behind. The pile of sacks was
redder than an altar.

After eating and when they had drunk wine, they were terrible
indeed! The latter indulgence was forbidden in the Punic armies
under pain of death, and they raised their cups towards Carthage
in mockery of her discipline. Then they turned back upon the
accountant slaves, and again began to kill. And the word 'strike',
though different in every tongue, was understood by all.

Gisco knew very well that his country had deserted him; but he
had no wish to dishonour her, for all her ingratitude. When the

Mercenaries reminded him that they had been promised ships, he swore by Moloch to provide them himself, at his own expense; and, pulling off his necklace of blue pearls, he threw it among the crowd as pledge of his oath.

The Africans then claimed the corn with which the Great Council had agreed to provide them. Gisco spread forth the accounts of the Syssitia, painted in violet upon sheep skins; and read out all the amounts that had come into Carthage month by month and day by day.

Suddenly he stopped with wide open eyes, as if he had read his death sentence among the figures.

The Elders had made fraudulent reductions; & the corn sold during the most disastrous period of the war was set down at so low a rate that no one who was not blind could possibly believe it.

'Speak!' they shouted. 'Louder! Ah, he is inventing some lie, the coward! Do not trust him!'

After some moments of hesitation, he went on with his task.

Without suspecting that they were being deceived, the soldiers accepted the accounts of the Syssitia as correct: and were thrown into a fury of jealousy on learning of Carthage's abundance. They broke open the sycamore chest; and it was three parts empty. They had seen such sums come forth from it that they thought it inexhaustible: Gisco must have buried some in his tent. Led by Matho, they clambered over the sacks; and to their cries of 'The money! The money!' Gisco at last replied:

'There is your general! Let him see to it!'

He faced them without speaking, with his great yellow eyes and his long face whiter than his beard. An arrow, checked by its feathers, hung in the large gold ring at his ear, & a thread of blood trickled from his tiara to his shoulder.

At a sign from Matho they all came forward. Gisco spread his arms; and Spendius caught his wrists together with a slip knot; someone else knocked him down, and he disappeared in the confusion of the mob which was tumbling over the sacks.

They pillaged his tent, and found nothing save bare necessaries; but, on a closer search, they discovered three images of Tanit and, wrapped in an ape's skin, a black stone fallen from the moon. Many Carthaginians had chosen to accompany him; and they were notable men, all belonging to the war party.

These were dragged out of their tents and thrown into the cess-pit. They were bound to solid stakes by iron chains about their bellies, and food was held out to them on a javelin point.

Autharitus, who watched over them, loaded them with vituperation; but as they knew nothing of his language, they did not answer; and the Gaul from time to time threw stones at their faces to make them cry out.

Next day a sort of languor fell upon the army, and disquieting thoughts began to trouble them now that their anger was over. Matho was feeling vaguely depressed: for it seemed to him that he had indirectly outraged Salambo, that these Rich men were in some sort a part of her person. He sat down at night on the edge of their pit, and in their groans he recaptured some note of that voice which filled his heart.

Meanwhile they were all united in bitterness against the Libyans, who alone had been paid. But while national antipathies and personal hatreds again became lively, they saw the danger of giving way to them. There would surely be terrible reprisals after such an outrage; they must forestall the vengeance of Carthage. They held countless secret meetings, and made interminable speeches. Everyone spoke, but no one listened; and Spendius, who usually had so much to say, shook his head at each proposal.

One evening he carelessly asked Matho whether there were no water-springs inside the city.

'Not one!' answered Matho.

Next day Spendius drew him to the shore of the lake.

'Master!' said that former slave. 'If you have a stout heart, I will lead you into Carthage.'

'How?' gasped the other.

'Swear to do all that I bid you, and to follow me like a shadow!'

Matho raised his arm towards the planet Shabar, and exclaimed:

'By Tanit, I swear to do so!'

Spendius continued:

'To-morrow after sunset you must wait for me at the foot of the aqueduct between the ninth and tenth arches. Bring an iron pick, and wear a helmet with no plume, and leather sandals.'

The aqueduct of which he spoke ran obliquely across the entire isthmus, a notable piece of workmanship that was afterwards enlarged by the Romans. In spite of her contempt for other nations, Carthage had awkwardly borrowed this novel invention from Rome; just as Rome herself had imitated the Punic galleys. Five tiers of superposed arches in a squat, stumpy kind of architecture, with buttresses at their base and lions' heads on top, abutted on the western side of the Acropolis, where they sank under the town to pour what was almost a river into the cisterns of Megara.

Spendius met Matho here at the appointed hour. He tied a sort of harpoon to the end of a rope, and whirled it rapidly like a sling: the iron caught, and they began to climb up the wall, one after the other.

But when they had reached the first tier the cramp-hook fell back each time they threw it, and to find some fissure for it in the masonry they had to walk along the edge of the cornice. They found that this grew narrower at each successive tier of arches. Sometimes the rope slackened, & several times it nearly broke.

At last they reached the topmost platform. Spendius kept stooping to feel the stones of it with his hand.

'This is the place,' he said. 'Let us begin!'

And, by leaning hard on the pick which Matho had brought, they succeeded in prising up one of the flagstones.

In the distance they perceived a troop of riders galloping upon unbridled horses. Their golden bracelets leaped in the loose drapery of their cloaks, and at their head was a man crowned with ostrich plumes, riding with a lance in either hand.

'Narr'Havas!' cried Matho.

'What does it matter?' answered Spendius.

And he jumped down into the hole they had just made by displacing the flagstone.

Matho, at his bidding, endeavoured to lever out one of the blocks of stone: but he had no space to move his elbows.

'We shall come back,' said Spendius. 'Go on in front.'

Then they ventured into the conduit.

The water came up to their waists, and soon they were staggering and forced to swim. They barked their limbs against the walls of the narrow duct: the water ran almost at the level of the stones that roofed it in, and these tore their faces. Then they were carried along by the current. An atmosphere heavier than that of the tomb weighed down upon their lungs; stretching themselves out as much as possible, with their heads between their arms and their knees pressed close together, they passed like arrows into the darkness, choking, gasping, and almost overcome. Suddenly everything went black before them, and the water redoubled its speed. They fell.

When they came to the surface again, they remained for some minutes floating on their backs, taking delicious draughts of air. Line behind line of wide walls pierced with archways divided the basins. These were all full, and the whole length of the cisterns was one unbroken sheet of water. The air-holes in the cupolas of the roofing filtered pale discs of light upon the water, and the darkness thickened towards the walls, making them seem indefinitely distant. The slightest noise set up a loud echoing.

Spendius and Matho started to swim again and, passing through the arches, crossed several chambers in succession. A chain of smaller basins ran on each side of them. They lost themselves, turned and came back again. At last their feet met something solid. It was the stone ledge which ran alongside the cisterns.

Proceeding very cautiously, they felt along the wall for an outlet; but their feet kept slipping, and they fell back into the deep basins. They had to climb up again, & again fell back. They were terribly weary, and felt as if their limbs had melted in the water as they swam. Their eyes closed, and they felt all the agony of death.

Spendius struck his hand against the bars of a grating. They both shook it, and it gave way; and they found themselves upon some steps. At the top of these there was a closed door of bronze; but with the point of a dagger they lifted the bar which held it on the other side, and suddenly pure open air was about them.

The night was filled with silence, and the heavens were infinitely high. Clusters of trees topped the long lines of walls. The whole town was asleep. The fires of the outposts shone like lost stars.

Spendius, after three years in the slave prison, had only an imperfect knowledge of the quarters of the city. Matho reckoned that, to reach Hamilcar's palace, they should strike to the left and cross the Mappales district.

'No,' said Spendius. 'Lead me to the temple of Tanit.'

Matho opened his mouth and was about to speak.

'Remember!' said the one-time slave.

And, raising his arm, he pointed to the planet Shabar shining in heaven.

Matho turned silently towards the Acropolis.

They crept along the nopal hedges bordering the path. The water dripped on to the dust from their bodies; their wet sandals made no sound. Spendius searched the bushes at every step, with eyes brighter than torches; he walked behind Matho, & his hands rested on two daggers in a leather band below his arm-pits.

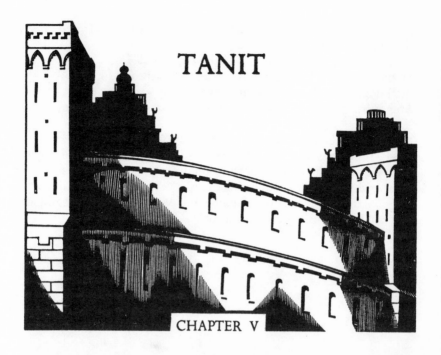

TANIT

CHAPTER V

AFTER LEAVING THE GARDENS THEY FOUND THEIR
way barred by the high wall enclosing Megara; but they soon discovered a breach and passed within.

The ground sloped downwards in a sort of broad and open valley.

'Listen,' said Spendius, 'and first of all, have no fear! ... I shall
fulfil my promise ... '

He broke off and seemed to reflect, as if he were feeling for words.

'Do you remember that time at sunrise, on Salambo's terrace,
when I showed you Carthage? We were strong then; but you
would not listen to me!'

Then in a graver tone:

'Master, in the sanctuary of Tanit there is a mysterious veil, which
fell from heaven and covers the Goddess.'

'I know,' said Matho.

Spendius continued:

'It is in itself divine, for it is part of her. The gods dwell where

70

their images are set. It is because Carthage possesses this veil that Carthage is powerful.'

Then, whispering into his ear:

'I have brought you with me to ravish it away!'

Matho recoiled in horror.

'Go! Find someone else! I will have no part with you in such an execrable deed!'

'But Tanit is your enemy,' insisted Spendius. 'She persecutes you, her wrath is killing you. You can be avenged upon her. She will obey you; you will be well-nigh immortal and invincible.'

Matho bowed his head; and Spendius went on:

'We may be worsted; the army may bring about its own destruction. We have no escape to hope for, no help, no pardon! Why need you fear punishment from the gods, when you have their power in your own hands? Would you rather die miserably under a bush in a night of defeat, or be burned at the stake amid the jeers and insults of the crowd? Master, one day you will enter Carthage escorted by the colleges of the priests, & they will kiss your sandals; if the veil of Tanit still weighs upon you then, you can restore it to its temple. Come! Follow me, and take it!'

Matho was devoured by a terrible yearning. He would have liked to possess the veil, and at the same time to avoid the sacrilege. He told himself that perhaps he might acquire its virtue without necessarily seizing it. He did not plumb the bottom of his thought, but stopped at the point where it began to frighten him.

'Let us go!' he said.

And they strode quickly away side by side, without speaking.

The ground rose again, and houses became more frequent. They turned into narrow, dark streets. Rags of esparto-grass door coverings flapped against the walls; camels chewed the cud in a square, with some heaps of cut grass beside them. Then they passed under a leaf-covered balcony, and a pack of dogs barked at them. Suddenly they came into a wider space, and recognized the western face of the Acropolis. At the foot of Byrsa lay a long black mass which was the temple of Tanit, an accumulation of monuments and gardens, courts and fore-courts, bounded by a low wall of unmortared stones. Spendius and Matho vaulted over it.

This first barrier enclosed a wood of plane-trees, planted as a protection against the plague and tainted air. Tents were scattered here and there in which, by day, were sold depilatory pastes, and scents and garments and moon-shaped cakes, images of the Goddess and models of the temple carved from blocks of alabaster.

They had nothing to fear, for on nights when there was no moon the rites were suspended: nevertheless Matho shortened his pace, and stopped before the three ebony steps which led to the second enclosure.

'Go on!' said Spendius.

Pomegranates, almond trees, cypresses and myrtles stood in regular succession, as still as if their leaves were made of bronze: the path was paved with blue pebbles, and crunched under their feet; and there was a hanging bower of full-blown roses over the whole length of the avenue. They came to an oval opening protected by a grate. Matho, appalled by the silence, said to Spendius:

'It is here that they mix the Sweet with the Bitter Waters.'

'I have seen all that,' returned the former slave, 'in Syria, in the town of Maphug.'

And they climbed six silver steps into the third enclosure.

The middle of this was occupied by a mighty cedar, the lower branches of which were hidden beneath scraps of stuff and necklaces hung upon them by the faithful. They went a few steps further, and the front of the temple came in view.

Two long porticoes, with their architraves resting on squat columns, flanked a square tower, the platform of which was adorned with a crescent moon. At the angles of the porticoes & at the four corners of the tower stood vases of burning aromatics. The capitals were charged with pomegranates and colocynths, and the walls decorated with a pattern of twined knots, lozenges, and rows of pearls; a hedge of silver filigree made a wide semi-circle in front of the brass staircase which led down from the vestibule.

At the entrance, between a golden stele and one of emerald, stood a cone of stone; and Matho kissed his right hand as he passed it.

The first chamber was very lofty; its vaulted roof was pierced by countless openings, & on looking upwards one could see the stars. All round the wall were rush baskets heaped up with beards and hair, the firstlings of adolescence; and in the middle of the round hall there was a case covered with paps, from which protruded the body of a woman. Fat, bearded, and with lowered eye-lids, she seemed to be smiling; and her hands were crossed upon the bottom of her great belly, which was polished by the kisses of the people.

Then they found themselves once more in the open air, in a transverse corridor, where a little altar stood against an ivory door beyond which it was impossible to go: only the priests could open that door; for the temple was not a meeting-place for the multitude, but the particular abode of a Divinity.

'It is impossible,' said Matho. 'You had not thought of this! Let us go back!'

Spendius was examining the walls.

He wanted the veil, not because he had faith in its virtue (Spendius believed only in the Oracle), but because he was persuaded that the Carthaginians would fall into a panic on finding themselves without it. They walked all round the back, and looked for an opening.

Under clusters of terebinths they saw variously shaped pavilions. Here and there stood up a stone phallus, and great stags wandered peacefully, spurning the fallen fir-cones with their cloven hoofs.

They made their way back between two long parallel galleries with little cells opening out from them, which had tambourines and cymbals hooked from top to bottom of their cedar columns. On mats outside the cells women were sleeping. Their bodies were greasy with unguents, and redolent of spices and burned-out censers; and they were so covered with tattooings, and necklaces and rings, and vermilion & antimony, that but for the moving of their breasts they might have been idols thus lying upon the ground. There was a lotus-fringed fountain in which fish like Salambo's were swimming: and spread against the temple wall in the background was a vine, whose branches were of glass and the grapes of emerald. Splashes of light from the precious stones played through the painted columns upon the sleeping faces.

Matho felt stifled in the warm atmosphere which beat out at him from the cedar partitions. All these symbols of fecundation, these perfumes, these radiations and exhalations overwhelmed him. In this mystic maze his thoughts turned to Salambo. She became confused in his mind with the Goddess herself; and his love spread forth the more strongly, like great lotuses upon deep waters.

Spendius was calculating how much he would once have made by the sale of these women; and, with a rapid glance as he passed by, estimated the weight of the golden necklaces.

From this side as from the other, the temple was impenetrable; and they returned to behind the first chamber. While Spendius was searching and ferreting, Matho lay prone before the door and supplicated Tanit. He besought her not to permit this sacrilege, and strove to soothe her with such soft words as are used to an angry woman.

Spendius descried a narrow aperture above the door.

'Get up!' he said to Matho, and made him stand upright with his back against the wall.

Then, placing one foot in his hands and the other upon his head, he reached and climbed into the air-hole, and disappeared. Then there fell upon Matho's shoulders the knotted cord which Spendius had coiled about his body before entering the cisterns; & climbing up it with both hands, he soon found himself with the other in a large and shadowy hall.

An outrage of this sort was something extraordinary. That the precautions against it were so inadequate was clear proof that it was considered impossible. It was awe, rather than their walls, which kept the sanctuaries inviolate. Matho expected death at every step.

A light was glimmering far in the darkness, and they went up to it. It came from a lamp burning in a shell on the pedestal of a statue which wore the cap of the Kabiri. There were diamond discs scattered about her long blue robe, & her heels were fastened to the ground by chains let into the stone paving. Suppressing a cry, Matho stammered:

'Ah, there she is! There she is!'

Spendius took up the lamp to light their way.

'How impious you are!' murmured Matho; but he followed nevertheless.

In the chamber which they next entered there was nothing but the black painting of another woman. Her legs reached the top of the wall, and her body filled the entire ceiling; a huge egg hung by a thread from her navel; and she fell head downwards upon the other wall, to touch the floor stones with her pointed fingers.

They drew aside a hanging, meaning to go further; but a draught of wind blew out the light.

They groped among the mazes of the architecture, and all at once felt something strangely soft under their feet: sparks were flashing and dancing, and it was as if they walked in fire. Spendius touched the floor and found it to be carefully carpeted with lynx skins. Then they felt something like a great rope, wet and cold and slimy, slipping between their legs. Thin white rays fell through the slits cut in the walls, and gave them an uncertain light as they went on. At last they made out the form of a vast black serpent; it darted quickly away and disappeared.

'Let us flee!' exclaimed Matho. 'It is she! I feel her: she is coming.'

'No, no!' answered Spendius. 'The temple is empty.'

A dazzling light made them lower their eyes, and then, all about them, they saw innumerable beasts, lank and panting, with hooked claws, mingling one above another in a mysterious and frightful confusion. There were serpents with feet, and winged bulls; man-headed fishes were eating fruits; flowers blossomed in the jaws of crocodiles; and elephants with uplifted trunks floated through the air, in all the pride of eagles. Their imperfect or manifold limbs were swollen with terrible effort: as they thrust out their tongues, they looked as if they would send forth their souls. Every sort of shape was there, as if the very repository of life had suddenly hatched and burst and emptied itself upon the walls of the hall.

About the walls stood twelve globes of blue crystal, supported by tiger-like monsters. Their eyes stood out like a snail's, and they were twisted round upon their squat loins that they might look backwards to where, splendid upon an ivory chariot, shone Rabbet the Supreme, the Omnifecund, the Last-conceived.

She was covered as far as the belly with shells and feathers, flowers and birds. Her earrings were silver cymbals, beating against her cheeks. Her great eyes gazed fixedly upon you; and a luminous stone, set in an obscene symbol upon her brow, lit the whole hall with its reflection from red copper mirrors set above the door.

As Matho took a step forward, a stone gave under his feet; and immediately the globes began to revolve and the monsters to roar; there rose a tuneful & swelling music, like the harmony of planets; and the tumultuous soul of Tanit was poured streaming forth. She was about to rise as huge as the hall, with open arms. Suddenly the monsters closed their jaws, & the crystal globes revolved no longer.

A mournful modulation lingered on the air for a time, and at last died away.

'The veil?' asked Spendius.

It was nowhere to be seen. Where could it be? How could it be found? And what if the priests had hidden it? Matho felt his heart rent, as if all his faith were shattered.

'This way!' whispered Spendius.

Guided by inspiration, he led Matho behind Tanit's chariot, where they found a cleft a cubit wide, cutting the wall from top to bottom.

They came through it into a small round chamber, so high that it was like the inside of a pillar. In the midst was a great black stone in the shape of a half sphere, like a kettle-drum: there were flames burning upon it, and an ebony cone, bearing a head and two arms, stood up behind it.

Beyond it was that which might have been a cloud with stars glittering athwart it: they could distinguish shapes in its deep folds; Eshmun with the Kabiri, & some of the monsters they had already seen; sacred beasts of the Babylonians, and others which were unknown to them. It passed like a mantle under the idol's face, and rose in a spread upon the wall, to which it was fastened by the corners; it was at the same time blue as night, and yellow as the dawn, and purple as the sun, shadowy, diaphanous, sparkling, impalpable. This was the mantle of the Goddess, the holy zaimph upon which none might look. They both turned pale.

'Take it!' said Matho at last.

Spendius did not hesitate. Leaning upon the idol, he unfastened the veil; and it sank to the ground. Matho laid his hand upon it; then he put his head through its opening and wrapped it about his body, spreading out his arms the better to view it.

'Let us go!' said Spendius.

Matho stood panting, his eyes upon the pavement. Suddenly he cried:

'What if I went to her? I am no longer afraid of her beauty! What could she do against me? I am more than a man now. I could pass through flames! I could walk upon the sea! I am rapt out of myself! Salambo! Salambo! I am your master!'

His voice was like thunder, and he seemed to Spendius to have grown taller and to have become transfigured.

Footsteps were heard approaching, a door opened, and a man appeared, a tall-capped priest with staring eyes. Before he could make a movement Spendius had rushed upon him and, clasping his arms about him, had buried both his daggers in his sides. His head rang upon the pavement.

They stood listening for a while, as still as the corpse itself. They could hear nothing but the wind murmuring through the half-open door.

This gave upon a narrow passage, which Spendius entered, followed by Matho; and they found themselves almost at once in the third enclosure, between the flanking lines of porticoes which held the dwellings of the priests.

There must surely be a shorter way out behind these cells. They hurried forward.

Spendius squatted down at the edge of the fountain and washed his bloody hands. The women were asleep, and the emerald vine still glittered. They went on their way.

Someone seemed to be running behind them under the trees; and Matho, who was still wearing the veil, several times felt it pulled very gently from below. The thing was a great baboon, one of those which lived at large within the enclosure of the Goddess. It clung to the mantle as if it knew that it was being stolen; but they did not dare to strike it, for fear that it might redouble its cries. Suddenly its rage subsided, & it trotted close beside them, swinging its body between its hanging arms. At the barrier it gave one bound into a palm tree.

When they had left the last enclosure, they turned towards Hamilcar's palace; for Spendius understood the futility of trying to turn Matho from his purpose.

They went by the Street of the Tanners, the Square of Muthumbal, the Herb Market and the Crossways of Cynasyn. At the corner of a wall a man drew back, frightened by this sparkling thing which moved through the darkness.

'Hide the zaimph!' said Spendius.

Other people passed them; but they escaped detection.

At last they recognized the houses of Megara.

The pharos, standing in the background on the top of the cliff, lit up the heavens with a great red glow; & the shadow of the palace, with its terraces rising one above the other, fell upon the gardens like a monstrous pyramid. They entered through the hedge of jujube plum trees, cutting their way through the branches with their daggers.

Traces of the Mercenaries' feast were everywhere still manifest. The parks were broken up, the trenches drained, and the doors of the slave prison stood open. No one was to be seen about the kitchens or cellars. They were amazed at this silence, which was broken occasionally by the hoarse breathing of elephants moving in their shackles, and by the crackling of the beacon of aloes on the pharos.

Matho meanwhile kept saying:

'Where is she? I want to see her! Show me!'

'It is madness!' Spendius kept answering. 'She will call out, her slaves will come; and, in spite of your strength, you will be killed!'

So they came to the stairway of the galleys. Matho raised his head and thought that he could see an indistinct glow far above him, radiant and soft. Spendius tried to hold him back; but he dashed up the steps.

Back again in places where he had once seen her, he forgot all about the time that had intervened. But a moment ago she was singing among the tables; she had disappeared, and he had been climbing these stairs ever since. The sky was all fire above his head; the horizon was filled by the sea; each step brought him into a greater immensity of space; and he went on climbing with that strange ease that comes to us in dreams.

The rustling of the veil against the stones recalled his new power to him: his hopes so overflowed that he no longer knew what he should do; he was alarmed by this uncertainty.

From time to time he pressed his face against the square windows of the closed apartments, and in some of them he thought he could see people asleep.

The last storey was narrower, and formed a sort of dado on the top of the terraces. Matho walked slowly round it.

The sheets of talc over the little openings in the wall were filled with a milky light; and in their symmetrical arrangement they looked like rows of fine pearls in the darkness. He recognized the red door with the black cross. His heart beat faster. He would have liked to run away. He pushed the door, and it opened.

A lamp shaped like a galley hung burning at the back of the room; and from its silver keel three pencils of light trembled upon the high wainscoting, which was painted red with black bars. The ceiling was a cluster of small beams, with amethysts and topazes, amid their gilding, in the knots of the wood. By each of the longer walls of the apartment stood a very low bed made of white leather bands; and above each was a shell-like half-circle cut from the thickness of the wall and holding articles of apparel, some of which hung to the ground.

There was an oval bath with a margin of onyx; delicate snake-skin slippers were standing on its edge beside an alabaster flagon. A little further on was the mark of a wet foot. Exquisite perfumes fainted there.

Matho tip-toed over the floor-stones, which were encrusted with gold and glass and mother-of-pearl; and in spite of their polished smoothness, his feet seemed to sink into them as if he were walking on sand.

Behind the silver lamp he had noticed a large azure-coloured square suspended by four cords; and he went towards it, crouching and open-mouthed.

Flamingoes' wings, fitted on branches of black coral, trailed among purple cushions and tortoiseshell strigils, cedar boxes and ivory spattles. There were antelopes' horns with rings & bracelets slipped upon them; and in the cleft of the wall clay vases stood to cool in the wind on a lattice-work of reeds. Several times he stubbed his feet; for the floor was of varying levels, dividing the room, as it were, into a series of apartments. At the back was a flower-painted carpet with a silver balustrade about it. At last he came to the hanging bed; an ebony stool stood near from which to climb into it.

The light reached no further than its edge; and the shadow, like a great curtain, hid all but a corner of the red mattress and the tip of a little bare foot resting upon its ankle. Very gently, Matho took up the lamp.

She was sleeping with her cheek in one hand, and the other arm stretched out. The rings of her hair were heaped about her in such profusion that she might have been couched upon black feathers; and her wide white tunic fell in soft draperies to her feet, following the inflexions of her body. Her eyes could just be seen under her half-closed eyelids. The straight falling curtains threw a blue shadow about her; & the motion of her breathing made the cords sway a little, so that she seemed to be rocked in air. A large mosquito was humming there.

Matho stood motionless, holding the silver galley at arm's length. Suddenly the mosquito-net caught fire & vanished. And Salambo awoke.

The fire had burned itself out. She did not speak. The lamp caused a great watery light to flicker on the wainscots.

'What is it?' she said.

And he answered:

'It is the veil of the Goddess!'

'The veil of the Goddess!' cried Salambo.

And supporting herself on her two hands, she leaned shudderingly outward. He went on:

'I have been to fetch it for you from the inmost depths of the sanctuary! Look!'

The zaimph was a glittering nexus of rays.

'Do you remember?' said Matho. 'You came to me at night in my dreams; but I did not understand the silent bidding of your eyes!'

She put one foot upon the ebony stool.

'Had I understood, I should have run to you; I should have forsaken the army; I should not have left Carthage. At your command I would go down through the caverns of Hadrumetum into the kingdom of the Shades!... Forgive me! There were mountains weighing upon my days; and yet something drew me on! I sought to come to you! Should I ever have dared, unless the gods were with me? Let us go! You must follow me! Or, if you do not wish that, I will remain. What does it matter to me? . . . Drown my soul in the breath of your breathing! Let my lips be bruised with kissing your hands!'

'Let me see it!' she said. 'Nearer! Nearer!'

Day was breaking, and the sheets of talc in the walls were filled with winy colour. Salambo leaned back faintly against the cushions of the bed.

'I love you!' cried Matho.

She stammered: 'Give it me!'

And they drew closer together.

She kept coming forward, clothed in her trailing white simar, her great eyes fastened upon the veil.

Matho gazed at her, dazzled by the glory of her head; holding out the zaimph towards her, he made as if to enfold her. She was holding out her arms. Suddenly she stopped, and they stood gaping at each other.

Without understanding what he asked, she was seized with horror. Her slim eyebrows rose, and her lips opened. She trembled. At last she struck one of the brass pateras which hung at the corners of the red mattress, crying:

'Help! Help! Back, sacrilegious one! Infamous and accursed! Help! Taanash, Krum, Ewa, Micipsa, Shaul!'

And the scared face of Spendius, appearing in the wall between the clay flagons, hurled these words:

'Fly! They are coming!'

The stairs were shaken by a great tumult, and a flood of women, serving-men, and slaves poured into the room with spears and maces, cutlasses and daggers. They were stricken motionless with indignation at seeing a man: the women made funeral wailing, and the eunuchs grew pale under their black skin.

Matho was standing behind the balustrades. Wrapped about with the zaimph, he looked like a stellar god clothed in the firmament. The slaves were about to fall upon him; but she checked them:

'Do not touch it! It is the mantle of the Goddess!'

She had drawn back into a corner; but now took a step towards him, stretching out one bare arm:

'A curse upon you, who have plundered Tanit! Hatred and vengeance, slaughter and sorrow! May Gurzil, god of battles, rend you!

May Mastiman, god of the dead, choke you! May that Other—whose name may not be said—now burn you!'

Matho uttered a cry, as if he had received a sword thrust.

She kept on saying:

'Begone! Begone!'

The crowd of servants gave way, and Matho, with lowered head, passed slowly through them: at the door he stopped, for the fringe of the zaimph had caught on one of the golden stars which paved the flagstones. He jerked it off with a rough movement of his shoulder, and went down the stairways.

Spendius, leaping from terrace to terrace and jumping the hedges and trenches, had escaped from the gardens, and reached the foot of the pharos. The wall was discontinued here, so inaccessible was the cliff. He went up to the edge, lay down on his back, and let himself slide feet foremost, down its whole length, to the bottom. Then he swam to the Cape of the Tombs, made a wide detour by the salt lagoon, and re-entered the Barbarians' camp at evening.

The sun had risen: and like a retreating lion Matho came down the paths, casting terrible glances about him.

A vague clamour came to his ears. It had started from the palace, and was beginning afresh in the distance towards the Acropolis. Some said that the treasure of the Republic had been seized from the temple of Moloch; others spoke of the assassination of a priest. It was thought also that the Barbarians had entered the city.

Matho, not knowing how to make his way out of the enclosures, walked straight before him. He was seen, and an outcry raised. Everyone understood at last; there was first consternation, & then unmeasured anger.

From the back of the Mappales quarter, from the heights of the Acropolis, from the catacombs, from the borders of the lake, the multitude came running. Patricians left their palaces, merchants their shops; women abandoned their children. They seized on swords, axes and clubs; but were checked by the same obstacle which had stayed Salambo. How could the veil be retrieved when but to look upon it was a crime? It was of the nature of the gods, and to touch it was death.

Priests were wringing their hands in despair on the peristyles of the temples. The guards of the Legion galloped at random; the people climbed up on the houses, on the terraces, on the shoulders of colossi and the masts of ships. Still he went on, and at each of his steps their rage increased, their panic also. The streets emptied at his approach, & this torrent of fleeing men streamed up from both sides to the tops of the walls. He saw nothing anywhere but eyes opened wide as if to devour him, gnashing teeth, and clenched fists; and Salambo's curses were re-echoed and multiplied against him.

Suddenly a long arrow whistled by him, then another, & stones began to hum about him: but these missiles were badly aimed, since men were afraid of hitting the zaimph, and passed over his head. Moreover, he used the veil as a shield, holding it to right, to left, before him and behind him; and they could think of no plan. He walked more and more quickly as he entered the open streets. These were barred with ropes and chariots and snares; and every time he turned aside he found himself retreating. At last he entered the Square of Khamon, where the Balearic slingers had perished: here Matho stopped, and grew pale as one about to die. This time he was surely lost; and the crowd clapped their hands.

He ran up to the great closed gate. It was very high, and made throughout with heart of oak; it was studded with iron & sheathed in brass. Matho hurled himself against it. The people stamped their feet with joy as they saw the impotence of his fury. Then he took off his sandal, spat upon it, and beat the immovable panels with it. The whole city yelled. The veil was forgotten now, and they were ready to crush him. Matho cast wide troubled eyes upon the crowd. The pulses in his temples throbbed as if they would stun him; he felt fallen into the torpor of the drunk. Suddenly he caught sight of the long chain that was used to work the levers of the gate. With a bound he grasped it, stiffening his arms and buttressing himself with his feet; and at last the huge leaves swung open a little.

When he was outside he took the great zaimph from his neck and raised it as high as he could above his head. The stuff of it, upborne by the sea breeze, flashed its colours, its gems, and the figures of its gods to the sun. Matho carried it thus across the whole plain, as far as the soldiers' tents; and the people on the walls watched the passing of the fortune of Carthage.

HANNO

CHAPTER VI

'I OUGHT TO HAVE BORNE HER AWAY!' HE SAID TO
Spendius that evening. 'I should have seized her, torn her from
her house! No one would have dared aught against me!'
Spendius was not listening to him. He was stretched on his back
deliciously resting, beside a large jar of honied water, into which
he plunged his head from time to time to drink more copiously.
   Matho continued:
'What is to be done? ... How can we re-enter Carthage?'
'I do not know,' said Spendius.
Matho was exasperated by this impassivity, and cried:
'It is your fault! You drag me there, and then forsake me, O coward
that you are! Why should I obey you? Do you think you are my
master? Ah, you pimp! You slave, and son of a slave!'
He ground his teeth and lifted his great hand against Spendius.
The Greek did not answer. A light was burning gently in an
earthenware sconce against the tent-pole, where the zaimph shim-
mered among the hanging armour.
Suddenly Matho put on his buskins, buckled his brazen coat of
mail upon him, and took his helmet.

'Where are you going?' asked Spendius.
'I am going back! Let me be! I shall bring her away! And if they oppose me I will crush them like vipers! I will put her to death, Spendius!'
And again he said:
'I will kill her! You shall see, I will kill her!'
Spendius, whose ears were on the alert, suddenly caught up the zaimph and, throwing it into a corner, covered it over with fleeces. A murmur of voices came to them; there was a gleam of torches, and Narr'Havas entered, followed by some twenty men.
They wore white woollen cloaks, long daggers, and leather collars, wooden eardrops, & boots of hyena skin; halting on the threshold, they leaned upon their lances like resting shepherds. Narr'Havas was the handsomest of them all; there were pearl-crusted bands about his slender arms, and in the hoop of gold which fastened his ample robe about his head was an ostrich plume, which swept downward over his shoulder behind; his teeth showed in a continual smile; his eyes looked sharp as arrows; all about him there was an air of light alertness.
He explained that he had come to join the Mercenaries, because the Republic had long been threatening his kingdom. It was therefore to his interest to help the Barbarians, and he might also be of use to them.
'I will provide you with elephants (my forests are full of them), and with wine, oil, barley and dates; and with pitch and sulphur for your sieges; and I can bring you twenty thousand foot-soldiers and ten thousand horse. If I address myself to you, Matho, it is because the possession of the zaimph has made you the first man in the army.'
And he added:
'Besides, we are old friends.'
Matho looked at Spendius, who was sitting on his sheepskins, listening and giving little nods of assent. Narr'Havas went on speaking, calling his gods to be his witness, and cursing Carthage. He broke a javelin in the heat of his imprecation; and his men gave a loud shout. Matho, carried away by their passion, cried out that he accepted their alliance.

They brought a white bull and a black sheep, symbols of day and night, and cut their throats over a trench. When it was full of blood they plunged their arms into it. Then Narr'Havas placed his open hand upon Matho's breast, and Matho his on the breast of Narr'Havas; and they repeated this blood sign on their tent-cloths. Afterward they passed the night in eating, & burned what was left of the meat, together with the skin and bones, and horns and hoofs.

A mighty burst of applause had greeted Matho when he returned wearing the veil of the Goddess; even those who were not of the Canaanite religion felt with a vague thrill the advent of a Spirit. As for trying to seize the zaimph, no one ever dreamed of this; for, to the Barbarian mind, the mysterious manner in which he had won it had sufficiently established his claim to it. So thought the soldiers of the African race. The others, whose hatred of Carthage was of more recent birth, could not make up their minds. If they had had any ships, they would have departed at once.

Spendius, Narr'Havas and Matho despatched envoys to all the tribes within the Punic territories.

Carthage was draining these nations. She wrung exorbitant taxes from them; and any tardiness of payment, any murmuring even, was punished with imprisonment, decapitation or crucifixion. They were made to cultivate whatever suited the Republic's requirement, and to provide whatever she demanded: no one was allowed to own a weapon: when a village rebelled, its inhabitants were sold into slavery; the worth of a governor was reckoned like that of a wine-press, by the quantity which he could squeeze from them. Then, beyond the regions immediately subject to Carthage, lay allies who paid only a moderate tribute; and behind these allies roamed the Nomads, who might at any time be let loose upon them. This system assured that the crops were always abundant, the studs skilfully managed, and the plantations superb. The elder Cato, an expert in matters of tillage and slave culture, was amazed at these things ninety-two years later; and his oft repeated demand at Rome for the destruction of Carthage was but an exclamation of jealousy and greed.

During the last war these impositions had been doubled, so that the towns of Libya had nearly all surrendered to Regulus. As a punishment, they had been compelled to pay a thousand talents, twenty thousand oxen, and three hundred bags of gold dust; considerable advances of corn had been exacted from them, and the chiefs of the tribes had been crucified or thrown to the lions.

Tunis above all execrated Carthage. Older than the metropolis, it could not forgive her her greatness: it fronted her walls, crouching in the mire on the water's edge like a venomous beast watching her. It survived all transportations, massacres, and epidemics. It had supported Archagathas, the son of Agathocles. The Eaters of Unclean Things very quickly found weapons there.

Even before the couriers had set forth, a universal rejoicing broke out in the provinces. They incontinently strangled the stewards of the houses and the functionaries of the Republic in the baths; they brought their old weapons out of the caves where they had hidden them; they beat their ploughshares into swords; the children sharpened javelins on the door stones, and the women gave their necklaces, rings, ear-rings, and indeed all that could help towards the destruction of Carthage. Everyone was eager to do his share. Piles of lances were stacked up in the towns like sheaves of maize. Cattle and money were despatched, so that Matho speedily paid the Mercenaries their arrears: and for this, which was the idea of Spendius, he was appointed general-in-chief, the schalischim of the Barbarians.

Reinforcements of men poured in at the same time. First came the aborigines, & then the slaves from the fields. Caravans of Negroes were seized and armed; and merchants on their way to Carthage associated themselves with the Barbarians, hoping for surer profit. There was a continual influx of large bodies of men. From the heights of the Acropolis the army could be seen growing.

The guards of the Legion were posted as sentries on the platform of the aqueduct; & brazen vats full of boiling pitch stood near them at regular intervals. The great host in the plain below remained in a tumult of movement. They were undecided, and in that state of embarrassment which always comes to Barbarians when they are faced by fortifications.

Utica and Hippo-Zaritus refused their alliance. They were Phoe-

nician colonies themselves like Carthage, and though they were
self-governing, and had always inserted in the treaties concluded
by the Republic clauses to distinguish themselves from her, they
nevertheless respected this stronger sister who protected them, and
did not think that a horde of Barbarians would be capable of con-
quering her; but rather that they would be exterminated. They
desired to remain neutral and to live at peace.

But their position rendered them indispensable. Utica, standing at
the foot of a gulf, was conveniently placed for bringing help to Carthage from without. If Utica alone were captured, Hippo-Zaritus,
six hours further along the coast, would take its place, & the metropolis, being revictualled in this way, would prove impregnable.

Spendius wished to begin the siege at once; but Narr'Havas opposed
this plan in favour of first making an advance upon the frontier.
This was the opinion of the veterans and of Matho himself; and it
was decided that Spendius should attack Utica, and Matho Hippo-
Zaritus, while the third division of the army under Autharitus
should occupy the plain of Carthage, with Tunis as its base. As
for Narr'Havas, he was to return to his own kingdom to procure
elephants, and to patrol the roads with his cavalry.

The women cried out aloud at this decision; for they were covetous
of the jewels of the Punic ladies. The Libyans also protested: they
had been appealed to for help against Carthage & now were marching away from it! The soldiers set out almost alone. Matho was in
command of his own countrymen, together with the Iberians,
Lusitanians, the men of the West and of the Islands; all those who
spoke Greek had asked for Spendius to lead them, on account of
his mental quickness.

The sight of the army suddenly moving away caused utter amazement. It stretched out under the mount of Ariana along the seaside
road to Utica. Part of it remained before Tunis; and the rest disappeared, to come into view again at the other side of the gulf on
the skirts of the woods, into which it was swallowed.

They were perhaps eighty thousand strong. The two Tyrian cities
would offer no resistance; and they would return against Carthage,
which was already cut off by a considerable army that occupied
the base of the isthmus: it would soon be starved out, for it could

not live without help from the provinces, since the citizens paid no contributions as they did at Rome. Carthage was lacking in political genius. Her eternal lust for gain debarred her from that wisdom which comes from nobler ideals. She was no more than a galley anchored on the Libyan sands, and it was by dint of hard labour that she maintained her position. The nations roared about her like waves, & the slightest storm rocked this formidable vessel.

The treasury was exhausted by the Roman war and by all that had been squandered and lost in chaffering with the Barbarians. Meanwhile the Republic had dire need of soldiers, and not a single government would trust her! Ptolemy had lately refused her a loan of two thousand talents. Moreover, she was disheartened by the rape of the veil, as Spendius had wisely foreseen.

But this nation, knowing herself to be hated, clasped her money and her gods to her heart; and her patriotism was kept alive by the very constitution of her government.

In the first place, the power was shared by all in common, without any one man being strong enough to engross it. Private debts were treated as public debts. The men of Canaanite race had a monopoly of commerce; and through multiplying by usury the profits they gained from piracy, by harsh exploitation of lands and slaves and of the poor, they not seldom achieved riches. Wealth was the sole key to public office; and although authority and money always rested with the same families, people tolerated this oligarchy because there was always the hope of winning to a share in it.

The legislature was formed by the merchant guilds, who elected the intendants of finance; & these, at the end of their term of office, nominated the hundred members of the Council of Elders, who were themselves responsible to the Grand Assembly, or general convention of all the Rich. As for the two Suffetes, those relics of the monarchy, who were of less account than consuls; they were chosen from two distinct families on the same day; and it was contrived that there should be every sort of rivalry & personal enmity between them, so that they might frustrate and weaken each other. They had no voice in matters of war or peace; but if they were defeated the Grand Council crucified them.

Hence the central power in Carthage was the Syssitia, that is to say a great court in the middle of Malqua, at the place where the Phoenician sailors were said to have beached their first vessel at a time when the sea had flowed much further inland. It was a collection of little rooms of archaic architecture, built of palm trunks with stone corner-pieces, & separated from one another so as to ensure privacy for each of the various companies. The Rich assembled there all day to discuss their own concerns and those of the government, from the procuring of pepper to the extermination of Rome. Three times every moon they had their couches taken up to the high terrace bordering upon the wall of the court, and from below might be seen at table in mid-air, unbooted and uncloaked, with their diamond-covered fingers moving over the dishes, and their great ear-rings hanging down among the flagons: all fat and lusty, half-naked, laughing and eating in the blue of the sky, like great sharks sporting in the sea.

But just now they could not disguise their anxiety, so pale they were, and the crowd which waited for them at the gates escorted them back to their palaces, in the hope of learning some news from them. Every house was shut, as they were in times of plague; the streets would fill and suddenly empty again; certain folk went up to the Acropolis or ran to the harbour; and the Great Council deliberated every night. At last the people were convened in the Square of Khamon, and it was decided to put matters under the control of Hanno, the conqueror of Hecatompylos.

This was a pious and crafty man, one pitiless towards the people of Africa, and a true Carthaginian. His revenues equalled those of the Barcas. No one had greater administrative experience.

He ordered the enrolment of all able-bodied citizens, placed catapults on the towers, and exacted exorbitant supplies of weapons; he even ordered the construction of fourteen galleys of which there was no need: he saw that everything was registered and carefully set down in writing. He had himself conveyed to the arsenal, the pharos, and the temple treasuries; his great litter was continually to be seen swinging from step to step as it went up the stairways of the Acropolis. And in his palace at night, since he could not sleep, he would prepare himself for battle by shouting out army commands in a terrible voice.

Overpowering fear made a hero of every man, and the Rich drew up in line along the Mappales at cockcrow and, tucking up their robes, practised the use of the pike. But, for want of an instructor, they would have arguments about it, and sit down breathless upon the tombs, and begin again. Several even subjected themselves to a diet. Some thought that they must eat a great deal in order to gain strength, and gorged themselves; while others, who were incommoded by their corpulence, weakened themselves by fasting in an attempt to become slim.

Utica had already called several times upon Carthage for help; but Hanno would not move until the last screw was driven home in his engines of war. He lost three further moons in equipping the hundred and twelve elephants stabled among the ramparts. These were the conquerors of Regulus, and the people loved them; no treatment was too good for such old friends. Hanno had their brazen breast-plates recast, their tusks gilt, and their towers enlarged, and had most heavily fringed caparisons cut for them from the finest purple. Finally, as their drivers were called Indians (no doubt because their first drivers had come from the Indies), he ordered them all to be dressed after the Indian fashion; that is, with white turbans, and little byssus breeches which, with cross folds, hung from their hips like the two valves of a shell.

All this time the army of Autharitus lay before Tunis, hidden behind a wall built of mud from the lake and protected at the top by thorn bushes. Some of the Negroes had stuck horrible faces on tall sticks at intervals along it; human masks made of birds' feathers, & jackals' or serpents' heads, to gape at the enemy and terrify them, and the Barbarians, thinking that this rendered them invincible, danced, wrestled & juggled, in the conviction that Carthage would soon fall. Anyone but Hanno would easily have crushed this horde, hampered as it was by herds and women. Moreover, they had no military skill, and Autharitus was so disheartened that he had ceased to expect it of them.

They drew aside when he passed, rolling his great blue eyes. On reaching the edge of the lake he would take off his sealskin tunic, unfasten the cord which tied up his long red hair and soak it in the water. He regretted not having deserted to the Romans along with the two thousand Gauls of the temple of Eryx.

Often in the middle of the day the sun would suddenly be blotted out, and the gulf and the open sea would seem as motionless as molten lead. A cloud of brown dust whirled forward in a straight column; the palm trees bent and the sky was hidden, and stones were heard rattling upon the flanks of the animals: the Gaul would glue his lips to the holes in his tent, and gasp in his exhaustion and melancholy. He was thinking of the scent of pastures on autumn mornings, of snowflakes, and of the lowing of the aurochs in the fog; when he closed his eyes, he thought he saw the fires in the long straw-thatched cottages, flickering on the marshes in the depth of the woods.

There were others, as well as he, who longed for their native land, although it was not so distant; the Carthaginian captives could make out the awnings spread over the courtyards of their houses beyond the gulf, on the slopes of Byrsa. But they were constantly patrolled by sentries, and all were fastened together by one chain; each of them wore an iron carcanet; and the crowd was never tired of coming to gaze at them. The women would show their little children the fine robes that hung in rags from their wasted limbs.

Whenever Autharitus looked at Gisco he was seized with rage at the thought of the injury he had received, and would have killed him but for the oath he had sworn to Narr'Havas. Then he would go back to his tent and drink a mixture of barley and cumin until he lost his senses in drunkenness, from which he would awake in broad daylight, consumed with a horrible thirst.

Matho, meanwhile, was besieging Hippo-Zaritus.

But the town was protected by a lake communicating with the sea. It had three lines of circumvallation, & around the heights dominating it ran a wall fortified with towers. He had never been in command of such an enterprise before. Besides, the thought of Salambo obsessed him; & he dreamed as much of the pleasures of her beauty as of the delights of a vengeance which carried him away with pride. He felt a biting, furious, unceasing need to see her again. He even thought of presenting himself as an ambassador, in the hope that, once inside Carthage, he might find his way to her. Often he would sound the assault and rush incontinently upon the mole which the enemy was trying to build into the sea. He would snatch up the stones in his hands, overthrowing, striking & thrusting with his sword on every side. The Barbarians charged pell-mell; the ladders broke with a loud crash, & masses of men tumbled into the water, sending up red splashes against the walls: then the tumult would subside, and the soldiers retire but to begin again.

Matho would go and sit outside the tents: he wiped his blood-spattered face with his arm, and gazed at the skyline in the direction of Carthage.

In front of him, among the olives and palms, the myrtles and plane trees, lay two wide pools which met another lake, the contours of which could not be seen. There was a mountain, with other mountains towering behind it; and in the middle of the immense lake stood an island, perfectly black and shaped like a pyramid. On the left, at the end of the gulf, the sand-heaps showed as great pale waves stopped in their motion; while the sea, as flat as a pavement of lapis, rose imperceptibly to the edge of the sky. The greenery of the country was lost in places under long patches of yellow; carobs shone like coral studs; vine branches hung down from the tops of the sycamores; the murmur of water could be heard; crested larks hopped hither and thither, and as the tortoises came from the reeds to taste the breeze the sun's last fire gilded their shells.

Matho heaved great sighs. He lay flat on his stomach, digging his nails into the ground and weeping: he felt wretched, abject, forsaken. He would never possess her. He could not even take a town.

Alone in his tent at night he would gaze at the zaimph. What good was this thing of the gods to him? Doubts arose in the Barbarian's mind. At other times it would seem to him that the robe of the Goddess was inseparable from Salambo herself, and that a part of her soul hovered about it, more subtle than a breath; he would feel it, breathe it, bury his face in it and, sobbing, kiss it. He would cover his shoulders with it to delude himself into believing he was near her.

Sometimes he would suddenly break away, step over the soldiers sleeping in their cloaks, spring upon a horse and, two hours later, be in Spendius' tent at Utica.

At first he would speak of the siege; but he had only come to comfort his sorrow by talking about Salambo. Spendius urged him to be prudent.

'Rid your soul of this unmanly sorrow! Once you had to obey

others; now you command an army. Even if Carthage is not conquered, we shall have provinces assigned to us: we shall be kings!'

But how was it that the possession of the zaimph did not give
them victory? According to Spendius, they must wait.

Matho fancied that the veil had virtue only for those of Canaanite
race, & with Barbaric subtlety said to himself: 'So the zaimph will
do nothing for me; but, since they have lost it, it will do nothing
for them.'

Afterwards he was troubled by a scruple. He was afraid lest by
worshipping Aptuknos, the God of the Libyans, he should offend
Moloch, and he timidly asked Spendius to which of the gods it
would be well to sacrifice a man.

'I should sacrifice all round!' laughed Spendius.

Matho, who could not understand such indifference, suspected the
Greek of having a Spirit of whom he would not speak.

Every religion as well as every race was to be met with in these
Barbarian armies; and other men's gods were respected, since they
were also feared. Many observed foreign rites in combination with
their own religion. Men might not be star worshippers, but such
or such a constellation was fatal or favourable, and so they offered
it sacrifice: an unknown amulet, found by chance in a moment of
peril, became a divinity; or it might be a name, no more than a
name, they would repeat it without trying to understand what it
meant. But, having looted temples and seen countless nations and
massacres, many of them no longer believed in anything but
destiny and death; and every evening these fell asleep as care-free
as wild beasts. Spendius would have spat upon the image of Olym-
pian Jupiter; yet he was afraid to speak aloud in the dark, nor did
he fail each day to put on his right boot first.

He was building a long quadrangular terrace in front of Utica; but
the higher it grew, so also was the rampart heightened: and what
was battered down by one side was almost immediately raised
again by the other. Spendius spared his men; he devised plans, and
tried to remember the stratagems he had heard described in his
travels. Why did Narr'Havas not return? There was ample cause
for anxiety.

Hanno had concluded his preparations. One moonless night he

transported his elephants and soldiers on rafts across the gulf of Carthage. Then they rounded the mountain of the Hot Springs so as to avoid Autharitus, and continued their march so slowly that instead of surprising the Barbarians in the morning as the Suffete had calculated, they did not reach them until broad daylight on the third day.

To the east of Utica was a plain stretching to the great lagoon of Carthage; behind it a valley ran at right angles between two low, abruptly terminating mountains. The Barbarians were encamped further to the left, in such a way as to blockade the harbour, and were sleeping in their tents (for on that day both sides were too weary to fight, and rested) when the Carthaginian army appeared round the bend of the hills.

Camp followers armed with slings were posted on the wings of it. The guards of the Legion, in golden scale armour, formed the first line, mounted on great horses which were shorn of mane, hair and ears, and had silver horns in the middle of their foreheads to make them look like rhinoceroses. Between their squadrons came youths in small helmets, poising an ashen javelin in each hand: & the long pikes of the heavy infantry brought up the rear. All these merchant soldiers had loaded their bodies with as many weapons as possible: there were some who carried a lance, an axe, a club, & two swords; others bristled with darts like porcupines, their arms stuck out from cuirasses made of sheets of horn or iron plates. Finally came the towering scaffolds of the war engines: carrobalistas, onagers, catapults and scorpions, rocking on cars drawn by mules and quadrigas of oxen: and as the army deployed the captains ran breathlessly right and left to give orders, to close up the files and maintain the proper intervals. Such of the Elders as held commands had come in purple gowns, the magnificent fringes of which got caught in their buskin straps. Their faces were daubed all over with vermilion & glistened under their huge helmets, which were crested with gods; and their shields, with ivory rims covered in precious stones, might have been suns passing over walls of brass.

The Carthaginians manœuvred so clumsily that the soldiers derisively invited them to sit down, calling out that they would soon purge their fat bellies, dust the gilding of their skins, and give them iron to drink.

At the top of the pole planted before Spendius' tent a strip of green cloth fluttered forth as a signal. The Carthaginian army answered it with a great noise of trumpets, cymbals, ass-bone flutes, and drums. The Barbarians had already leaped outside the palisades, and were facing the enemy within a javelin's throw.

A Balearic slinger took a step forward, put one of his clay balls into his sling and swung his arm. An ivory shield was shattered, and the two armies closed.

By pricking the horses' nostrils with the points of their lances, the Greeks made them rear and fall back upon their riders. The slaves detailed to hurl stones had picked ones that were too big & could only cast them so that they fell quite near themselves. The Punic soldiers, in making cutting strokes with their long swords, exposed their right sides. The Barbarians broke their lines, and had full sword room to cut their throats; they stumbled over the dying and dead, quite blinded by the blood that spurted into their faces. The confused mass of pikes and helmets, cuirasses and swords and human limbs, whirled over and over, widening and narrowing like elastic. Gaps appeared more and more frequently in the Carthaginian cohorts; & the engines stuck in the sand: finally the Suffete's litter, his great litter with the crystal pendants which had been seen from the beginning, tossing among the soldiers like a bark on the waves, suddenly foundered. He was surely dead. The Barbarians found themselves alone.

The dust about them was settling and they were beginning to sing, when Hanno himself appeared before them mounted high upon an elephant. He was bare-headed under a parasol of byssus, which was carried by a negro behind him. His necklace of blue plaques dangled against the flowers on his black tunic; there were diamond bracelets about his arms; his mouth was open, and he brandished a colossal spear, which spread at the end like a lotus and shone more brightly than a mirror.

Immediately the earth shook, and the Barbarians saw all the elephants of Carthage charging upon them in one line: they had gilt tusks and blue-painted ears, and were sheathed in bronze; on top of their scarlet caparisons rocked their leather towers, in each of which knelt three archers bending a great bow.

The soldiers had barely time to take up their arms, and formed up at random. They were frozen with terror, and did not know what to do.

Javelins, arrows, fire-darts and masses of lead were already being showered upon them from the towers. Some of them clung to the fringes of the caparisons, in an attempt to climb up; but their hands were struck off with cutlasses and they fell back upon the sword points. Their pikes were too frail, and broke; and the elephants passed through their phalanxes like wild boars through tufts of grass; they plucked up the stakes of the camp with their trunks, and went from one end to the other of it, overturning the tents with their breasts. The Barbarians had all fled, and were hiding in the hills bordering the valley by which the Carthaginians had come upon them.

The victorious Hanno presented himself before the gates of Utica. He had a trumpet sounded. The three Judges of the town appeared at the top of a tower in the opening of its battlements.

The people of Utica had no wish to admit such well-armed guests. Hanno flew into a rage; and at last they consented to receive him and a small escort.

The streets proved to be too narrow for the elephants, and they had to be left outside.

As soon as the Suffete was in the town the principal men came to greet him. He had himself taken to the baths, and summoned his cooks.

Three hours later he was still immersed in the cinnamon oil with which the bath had been filled; and while he bathed he ate flamingoes' tongues and poppy seeds seasoned with honey, served upon an ox-hide stretched before him. Beside him his Greek physician, motionless in a long yellow robe, directed the periodical re-heating of the bath; and two young boys leaned over its steps and rubbed his legs. But the care of his body did not interfere with his zeal for public affairs; for he was dictating a letter to the Great Council; also, as some prisoners had just been taken, he was taxing his powers of invention to find some terrible punishment for them.

'Stop!' he said to a slave who stood writing in the hollow of his hand. 'Let some of them be brought to me! I wish to see them!'

And from the end of the hall, which was filled with a whitish vapour stained red in places by the torches, three Barbarians were thrust forward: a Samnite, a Spartan, and a Cappadocian.

'Proceed!' said Hanno.

' "Rejoice, O light of the Baalim! Your Suffete has exterminated the ravenous dogs! Blessings upon the Republic! Give order for prayer!" '

Then, seeing the prisoners, he burst out laughing: 'Aha, my fine fellows of Sicca! You are not shouting so loud to-day! It is I! Do you know me? And where are your swords? What terrible fellows, to be sure!'

And he pretended to hide himself, as if he were afraid of them.

'You would ask for horses and women and land, and no doubt for magistracies and priesthoods! Why not? Very well, I will give you land, such land as you will never leave! You shall be married to fine new gallows! Your pay? It shall be cast in your mouths in ingots of molten lead! And I shall raise you to excellent and very exalted positions among the clouds, to bring you near the eagles!'

The three long-haired and ragged Barbarians looked at him without understanding what he said. They had been wounded in the knees and caught by ropes thrown over them; the ends of the great chains on their hands trailed upon the pavement. Hanno was indignant at their impassivity.

'On your knees! On your knees! Jackals, dirt, vermin, dung! And they do not answer me! Enough, then! Be silent! Let them be flayed alive! Not now, but presently!'

He was puffing like a hippopotamus and rolling his eyes. His great carcase made the perfumed oil to overflow, and it clung to the scales on his skin, making it look pink in the torch light.

He went on dictating:

' "For four days we suffered greatly from the sun. Some mules were lost in crossing the Makar. In spite of their position, with extraordinary courage ..." Ah, Demonades! How I suffer! Have the bricks re-heated, and let them be red-hot!'

There was a noise of raking from the furnaces. Thicker clouds of incense arose from the great perfuming-pans; and the naked rubbers, who were sweating like sponges, kneaded into his joints a paste composed of wheat, sulphur, black wine, bitch's milk, galban and storax. He had a raging and incessant thirst; but the man in tne yellow robe would not indulge it, & offered him a golden cup of smoking viper broth.

'Drink!' he said, 'that the strength of serpents born in the sun may penetrate to the marrow of your bones; take courage, O reflection of the gods! You know that a priest of Eshmun is watching those cruel stars round the Dog, from which your malady is derived. They are growing pale like the spots on your skin; and you are not to die of it.'

'Ah, yes! That is so, is it not?' repeated the Suffete. 'I am not to die of it!'

And from his purple lips escaped a breath more fetid than the exhalation from a corpse. Two coals seemed to burn in the place of his eyes, which were bare of eyebrows; folds of wrinkled skin hung down upon his forehead; his ears stood out from his head and were beginning to swell; and the deep wrinkles which made half circles about his nostrils gave him a strange & terrifying appearance, like that of a wild beast. His voice was an unnatural roar; and he said:

'Perhaps you are right, Demonades. In fact there are many ulcers which have closed here. I feel strong. Look! See how I can eat!'

And, not so much from gluttony as in ostentation, and to convince himself that he was in good health, he made an onslaught upon cheeses forced with marjoram, boned fish, gourds & oysters; upon eggs, horse-radishes, truffles and small birds on the spit. As he looked at the prisoners, he took a delight in imagining their torture: the memory of Sicca returned to him, and at the thought of all his sufferings he vented his fury in abusing these three men.

'Ah, traitors! Infamous, accursed wretches! And it was I whom you outraged! I, the Suffete! "Their services," say they! "The price of their blood!" Ah, yes! Their blood! Their blood!'

Then, speaking to himself:

'They shall all die! Not one shall be sold! It would be better to take them to Carthage! The people would see me ... But, I doubt, I have not brought enough chains? Write: "Send me..." How many of them are there? Go and ask Muthumbal! Go! No mercy! And bring me all their hands in baskets!'

But strange cries, at once hoarse and shrill, now reached the hall, drowning Hanno's voice and the rattling of the dishes that were being placed about him. The noise increased, and suddenly the furious trumpeting of elephants burst forth, as if the battle were beginning again. The city was beset by a great tumult.

The Carthaginians had not attempted to pursue the Barbarians. They had taken up their quarters at the foot of the walls with their baggage, their serving-men, and all the retinue of their satraps; and they were making merry in their fine pearl-bordered tents, while the Mercenaries' camp was no more than a heap of ruins on the plain. Spendius had recovered his courage. He despatched Zarxas to Matho, scoured the woods, and rallied his men, whose losses had been inconsiderable. They were re-forming their lines, in a great anger at having been beaten without a fight, when they discovered a vat of petroleum which had no doubt been abandoned by the Carthaginians. Then Spendius took pigs from the farms, smeared them with the bitumen, set them on fire and drove them towards Utica.

The elephants were terrified by the flames, and fled. The ground sloped upwards, and they were driven back again by the javelins hurled at them; with great strokes of their tusks, and trampling them under foot, they disembowelled and crushed and flattened the Carthaginians. The Barbarians came down the hill behind them; and the Punic camp, having no entrenchments, was sacked at the first rush. The Carthaginians were crushed against the gates, which the citizens would not open for fear of the Mercenaries.

Day broke, and Matho's foot-soldiers came up from the west. At the same time Narr'Havas appeared with his Numidian cavalry, leaping ravines and bushes to run down the fugitives, like greyhounds coursing hares. This change of fortune interrupted the Suffete. He called for someone to help him out of the bath.

The three captives still stood before him. A negro (the same that had carried his parasol in the battle) whispered in his ear.

'What is it?' answered the Suffete slowly.

'Oh, kill them!' he added abruptly.

The Ethiopian drew a long knife from his belt, and the three heads fell. One of them bounded among the remains of the feast and leaped into the bath, where it floated for some time with open mouth and staring eyes. The morning light came through the slits in the wall: the three bodies lay on their breasts and spurted great bubbles, like three fountains; a sheet of blood flowed over the mosaics, which were sanded with blue powder. The Suffete dipped his hand into this warm mud and rubbed his knees with it. It was a cure.

When evening came he stole away from the town with his escort, and made his way into the mountains to rejoin his army.

He found what was left of it.

Four days later he was at the head of a defile at Gorza, when the troops under Spendius appeared below him. Twenty stout lances might easily have checked them by attacking the head of their column; but the stunned Carthaginians watched them pass by. Hanno recognized the king of the Numidians in the rear guard. Narr'Havas bowed his head to salute him, and in doing so made a sign he did not understand.

Their return to Carthage was attended by every kind of terror. They marched only by night, hiding in the olive woods during the day. At every halt some of them died, and very often they thought they were lost. At last they reached Cape Hermaeum, from which they were taken off by ships.

Hanno was so weary, so desperate, and above all so overwhelmed by the loss of the elephants, that he asked Demonades to give him poison to end it all. He could already feel himself stretched upon the cross.

Carthage had not the energy to be indignant with him. She had lost four hundred thousand nine hundred and seventy-two shekels of silver, fifteen thousand six hundred and twenty-three shekels of gold, eighteen elephants, fourteen members of the Great Council, three hundred of the Rich, eight thousand citizens, three moons' supply of corn, a considerable quantity of baggage, and all her engines of war! The defection of Narr'Havas was certain, and both the sieges were being resumed. The army under Autharitus now stretched from Tunis to Rhades. From the top of the Acropolis men could see long columns of smoke in the country, rising to the sky from the burning mansions of the Rich.

One man, and one man only, could have saved the Republic. They regretted their lack of appreciation for him, and the peace party itself voted holocausts for Hamilcar's return.

Salambo had been overcome by the sight of the zaimph. At night she thought she could hear the footsteps of the Goddess, & would wake terrified & screaming. Every day she sent food to the temples. Taanach was worn out with executing her orders, and Shahabarim never left her.

HAMILCAR BARCA

CHAPTER VII

THE ANNOUNCER OF THE MOONS, WHO WATCHED
the planet's different movements each night on the top of the
temple of Eshmun in order to signal with his trumpet, saw in the
west one morning as it were a bird skimming the surface of the sea
with its long wings.

It was a ship with three banks of oars, and there was a carven horse
at the prow. The sun was rising; the Announcer of the Moons
shaded his eyes with his hand; and then, grasping his clarion at
arm's length, sent a great brazen cry over Carthage.

People came out of every house, unable to believe his message, dis-
puting with one another, and crowding upon the mole. At last
they recognized Hamilcar's trireme.

She came on proudly like a wild thing, her yard-arm straight and
her sail bellying throughout the length of her mast, cleaving the
foam around her; her huge oars kept time as they struck the water;

every now and then the end of her keel would appear, shaped like a plough-share; and the ivory-headed horse, rearing its two feet under the spur at the end of the prow, seemed to be galloping on the plains of the sea.

On rounding the promontory she ran out of the wind, and her sail fell; a man was seen standing bareheaded beside the pilot. It was he, the Suffete Hamilcar! About his sides he wore shining plates of iron, a red cloak hung from his shoulders, leaving his arms free; two pearls of great length depended from his ears; and his black, bushy beard was sunken upon his breast.

Meanwhile the galley, tossing amid the rocks, coasted the mole; and the crowd followed her along the stones, shouting:

'Greeting and blessing, O Eye of Khamon! Ah, deliver us! The Rich are to blame! They want to put you to death! Have a care for yourself, O Barca!'

He made no reply, as if the clamour of oceans and battles had deafened him completely. But when he was below the stairway leading down from the Acropolis, Hamilcar raised his head and, folding his arms, looked up at the temple of Eshmun. He looked higher yet, at the great clear sky; then in a harsh voice he shouted an order to his sailors, and the trireme leaped forward. She grazed the idol set up at the corner of the mole to ward off storms; and once in the merchant harbour, which was full of filth and bits of wood and fruit rinds, she jostled aside and ripped open the other ships that were moored to stakes there, with prows like crocodile jaws. The people ran behind, some diving into the water to swim to her. Now she was at the head of the harbour, before the nail-studded gate. The gate rose, and the trireme disappeared under the deep arch.

The Military Harbour was completely separated from the town; when ambassadors arrived, they had to pass between two walls, through a passage which opened to the left in front of the temple of Khamon. This great basin of water was as round as a cup, and on the quays which bordered it were the docks for ships. Before each of these rose two pillars bearing the horns of Ammon on their capitals & forming a continuous portico all round the basin. On an island in the midst stood a house for the Suffete of the Sea.

The water was so clear that the white pebbles paving the bottom were easily visible. The noise of the streets did not reach so far as this. Hamilcar, as he passed, recognised the triremes he had once commanded.

Not more than perhaps twenty remained of them, ashore in dock, resting on their sides or standing upright on their keels, with lofty poops and curved prows, and covered with gilding and mystic symbols. The chimaeras had lost their wings, the Pataec Gods their arms, and the bulls their silver horns. They had all parted with half their paint and lay still and rotting; but their past yet lived about them and they were redolent of old voyages: like disabled soldiers seeing their captain once again, they seemed to say to him: 'It is we! It is we! And you, you also were conquered!'

No one but the Suffete of the Sea might enter the admiral's house: & so long as there was no proof of his death he was assumed to be still living. Thus the Elders avoided the embarrassment of having yet another master, and had not failed to observe this custom in the case of Hamilcar.

The Suffete entered the deserted chambers, and at every step found armour and furniture and well-known things that nevertheless astonished; in a perfuming-pan in the vestibule remained the ashes of the incense, even, that had been burned on his departure to invoke Melkarth. It was not thus he had hoped to return. All that he had done, all that he had seen, now pictured itself in his memory: the assaults and burnings, the legions and the tempests; Drepanum and Syracuse, Lilybaeum and Mount Etna and the plateau of Eryx, five years of fighting and the loss of Sicily, and the fatal day when he laid down his arms. And then he saw woods of citron trees again, and herdsmen with their goats on grey mountains; his heart leaped at the thought of making another Carthage yonder. His projects & his recollections sang through his head, which was still dizzy from the pitching of the vessel; an anguish gripped him, and he felt a sudden weakness and a need to draw near to the gods.

Then he went up to the highest story of his house and, taking a nail-studded spattle from a golden shell which hung from his arm, opened a small oval chamber.

It was softly lighted by delicate black rondles let into the wall, as translucent as glass. Between these regular rows of discs were hollowed niches, such as are used for urns in the columbaria. Each of these contained a round dark stone, and this appeared to be very heavy. Only the more noble-minded paid honour to these Abaddirs, which had fallen from the moon. By their fall they symbolised the stars and the sky and fire; by their colour, the darkness of night; and by their density, the cohesion of all earthly things. The atmosphere of this mystic place was stifling. The round stones lying in the niches were a little white with sea-sand, blown, no doubt, through the doorway by the wind. Hamilcar counted them one by one with the tip of his finger; then he hid his face in a saffron coloured veil and, falling on his knees, threw himself to the ground with outstretched arms.

The daylight outside beat on the leaves of the black lattice-work, causing tree-like growths and hillocks, eddies and ill-defined animals to appear upon its diaphanous substance; and the light came terrifying yet peaceful; as it must needs be behind the sun, in the gloomy regions of unborn creation. He strove mentally to banish every shape or symbol or name of the gods, the better to grasp their unchanging spirit unmasked by outward appearance. Something of the vitality of the planets entered into him, bringing him a wiser and more intimate contempt for death and all the chances of life. When he rose, he was filled with a serene fearlessness, proof against pity or dread; his breast was choking, & therefore he went to the top of the tower that overlooked Carthage.

The town sank downwards in a long hollow curve of cupolas and temples, of golden roofs and houses, of clusters of palm trees here and there, and of glass balls shooting fire; and the ramparts formed as it were the gigantic rim of this horn of plenty which poured itself out before him. Down below him he could see the harbours, the squares, and the interiors of courts, the plan of the streets and pigmy men who seemed but little higher than the pavement. Ah! if Hanno had not arrived too late that morning at the Islands of the Aegates! His eyes pierced the distant horizon, and he held out his trembling arms towards Rome.

The people were crowding on the steps of the Acropolis. In the Square of Khamon they jostled one another to see the Suffete come forth, and the terraces were gradually thronged with people. Some of them recognised him, and he was cheered; but he retired again, so as further to excite the people's impatience.

In the hall below, Hamilcar found the most important men of his party: Istatten, Subeldia, Hictamon, Yeubas and others. They told him all that had happened since the conclusion of peace: of the greed of the Elders, the soldiers' departure, their return, their demands, the capture of Gisco, the theft of the zaimph, the relief and subsequent abandonment of Utica. But no one dared to tell him of the events which concerned himself. At last they separated, to meet again during the night at the assembly of Elders in the temple of Moloch.

They had just gone out when a tumult arose beyond the door. Some one was trying to enter in spite of the servants; and as the disturbance increased Hamilcar ordered the stranger to be admitted.

An old negress made her appearance, broken, wrinkled, trembling, stupid looking, and wrapped to the heels in wide blue veils. She came forward and faced the Suffete, and they looked at each other for some time. Suddenly Hamilcar gave a start; and at a wave of his hand the slaves withdrew. Then, signing to her to walk cautiously, he drew her by the arm to a remote apartment.

The negress threw herself upon the ground to kiss his feet; but he raised her brutally.

'Where have you left him, Iddibal?'

'Down yonder, Master.'

And, throwing off her veils, she rubbed her face with her sleeve; the black colour, the senile trembling, the bent figure, all had vanished, and she stood forth a vigorous old man, whose skin seemed tanned by sand and wind and sea. A tuft of white hair stood up on his head like the crest of a bird. He glanced ironically at his disguise as it lay upon the ground.

'You have done well, Iddibal! It is good!'

Then, as if he would pierce him through with his keen gaze:

'No one suspects?'

The old man swore to him by the Kabiri that the secret was still kept. They never left their cottage, three days' journey from Hadrumetum, where the shore was peopled with turtles and there were palm trees growing on the dunes.

'And, as you bade me, Master, I am teaching him to hurl the javelin and to manage a team of horses.'

'He is strong, is he not?'

'Yes, Master, and fearless, too! He is not afraid of serpents or thunder or phantoms. He runs bare-foot like a herdsman along the brinks of the precipices.'

'Tell me of him! Speak!'

'He devises snares for the wild beasts. A moon or so ago, would you believe it? he trapped an eagle; he dragged it away, and blood from the bird and the child mingled in the air in large drops like wind-driven roses. The maddened creature wrapped him about with its beating wings; but he hugged it against his breast, and as it died his laughter grew louder, ringing and proud like the clashing of swords.'

Hamilcar bent his head, awed by such presages of greatness.

'But for some time he has been restless and uneasy. He watches the sails passing in the distance; he is sad and refuses his food, he asks about the gods, and wishes to know Carthage.'

'No, no! Not yet!' cried the Suffete.

The old slave seemed to understand the danger which alarmed Hamilcar, and he resumed:

'How can I restrain him? Already I have to make him promises; I have come to Carthage only to buy him a dagger with a silver handle encircled with pearls.'

Then he told how, seeing the Suffete on the terrace, he had passed himself off on the harbour guards as one of Salambo's women, so as to gain access to him.

For a long time Hamilcar seemed lost in meditation, till at last he said:

'To-morrow at sunset you must be behind the purple factories in Megara, and cry three times like a jackal. If you do not see me, you will return to Carthage on the first day of every moon. Forget nothing! Love him! You may speak to him now about Hamilcar.'

The slave resumed his disguise, and together they left the house and the harbour.

Hamilcar took his way alone and on foot, without an escort; for the meetings of the Elders were, at times of crisis, always secret, and the members avoided any publicity as they went to attend them.

At first he skirted the western front of the Acropolis, and then passed through the Herb Market, the galleries of Kinisdo, and the Perfumers' Suburb. The scattered lights were being extinguished, silence was falling upon the wider streets, and there came shadows gliding through the darkness. These followed him and others came behind, and all, like him, made towards the Mappales.

The temple of Moloch was built in a sinister spot at the foot of a steep defile. Nothing could be seen from below save high walls rising indefinitely like the sides of a monstrous tomb. The night was gloomy; a grey mist seemed to weigh upon the sea, as it beat against the cliff with a noise of râle and sobbing. And the shadows gradually vanished, as if they had passed through the walls. But, once having crossed the threshold of the door, they found themselves in a vast quadrangular court bordered by arcades. In the midst rose a massive structure with eight equal faces, and topped by cupolas ranged round a second story which supported a kind of rotunda; and from this there rose a cone with inward curving sides, bearing a ball on its point.

Fires were burning in filigree cylinders which men carried upon poles; and their light flickered in the gusts of wind and reddened the golden combs that fastened their plaited hair behind their necks. They ran forward, calling to one another to receive the Elders.

Here & there on the flag-stones crouched huge lions like sphinxes, living symbols of the devouring sun. They were sleeping with half closed eyes: but, roused by the footsteps and voices, they rose slowly, & came towards the Elders whom they recognized by their dress, & rubbed themselves against their thighs, arching their backs and yawning sonorously; the steam of their breath floated across the torchlight. There was more bustling to and fro, and closing of doors; then all the priests fled, and the Elders disappeared under the columns which formed a deep vestibule about the temple.

These columns were so arranged, in circles one within the other, as to show the Saturnian period with its years, the years with their months, and the months with their days; and finally they touched the walls of the sanctuary.

It was here that the Elders laid aside their narwhal-horn staves; for by an infrangible law, no one, on pain of death, might bring any sort of weapon to their meetings. Several of them had a tear at the bottom of their robes, stopped by a strip of purple braid, to show how they had neglected their garments while mourning for their relatives; & this proof of their grief prevented the slit from spreading. Others had their beards cased in little bags of violet skin, fastened to their ears by two cords. All greeted and embraced each other breast to breast. They crowded round Hamilcar to offer him their congratulations. They might have been brothers meeting a brother again.

Most of these men were thick-set, with hooked noses like the Assyrian colossi. But some of them, by their more prominent cheek bones, greater stature and more slender feet, betrayed an African origin and Nomad ancestors. Those who lived shut up in their counting-houses had pale faces; others preserved something of the severity of the desert about them, and strange jewels sparkled on every finger of their hands, which were tanned by unknown suns. Sailors could be distinguished by their rolling gait; while farmers smelled of the wine-press, dried grass, & the sweat of mules. These old pirates held land under tillage, these money-makers had fitted out ships, these landed proprietors maintained slaves who were skilled craftsmen. They were all learned in religious discipline, expert schemers, pitiless and rich. Their long-standing cares had given them an air of weariness. Suspicion looked out from their flaming eyes; and their habits of journeying and lying, of bargaining and commanding, clothed them with an appearance of cunning and violence, a sort of discreet and convulsive brutality. Also, the influence of the God cast a heaviness upon them.

First they passed through a vaulted hall shaped liked an egg. Seven doors, corresponding with the seven planets, showed seven squares of different colours against the wall. After crossing a long apartment, they entered another similar hall.

A candelabrum completely covered with sculptured flowers was burning at the far end, and each of its golden branches bore a wick of byssus in a diamond cup. It stood upon the last of the long steps leading to a great altar, from the corners of which rose brazen horns. At each side were steps leading to the flat top of the latter;

the stones of it could not be seen, for it was a mountain of heaped cinders, and a vague smoke hovered slowly above it. Further back, higher than the candelabrum and much higher than the altar, rose the Moloch, who was all of iron and had yawning cavities in his human breast. His open wings spread out over the wall, and his long hands reached to the ground; three black stones with yellow rims made three eyes in his brow; and his bull's head strained upward in a terrible effort, as if about to bellow.

Ebony stools were ranged about the hall, behind each of which a bronze standard, resting upon three claws, supported a torch. All these lights were reflected in the mother-of-pearl lozenges which paved the hall. This was so lofty that the red of its walls grew black as they soared towards the vaulted roof; and the three eyes of the idol showed far above, like stars half lost in the night.

The Elders sat down on the ebony stools, having thrown the ends of their robes over their heads. They remained motionless with their hands crossed inside their wide sleeves, and the mother-of-pearl paving was like a luminous river flowing from the altar to the door, under their naked feet.

The four pontiffs were seated in the middle, back to back on four ivory seats arranged in a cross: the high priest of Eshmun in a hyacinth robe, the high priest of Tanit in a white linen robe, the high priest of Khamon in a tawny woollen robe, and the high priest of Moloch in a purple robe.

Hamilcar advanced towards the candelabrum. He walked all round it, examining the burning wicks; then he threw a scented powder upon them, and violet flames showed at the ends of the branches.

A shrill voice rose, and was answered by another; the hundred Elders, the four pontiffs, & the standing Hamilcar, intoned a hymn together; and their voices, ever repeating the same syllables and growing in volume, swelled into a burst of sound, became terrible, and then, abruptly, ceased.

They waited for some moments. At length Hamilcar drew from his bosom a little three-headed statuette, as blue as sapphire, and placed it before him. It was the image of Truth, the very spirit of his speech. Then he replaced it in his breast; and all, as if seized with a sudden rage, cried out:

'They are good friends of yours, these Barbarians! Traitor! Infamous wretch! You have come back to watch us perish, have you
not? Let him speak!—No! No!'

They were compensating themselves for the constraint under
which they had been placed till then by political ceremonial: and
although they had wished for Hamilcar's return, they were now
indignant because he had not prevented their disasters, or rather
because he had not suffered in them as well as they.

When the tumult had subsided, the high priest of Moloch rose:

'We would know why you did not return to Carthage.'

'What is that to you?' answered the Suffete disdainfully.

Their outcries redoubled.

'Of what do you accuse me? I managed the war badly, perhaps?
You have seen how I order my battles, you who conveniently leave
such things to the Barbarians ...'

'Enough! Enough!'

He went on in a deeper voice, so as to be heard the better:

'Ah, true! I am wrong, O lights of the Baalim; there are brave men
among you! Gisco, arise!'

And moving along the altar step with half closed eyes, as if looking
for someone, he repeated:

'Rise, Gisco! You can accuse me; they will defend you! But where
is the man?'

Then, as if bethinking himself:

'Ah, he is in his house, no doubt, surrounded by his sons, giving
orders to his slaves, happy, and counting the necklets of honour
upon the wall, the necklets his country has conferred upon him!'

They shuffled and lifted their shoulders, as if they were being
lashed with thongs.

'You do not even know whether he is alive or dead!'

And without heeding their clamour, he told them that in deserting
the Suffete they had deserted the Republic. So, too, the peace with
Rome, however advantageous it might seem to them, was more
fatal than twenty battles. A few—the least wealthy members of
the Council, who were suspected of continually leaning towards
the people or towards a tyranny—applauded him. Their oppo-
nents, administrators and chiefs of the Syssitia, overbore them by
dint of numbers; the more notable of these had ranged themselves

close by Hanno, who sat at the other end of the hall before the
lofty door, which was closed by a hyacinth tapestry.

He had painted the ulcers on his face with cosmetic. But the gold
dust from his hair had fallen upon his shoulders, where it made
two shining patches, so that the hair itself looked whitish and thin
and frizzed like wool. His hands were wrapped in linen, saturated
with a greasy perfume which dripped upon the pavement; and his
disease had obviously made considerable progress, for the folds of
his eyelids fell down over his eyes and hid them. He had to throw
back his head in order to see. His partisans urged him to speak:
and at last, in a hoarse and hideous voice, he said:

'Less arrogance, O Barca! We have all been conquered! Each one
of us has his misfortune. Now be resigned to yours!'

'Tell us rather,' said Hamilcar, smiling, 'how it was that you steered
your galleys into the Roman fleet?'

'I was driven before the wind,' answered Hanno.

'You are like a rhinoceros trampling its own dung: you expose
your folly! Be silent!'

And they began to accuse each other about the battle of the Aegates.

Hanno blamed him for not having come to join forces with him.

'But that would have left Eryx undefended! Your right course
was to take to the open sea. Who hindered you? Ah, I forgot! All
elephants are afraid of the sea!'

Hamilcar's followers thought this jest so good that they burst into
loud laughter, making the vaulted roof echo as if with the beating
of drums.

Hanno denounced the unworthiness of such an insult; he had contracted his disease as a result of a chill taken at the siege of Hecatompylos: and tears rolled down his face like winter rain upon a
ruined wall.

Hamilcar went on:

'If you had loved me as much as you love that man, there would
be great joy in Carthage now! How many times have I not appealed to you; and you always refused me money!'

'We had need of it,' said the chiefs of the Syssitia.

'And when matters were desperate with me — we have drunk
mules' piss and eaten the straps of our sandals—when I could have
wished that the blades of grass were soldiers, and that battalions

could be kneaded from our rotting dead, you recalled what vessels I had left!'

'We could not risk everything,' replied Baal-Baal, who owned gold mines in Darytian Gaetulia.

'Meanwhile, what were you doing here at Carthage, in your houses, behind your walls? There are Gauls on the Eridanus who ought to have been roused, Canaanites at Cyrene who would have come; and while the Romans sent Ambassadors to Ptolemy ...'

'He is praising the Romans to us now!'

Some one shouted out to him:

'How much have they paid you to defend them?'

'Ask that of the plains of Bruttium, of the ruins of Locri, of Metapontum, and of Heraclea! I have burned all their trees; I have pillaged all their temples; and even to the death of their grandsons' grandsons ...'

'Why! You are declaiming like an orator!' said Kapuras, a very illustrious merchant. 'What is it you mean?'

'I say that you must be either more cunning or more terrible! If the whole of Africa is throwing off your yoke, it is because you do not know, weak masters that you are, how to fasten it upon her shoulders! Agathocles, Regulus, Coepio, any bold man has only to land, and she is his; and when the Libyans in the east join with the Numidians in the west, and the Nomads come from the south, and the Romans from the north ...'

A cry of horror rang out.

'Oh! You may beat your breasts, and roll in the dust, and tear your cloaks! It will not avail you! You will have to go and turn mill-stones in the Suburra, and gather the vintage on the hills of Latium.'

They smote their right thighs to mark their scandalised offence, and the sleeves of their robes rose like the great wings of flustered birds. Hamilcar, in the grip of an inspiration, spoke straight on, standing upon the highest step of the altar, quivering and terrible: he raised his arms, & the rays from the candelabrum which burned behind him shot between his fingers like gold javelins.

'You will lose your ships, your estates, your chariots, your hanging beds, and the slaves who rub your feet. Jackals will lie in your palaces, and the ploughshare will turn up your graves. There will be nothing left but the eagles' cry and a heap of ruins. Thou wilt fall, O Carthage!'

The four pontiffs put out their hands to avert this anathema. Every man had risen. But the Suffete of the Sea, who held a priestly office under the protection of the Sun, was inviolable until the assembly of the Rich had judged him. There was an awfulness about the altar; and they drew back.

Hamilcar spoke no more. With fixed eyes, and face as pale as the pearls of his tiara, he panted and was almost frightened at himself; his spirit was lost in visions of death. From the height on which he stood, all the torches on the bronze standards seemed to him a vast wreath of fire, laid flat on the pavement; black smoke came up from them and rose into the darkness of the dome; and for some minutes the silence was so profound that the sea could be heard sounding in the distance.

Then the Elders began to consult together. Their interests, their very lives, were threatened by the Barbarians. But it was impossible to conquer them without the help of the Suffete; and, in spite of their pride, this outweighed all other considerations. They took his friends aside; and there were interested reconciliations, understandings & promises. Hamilcar was unwilling to take any further part in any government. They implored and besought him; and, as they again made use of the word treason, he flew into a passion. The sole traitor was the Great Council: for since soldiers were engaged only for the period of the war, they became free as soon as the war had finished. He even extolled their bravery and all the advantages which might accrue from interesting them in the Republic by gifts and the grant of privileges.

Then Magdassan, a former provincial governor, rolled his yellow eyes and said:

'Surely, Barca, your travels have turned you into a Greek or a Latin, or I know not what! You speak of rewards for these men? Let ten thousand Barbarians perish, rather than a single one of us!'

The Elders nodded approval, murmuring:

'Yes, why need we trouble so about them? We can always find others!'

'And they are easily got rid of, are they not? They can be abandoned, as they were in Sardinia. You have but to apprise the enemy of the road they will take, as you did in the case of those Gauls in Sicily; or you may even disembark them in the middle of the sea. On my way back I saw that rock all white with their bones!'

'What a misfortune!' said Kapuras impudently.

'Have they not gone over to the enemy a hundred times?' cried others.

'Why, then, did you recall them to Carthage in violation of your laws?' exclaimed Hamilcar. 'And when they are in your city, poor and numerous in the midst of all your riches, it does not occur to you to weaken them by the slightest division of their forces! Afterwards you dismiss the whole of them, with their women and children, and do not keep a single hostage! Did you suppose that they would massacre themselves to save you the trouble of keeping your oaths? You hate them because they are strong! Still more do you hate me, who am their master! Oh! I felt it just now, when you kissed my hands, and all had much to do to keep from biting them!'

If the lions sleeping in the court had come in roaring, the din could not have been more frightful. But the pontiff of Eshmun rose and, standing straight upright with his knees pressed together, his elbows close to his body, and his hands half open, said:

'Barca, Carthage needs you to take general command of the Punic forces against the Mercenaries!'

'I refuse,' answered Hamilcar.

'We give you full authority,' cried the chiefs of the Syssitia.

'No!'

'Uncontrolled and undivided authority, with all the money you require, all the captives, all the booty, and fifty zereths of land for each enemy corpse.'

'No! No! Because victory is impossible with such as you!'

'He is afraid of them!'

'Because you are cowardly, miserly, ungrateful, pusillanimous and mad!'

'He is nursing the enemy's interests!'

'To put himself at their head,' said some one.

'And return against us,' added another.

And Hanno yelled from the bottom of the hall:

'He wants to make himself king!'

Then they leaped to their feet, overturning the seats & the torches; they rushed in a body towards the altar, brandishing daggers. But Hamilcar felt within his sleeves & drew forth two broad cutlasses; and half stooping, his left foot advanced, his eyes flaming and his teeth clenched, he defied them, standing motionless beneath the gold candelabrum.

As a precaution, then, they had brought weapons with them. This was a crime; and they looked at one another in terror. But since all were guilty, each was quickly reassured; & by degrees they turned their backs on the Suffete and came down again, angry and humiliated. For the second time they had recoiled before him. They remained standing for some moments, & several who had wounded their fingers put them to their mouths or rolled them gently in the hem of their mantles; they were on the point of departing, when Hamilcar heard these words:

'Why! It is a point of delicacy, to avoid distressing his daughter!'

A louder voice was raised:

'Without a doubt: for she takes her lovers from among the Mercenaries!'

At first he tottered; then his eyes rapidly sought Shahabarim. The priest of Tanit had alone remained in his place; and Hamilcar could only see his tall cap in the distance. They were all sneering in his face, and as his anguish increased their joy was redoubled; those who were in the rear shouted amid the hootings:

'He was seen coming out of her room!'

'One morning in the month of Tammuz!'

'It was the thief of the zaimph!'

'A very handsome man!'

'Taller than you!'

He snatched off his tiara, the badge of his rank—his tiara of eight mystic rows, with an emerald shell in the middle—and with both hands & all his strength dashed it to the ground; the golden circles rebounded as they broke, and the pearls clattered upon the paving. This exposed upon the whiteness of his brow a long scar, turning like a serpent between his eyebrows. All his limbs were trembling. He went up one of the side stairs which led on to the altar, and walked upon it! To do this was to devote himself to the God, to offer himself as a holocaust. The motion of his mantle shook the flames of the candelabrum, which burned below the level of his sandals, and the fine dust raised by his footsteps enveloped him like a cloud to the waist. He stopped between the legs of the iron colossus and took up two handfuls of that dust, the mere sight of which made every Carthaginian shudder with horror. Then he said:

'By the hundred brands of your Intelligences! By the eight fires of the Kabiri! By the stars, the meteors, and the volcanoes! By all that burns! By the thirst of the Desert and the salt of the Sea! By the cave of Hadrumetum and the kingdom of Souls! By death! By the ashes of your sons, and the ashes of your forefathers' brethren, with which I now mingle my own! You, the Hundred of the Council of Carthage, have made a lying accusation against my daughter! And I, Hamilcar Barca, Suffete of the Sea, Chief of the Rich and Ruler of the people, now before bull-headed Moloch swear ...'

They expected some terrible oath: but he continued in a louder yet calmer voice:

'That I will not even speak to her of the matter!'

The sacred servitors entered wearing their golden combs, some with purple sponges & others with branches of palm. They raised the hyacinth curtain spread before the door; and through the opening of this corner the great rose-coloured sky could be seen beyond the other halls like a continuation of the vaulted roof, coming to rest on the blue sea at its horizon. The sun was rising from the waves, and suddenly struck upon the breast of the iron colossus, which was divided into seven compartments closed by gratings. His red-toothed jaws opened in a horrible yawn; his huge nostrils dilated; the broad daylight made him alive and gave him a terrible and impatient look, as if he wished to leap into the open air and mingle with the star, the God, and travel the immensities of space with him.

The torches scattered upon the ground were still burning, and casting here and there upon the mother-of-pearl pavement stains as of blood. The Elders were reeling with exhaustion; they filled their lungs with full draughts of the fresh air, & the sweat streamed down their livid faces; they had shouted so much that they could scarcely make their voices heard. But their rage against the Suffete was no whit abated; they hurled threats at him by way of farewell;

and Hamilcar answered them.

'Until to-morrow night, Barca, in the temple of Eshmun!'

'I shall be there!'

'We will have you condemned by the Rich!'

'I shall have the people condemn you!'

'Take care lest you end upon the cross!'

'And you, lest you be torn to pieces in the streets!'

As soon as they reached the threshold of the court, they resumed a demeanour of serenity and calm.

Their runners & charioteers were awaiting them at the door. Most of them departed on white mules. The Suffete leaped into his chariot and took the reins; the two animals, arching their necks and rhythmically beating the flying pebbles, went up the whole of the Mappales road at full gallop; and the silver vulture at the end of the pole seemed to be flying, so quickly did the chariot rush by.

The road crossed a field planted with long stones which tapered to their tops like pyramids, each with an open hand carved out in the middle, as if the dead lying beneath were reaching out towards heaven to take something back. Then came scattered huts of mud and branches and rush-hurdles, all conical in shape. Little pebble walls, runnels of spring water, esparto-grass ropes, and nopal hedges formed irregular boundaries between these dwellings, which grew more and more frequent as the ground rose towards the Suffete's gardens. But Hamilcar's eyes were fixed upon a great tower, the three storys of which were three monstrous cylinders. The first of these was built of stone, the second of brick; the third, which was all of cedar, supported a copper cupola upon twenty-four juniper pillars, from which hung little interlacing chains of brass like garlands. This lofty structure towered over the buildings which lay to the right, the warehouses and the counting-house; while the women's palace rose at the end of the cypress trees, which stood in a double line like walls of copper.

Passing through the narrow gate, the rumbling chariot stopped under a wide shed, in which were tethered horses munching at heaps of chopped grass.

All the servants hastened up. There was a great crowd of them, since the field workers had been brought into Carthage for fear of the soldiers. The farm labourers were clad in beast skins & dragged chains riveted to their ankles; the arms of the workers in the purple factories were as red as an executioner's; the sailors wore green bonnets; the fishermen had coral necklaces; the huntsmen carried nets on their shoulders; and the people of Megara wore black or white tunics, leather breeches, and caps of straw, felt, or linen, according to their various employments or occupations.

Behind them pressed a ragged mob who had neither work nor dwelling, who slept at night in the gardens, and ate the refuse from the kitchens; a human mildew spawning in the shadow of the palace. Hamilcar tolerated them from motives of prudence rather than contempt. Every one of them had put a flower in his ear in token of joy; though many of them had never even seen him.

But men with their heads dressed in sphinx fashion & armed with great cudgels, dashed into the crowd, striking right and left, to drive back the slaves, who were curious to see their Master, lest he should be jostled by their numbers or inconvenienced by their smell.

Then they all threw themselves flat on the ground, crying:

'O Eye of Baal, may your house prosper!'

And through these men as they lay thus on the ground in the cypress avenue, Abdalonim, the Steward of the stewards, came towards Hamilcar wearing a white mitre, & with a censer in his hand.

Salambo was descending the galley stairway. All her women followed behind her, taking a pace downward in unison with each of her steps. The heads of the negresses made great black dots in the line of golden plaques which adorned the fillets about the Roman women's brows. Others wore silver arrows in their hair, or emerald butterflies, or long bodkins spread like suns. Rings, clasps and necklaces, fringes and bracelets glittered amid the medley of white and yellow and blue; there was a rustling of fine draperies; the pattering of sandals chimed with the dull sound of naked feet on wood: and here and there a tall eunuch, standing head and shoulders above them, held up his face and smiled. When the shouts of the men had died down, the women hid their faces in their sleeves and together uttered a strange cry like the howling of a she-wolf, so wild and strident that it seemed to set the great thronged ebony stairway vibrating from top to bottom like a lyre.

Their veils were lifted by the wind, and the papyrus plants swayed gently on their long stems. It was the month of Shebat, in mid-winter. The pomegranates spread their blossom against the azure of the sky, and through their branches could be seen the sea, and a distant island half lost in the mist.

On perceiving Salambo, Hamilcar stopped. She had come to him after the death of several male children, and the birth of a daughter was considered a calamity among the Sun worshippers. The gods had afterwards sent him a boy; but he still retained some sense of a hope betrayed and, as it were, the shock of the curse which he had uttered against her. Salambo meanwhile continued to advance.

Divers-coloured pearls hung in long clusters from her ears to her shoulders and down to her elbows. Her hair was crisped till it looked like a cloud. Round her neck she wore little square golden plaques, each representing a woman between two rampant lions; and her dress was in all respects a reproduction of the equipment of the Goddess. Her wide-sleeved hyacinth robe clung close to her form, broadening as it descended. The whiteness of her teeth was heightened by the vermilion of her lips, and the antimony on her eyelids made her eyes seem very long. Her sandals of birds' plumage had high heels, and she was more than ordinarily pale on account, no doubt, of the cold.

At last she came near to Hamilcar and, without looking at him, without raising her head, spoke thus:

'Greeting, O Eye of the Baalim! Eternal glory and triumph! Rest, contentment and wealth be with you! Long has my heart been sad and the house languished. But when the Master returns, it is as if Tammuz lived again; and under your countenance, O father, life and gladness and existence everywhere blossom anew!'

And, taking from Taanach's hand a little oblong vessel in which fumed a mixture of meal. butter, cardamom and wine:

'Drink freely,' she said, 'of the welcoming cup which your servant has prepared!'

He answered:

'A blessing upon you!'

And mechanically he grasped the golden vase which she held out to him.

Meanwhile he was scrutinising her so sharply and keenly that Salambo was troubled, and stammered forth:

'They have told you, O Master!'

'Yes! I know!' said Hamilcar in a low voice.

Was this a confession? Was she speaking of the Barbarians? He added a few vague words upon the public embarrassments which he hoped to remedy single handed.

'O father!' exclaimed Salambo, 'you can never efface what is irreparable!'

He started back, and Salambo was astonished at his consternation; for she was not thinking of Carthage, but of the sacrilege to which she felt herself accessory. This man before whom legions trembled, and whom she scarcely knew, terrified her as if he were a god. He had guessed, he knew all: something frightful was about to happen. She cried out:

'Mercy!'

Hamilcar slowly bowed his head.

Although she desired to accuse herself, she dared not open her lips; yet she was bursting to pour out her complaint, & to be consoled. Hamilcar fought against a longing to break his oath. He kept it out of pride, or because he feared to put an end to his uncertainty; he looked her in the face, trying with all his might to grasp what she was hiding in her heart.

Little by little the panting Salambo, crushed with the weight of his gaze, sank her head between her shoulders. He was sure now that she had sinned in the embrace of a Barbarian; he shuddered, and raised his two fists. She gave a cry, and fell among her women, who crowded about her.

Hamilcar turned on his heel, and all the stewards followed him.

The warehouse doors were thrown open, & he entered a vast round hall from which long passages, leading to other halls, branched away like spokes from the nave of a wheel. A stone disc stood in the middle, with balustrades to support cushions heaped up on carpets.

At first the Suffete walked with long rapid strides, and breathed heavily; he stamped on the ground with his heel, and brushed his hand across his forehead like a man tormented by flies. Then he gave his head a shake and, as he saw the accumulation of his riches, grew more calm; his thoughts were drawn down the perspective of the corridors, and dwelt on the rarer treasures in the other halls. Bronze plates, silver ingots, and iron bars alternated with blocks of tin brought over the Shadowy Sea from the Cassiterides; gums from the land of the Negroes overflowed their sacks of palm-tree bark; and the gold dust heaped up in leather bottles filtered imperceptibly through the worn-out seams. Delicate filaments spun from sea plants hung amid flax from Egypt and Greece, Taprobane and Judaea; madrepores bristled like great bushes at the foot of the walls; and an indefinable odour hung upon the air, an exhalation from the perfumes, the leather, and the spices, and from the ostrich plumes which were tied in great bunches & piled to the domed roof. Before each passage stood elephant tusks with their tips meeting, to form an arch above the door.

At last he mounted upon the stone disc, and all the stewards stood with arms folded & heads bent, while Abdalonim lifted his pointed mitre with an imposing air.

Hamilcar questioned the Chief of Ships, who was an old pilot with eyelids reddened by the wind, and tufts of white falling to his hips, as if the foam of tempests had lingered in his beard.

He answered that he had sent a fleet by Gades and Thymiamata to try to reach Eziongaber by rounding the Southern Horn and the promontory of Aromata.

Other ships had sailed on westward for four moons without finding any shore; their prows had become entangled in weed, the horizon had echoed continually with the thunder of cataracts, blood-coloured mists had darkened the sun, and a heavily scented breeze had overcome the crews with sleep; their memories were so troubled that they were at present unable to make their report. Some of his ships, however, had ascended the rivers of Scythia, had made their way into Colchis and into the countries of the Jugrians and of the Estians, had carried off fifteen hundred virgins in the Archipelago, and had sunk all foreign vessels sailing beyond Cape Oestrymon, so that the secret of the routes should not become known. King Ptolemy was keeping back the incense from Shesbar; Syracuse, Elathia, Corsica and the Islands had furnished nothing:

and the old pilot lowered his voice to announce that a trireme had
been taken at Rusicada by the Numidians:
'For they are siding with them, Master.'
Hamilcar knit his brows; then he signed to the Chief of Journeys
to speak. This man was wrapped in a brown robe without a girdle,
and his head was bound with a long scarf of white stuff passing
by his mouth and falling over his shoulder behind.

The caravans had set out regularly at the winter equinox. But of
fifteen hundred men who had started for farthest Ethiopia with
excellent camels, new water bottles, and supplies of painted cloth,
one only had returned to Carthage: the rest had died of fatigue or
been driven mad by the terrors of the desert. This survivor reported
that far beyond the Black Harush, beyond the Atarantes and the
country of the great apes, he had seen vast realms wherein the
meanest utensils were all of gold, a river of the colour of milk & as
wide as a sea, forests of blue trees, hills of aromatics, monsters with
human faces growing like plants upon rocks, whose eyes opened
like flowers to look at you; and lastly, behind dragon-infested lakes,
crystal mountains that held up the sun. Others had returned from
India with peacocks, pepper, and woven stuffs. As for those who
had gone by way of the Syrtes and the temple of Ammon to purchase chalcedonies, they had no doubt perished in the sands. The
caravans from Gaetulia and Phazzana had brought in their usual
supplies. But he, the Chief of Journeys, did not dare to fit out any
caravan at the present moment.

Hamilcar understood: the Mercenaries were in occupation of the
country. He leaned upon his other elbow with a hollow groan;
and the Chief of Farms was so afraid to speak that he trembled
horribly, in spite of his thick shoulders and his great red eyes. His
face, which was as snub-nosed as a bulldog's, was surmounted by a
network of bark fibre; he wore a belt of leopard's skin with all the
hair intact, in which gleamed two formidable cutlasses.

As soon as Hamilcar turned towards him he began to cry aloud
and invoke the Baalim. It was not his fault! He could do nothing!
He had observed the temperature, the soil, & the stars; had planted
at the winter solstice and pruned at the waning of the moon; had
inspected the slaves and been economical with their clothes.

Hamilcar was irritated by this loquacity. He clicked his tongue;
and the man with the cutlasses spoke on rapidly:

'Ah, Master! they have pillaged everything, sacked and destroyed
everything! Three thousand feet of timber have been cut down at
Mashala, and at Ubada the granaries have been broken open and
the cisterns all laid waste! At Tedes they have carried off fifteen
hundred omers of meal; at Marrazana they have killed the shepherds, eaten the flocks, and burned your house, your beautiful
house with cedar beams where you used to come in summer! The
slaves who were reaping barley at Tuburbo fled to the mountains;
and the asses, the pack mules and working mules, the oxen from
Taormina, and the antelopes,—not one is left. They are all carried
off! It is a curse! I shall not survive it!'

He continued in tears:

'Ah, if you knew how full the store-houses were, and how the
ploughshares shone! Ah, the fine rams! The splendid bulls!'

Hamilcar was choking with his rage, and now it burst forth.

'Be silent! Am I a pauper, then? No lies! Tell me the truth! I wish
to know the full extent of my losses to the last shekel, to the last
cab! Abdalonim, bring me the accounts of the ships, of the caravans, of the farms, and of my household! And if your consciences
are troubling you, woe to your heads! Leave me!'

The stewards retired, walking backwards and bowing till their
fingers touched the ground.

From the middle of a rack upon the wall Abdalonim brought out
knotted cords, strips of linen and papyrus, and sheeps' shoulder-
blades covered with fine writing. He laid these at Hamilcar's feet,
placed in his hands a wooden frame enclosing three wires on which
balls of gold, silver, and horn were strung; and then began:

'One hundred and ninety-two houses in the Mappales let to the
New Carthaginians at the rate of one beka a moon.'

'No! That is too much! Be lenient to the poor! Also make a list of
the names of those you consider the boldest, & try to learn whether
they are attached to the Republic. What next?'

Abdalonim hesitated, surprised by such generosity.

Hamilcar snatched the strips of linen from his hands.

'What is this? Three palaces round Khamon at twelve kesitahs a

month! Make it twenty! I do not wish to be devoured by the Rich!'
The Steward of the stewards resumed, after a long obeisance:
'Lent to Tigillas until the end of the season, two kikars at thirty-
three and a third per cent., maritime interest; to Bar-Malkarth fifteen hundred shekels on the security of thirty slaves. But twelve
died in the salt marshes.'
'Because they were not strong,' laughed the Suffete. 'No matter!
If he is in want of money, let him have it! We must always lend,
and at different rates according to a man's means.'
Then the servant hastened to read all the yield from the iron mines
of Annaba, the coral fisheries, the purple factories, the farming of
the tax on the resident Greeks, the export of silver to Arabia where
it was worth ten times as much as gold, & that from captured ships,
after a tithe had been deducted for the temple of the Goddess.
'In each case, Master, I declared a quarter less than the amount!'
Hamilcar was reckoning with the balls, and they rattled under his
fingers.
'Enough! What have you paid out?'
'To Stratonicles of Corinth and to three Alexandrian merchants
on these letters (which have been realised), ten thousand Athenian
drachmas and twelve Syrian talents of gold. The food for the crews,
amounting to twenty minae a month for each trireme ...'
'I know! How much has been lost?'
'Here is the account on these sheets of lead,' said the steward. 'As
to the ships chartered in common, it has often been necessary to
throw the cargoes into the sea, and the unequal losses have been
shared by the partners. For cordage borrowed from the arsenals,
which it was impossible to restore, the Syssitia exacted eight hundred kesitahs before the expedition to Utica.'
'Those men again!' cried Hamilcar, lowering his head; & he stayed
thus for some time, as if crushed by the weight of all the hatreds
he could feel pressing about him.
'But I do not see the Megara expenses?'
Abdalonim turned pale and went to another rack, from which he
took some tablets of sycamore strung in bundles on leather thongs.
    Hamilcar listened, his interest chained by the domestic details
and his mind soothed by the monotonous enumeration of figures.

Abdalonim's reading grew slower and slower. Suddenly he let the wooden sheets fall to the ground and threw himself flat on his face with his arms outstretched, in the posture of a man condemned. Hamilcar, quite unmoved, picked up the tablets; & his lips parted and his eyes grew larger when he saw entered as a single day's expense an exorbitant consumption of meat, fish, birds, wines and aromatics, together with broken vessels, dead slaves, and ruined napery.

Abdalonim, still prostrate, told him of the Barbarians' feast. He had not been able to evade the command of the Elders. Moreover, Salambo had desired money to be spent lavishly, for the better entertainment of the soldiers.

At his daughter's name Hamilcar leaped to his feet. Then, with compressed lips, he crouched down again upon the cushions, tearing their fringes with his nails, panting, and staring before him with fixed eyes.

'Rise!' he said, and stepped down.

Abdalonim followed him, trembling at the knees; then, seizing an iron bar, and working like a madman, he began to loosen the tiles of the pavement. A wooden disc sprang up, and soon a quantity of the large covers used for stopping up the pits of stored grain showed all along the passage.

'You see, O Eye of Baal,' said the trembling servant, 'they have not yet taken everything! These are each fifty cubits deep and filled to the brim! During your absence I had them dug in the arsenals, in the gardens, everywhere! Your house is as full of corn as your heart of wisdom.'

A smile passed over Hamilcar's face.

'It is well, Abdalonim!'

Then, whispering in his ear:

'You will have corn brought from Etruria, from Brutium, whence you will, and no matter at what price! Heap it up and keep it! I must hold all the corn in Carthage.'

When they were at the end of the passage Abdalonim, with one of the keys that hung at his girdle, opened a large square chamber divided in the middle by cedar-wood pillars. Here gold, silver and bronze coins were set out on tables or packed along the four walls in niches which rose to the joists of the roof. In the corners were huge baskets of hippopotamus hide bearing whole tiers of smaller bags; there were hillocks of heaped bullion on the floor, and here and there too high a pile had toppled over and now looked like some ruined column. The large Carthaginian coins, stamped with the figure of Tanit and a horse under a palm tree, mingled with those from the colonies, which were marked with a bull, a star, a globe or a crescent. Next, ranged in unequal sums, came pieces of all values, of all sizes & of every age, from ancient coins of Assyria, as thin as a finger nail, to ancient coins of Latium, which were thicker than a man's hand: buttons of Egina, tablets of Bactria, and the short bars of ancient Lacedaemon. Many were rusty, or grimy, covered with verdigris by water, or blackened by fire, as they had been fished up in nets or rescued from the ruins of captured towns after some siege. The Suffete had very speedily calculated whether the sums present corresponded with the gains and losses which had just been read to him; he was on the point of departing, when he saw that three of the brass jars were completely empty. Abdalonim averted his head in horror. Hamilcar resigned himself in silence.

They went through other passages and halls, and came at last to a door where, to ensure its being well guarded & following a Roman custom lately introduced into Carthage, a man was fastened by the waist to a long chain let into the wall. His beard and his nails had grown to an immoderate length, and he kept rocking from right to left with the ceaseless swaying motion of a captive animal. As soon as he recognised Hamilcar he darted towards him, crying: 'Mercy, O Eye of Baal! Pity! Kill me! For ten years I have not seen the sun! In your father's name, mercy!'

Without answering him, Hamilcar clapped his hands and three men appeared; all four together strained their arms and drew back from its rings the enormous bar which closed the door. Hamilcar took a torch and disappeared into the darkness.

This was believed to be the family sepulchre; but nothing would have been found in it save a wide well, which had been dug out merely to throw thieves off the scent, & concealed nothing. Hamilcar passed along beside this, and then, stooping down, turned a very heavy millstone upon its rollers; through the opening thus made he entered an apartment built in the shape of a cone.

The walls were covered with bronze scales; and in the midst, on a granite pedestal, stood the statue of one of the Kabiri called Aletes, the discoverer of the mines in Celtiberia. On the ground, at its base, and arranged in the form of a cross, lay broad gold shields and monstrous silver vases with closed necks, of extravagant shape and of no possible use; it was customary to cast quantities of metal in this form, so as to make it almost impossible to embezzle or even to move.

With his torch he lit a miner's lamp fastened to the idol's cap; and at once green, yellow, blue and violet fires, wine-coloured and blood-coloured fires flamed about the hall. It was filled with jewels disposed in gold calabashes hung like sconces from the bronze panelling, or standing in their native blocks at the foot of the wall. There were turquoises which had been shot from the mountains with slings, carbuncles formed of lynx's urine, glossopetrae fallen from the moon, tyanos, diamonds, sandastra and beryls; the three kinds of ruby, the four kinds of sapphire, and the twelve kinds of emerald. They flashed like splashes of milk, like blue icicles or silver dust, sending out their light in sheets and rays and stars. Thunder-engendered ceraunites glittered by the side of chalcedonies, which are an antidote for poison. There were topazes from Mount Zabarca to ward off terrors; opals from Bactria to prevent abortion; and those horns of Ammon which are placed under the bed to induce dreams.

The fires from the stones and the flames from the lamp were mirrored in the great gold shields. Hamilcar stood smiling, with folded arms, taking less delight in the sight than in the knowledge of his riches. They were inaccessible, inexhaustible, infinite. His ancestors, sleeping beneath his feet, sent up something of their eternity to his heart. He felt very near to the subterranean deities, and a joy akin to that of the Kabiri; the great luminous rays which beat upon his face seemed to him to be the end of some invisible network stretched across the abysses to link him with the centre of the world.

Suddenly he was struck by a thought which made him shudder; taking up a position behind the idol, he walked straight forward to the wall. Then he examined amid the tattooings on his arm a horizontal line and two perpendicular ones, which in Canaanite

figures signified thirteen. He counted up to the thirteenth of the
bronze panels, once more drew up his wide sleeve and, with his
right hand stretched, read other more complicated lines on another
part of his arm, moving his fingers delicately like one playing upon
a lyre. Finally he struck seven blows with his thumb, and an entire
section of the wall swung round in a single block.

This masked a sort of cellar containing mysterious matters which
had no name and were of incalculable value. Hamilcar went down
the three steps, took up an antelope hide which was floating on a
black liquid in a silver vat, and then came up again.

Abdalonim now began to walk in front of him once more, striking
the pavement with his tall cane, which had bells upon its pommel;
he cried the name of Hamilcar aloud before each apartment, and
embroidered it with praise and benediction.

Along the walls of the circular gallery, from which all the passages
radiated, were piled little blocks of algum-wood, sacks of henna,
cakes of Lemnos-earth, and tortoise-shells filled with pearls. The
Suffete brushed them with his robe as he passed, and did not even
glance at certain gigantic pieces of amber, that almost divine substance formed by the rays of the sun.

A cloud of scented vapour burst forth upon them.

'Open the door!'

They went in.

Naked men were kneading pastes, pounding herbs, and stirring
coals, pouring oil into jars, and opening and shutting little oval
cells hollowed in the whole surface of the wall and so numerous
that the chamber seemed to be honey-combed like a hive. These
cells were overflowing with myrobolan, bdellium, saffron & violets.
Gums and powders, roots and glass phials, branches of dropwort
and rose-petals were scattered everywhere; and the scent of these
things was stifling in spite of the clouds from the storax crackling
upon a brazen tripod in the centre.

The Chief of Sweet Perfumes, who was as pale and tall as a waxen
taper, came up to Hamilcar to crush a roll of metopion gum over
his hands, while two others rubbed his heels with baccar leaves. He
repulsed these last, who were Cyrenians of unspeakable morals,
tolerated on account of their secret knowledge.

To show his vigilance the Chief of Perfumes offered the Suffete a little malobathrum to taste in an amber spoon; then he pierced three Indian bezoars with an awl. The Master, who was familiar with all artifices, took a horn full of balm and, after holding it near the coals, tilted it over his robe: a brown spot appeared, proving it to be adulterated. Then he looked fixedly at the Chief of Perfumes and, without saying a word, flung the gazelle's horn full in his face.

Yet however indignant he might be at adulterations made to his own detriment, when he saw some parcels of nard which were being packed for over-sea exportation, he ordered antimony to be mixed with it to make it heavier.

Then he asked where three boxes of psagdas were which had been destined for his personal use.

The Chief of Perfumes confessed that he did not know: soldiers had come in howling and brandishing knives, and he had opened the boxes for them.

'So you are more afraid of them than of me!' cried the Suffete.

His eyes flamed through the smoke like torches upon the tall pale man, and the latter began to understand what was in store for him.

'Abdalonim! Before sunset you will make him run the gauntlet; cut him up well!'

This loss, which was insignificant compared with the others, exasperated him: for, in spite of all his efforts to banish them from his thought, he was continually being reminded of the Barbarians. Their excesses inevitably recalled his daughter's shame, and it irked him that all his household knew of this & would not speak to him of it. But something impelled him to sink himself, as it were, deeper in his misfortune; and he visited the sheds behind the counting-house in a fury of investigation, to inspect the supplies of bitumen and wood, anchors and cordage, honey and wax, and the cloth warehouse, the food stores, the marble yard & the silphium granary.

Then he went to the other side of the gardens to inspect the huts of his household artisans, who made things for sale. There were tailors there embroidering cloaks; others were knotting nets, painting cushions or cutting out sandals; Egyptian workmen were polishing papyrus with a shell. There was a clatter of weavers' shuttles and a clang of armourers' anvils.

Hamilcar said to these last:

'Forge swords! Nothing but swords! I shall need them.'

And he drew from his bosom that antelope's hide which had been steeping in poisons, to have it cut into a cuirass more solid than brass and proof against steel or flame.

As soon as he approached the workmen, Abdalonim tried to divert his master's wrath from himself by muttering disparaging remarks about their work.

'What a sorry performance! What shame! Surely the Master is too good.'

Hamilcar moved away without listening to him.

He walked more slowly now, for the paths were barred by great trees charred from head to foot, such as may be found in woods where shepherds have encamped; the palings were broken, the water drained from the trenches, and fragments of glass and the bones of apes were lying in muddy puddles. A scrap of cloth hung here and there on the bushes; and the flowers rotting under the citron trees made a heap of yellow manure. The servants had neglected everything, thinking that the Master would never return.

At each step he discovered some fresh disaster, some further proof of this thing which he had forbidden himself to learn. He was fouling his purple boots at this very moment as he trod the filth under foot; and yet he had not these men before him at the end of a catapult, to send flying in fragments! He felt humiliated at having defended them; for their conduct was a treachery and a treason. As he could not avenge himself upon the soldiers, nor upon the Elders, nor upon Salambo, nor upon anybody, and since his wrath must needs have a victim, he condemned all the garden slaves to the mines, at a single stroke.

Abdalonim trembled every time he saw him approaching the parks. But Hamilcar took the path towards the mill, from which came a mournful sound of singing.

The heavy mill-stones were revolving in the dust, two cones of porphyry laid one upon the other, the upper, which had a funnel, being turned upon the lower by means of strong bars which men pushed with their breasts and arms, while others were yoked to them and pulled. The friction of the straps had caused purulent sores about their arm-pits, such as are seen on asses' withers; and the ends of the limp black rags which barely covered their loins hung down and flapped against their houghs like long tails. Their eyes were red, the shackles clanked about their feet, and all their breasts rose & fell in unison. They were muzzled to prevent them from eating the meal, and their hands were enclosed in gauntlets without fingers so that they could not pick it up.

At the Master's entrance the wooden bars creaked yet more loudly. The grain made a grating sound as it was being crushed. Several of the slaves fell to their knees; the others walked over them and went on with their work.

He asked for Giddenem, the governor of the slaves; and that personage appeared, displaying his dignity by the richness of his dress. His tunic of fine purple was slashed up the sides; his ears were drawn down by heavy rings; and the strips of cloth about his legs were bound together by a lacing of gold which wound him from ankles to hips, like a serpent round a tree. In his ring-laden fingers he held a necklace of jet beads, by which he could distinguish which men were subject to the accursed disease.

Hamilcar signed to him to unfasten the muzzles. With cries like famished animals, they all rushed upon the meal and devoured it, their faces buried in the heaps.

'You are weakening them!' said the Suffete.

Giddenem answered that this was necessary in order to tame them. 'It was scarcely worth while sending you to the slaves' school at Syracuse. Summon the others!'

All the cooks and butlers, grooms and runners, litter-carriers and bath attendants, and the women with their children, drew up in a single line in the garden, stretching from the counting-house to the deer park. They held their breath. A vast silence filled all Megara. The sun was slanting across the lagoon, at the foot of the catacombs. The peacocks were screeching. Hamilcar moved along the line, step by step.

'What use to me are these old men?' he cried. 'Sell them! There are too many Gauls: they are drunkards! And too many Cretans: they are liars! Buy me Cappadocians, Asiatics, and Negroes!'

He was astonished at the small number of children.

'There ought to be births in the household every year, Giddenem. You will leave the huts open every night so that they may mix freely.'

He then had the thieves, the idle, and the mutinous pointed out to him, and ordered punishments, each time reproaching Giddenem in the same breath; and Giddenem, like a bull, drooped his low forehead with its great intercrossing eyebrows.

'See, O Eye of Baal,' he said, pointing out a sturdy Libyan. 'Here is one who was caught with a rope round his neck.'

'Ah! You wish to die?' asked the Suffete disdainfully.

'Yes!' the slave boldly answered.

Then, without caring for the precedent or the pecuniary loss, Hamilcar said to the serving-men:

'Take him away!'

Perhaps he had the idea of a sacrifice in mind, and that by inflicting this misfortune upon himself he might avert more terrible disaster. Giddenem had hidden those who were mutilated behind the others, but Hamilcar saw them:

'Who cut off your arm?'

'The soldiers, O Eye of Baal.'

Then to a Samnite who limped like a wounded heron:

'And you, who did that to you?'

The governor had broken his leg with an iron bar.

This idiotic atrocity angered the Suffete, and he snatched the jet necklace from Giddenem's hands.

'Cursed be the dog that wounds the flock! Gracious Tanit! A slave crippler! Ah, you are ruining your master! Let him be smothered in the dung-heap. And the missing? Where are they? Did you join the soldiers in murdering them?'

His face was so terrible that all the women fled. The slaves drew back, forming a large circle about them: Giddenem frantically kissed his sandals, while Hamilcar stood with his two arms raised above him.

He was as clear minded as in the sternest of his battles, and recalled a thousand odious matters, ignominies from which he had turned aside; and by the light of his wrath, as in the lightnings of a storm, he could visualise the sum of all his disasters in a single flash. The governors of the country estates had fled through terror of the soldiers, and possibly in connivance with them: they were all deceiving him; he had restrained himself too long.

'Let them be fetched!' he cried. 'And brand them on the forehead with a red-hot iron as cowards!'

Fetters, carcanets, and knives were brought and spread out in the middle of the garden, with chains for those condemned to the mines, boots for leg crushing, and instruments for pressing in the shoulders; also scorpions, or whips with three thongs ending in brass claws.

All the slaves were placed facing the sun, towards Moloch the Devourer, and stretched on their stomachs or their backs upon the ground; those condemned to be flogged were stationed upright against the trees with two men beside each of them, one to count the blows and the other to give them.

This last used both his arms to strike, and the whistling thongs flicked the bark off the plane-trees. Blood sprayed like rain over the leaves, and writhing red masses howled at the foot of the trees. Those who were being branded tore their faces with their nails. There was a creaking of wooden vices, a sound of dull knockings: at times a sudden sharp scream would pierce the air. Towards the kitchens men in tattered rags and with disordered hair were fanning the live coals, and a smell of burning flesh was wafted by. Those who were being scourged fainted away, but were held up by the bonds on their arms, & rolled their heads upon their shoulders, with closed eyes. The others who were watching them began to shriek with terror; and the lions, remembering the feast perhaps, came forward toward the edge of their pits, yawning.

Then Salambo appeared on the platform of her terrace, and ran backwards and forwards upon it, in a wild terror. Hamilcar saw her: and it seemed to him that she was holding out her arms towards him to ask for mercy. With a gesture of horror he plunged into the elephants' park.

These animals were the pride of all great Punic houses. They had carried the Ancestors, had triumphed in the wars, & were venerated as favourites of the Sun.

Those of Megara were the strongest in Carthage. Before he went away, Hamilcar had required Abdalonim to swear an oath that he would watch over them. But they had died from their mutilations; and only three remained, lying in the middle of the court in the dust, before the ruins of their mangers.

They recognized and came up to him.

One had his ears horribly slit, another a large wound in his knee, and the third had his trunk cut off.

They looked pitifully at him, like reasonable beings; and the one that had lost his trunk lowered his great head and bent his hams, as he tried to stroke his master gently with his hideous stump.

Two tears started to his eyes at the caress of the beast, and he rushed upon Abdalonim.

'Ah, wretch! The cross! The cross!'

Abdalonim fell backward upon the ground in a swoon.

From behind the purple factories, with their slowly rising blue smoke, rang the yelp of a jackal. Hamilcar paused.

The thought of his son had suddenly calmed him, like the touch of a god. He seemed to see a prolongation of his might, an indefinite continuation of his personality: and the slaves could not understand what had brought him this sudden composure.

As he made his way towards the purple factories, he passed before the slave prison, a long house of black stone built in a square pit, with a narrow path running round it, and a stairway at each of the four corners.

Doubtless Iddibal was waiting until night to finish his signal. 'There is no hurry yet,' thought Hamilcar; and he went down into the prison. Some cried out to him:

'Come back!'

The boldest followed him.

The open door was swinging in the wind. The twilight filtered in through the narrow loopholes, and showed broken chains hanging from the walls.

This was all that remained of the war captives!

Hamilcar grew extraordinarily pale & those who were leaning over the pit outside saw him support himself with one hand against the wall to keep from falling.

But the jackal now uttered its cry thrice in succession. Hamilcar raised his head; he spoke no word & made no gesture. Then, when the sun was fully set, he disappeared behind the nopal hedge: and that evening, at the assembly of the Rich in the temple of Eshmun, he said as he entered:

'O Lights of the Baalim, I accept the command of the Punic forces against the Barbarian army!'

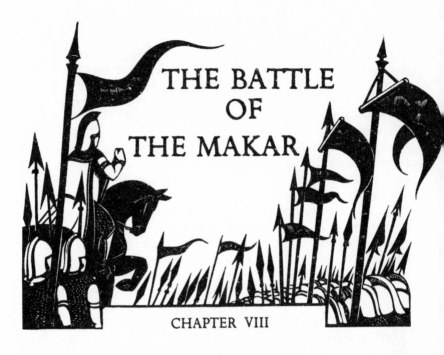

THE BATTLE OF THE MAKAR

CHAPTER VIII

ON THE FOLLOWING DAY HE DREW TWO HUNDRED and twenty-three thousand kikars of gold from the Syssitia, and levied a tax of fourteen shekels a head on the Rich, including even women and children: also he made a monstrous departure from Carthaginian custom by forcing the colleges of priests to furnish money.

He requisitioned all the horses, mules, and arms. He sold the property of any whom he found to have misrepresented his wealth; and, to shame the niggardliness of others, he himself gave sixty suits of armour and fifteen hundred omers of meal, which was as much as was given by the Ivory Company.

He sent into Liguria to buy soldiers, three thousand mountaineers used to fighting bears; and paid them for six moons in advance at the rate of four minae a day.

He still needed an army: but he did not, as Hanno had done, accept all citizens indiscriminately. First he rejected those engaged in sedentary occupations, & then those who were too fat in the paunch or had a faint-hearted appearance; and he admitted men of evil repute, the scum of Malqua, sons of Barbarians, and freed men. For reward, he promised full rights of citizenship to these New Carthaginians.

His first care was to reform the Legion. These splendid young men, who looked upon themselves as the military majesty of the Republic, governed their own affairs: but Hamilcar cashiered their officers; he treated them harshly, made them run and jump, climb the hill of Byrsa without a halt, hurl javelins, wrestle together, and sleep in the squares at night. Their families used to come to see them and commiserate with them.

He ordered shorter swords, & stouter boots. He limited the number of servants, and reduced the amount of baggage: and as there were three hundred heavy Roman javelins kept in the temple of Moloch, he commandeered these in spite of the pontiff's protests.

With those that had returned from Utica, and with others which were privately owned, he organised a phalanx of seventy-two elephants, and made a formidable force of them. He armed their drivers with mallet and chisel with which to split their skulls in the fight, if they should get out of control.

He firmly refused to allow the Grand Council to have the nomination of his generals; and when the Elders tried to object that this was their privilege by law, he overrode them. No one dared to murmur further, and all things yielded to the vehemence of his genius.

He assumed sole charge of the war, of the government, and of the finances; and to forestall any accusation, he insisted that the Suffete Hanno should be auditor of his accounts.

He set to work repairing the ramparts and had the old and now useless inner walls demolished to provide stones. But though the old racial hierarchy had disappeared, the descendants of the conquered were still kept separate from those of their conquerors by difference of fortune; and therefore the patricians viewed the destruction of these ruins with an angry eye, while the plebeians, without very well knowing why, rejoiced at it.

From morning till night armed troops defiled through the streets;

trumpets were sounding each minute, & chariots passed by loaded with shields, tents and pikes; the courts were full of women tearing up linen for bandages; enthusiasm spread from one to another, and Hamilcar's zeal pervaded the Republic.

He had disposed his soldiers in pairs, taking care to place the strong ones and the weak ones alternately throughout their files, so that the weaklings and laggards should be both led on and pushed forward by two others. But with his three thousand Ligurians, and the pick of the Carthaginians, he could only form one simple phalanx of four thousand and ninety-six hoplites, protected by bronze helmets, and each wielding an ash-wood Macedonian pike fourteen cubits long.

There were two thousand young men armed with sling and dagger, and wearing sandals; and these he reinforced by eight hundred others with round shields and Roman swords.

The heavy cavalry was composed of the nineteen hundred remaining guardsmen of the Legion, covered with red bronze mail, like the Assyrian Clibanarii. He had also four hundred of those mounted archers called Tarentines, with weasel-skin caps, two-edged axes, and leather tunics. Finally there were twelve hundred Negroes from the caravan quarter, and these were mingled with the Clibanarii, to run beside the stallions and hold to their manes with one hand. Everything was ready; yet Hamilcar did not start.

He would often go out of Carthage alone at night, and make his way beyond the lagoon towards the mouths of the Makar. Did he intend to join the Mercenaries? His house was surrounded by the Ligurians encamped in the Mappales.

The fears of the Rich appeared to be justified when, one day, three hundred Barbarians were seen approaching the walls, & the Suffete opened the gates to them. They were deserters, impelled either by fear or by loyalty to run to their master.

Hamilcar's return had not surprised the Mercenaries; for, to their minds, this man could not die. He had come back to keep his promises: and this was by no means an absurd expectation, having regard to the depth of the cleavage between the Republic and the Army. Besides, they did not see that they were at all to blame: they had forgotten the feast.

The spies whom they caught undeceived them, triumphantly vindicating the extremists and whipping even the lukewarm into a fury. Moreover, they were weary to death of the two sieges; they were making no progress, and would rather fight a pitched battle! Accordingly many of them had left the ranks to wander about the country. But the news of the preparations for war brought them back; and it made Matho leap for joy.

'At last! At last!' he cried.

His pent up resentment against Salambo found in Hamilcar a means of outlet. His hatred had now a definite prey in view; and as his revenge grew easier to visualise, he almost persuaded himself that he had already achieved it, and rejoiced in it already. He was possessed at the same time by a nobler tenderness and a more consuming lust. First he would see himself in the midst of his soldiers, brandishing the Suffete's head on a pike; & then he would be in the room with the purple bed, clasping the maid in his arms, covering her face with kisses, passing his hands over her long black hair: & this vision which he knew could never be realised was a torture to him. He swore to himself that, since his companions had made him schalishim, he would prosecute the war; and the certainty that he would never return from it urged him to make it a war without mercy.

He came to Spendius and said to him:

'Go and get your men! I will bring mine. Warn Autharitus! We are lost if Hamilcar attacks us! Do you hear me? Rise!'

Spendius was amazed by his air of authority; for as a rule Matho let himself be led, and his fits of passion had quickly died away. But now he appeared both calmer and more terrible; a proud determination shone in his eyes like the flame of a sacrifice.

The Greek paid no heed to his arguments. He was living in one of the pearl-embroidered Carthaginian tents, drinking cool drinks from silver cups, playing at cottabos, letting his hair grow, and conducting the siege in a leisurely manner. Besides, he had obtained information from the town and was unwilling to move, being sure that, before many days, it would open its gates.

Narr'Havas, who wandered about between the three armies, was with him at the time and backed his opinion, even going so far as to blame the Libyan for wishing to risk the wreck of their enterprise by his foolhardiness.

'Go home, if you are afraid!' cried Matho. 'You promised us pitch, sulphur, elephants, foot-soldiers and horses! Where are they?'

Narr'Havas reminded him that he had exterminated Hanno's last cohorts. As for the elephants, they were being hunted in the woods; he was arming the foot-soldiers, and the horses were on their way: the Numidian rolled his eyes like a woman and smiled in an irritating manner as he stroked the ostrich plume which fell behind his shoulder. Matho was at a loss how to answer him.

A man who was a stranger to them ran in dripping with sweat, dismayed, terrified, with bleeding feet & girdle unfastened; he panted so as well-nigh to burst his wasted sides and, speaking in an unintelligible dialect, opened wide eyes as if he were telling of some battle. The king sprang forth and called his horsemen.

They formed up on the plain in a circle before him. Narr'Havas, on his horse, bent his head and bit his lips. At length he divided his men into two halves, telling the first to wait; then. with an imperious gesture, he took the others off at a gallop and disappeared with them beyond the horizon towards the mountains.

'Master!' murmured Spendius, 'I do not like these strange doings, ... the Suffete's return, Narr'Havas going away ...'

'Why! What does it matter?' answered Matho disdainfully.

It was an added reason for forestalling Hamilcar by joining forces with Autharitus. But if the siege of the towns were raised, the inhabitants would come out and attack them in the rear, while they had the Carthaginians in front. After much discussion they decided upon the following measures, and immediately put them into execution.

Spendius proceeded with fifteen thousand men as far as the bridge built across the Makar, three miles from Utica, and fortified its corners with four great towers mounted with catapults. All the mountain paths and gorges were blocked with tree trunks, masses of rock, tangled thorns and stone walls: and they heaped mounds of grass on the peaks, to be lit as signals, and at intervals posted shepherds skilled in seeing to a great distance.

No doubt Hamilcar would not, as Hanno had done, advance by way of the mountain of the Hot Springs. He would be sure to think that Autharitus, being master of the interior, would block his path. Moreover, a check at the opening of the campaign would ruin him; while a victory gained at that point would soon have to be repeated when the Mercenaries had formed up further away. Or he might land at the Cape of Grapes and march upon one of the towns from there. But then he would find himself between the two armies, and with his inferiority in numbers he could not take such a risk. He must therefore skirt the base of Mount Ariana, then turn to the left to avoid the mouths of the Makar, and come straight to the bridge. It was there that Matho awaited him.

At night he used to supervise the pioneers by torchlight. He would rush off to Hippo-Zaritus or to the works on the mountains, he would come back again, and never took any rest. Spendius envied his energy; but in the management of spies, the choice of sentries, the working of the engines and all measures of defence, Matho quietly followed his companion's advice. They spoke no more of Salambo, one not thinking about her, & the other being prevented by a sense of shame.

Often he went towards Carthage, hoping to catch sight of Hamilcar's troops. His eyes would pierce the horizon; he would lie flat on his stomach, and believe that the beating of the blood in his arteries was the tramp of an army.

He told Spendius that if Hamilcar did not come within three days he would go out with all his men to meet him and offer battle. Two more days passed. Spendius still restrained him; but on the morning of the sixth day he departed.

The Carthaginians were no less eager for war than the Barbarians. In tent and house was the same longing and the same suspense; everybody was asking what delayed Hamilcar.

From time to time he mounted to the cupola of the temple of Eshmun, beside the Announcer of the Moons, and observed the wind.

One day, the third of the month of Tibby, he was seen coming down from the Acropolis with hurried steps. A great clamour arose in the Mappales. Soon the streets were astir, and on all sides the soldiers began to arm, surrounded by weeping women who clung to their breasts; then they hurried to the Square of Khamon and fell into rank. No one was allowed to follow them or even to speak to them, or to approach the ramparts; for some minutes the whole town was as silent as a great tomb. The soldiers, leaning upon their spears, were wrapped in thought; & those in the houses were sighing.

At sunset the army marched out by the western gate; but instead of taking the road to Tunis or making for the mountains in the direction of Utica, it continued along the sea coast & soon reached the Lagoon, where round patches, whitened with salt, glittered like huge silver dishes that had been left forgotten on the shore.

Then the pools of water grew more frequent. The ground gradually became softer, and their feet sank into it; but Hamilcar did not turn back. He went on ceaselessly at their head; and his horse, which was yellow-spotted like a dragon, scattered the foam about him as he strained mightily forward in the mire.

Night fell—a night of no moon. Some cried out that they would perish; he snatched their weapons from them and gave them to the servants.

The mud became deeper and deeper. They had to mount the baggage animals; others clung to the horses' tails; the strong pulled along the weak, and the Ligurian corps drove the infantry forward with the points of their pikes. The darkness thickened. They had lost their way. All halted.

Some of the Suffete's slaves went forward to find the buoys which he had ordered to be placed ahead at intervals. These shouted through the darkness, and the army made towards them at a distance.

At last they felt firm ground; a whitish curve vaguely appeared, and they found themselves on the bank of the Makar.

In spite of the cold, no fires were lighted.

In the middle of the night squalls of wind arose. Hamilcar had the soldiers roused, but not a trumpet was sounded: their captains tapped them softly on the shoulder.

A very tall man went down into the water. It did not come up to his girdle; so it was possible to cross.

The Suffete ordered thirty-two of the elephants to be posted in the river a hundred paces higher up; the others, lower down, would prevent any of the men from being carried away by the current; holding their weapons above their heads, they all crossed the Makar as it were between two walls. He had noticed that when the wind was in the west it drove up the sand, so as to obstruct the river by forming a natural causeway along it.

He was now on the left bank facing Utica, in a vast plain favourable to the elephants which constituted the strength of his army. This stroke of genius filled the soldiers with enthusiasm. They wished to advance against the Barbarians at once; but the Suffete made them rest for two hours. As soon as the sun appeared they moved across the plain in three lines: first the elephants, then the light infantry with the cavalry behind it, & the phalanx marching in the rear.

The Barbarians encamped at Utica and the fifteen thousand about the bridge were surprised to see the ground billowing in the distance. There was a very strong wind blowing; & it drove the sand before it in eddies, which rose as if snatched up from the ground in great pale strips, and then fell apart only to rise again, thus hiding the Punic army from the Mercenaries. The horns standing out from the helmets made some of the Barbarians imagine that it was a herd of oxen: others, deceived by the fluttering cloaks, pretended that they could distinguish wings; and those who had travelled much shrugged their shoulders & ascribed the whole phenomenon to the illusion of a mirage. Meanwhile some enormous object kept moving towards them. Little vapours, tenuous as a breath, ran across the surface of the desert; a harsh and, as it were, quivering glare made the sky more remotely deep, and permeated all things, in such a way that it prevented any judgment of distances. The immense plain stretched out of sight on every hand; and the almost imperceptible undulations of the soil ran to the extreme horizon, which was bounded by a great blue line men knew to be the sea.

The two armies left their tents and stood gazing: the people of Utica crowded upon the walls to see the better.

They made out several transverse bars of level bristling points, and these grew thicker and larger; they saw black hillocks swaying to and fro; and square thickets suddenly appearing. These things were elephants and lances. A single shout went up:

'The Carthaginians!'

Without waiting for any signal or word of command the soldiers at Utica and those at the bridge charged out pell-mell to fall in a body upon Hamilcar.

Spendius shuddered at this name, and breathlessly repeated:
'Hamilcar! Hamilcar!'
And Matho was not there! What was to be done? Flight was impossible! He was distracted by the unexpectedness of the event, his terror of the Suffete, & above all by the urgent need for immediate action: he saw himself pierced by a thousand swords, decapitated, dead. He was being called for; thirty thousand men would follow him; he was seized with fury against himself. To hide his pallor he smeared his cheeks with vermilion, then he buckled on his greaves and his cuirass, swallowed a bowl of unmixed wine, and ran after his men as they were hastening to join the troops from Utica.

The two divisions united so rapidly that the Suffete had no time to draw up his men in line of battle. Gradually he slackened his speed. The elephants stopped, swaying their heavy ostrich-feathered heads and striking their shoulders with their trunks.

Behind the elephants could be seen the light-armed cohorts, and further back the great helmets of the Clibanarii; iron weapons gleaming in the sun, cuirasses, plumes, and waving standards. The Carthaginian army, which was eleven thousand three hundred and ninety-six strong, seemed scarcely to muster so many; for it extended in an oblong narrow at the sides and much compressed.

Seeing them so weak, the Barbarians were seized with extravagant joy. They did not see Hamilcar. Perhaps he had stayed behind? In any case, what did it matter? The contempt which they felt for these tradesmen heightened their courage: & before Spendius had ordered the manoeuvre, they had all understood and were already executing it.

They deployed in a long straight line, overlapping the wings of the Punic army, so as to encompass it completely. But when they were within three hundred paces, the elephants turned about instead of advancing, the Clibanarii promptly wheeled about and followed them; and the surprise of the Mercenaries was crowned by seeing the archers running to join them.

So the Carthaginians were afraid, and were running away! A terrific outburst of hooting came from the Barbarian troops, and Spendius, from the top of his dromedary, cried out:
'Ah, I knew it! Forward! Forward!'
Then began a mighty shower of javelins, darts, and sling-shots. The

elephants, stung in the rump by the arrows, broke into a faster gallop: they were enveloped by a dense dust, and vanished like shadows in a cloud.

A heavy tramping of feet was heard from the rear, and trumpets furiously shrilling over all. The space in front of the Barbarians was full of eddy and tumult, and drew them like a whirlpool: some of them dashed forward into it.

Cohorts of infantry came into view, and closed their ranks; and at the same time the rest of the Barbarians saw the foot-soldiers running up with the galloping cavalry.

Hamilcar had ordered the phalanx to break section, letting the elephants, light troops and cavalry pass through and then extend swiftly outward toward the wings; & so well had he judged his distance from the Barbarians that, at the moment when they reached him, the entire Carthaginian army stood in one long straight line.

In the centre bristled the phalanx, composed of syntagmata, or solid squares of men sixteen a side. Every front rank man was hedged by the long sharp points which jutted irregularly past him; for the first six ranks held their spears by the middle and crossed them, and the ten rear ranks rested theirs upon the shoulders of the men immediately in front. Their faces were half hidden by the visors of their helmets, their right legs were protected by bronze greaves, and their broad cylindrical shields reached to their knees: and this formidable quadrangular mass moved as a single body, and seemed to combine the animation of a living thing with the qualities and functions of a machine. It was regularly flanked by two cohorts of elephants, which shook themselves to get rid of the arrow splinters sticking in their black hides. The Indians, squatting on their withers among the tufts of white feathers, controlled them with spoon-headed harpoons; while the towers held men, hidden to the shoulders, who worked great bows holding iron spindles loaded with flaming tow.

Right and left of the elephants hovered the slingers, with a sling round their loins, a second on their heads, and a third in their right hands. The Clibanarii, each of whom was flanked by a negro, pointed their lances between the ears of their horses, which, like themselves, were completely covered in gold. Beyond them were the light-armed soldiers in extended order, with shields of lynx

skin over which they thrust the points of the javelins they held in
their left hands; and either end of this wall of soldiers was rounded
off by the Tarentines, each of whom managed two horses yoked
together.

The Barbarian army, on the contrary, had not been able to keep in
line. There were waves and gaps along its unwieldy length; and the
men were panting and out of breath with running.

The phalanx swayed heavily as it thrust forth all its spears; and
the Mercenaries' line, which was too thin to resist this enormous
weight, gave in the centre.

The Carthaginian wings executed a flanking movement in order to
fall upon them; and the elephants followed up. The phalanx, with
obliquely pointed lances, cut the Barbarians into two great struggling masses, which were driven back again upon the phalangites
by the slingers and archers on the wings. They had no cavalry to
disperse these last, except two hundred Numidians who charged
the right squadron of the Clibanarii: the rest were unable to move
from the lines that hemmed them in. The peril was imminent.
There was urgent need of some resolute manoeuvre.

Spendius ordered a simultaneous attack upon the two flanks of the
phalanx, so as to pass clean through it. But the more closely packed
ranks slipped behind the longer ones and re-formed; and thus the
phalanx turned upon the Barbarians as formidable in flank as it
had just been at the front.

They struck at the spear shafts, but the cavalry in their rear embarrassed their attack; and the phalanx, supported by the elephants,
kept closing up and extending, taking in turn the form of a square,
a cone, a rhombus, a trapezium or a pyramid. A continual backward and forward movement went on throughout its entire depth,
as the rear files hurried forward to take the place of the front rank
men who dropped back weary or wounded. Sometimes wide cur-
rents swept down from one end to the other, and then up again;
while a heavy mass stood firm in the centre. The spears dipped and
rose in turn. Elsewhere the play of naked swords was so rapid
that only their points could be seen, and squadrons of cavalry kept
clearing wide circles, which closed again in eddies behind them.

Above the captains' voices, the blare of clarions and the twanging
of lyres, rose the whistling of lead bullets and almond-shaped clay

pellets, as they dashed a sword from the hand or flicked the brains from a skull. The wounded, using one arm to cover themselves with their shields, still held their swords forward by resting the hilts on the ground; & others, lying in pools of blood, would turn and bite their enemies' heels. The press was so dense, the dust so thick, and the tumult so great that it was impossible to distinguish anything at all, and cowards who offered to surrender were not even heard. Those who had lost their weapons crushed each other body to body; breast-bones cracked against cuirasses, and corpses, with the head hanging backwards, were held up by a pair of tensed arms. A company of sixty Umbrians, firmly planted upon their hams, and with their pikes held before their eyes, immovable and gritting their teeth, forced two syntagmata to give ground together. Some Epirote shepherds ran upon the left squadron of the Cliba-narii, seized the horses' manes and twisted them round with their staves, until the animals threw their riders and fled across the plain. The Punic slingers were scattered here and there, and stood gaping. The phalanx began to waver, the captains ran to and fro in distrac-tion, the rearmost files were pressing upon the other soldiers, and the Barbarians had re-formed; they came on again; the victory was theirs.

But a cry, an appalling cry broke forth, a bellow of pain and rage. The seventy-two elephants were charging in a double line. Hamil-car had waited until the Mercenaries were massed together in one spot before he loosed the elephants against them; and the Indians had goaded them so vigorously that the blood was trickling down their ears. Their trunks had been smeared with red lead, and stood out straight in the air like red serpents; their breasts were armed with a spear & their backs with a cuirass, their tusks were lengthened by steel blades curved like sabres, and, to make them more fero-cious, they had been intoxicated with a mixture of pepper and neat wine, and incense. They shook their collars of bells, and trum-peted. And the elephantarchs bent their heads to avoid the rain of fire-darts which was beginning from the tops of the towers.

The Barbarians rushed forward in a solid mass, the better to resist them; and the elephants flung themselves impetuously upon their midst. The spurs on their breasts, like ships' prows, clove through the cohorts, which then flowed surging back again. They throttled men with their trunks, or snatched them from the ground and passed them over their heads to the soldiers in the towers; they disembowelled them with their tusks and tossed them into the air; guts hung in long streams from their ivory points like festoons of rope from a mast. The Barbarians tried to gouge out their eyes or to ham-string them; others slipped under their bellies, plunged in their swords to the hilt, and were thereupon crushed to death; the most daring clung to the straps and sawed away at the leather amid flame and bullet and arrow, until the wicker tower collapsed like a tower of stones. Fourteen of the animals on the extreme right, maddened by their wounds, turned round upon the second rank; the Indians seized mallet and chisel, and struck with all their force upon the head joint.

The huge beasts sank down, falling one upon another in a mountain: and upon this heap of dead bodies and armour, a monstrous elephant named 'Fury of Baal', whose leg had become entangled in some chains, stood trumpeting until the evening with an arrow in its eye.

The others, like conquerors gloating in the extermination of their foes, kept turning and crushing and trampling and wreaking their fury upon the corpses and the general wreckage.

They pivoted on their hind feet as they advanced, swinging continually from side to side, to repel the serried columns of the maniples around them. The Carthaginians felt their vigour renewed, and the battle began again.

The Barbarians were weakening; some of the Greek hoplites threw down their arms. Spendius could be seen leaning forward upon his dromedary, and goading it in the shoulders with two javelins. Then they all broke for the wings and ran towards Utica.

The Clibanarii, whose horses were exhausted, did not attempt to overtake them. The Ligurians, who were overcome by thirst, clamoured to make for the river. But the Carthaginians, who were posted in the centre of the syntagmata & had suffered less, stamped their feet in their hunger for the revenge which was escaping them; they were already starting in pursuit of the Mercenaries, when Hamilcar appeared.

He checked his foaming, spotted horse with his silver reins. The streamers from the horns of his helmet cracked behind him in the wind, and he had placed his shield under his left thigh. With a motion of his three-pointed pike he checked the army.

The Tarentines swiftly dismounted and, leaping upon their spare horses, set off to right and left towards the river and the town.

All that remained of the Barbarians were killed off at leisure by the phalanx. As the swords reached them, some stretched out their throats and shut their eyes; others defended themselves to the last, and were battered down from a distance with flints, as if they had been mad dogs. Hamilcar had charged his men to take prisoners; but the Carthaginians obeyed him grudgingly, since it was so much pleasure to plunge their swords into the bodies of the Barbarians. As they were too hot, they set about their work with bare arms like mowers; and when they paused to take breath their eyes would follow some horseman galloping across the plain after a fleeing soldier. He would seize him at last by the hair, hold him thus for a while, and then fell him with a blow of his axe.

Night fell. Carthaginians and Barbarians alike had disappeared. Those elephants that had fled now roamed on the sky-line with their towers ablaze, burning here and there in the darkness like beacons half lost in mist; no movement was to be seen in the plain save the rippling of the river, swollen by the corpses it was bearing away to sea.

Two hours later, Matho arrived. By the starlight he could discern long uneven heaps lying upon the ground.

These were files of Barbarians. He stooped down; all were dead. He called; but no one answered.

That very morning he had left Hippo-Zaritus with his soldiers to march upon Carthage. At Utica the army under Spendius had just set forth, and the inhabitants were beginning to set fire to the engines. There had been a desperate general fight. But the tumult in the direction of the bridge was growing in an incomprehensible fashion, and Matho had struck across the mountain by the shortest road; thus, since the Barbarians were fleeing over the plain, he had met nobody.

In front of him were little pyramids rising in the shade; and closer to him, on the near side of the river, motionless lights showed level with the ground. The Carthaginians had in fact fallen back behind the bridge and, to deceive the Barbarians, the Suffete had stationed numerous posts upon the further bank.

Advancing still further, Matho thought that he could make out Punic ensigns; for he could see, in motionless silhouettes against the sky, horses' heads which had been fixed on top of invisible bundles of spear-shafts: he could hear a great clamour further off, a noise of songs, and a clashing of cups.

Then, not knowing where he was or how to find Spendius, smitten with anguish, scared and lost in the darkness, he returned with even greater haste by the same road. Dawn was growing white when, from the top of the mountain, he saw the town, with the fire-blackened carcases of the engines leaning like giant skeletons against its walls.

A strange silence and heaviness rested over all things. Among his soldiers outside the tents, men were sleeping nearly naked on their backs, or resting their heads upon their arms, their arms on their cuirasses. Some eased off the blood-stained bandages which had stuck to their legs. The dying were gently rolling their heads from side to side; and others dragged themselves along the ground to bring them drink. The sentries walked up and down along the narrow paths to warm themselves, or stood fiercely facing the horizon, their pikes on their shoulders.

Matho found Spendius sheltering beneath a rag of canvas supported on two sticks set in the ground, clasping his knees in his hands and with his head bowed down.

They remained for a long while without speaking.

At last Matho murmured:

'Beaten!'

And Spendius rejoined gloomily:

'Yes, beaten!'

And to all the other's questions he answered with gestures of despair.

Meanwhile the sound of moaning & of death-rattles came to them; and Matho drew the canvas a little aside. The sight of the soldiers reminded him of another disaster on the same spot, and he ground his teeth:

'Wretch! Once already ...'

Spendius interrupted him:

'You were not there, either.'

'There is a curse on me!' cried Matho. 'But I shall have him at last! I shall vanquish him! I shall slay him! Ah, if I had been there . . . !'

The thought of having missed the battle caused him an even greater despair than the defeat. He pulled out his sword and threw it on the ground.

'How did the Carthaginians beat you?'

The one-time slave began to describe each manoeuvre in turn, and Matho, as he visualised it, grew more and more angry. The army from Utica ought to have taken Hamilcar in the rear instead of stampeding for the bridge.

'Alas, I know it!' said Spendius.

'You ought to have made your ranks twice as deep; you should not have exposed your light troops to the phalanx, & you should have let the elephants pass right through. The whole situation could have been saved at the last moment: there was no need to run away.'

Spendius answered:

'I saw him pass along in his great red cloak with uplifted arms, high above the dust, like an eagle flying on the flank of the cohorts; and at each nod of his head they closed up or they charged forward; we were borne near to one another by the press, & he looked at me: it pierced my heart like cold steel.'

'It may be he waited for a propitious day?' muttered Matho to himself.

They questioned each other, trying to discover what it was that had brought the Suffete just when circumstances were most untoward. To palliate his failure, or to re-kindle his own courage, Spendius declared that there was still hope.

'And if there be none, it is no matter!' said Matho. 'I will carry on the war alone!'

'And I too!' cried the Greek, leaping to his feet.

He paced up and down with great strides; his eyes sparkled, and his jackal's face was wrinkled in a strange smile.

'We will make a fresh start: do not leave me again! I am not made for battles in broad daylight; the flashing of swords troubles my eyes; it is a disease, due to living too long in a slave prison. But give me walls to scale at night, and I will enter citadels; and the bodies will be cold before cock-crow! Show me anyone, anything, an enemy, a treasure, a woman.' And he repeated:

'A woman, no matter if she be a king's daughter, and I will quickly bring your desire to your feet. You reproach me for having lost the battle against Hanno, but I won it back again. Confess it! My herd of swine did more for us than a whole phalanx of Spartans.'

And yielding to his need to aggrandise himself & take his revenge, he recounted all he had done for the cause of the Mercenaries.

'It was I who urged on the Gaul in the Suffete's gardens! Later, at Sicca, I made them all mad with fear of the Republic! Gisco was sending them back; but I saw to it that the interpreters could not interpret further. Ah, how their tongues hung out of their mouths! Do you remember? I brought you into Carthage. I stole the zaimph. I led you to her. I shall do more yet: you shall see!'

He burst out laughing like a madman.

Matho looked at him with wide open eyes. He felt a kind of embarrassment in the presence of this man, who was at once so cowardly and so terrible.

The Greek went on in merry tones, snapping his fingers:

'Hurrah! After rain, the sun! I have worked in the quarries, and I have drunk Massic wine under a golden awning in my own ship, like a Ptolemy. Misfortune should teach us to manage things better. By hard work we can bend fortune to our will. She loves schemers. She will yield!'

He came back to Matho and took him by the arm.

'Master, at present the Carthaginians are sure of their victory. You have an entire army which has not fought; and you ... your men obey you. Place them in the van, & mine will follow for revenge's sake. I have still three thousand Carians, twelve hundred slingers, archers, and whole cohorts! We could even form a phalanx. Let us return!'

Matho, who had been stunned by the disaster, had hitherto thought of no means of repairing it. He listened open-mouthed, and the bronze plates which cased his sides rose and fell with the throbbing of his heart. He picked up his sword, crying:

'Follow me! Forward!'

When the scouts returned, they reported that the Carthaginian dead had been carried off, that the bridge was in ruins, and that Hamilcar had disappeared.

IN THE FIELD

CHAPTER IX

HAMILCAR HAD RECKONED THAT THE MERCENARIES would either wait for him at Utica or come back and attack him; and considering that he was not strong enough either to initiate or to withstand an assault, he had struck southwards along the right bank of the river, & thus at once placed himself beyond the danger of surprise.

His plan was, after first shutting his eyes to their revolt, to detach all the tribes from the cause of the Barbarians, who would thus be left quite isolated in the midst of the provinces: then he would fall upon and exterminate them.

In fourteen days he pacified the district between Thuccaber and Utica, with the towns of Tignicabah, Tesurah, Vacca, and others further to the west: Zunghar built in the mountains, Assuras celebrated for its temple, and Djeraado fertile in junipers; Thapitis and Hagur sent envoys to him. The country people came with their hands full of provisions, implored his protection, kissed his and the soldiers' feet, and voiced complaints against the Barbarians. Some brought sacks containing the heads of Mercenaries & offered them to him, saying that they had killed them; whereas they had in truth cut them from dead bodies: for many had perished in their flight, and were found dead here and there under the olive trees and among the vines.

To dazzle the people, Hamilcar had, on the day after his victory, sent to Carthage the two thousand captives taken on the battlefield. They arrived in long companies of a hundred men each, their arms fastened behind their backs with a bronze bar which caught them at the nape of the neck; and the wounded, bleeding as they were, had to run with the rest, being driven along by mounted men with whips.

The people were drunk with joy! It was repeatedly rumoured that there were six thousand Barbarians killed; the others would not hold out, the war was finished; they hugged one another in the streets, and rubbed the faces of the Pataec Gods with butter and cinnamon as a mark of their thanks. These gods, with their big eyes, their great bellies, and arms raised to their shoulders, seemed to come to life under this fresh painting, and to share the people's gladness. The Rich left their doors open; the city echoed with the rolling of drums; the temples were lit up every night, and the servants of the Goddess went down to Malqua and set up stages of sycamore wood at the cross-ways, and prostituted themselves there. Lands were voted to the victors, holocausts to Melkarth, and three hundred golden crowns to the Suffete, whose partisans proposed that new prerogatives and honours should also be bestowed upon him.

He had begged the Elders to approach Autharitus with an offer to exchange all, if necessary, of the Barbarians for the aged Gisco and his Carthaginian fellow captives. The Libyans & Nomads, of whom Autharitus' army was composed, hardly knew these Mercenaries, who were men of Italiote or Greek extraction; the Republic's offer of so many Barbarians for so few Carthaginians must surely mean that the former were worth nothing and the latter worth much. They suspected a trap. Autharitus refused.

The Elders ordered the execution of the captives, although the Suffete had written bidding them not to put these to death. He had intended to incorporate the best of them with his own troops and thus stir up defection among the enemy. But all considerations of policy were swept aside by hatred.

The two thousand Barbarians were bound to the stelae of the

tombs in the Mappales; pedlars, kitchen scrubs, embroiderers, and even women, the widows of the dead with their children, anyone who so wished, came to shoot them to death with arrows. They lingered over their aim, the better to prolong the torture, they kept lowering their weapons and then raising them again; and the yelling mob pressed forward. Paralytics had themselves carried thither on stretchers; many took the precaution of bringing food, & stayed until the evening; others spent the whole night there. Drinking booths had been set up, and many gained much profit by hiring out bows.

All these crucified corpses were left upright, looking like so many red statues on the tombs; and the excitement spread even to the people of Malqua, who were descended from aboriginal tribes and were usually indifferent to the affairs of their country. Out of gratitude for the pleasure it had been giving them they now interested themselves in its fortunes, and felt that they were Carthaginians: & the Elders thought it a subtle thing thus to have united the entire people in one act of vengeance.

The gods did not withhold their countenance: for crows swooped down from every quarter, and circled in the air with loud hoarse cries in a great cloud, continually whirling about and about itself. It could be seen from Clypea, from Rhades, and the promontory of Hermaeum. Sometimes it would break suddenly and spread into long black spirals, as an eagle swept through its midst and soared away again. Here and there on the terraces, the domes, the tops of the obelisks, and the pediments of the temples were huge birds with strips of human flesh in their reddened beaks.

The Carthaginians reluctantly unbound the corpses because of their stench. A few were burned, the rest were thrown into the sea; and the waves, driven by the north wind, washed them ashore at the end of the gulf before the camp of Autharitus.

This punishment had doubtless terrified the Barbarians; for from the roof of Eshmun they could be seen striking their tents, collecting their flocks, and hoisting their baggage upon asses; and on the same evening the whole army withdrew.

Its object was, by marching and counter-marching between the mountain of the Hot Springs and Hippo-Zaritus, to cut off the Suffete from the Tyrian towns & to prevent his return to Carthage.

Meanwhile the two other armies were trying to come up with him in the south, Spendius from the east, and Matho from the west, in such a way that all three should unite to surprise and entrap him. They received an unlooked-for reinforcement when Narr'Havas reappeared with three hundred camels bearing bitumen, twenty-five elephants, and six thousand horsemen.

It had been the Suffete's policy to weaken the Mercenaries by keeping the Numidian occupied in his own distant kingdom: and working from the heart of Carthage with this end in view, he had come to an understanding with Masgaba, a Gaetulian brigand who was seeking to make himself master of a kingdom, backed by Punic money; this man had raised the Numidian States by promising them freedom. But Narr'Havas, warned by his nurse's son, had fallen upon Cirta, poisoned its conquerors by contaminating the water of the cisterns, struck off a few heads, and restored order; now he was returning with an anger against the Suffete greater even than that of the Barbarians.

The chiefs of the four armies agreed upon their plan of campaign. It would be a long war, and every contingency must be foreseen.

It was decided first to appeal for help to the Romans, & this mission was offered to Spendius; but as a fugitive he dared not undertake it, and twelve men from the Greek colonies sailed from Annaba in a Numidian sloop. Then the chiefs exacted an oath of complete obedience from all the Barbarians. Every day the captains inspected clothes and boots; sentries were even forbidden to use a shield, since they would often prop it against their lance and fall asleep as they stood; those who were dragging any baggage about with them were forced to get rid of it; everything was to be carried in the Roman manner, on the back. As a precaution against the elephants, Matho instituted a corps of panoplied cavalry, both man and horse being shielded by a cuirass of hippopotamus hide bristling with nails, and to protect the horses' hoofs, shoes of plaited esparto grass were made for them.

It was forbidden to pillage the towns, or to oppress such inhabitants as were not of Punic race. Since the country was becoming drained, Matho ordered the rations to be distributed to the soldiers at so much a head, without troubling about the women: at first the men shared with these, so that many grew weak through lack of food. This provoked continual quarrelling & abuse, for many of the men enticed away other men's mistresses by the offer or even by the promise of their own portion. Matho ordered all the women to be driven forth without mercy, & they took refuge in Autharitus' camp; but the Gaulish and Libyan females treated them so outrageously that they were compelled to depart.

They then came under the walls of Carthage to implore the protection of Ceres and Proserpine; for in Byrsa were a temple and priests consecrated to these goddesses, in expiation of the horrors committed at the siege of Syracuse. The Syssitia, alleging their right to all strays, claimed the youngest in order to sell them; and some fair-haired Lacedaemonian women were taken by the New Carthaginians in marriage.

A few persisted in following the armies. They ran on the flank of the syntagmata, by the side of the captains, calling to their men, pulling them by the cloak, striking themselves on the breast and cursing, holding out at arm's length their little naked crying children. The Barbarians were unmanned by this sight, & the women became a nuisance and a danger. Several times they were driven off, but they came back again, until Matho ordered Narr'Havas's cavalry to charge them with lances. When some Balearic Islanders shouted out that they must have women, he retorted:

'I have none myself!'

Now he was possessed by the spirit of Moloch. In spite of a rebellious conscience, he did terrible deeds in the belief that he was obeying the voice of a god. When he could not ravage the fields, he threw stones upon them to make them barren.

He repeatedly sent messages urging Autharitus and Spendius to make haste. But the Suffete's operations were incomprehensible. He encamped at Eidus, Monchar, and Tehent in turn; some scouts believed that they saw him in the neighbourhood of Ishiil, near the frontiers of Narr'Havas, and it was learned that he had crossed the river above Teburba as if returning to Carthage. Scarcely was he in one place before he moved to another. They could never ascertain what routes he took. Without giving battle, the Suffete maintained his advantage; he had an appearance of leading the Barbarians when they were pursuing him.

These marches and countermarches were still more fatiguing to the Carthaginians; and Hamilcar's forces, receiving no reinforcement, diminished from day to day. The country people were now slower to bring him provisions. Everywhere he was met with hesitation and mute hatred: and in spite of his pleas to the Great Council no help was sent to him from Carthage.

It was said, and perhaps believed, that he did not need help: that he was merely making empty complaints, or else there was some plot behind his messages. To do him an ill turn, Hanno's partisans exaggerated the importance of his victory. He was very welcome to the troops already under his command; but they were not going to keep on supplying his demands. The war was quite burdensome enough, and had cost too much already! And the patricians of his own party, touched in their pride, gave him but slack support.

So, despairing of the Republic, Hamilcar took from the tribes by force all that he needed for the war: grain, oil and wood, cattle and men. The inhabitants lost no time in taking to flight, & the towns were empty when he passed through them; he ransacked the abandoned dwellings and found nothing. Soon the Punic army was compassed about by a terrifying solitude.

The infuriated Carthaginians set about devastating the provinces, filling up the cisterns and firing the houses. Sparks, borne by the wind, were scattered far and wide, so that whole forests burned on the mountains, ringing the valleys with a crown of flames; the army had to wait before it could cross them, and would resume its march under the flaming sun over the hot embers.

Sometimes they would see a thing like the eyes of a tiger-cat gleaming in a bush by the side of the road: a Barbarian crouching on his heels, smeared with dust so as to blend with the colour of the leafage. Or perhaps, as they went through a ravine, those on the wings would suddenly hear stones rolling, and, raising their eyes, would see a bare-footed man leaping through the mouth of the gorge.

Meanwhile Utica & Hippo-Zaritus were free, since the Mercenaries were no longer besieging them. Hamilcar bade them come to his assistance: but not daring to compromise themselves, they answered him equivocally, with compliments and excuses.

He turned abruptly northward again, resolved to open up one of the Tyrian cities, even if he had to lay siege to it. A coastal base was essential for him if he would draw supplies and men from the islands or from Cyrene, and he coveted the harbour of Utica since it was nearest to Carthage.

The Suffete therefore left Zuitin and cautiously skirted the lake of Hippo-Zaritus. Soon he was obliged to extend his regiments into column in order to climb the mountain separating the two valleys. They were descending at sunset into its hollow, funnel-shaped summit, when they saw before them, level with the ground, as it were she-wolves of bronze running upon the grass.

Suddenly great plumes rose into view, & a terrible song burst forth to the rhythm of flutes. It was the army of Spendius; for some Campanians and Greeks had, in their hatred of Carthage, assumed the ensigns of Rome. At the same time long pikes, leopard-skin shields, linen cuirasses and naked shoulders were seen on the left: these were the Iberians under Matho, the Lusitanians, Balearians and Gaetulians. The horses of Narr'Havas could be heard neighing; they spread about the hill. Then came the loose rabble commanded by Autharitus; Gauls, Libyans and Nomads; and among these the Eaters of Unclean Things could be distinguished by the fish bones which they wore in their hair.

The Barbarians had so well timed their marches that they thus arrived all together: but they were themselves taken aback, & stood motionless for some minutes considering what they should do.

The Suffete had massed his men together in a circular formation so as to offer equal resistance on every side. The infantry were walled round by their tall, pointed shields which they had stuck close together in the turf. The Clibanarii remained outside, and the elephants were stationed at intervals still further off. The Mercenaries were worn with fatigue, and would surely do better to wait till next day; the Barbarians, feeling certain of their victory, spent the whole night eating.

They had lit huge bright fires, which served only to dazzle them, and left the Punic army below them in shadow. Hamilcar caused a trench fifteen feet broad and ten cubits deep to be dug round his camp in the Roman manner, and with the earth thus thrown up raised a parapet on the inside & planted sharp inter-crossing stakes upon it. At sunrise the Mercenaries were amazed to perceive all the Carthaginians thus entrenched as if in a fortress.

They recognised Hamilcar among the tents, walking about and

giving orders. His body was clad in a brown cuirass cut in little scales; he was followed by his horse, and stopped from time to time to point out something with his right arm.

More than one recalled similar mornings when, amid the din of clarions, he had passed slowly before them, and his looks had strengthened them like draughts of wine: these were seized with an emotion of tenderness. Those, on the contrary, who did not know Hamilcar were mad with joy at having caught him.

If they all attacked at once in such a confined space they would injure one another. The Numidians could charge across; but the Clibanarii, who were protected by cuirasses, would surely crush them. And then, how were the palisades to be surmounted? As to the elephants, they were not well enough trained for the work.

'You are all cowards!' cried Matho.

And with the pick of his men he rushed against the entrenchment, only to be repulsed by a volley of stones; for the Suffete had taken the catapults they had abandoned on the bridge.

This failure produced an abrupt change of heart in the unstable Barbarians, & their exaggerated bravery melted away. They wished to conquer, but with the least possible risk. According to Spendius they must carefully preserve the position they now held, and starve out the Punic army. The Carthaginians began to dig wells and, as there were mountains surrounding the hill, they found water.

From the top of their palisade they launched arrows, earth, and dung, and stones which they tore up from the ground, while the six catapults were constantly wheeled to and fro along the entrenchment.

But the springs would naturally dry up in time; the provisions would become exhausted, and the catapults worn out; the Mercenaries, who were ten times their number, would triumph in the end. The Suffete planned to gain time by negotiating with the enemy, and one morning the Barbarians found a sheepskin covered with writing within their lines. He justified himself for his victory on the ground that the Elders had forced him into the war. To show them that he was keeping his word, he offered them the pillaging of either Utica or Hippo-Zaritus, whichever they chose; and he concluded by declaring that he did not fear them, because he had won over certain traitors, and thanks to them would easily manage all the rest.

The Barbarians were disturbed: this proposal of immediate booty set them dreaming. They were afraid of being betrayed, not suspecting any snare in the Suffete's boasting, and they began to regard one another with mistrust. A watch was kept upon every word and every step: they were wakened by terrors in the night. Many forsook their companions and attached themselves to the army of their inclination; the Gauls with Autharitus joined the men of Cisalpine Gaul, whose speech they understood.

The four chiefs met every evening in Matho's tent and, squatting round a shield, gave their minds to the moving up and down of those little wooden figures invented by Pyrrhus to represent military manoeuvres. Spendius pointed out Hamilcar's resources and, swearing by all the gods, begged them not to spoil their opportunity. Matho would get angry and stride to and fro gesticulating. The war against Carthage was his personal affair; he resented the others' meddling with it and yet not being willing to obey him. Autharitus guessed from his face what he did not say, & applauded. Narr'Havas raised his chin in disdain; there was not a proposal made which he did not consider fatal; and he no longer smiled. Sighs would escape him, as if he had just pressed back the anguish of an impossible dream, the despair of an unaccomplished enterprise.

While the Barbarians deliberated and came to no decision, the Suffete was strengthening his defences. He had a second trench dug within the palisades, raised a second wall and built wooden towers at its corners; and his slaves went right to the outposts to drive caltrops in the ground. But the elephants, whose rations had been reduced, struggled in their shackles. To economise grass he ordered the Clibanarii to kill the weakest of the stallions; and when some of these refused to do so, he had them beheaded. They ate the horses; and in the days that followed the memory of this fresh meat was a most sorrowful one.

From the bottom of the amphitheatre in which they were confined they could see the four Barbarian camps full of movement upon the heights around them. Women went about with leather bottles on their heads, goats strayed bleating under the stacked lances; sentries were relieved, and there was eating about the tripods. The tribes brought them abundance of provision, and they themselves had no idea how much their inaction alarmed the Punic army.

On the second day the Carthaginians had noticed in the Nomads' camp a troop of three hundred men who stood apart from the rest. These were the Rich who had been held as captives since the beginning of the war. Some of the Libyans placed them all in line along the edge of the trench, and used them as cover from behind which to hurl their javelins. The poor wretches' faces were so foul with vermin and mire that they could hardly be recognised: their hair had been plucked out in places, exposing the ulcers on their heads; and they were so lean and hideous that they looked like mummies in tattered shrouds. A few were dully and stupidly sobbing; the rest cried out to their friends to shoot at the Barbarians. There was one who stood quite still with lowered head, saying no word; his long white beard fell down to his manacled hands; and the Carthaginians felt in the depth of their hearts that the Republic was ruined, when they recognised this figure as Gisco. Disregarding the danger to which they exposed themselves, they pressed forward to see him. A grotesque tiara of hippopotamus hide incrusted with pebbles had been set on his head. This was Autharitus' idea; but Matho was not pleased with it.

In exasperation, and resolved to cut his way through no matter at what expense, Hamilcar had the palisades opened; and the Carthaginians charged furiously for three hundred paces, halfway up the hill. Such a flood of Barbarians descended upon them that they were driven back on their lines. One of the guards of the Legion stumbled among the stones before he could win away. Zarxas ran up, knocked him down, plunged a dagger into his throat and, drawing it out, threw himself upon the wound, glued his lips to it and, mumbling and jerking his whole body with delight, pumped up the blood in full draughts: then he quietly sat down on the corpse, raised his face and threw back his head the better to breathe in the air, like a hind that has just drunk at a mountain stream, and in a shrill voice chanted a Balearic song, a vague melody of prolonged modulations, with breaks and repetitions like echoes answering one another in the mountains. He was calling to his dead brothers, inviting them to a feast. Then he dropped his hands between his legs, slowly bent his head, and wept. This atrocious action affected the Barbarians, especially the Greeks, with horror.

After that the Carthaginians did not attempt any further sally; also they had no thought of surrender, being certain that they could expect nothing save an agonising death.

Meanwhile, in spite of Hamilcar's care, the provisions were diminishing at an alarming rate. There was no more left than ten k'hommers of wheat, three hins of millet, & twelve betzas of dried fruit for each man. No more meat, no more oil, no more salted food; and not a grain of barley for the horses; these might be seen reaching down their wasted necks into the dust for bits of trampled straw. Often the sentries on the parapet would see one of the Barbarians' dogs prowling below the entrenchment in the moonlight among the heaps of filth; then they would knock it over with a stone and, climbing down the palisades with the help of their shield straps, eat it without a word. Sometimes a terrible barking would be heard, and the man would not come up again. Three phalangites, in the fourth dilochia of the twelfth syntagma, knived one another to death in a quarrel over a rat.

All yearned for their families, and their houses; the poor for their hive-shaped huts with shells on the threshold and nets hanging outside, and the patricians for the blue shadows of their great halls where, at the idlest hour of the day, they would lie and listen to the vague murmur of the streets mingled with the rustling of the leaves in their gardens; to sink themselves more deeply in such thoughts and enjoy them better, they would close their eyes, until roused by the shock of a wound. Every minute there was some engagement, some fresh alarm; the towers burned, the Eaters of Unclean Things leaped upon the palisades; when their hands were chopped off with axes, others would hasten up to take their place; a hail of iron would fall upon the tents. Galleries of rush hurdles were raised as a protection against such missiles, and the Carthaginians shut themselves up behind these and no longer ventured forth.

Every day in its course over the hill the sun, after the first early hours, would forsake the bottom of the gorge and leave them in the shade. Before and behind them, covered with stones scantily spotted by lichen, rose grey slopes; and over their heads stretched the ever cloudless sky, smoother and colder to the eye than a metal dome. Hamilcar was so incensed against Carthage that he felt inclined to throw in his lot with the Barbarians & lead them against her. Moreover, the porters, sutlers and slaves were beginning to grumble; and neither the people, nor the Great Council, nor anyone sent him the least word of hope. The situation was intolerable, and was rendered the more so by the thought that it must become worse.

At the news of the disaster Carthage had, as it were, started into sudden anger and hate: the Suffete would have been less execrated if he had let himself be beaten from the first.

But there was no time and no money to buy other Mercenaries; and as for raising soldiers in the city, how were they to be equipped? Hamilcar had taken all the arms! And who would command them? The best captains were away with him yonder! Some messengers from the Suffete came shouting into the streets and disturbed the Great Council, who arranged for their disappearance.

This was an unnecessary precaution; for everyone accused Barca of having acted half-heartedly. He ought to have annihilated the Mercenaries after his victory. What had been the use of his ravaging the tribes? They had already made heavy enough sacrifices; and the patricians deplored their contribution of fourteen shekels, and the Syssitia their two hundred and twenty-three thousand kikars of gold: those.who had given nothing lamented as loudly as the rest. The populace was jealous of the New Carthaginians, to whom he had promised full rights of citizenship; and even the Ligurians, who had fought so valiantly, were confounded with the Barbarians and cursed like them: their very nationality was a crime, a complicity. The merchants at their shop doors, workmen passing with their leaden rules in their hands, pickle sellers rinsing their baskets, attendants in the vapour baths and vendors of hot drinks, each and all discussed the operations of the campaign. They would trace plans of battle in the dust with their fingers; and there was no beggar so vile that he could not have corrected Hamilcar's mistakes.

It was a punishment, said the priests, for his long continued impiety. He had offered no holocausts; he had not purified his troops;

he had even refused to take augurs with him; and thus to the violence of suppressed hatred and the rage of hopes betrayed was added the scandal of sacrilege. People recalled the Sicilian disasters, and all the burden of his pride that they had borne for so long! The colleges of the pontiffs could not forgive him for having seized their treasure, and they exacted from the Great Council a pledge to crucify him should he ever return.

The excessive heat, that year, of the month of Elul was another calamity. A nauseous stench rose from the shores of the lake, and was wafted through the air together with the fumes of aromatics circling upwards at the street corners. There was a continual singing of hymns. The people flocked on to the temple stairways: the walls were covered with black veils; candles burned upon the brows of the Pataec gods; and the blood of sacrificed camels ran down the flights of the steps in red cascades. Carthage was shaken by a delirium of lamentation. From the depths of the narrowest lanes, from the blackest dens, came pale faced men with viperine profiles, grinding their teeth. The houses were filled with the shrill crying of women, and this, escaping through the lattices, made those who stood talking in the squares turn round in wonder. Sometimes it was thought the Barbarians were coming; they had been seen behind the mountain of the Hot Springs; they were encamped at Tunis: the voices of the people would multiply and swell, and be blended into one single clamour. Then silence would drop over all, and some remained where they had climbed upon the frontals of the buildings, screening their eyes with their open hands, and others lay flat on their faces at the foot of the ramparts, straining their ears. When their panic had passed, their anger would be born again. But the conviction of their own impotence would soon plunge them once more into their former sadness.

This was intensified every evening, when all went up on the terraces and, bowing down nine times, uttered a loud cry in salutation of the sun as it sank, slowly, behind the Lagoon, and then suddenly disappeared among the mountains in the direction of the Barbarian armies.

They were waiting for the thrice holy festival when, from the top of a pyre, an eagle was flown heavenwards as a symbol of the resurrection of the year and a message from the people to their supreme Baal; for they regarded this as a sort of union, a means of joining themselves with the might of the sun. Moreover, filled with their present hatred, they turned frankly towards Moloch the Slayer, and all forsook Tanit. Rabbet, having lost her veil, was as it were despoiled of part of her virtue. She denied the blessing of her waters; she had abandoned Carthage; she was a deserter, an enemy. Some threw stones at her to insult her. But many pitied her even as they cursed her; she was still loved, and perhaps more deeply than ever.

All their misfortunes, therefore, were due to the loss of the zaimph. Salambo had indirectly been accessory to this, and she was included in the general ill will; she must be punished. The vague idea of a sacrifice spread among the people. To appease the Baalim it was without doubt necessary to offer them something of incalculable worth, a beautiful being, young, virgin, of old family, a descendant of the Gods, a human star. Every day the gardens of Megara were invaded by strange men; the slaves, trembling for their own safety, dared not resist them. Yet they did not pass beyond the galley stairway. They remained below with their eyes raised towards the highest terrace: they were waiting for Salambo, and they would cry out against her for hours, like dogs baying up at the moon.

THE
SERPENT

CHAPTER X

THIS CLAMOURING OF THE POPULACE DID NOT ALARM
Hamilcar's daughter.

Higher things were troubling her: her great serpent, the black
Python, was failing in health; and, to the Carthaginians, this serpent was both a national and a private fetish. It was believed to be
engendered of the slime of the earth, since it emerges from its
depth and has no need of feet to traverse it; its going was like the
undulation of rivers, the heat of its body was that of the primeval
ooze of fecund darkness, and the circle that it made when biting
its tail recalled the harmony of the planets, the intelligence of
Eshmun.

Salambo's serpent had now several times refused the four live
sparrows which were offered to it at the full moon and at every
new moon. Its beautiful skin, covered like the firmament with
golden spots upon a dead black ground, was now yellow & flabby,
wrinkled and too large for its body. A cotton-like mould was

spreading round its head; and in the corners of its eyes were little red specks which seemed to move. From time to time Salambo went up to its silver filigree basket and drew aside the purple curtains, the lotus leaves, and the down bedding; but it lay always curled up, more still than a withered bindweed: and from much looking at it she came at last to feel a kind of spiral in her heart, another serpent, as it were, mounting slowly upwards to her throat and strangling her.

She was in despair at having seen the zaimph, yet it gave her a sort of joy, an intimate pride. There was a lurking mystery in the splendour of its folds; it was the cloud that wrapped the gods about, the secret of universal existence; and Salambo, though stricken with horror at herself, regretted that she had not lifted it up.

She nearly always crouched now at the back of her apartment, with her left leg curled up and clasped in her hands, her mouth a little open, her chin lowered and her eyes in a fixed stare. She remembered her father's face with terror; she wished to go away into the mountains of Phoenicia, on a pilgrimage to the temple of Aphaka, where Tanit descended in the form of a star; she was fascinated and appalled by every sort of imagining; moreover she was compassed by a solitude which grew greater each day. She did not even know what had become of Hamilcar.

Weary of her thoughts she rose and, with the soles of her little sandals flipping against her heels at every step, walked aimlessly about the vast silent room. The amethysts and topazes scattered upon the ceiling were shimmering spots of light, & as she walked Salambo turned her head a little to look at them. She handled the hanging amphoras by their necks; she cooled her breast under the broad fans, or would amuse herself by burning cinnamon in hollow pearls. At sunset Taanach would draw back the black felt lozenges which closed the openings in the wall; then her doves, that were rubbed with musk like the doves of Tanit, entered immediately, and their pink feet glided over the glass paving among the grains of barley she threw to them in handfuls, like a sower in a field. Suddenly she would burst into sobs and lie full length upon the great bed of ox hide straps, making no movement, ever repeating the same word, with open eyes, pale as the dead, insensible and cold; and all the time she could hear the apes crying in the clumps of palm trees, and the continual grinding of the great wheel as it raised a flow of pure water to the porphyry basin in the highest story.

Sometimes she would refuse to eat for several days. She could see, as in a dream, troubled stars wandering beneath her feet. She would call Shahabarim, and when he came have nothing to say to him.

She could not live without the solace of his presence. But inwardly she rebelled against this domination; her feeling for the priest was one at once of terror and jealousy, hatred and a kind of love born of gratitude for the strange pleasure she experienced when he was near her.

Skilled in the knowledge of the maladies sent by the different gods, he had recognised the influence of Rabbet; and, in order to cure Salambo, he had her apartment sprinkled with lotions of vervain & maidenhair: she ate mandrake every morning; she slept with her head on a cushion filled with aromatics which had been blended by the pontiffs; he had even used baaras, a fiery coloured root which banishes baleful spirits to the north; lastly, turning towards the polar star, he thrice murmured the mysterious name of Tanit. But Salambo went on suffering, and his anguish grew deeper.

No one in Carthage was so learned as he. In his youth he had studied at the College of the Mogbeds, at Borsippa, near Babylon; he had then visited Samothrace, Pessinus, Ephesus, Thessaly, Judaea, and the temples of the Nabathae which are lost in the sands; he had travelled on foot along the banks of the Nile from the cataracts to the sea. With a veil over his face and brandishing torches, he had cast a black cock upon a fire of sandarach before the breast of the Sphinx, the Father of Terror. He had been down into the caverns of Proserpine; he had seen the five hundred pillars revolving in the labyrinth of Lemnos, and the splendour of the candelabrum of Tarentum, which bore on its shaft as many sconces as there are days in the year; sometimes at night Greeks would visit him, and he would question them. He concerned himself with the constitution of the world no less than with the nature of the gods: he had observed the equinoxes with the armils placed in the portico of Alexandria, and had journeyed as far as Cyrene with the bematists of Evergetes, who measure the sky by calculating the number of their steps; so that now a religion of his own was growing in his thought, with no distinct formula, and on that very account fulfilled with ecstacy and fervour. He no longer believed that the earth was formed like a fir-cone; he believed it to be round & eternally falling through immensity with such prodigious speed that its fall could not be felt.

From the position of the sun above the moon he inferred the predominance of Baal, of whom the star itself is but the reflection and image; moreover, every terrestrial sign apparent to him compelled him to recognise the male principle of destruction as supreme. Secretly, too, he blamed Rabbet for the misfortune of his life. Was it not for her that the high priest had stepped forward amid the clash of cymbals, & had robbed him of his future manhood? And he gazed sadly after the men who disappeared with the priestesses into the depths of the terebinth trees.

His days were spent in inspecting the censers, the gold vases, the tongs, the rakes for the ashes on the altar, and the robes of all the statues; even down to the bronze bodkin used to curl the hair of an old Tanit in the third pavilion near the emerald vine. Regularly at the same hour he would raise the great hangings before the same swinging doors; would stand with arms outspread in the same attitude; or would pray prostrate on the flag-stones, while a colony of priests moved barefooted about him through the eternal twilight of the passages.

In the barrenness of his life Salambo was like a flower in the chink of a tomb. Nevertheless he was hard towards her, and spared her neither penances nor bitter words. His condition established between them, as it were, an equality and community of sex, and his resentment against the girl was due less to his inability to possess her than to her being so beautiful and, above all, so pure. Often he saw that she could not, for all her effort, follow his thought: then he would turn from her, sadder than ever; he would feel himself more completely forsaken, more lonely, more empty.

Strange words fell from him at times, which passed before Salambo like great lights illuminating her abysses. This was at night on the terrace when they two, alone, were gazing upon the stars, and Carthage lay beneath their feet, with the bay and the open sea melting vaguely into the darkness.

He explained to her the theory of souls descending upon the earth, following the same path as the sun through the signs of the zodiac. Stretching out his arm, he pointed to the gate of human generation in the Ram, and that of the return to the gods in Capricorn; and Salambo strove to see them, for she took these conceptions for realities; she accepted pure symbols and even figures of speech as literally true; and the distinction was not always very clear even to the priest.

'The souls of the dead,' he said, 'become merged into the moon, as do their bodies into the earth. Her humidity is made of their tears; it is a dark abode, where all is mire and wreck and tempest.'

She asked what would become of her there.

'At first you will languish, light as a mist hovering over the waves; and after prolonged trials and agonies you will pass into the centre of the sun, at the very source of the Intelligence!'

He did not, however, speak of Rabbet. Salambo imagined that this was through shame for his vanquished goddess, and, calling her by a common name which designated the moon, she poured forth blessings upon the fertile and benign planet. At last he exclaimed: 'No, no! She draws all her fruition from the other! Do you not see her circling about him like an amorous woman running after a man in a field?'

And he did not cease to extol the virtue of light.

Far from repressing her mystic yearnings, he encouraged them; he even seemed to delight in grieving her with his revelations of an inexorable doctrine. In spite of the pains of her love, Salambo gave herself entirely to them.

But the more Shahabarim felt himself doubting Tanit, the more he wished to believe in her. Far down in his soul there was a remorse which gave him pause. He ought to have had some proof, some manifestation from the gods, and in the hope of obtaining this he devised an enterprise which might possibly save at once his country and his faith.

Thenceforward he set himself, before Salambo, to deplore the sacrilege and the misfortunes which came from it even in the places of the sky. Then he told her on a sudden of the Suffete's danger, and how he was assailed by three armies under the command of Matho: for because of the veil, Matho was, in the eyes of the Carthaginians, as it were the king of the Barbarians. And he added that the safety of the Republic and of her father depended upon her solely.

'Upon me!' she exclaimed. 'How can I . . .?'

But the priest, with a disdainful smile, said:

'You will never consent!'

She entreated him, and at last Shahabarim said to her:

'You must go to the Barbarian camp and recover the zaimph!'

She sank down upon the ebony stool and remained with her arms stretched upon her knees, trembling in all her limbs, like a victim at the foot of the altar awaiting the fatal blow. There was a buzzing in her temples, and she could see whirling rings of fire, and, in her stupor, she could no longer understand anything save the fact that she was certainly soon to die.

But if Rabbet triumphed, if the zaimph were restored & Carthage delivered, what mattered a woman's life, thought Shahabarim! Moreover, she might perhaps obtain the veil and yet not perish.

For three days he did not come back to her: and on the evening of the fourth, she sent for him.

To inflame her heart the more, he repeated all the abuse that was openly howled against Hamilcar in the Council; he told her that she had erred, that she must make reparation for her crime, & that Rabbet demanded this sacrifice.

Often a great uproar rang across the Mappales to Megara; & Shahabarim and Salambo would go out quickly and gaze from the top of the galley stairway.

The people in the Square of Khamon were clamouring for arms. But the Elders would not provide these, considering that such an effort would be useless, since others who had set out without a general had been massacred. At last they were given permission to depart, and as a sort of homage to Moloch or from a vague need of destroying something, tore up tall cypress trees in the temple groves and, kindling them at the torches of the Kabiri, carried them singing through the streets. These monstrous flames as they advanced swayed gently, shooting fire into the glass globes on the crests of the temples, and upon the ornaments of the colossi and the beaks of the ships; they passed beyond the terraces and were as suns rolling through the town. They descended the Acropolis. The gate of Malqua opened.

'Are you ready?' exclaimed Shahabarim. 'Or have you charged them to tell your father that you forsake him?'

She hid her face in her veils, and the great flares receded into the distance, slowly sinking to the edge of the waves.

An indefinable dread held her back; she was afraid of Moloch, and of Matho. This man of giant stature who was master of the zaimph dominated Rabbet as much as did the Baal, and seemed to her to be invested with the same splendours as he: and the spirits of the gods did sometimes visit the bodies of men. Had not Shahabarim, in speaking of him, said that it was her task to vanquish Moloch? They were merged into each other; she confused them together; both of them were pursuing her.

She wished to know the future, and approached the snake; for auguries were drawn from the attitudes of serpents. The basket was empty, and Salambo became distraught.

She found it with its tail coiled round one of the silver balustrades beside the hanging bed, against which it was rubbing itself to cast its old yellow skin, while its body stretched forth gleaming and clear like a sword half drawn from its sheath.

On the following days, in proportion as she let herself be persuaded and grew more disposed to succour Tanit, the python recovered and grew, and seemed to gain new life.

Her conscience then became convinced that Shahabarim was expressing the will of the gods. One morning she awoke with her mind resolved, and asked what she must do to make Matho restore the veil.

'Demand it,' said Shahabarim.

'But if he refuses?'

The priest looked at her fixedly with a smile such as she had never seen.

'Yes, what can I do?' repeated Salambo.

His fingers twisted in the ends of the bands which fell from his tiara upon his shoulders, he stood motionless with downcast eyes. At last, seeing that she did not understand:

'You will be alone with him.'

'Well?' she asked.

'Alone in his tent.'

'What then?'

Shahabarim bit his lips. He sought some round-about way of expressing himself.

'If you are to die, it will be later,' he said, 'later! Fear nothing! And whatever he may attempt to do, do not call out, do not be frightened! You will be humble, you understand, submissive to his desire, for it is ordained of heaven!'

'But the veil?'

'The gods will take thought for it,' answered Shahabarim.

'If you were to come with me, father?'

'No!'

He made her kneel down, and, with his left hand raised and stretching out his right, he swore on her behalf to bring back the mantle of Tanit to Carthage. With terrible oaths she devoted herself to the gods, and every word that Shahabarim pronounced she falteringly repeated.

He told her all the purifications and fastings she was to observe, and how she was to reach Matho, Moreover, a man who knew the road was to accompany her.

She felt as if she had been set free. She thought only of the joy of seeing the zaimph again, and now she blessed Shahabarim for his exhortations.

It was the season when the doves of Carthage migrated to Mount Eryx in Sicily, to the temple of Venus. For several days before their departure they went seeking and calling to one another, that they might gather together; and one evening they flew away. The wind blew them along, & they glided in a great white cloud across the sky high up above the sea.

The horizon was flooded with the colour of blood. They seemed to sink slowly towards the waves; then they disappeared as if swallowed up and falling, of their own will, into the jaws of the sun. Salambo, as she watched them vanish, bent her head; and Taanach, believing that she had guessed her sorrow, said gently to her:

'But they will come back, Mistress.'

'Yes! I know.'

'And you will see them again.'

'Perhaps!' she sighed.

She had not confided her resolution to anyone. For the sake of ensuring secrecy, instead of giving the stewards orders for them, she sent Taanach to the suburb of Kinisdo to buy all the things she required: vermilion, aromatics, a linen girdle, and new garments. The old slave was amazed at these preparations, but did not dare to ask any question; and the day fixed by Shahabarim came at length, when Salambo was to set forth.

About the twelfth hour she saw, at the lower end of the sycamore trees, a blind old man with one hand resting on the shoulder of a child who walked before him, while with the other he carried a kind of cithara of black wood against his hip. The eunuchs, slaves and women had been scrupulously sent away; no one might know the mystery that was preparing.

Taanach kindled four tripods, filled with strobus & cardamom, in the corners of the apartment; then she unfolded large Babylonian tapestries, and hung them on cords all round the room; for Salambo did not wish to be seen even by the walls. The kinnor-player squatted behind the door, & the young boy stood with a reed flute to his lips. In the distance the roar of the streets was dying away, violet shadows lengthened before the peristyles of the temples, and on the other side of the gulf the mountain bases, the fields of olive trees, and the vague yellow lands rolled out indefinitely and were blended in a bluish haze; not a sound was to be heard, an untellable oppression weighed upon the air.

Salambo crouched down upon the onyx step by the rim of the basin; she drew up her wide sleeves, fastened them behind her shoulders, and began her ablutions methodically, according to the sacred rites.

Then Taanach brought her in an alabaster phial something that was both liquid and coagulate: the blood of a black dog slaughtered by barren women on a winter's night among the ruins of a tomb. She rubbed it upon her ears, her heels, and the thumb of her right hand; even her nail remained a little red, as if she had crushed a fruit.

The moon rose; the cithara and the flute began to play at the same time.

Salambo unfastened her earrings, and then her necklace, her bracelets, and her long white simar; she unknotted the fillet from her hair, and shook it for a few minutes softly over her shoulders to cool herself by this spreading of it. Outside, the music continued, ever the same three notes, hurried and frenzied; the strings grated, the flute trilled; Taanach kept time with a clapping of her hands; Salambo, swaying her whole body, chanted prayers, and her garments dropped one after another about her.

The heavy tapestry shook, and over the cord that supported it appeared the python's head. The snake came slowly, like a drop of water trickling down a wall, & crawled among the scattered stuffs; then, with its tail planted firmly upon the floor, it rose utterly erect; and its eyes, more brilliant than carbuncles, darted upon Salambo.

A cold shudder, or perhaps a feeling of shame, at first caused her to hesitate. But she recalled Shahabarim's orders, and stepped forward. The python lowered itself and, resting the centre of its body upon the nape of her neck, let its head and tail hang trailing to the ground, like the two ends of a broken necklace. Salambo wound it about her sides, under her arms and between her knees; then, taking it by the jaw, she brought the little three-cornered mouth near to her teeth and, with half-shut eyes, bent herself back beneath the rays of the moon. The white light seemed to envelop her in a silver mist, the marks of her wet feet shone upon the stones, stars glittered in the depth of the water. The python tightened its black rings about her, flecked with scales of gold. Salambo panted under the too great weight, her loins gave, and she felt herself dying; with the tip of its tail the serpent gently beat her thigh; then the music ceased, and it dropped away from her.

Taanach drew near her and arranged two candelabra, the lights of which burned in crystal globes filled with water; then she tinted the palms of her hands with henna, put vermilion upon her cheeks, pencilled her eyelids with antimony, and lengthened her eyebrows with a mixture of gum and musk, ebony & the crushed legs of flies.

Salambo, seated on a chair with uprights of ivory, gave herself up to the slave's attention. These touches, and the scent of the aromatics, and the fasts she had undergone, all enervated her. She grew so pale that Taanach stopped.

'Go on!' said Salambo.

And, drawing herself together, she suddenly came to life. Then she was seized with impatience; she urged Taanach to make haste, and the old slave grumbled:

'Well, well, Mistress! It is not as if you had someone waiting for you!'

'Yes!' said Salambo. 'Someone is waiting for me.'

Taanach drew back in surprise and, in order to learn more, asked:

'What orders do you give me, Mistress? For if you are to remain away . . .'

Salambo broke into sobs, and the slave exclaimed:

'You are suffering! What is the matter? Do not go away! Take me with you! When you were quite little and used to cry, I took you to my heart and made you laugh with the nipples of my breasts. You sucked them dry, Mistress!'

She struck herself upon her withered bosom.

'Now I am old! I can do nothing for you! You love me no longer! You hide your sorrows from me, and despise your nurse!'

Tears of tenderness and vexation flowed down her cheeks, following the scars of her tattoo marks.

'No!' said Salambo. 'No, I love you! Be comforted!'

With a smile like the grimace of an old ape, Taanach resumed her task. Following Shahabarim's recommendation, Salambo had ordered the slave to make her magnificent; & Taanach complied with a barbaric taste which was full of both refinement and ingenuity.

Over a first delicate, wine-coloured tunic she passed a second, embroidered with birds' feathers. A wide girdle of golden scales clung to her hips, and from this her blue, silver-starred drawers hung down in billowy folds. Next Taanach put upon her a long white green-striped robe of Seric silk. She fastened to her shoulder a square of purple weighted at the hem with sandastrum seeds, and over all passed a black mantle with a flowing train: then she contemplated her and, in the pride of her work, could not prevent herself from crying:

'You will not be more beautiful on your bridal day!'

'My bridal!' repeated Salambo.

She rested her elbow upon the ivory chair, and was musing.

Taanach set a copper mirror before her, so broad and so high that she could see all of herself within it. Then she rose and, with a light touch of her finger, raised a lock of hair which fell too low.

Her hair was covered with gold dust, and curled in front, and hung down her back in long plaits with pearls upon the ends of them. The light of the candelabra heightened the colour of her cheeks, the gold of her garments, and the whiteness of her skin: about her waist, and upon her arms, and hands and toes, she had such a wealth of jewels that the mirror flashed back their rays upon her like a sun; Salambo, standing by the side of Taanach, who leaned over to look at her, smiled among all this glittering.

Then she walked to and fro, fretting at the time she must still wait.

Suddenly and loudly a cock crew. She swiftly pinned a long yellow veil over her hair, passed a scarf about her neck, thrust her feet into little blue leather boots, and said to Taanach:

'Go and see whether there be not a man with two horses under the myrtles.'

Taanach had hardly returned to her before she was descending the galley stairway.

'Mistress!' cried the nurse.

Salambo turned round with a finger to her mouth, as a sign to her to be discreet and still.

Taanach stole softly along the prows to the foot of the terrace, and from a distance could now distinguish a gigantic shadow passing obliquely under the moonlight in the cypress avenue to the left of Salambo: this was a sign of death.

Taanach climbed again to the room & threw herself down, lacerating her face with her nails; she tore out her hair, and uttered piercing screams at the top of her voice.

Then she bethought her that she might be heard, and hushed her crying.

She sobbed very softly with her head in her hands and her face pressed to the floor.

IN THE TENT

CHAPTER XI

THE MAN WHO WAS GUIDING SALAMBO LED HER UP
beyond the pharos towards the Catacombs, and then down through
the steep lanes of the long suburb of Moluya. The sky was beginning to pale. Now & again they had to stoop under palm branches
jutting from the walls; the two horses went at a walk, and kept
slipping; and thus they reached the Teveste gate.

Its ponderous leaves were half open; they passed through, and it
closed behind them.

They followed the foot of the ramparts for a time and, reaching
the level of the cisterns, went along the Taenia, a narrow ribbon of
yellow land separating the gulf from the lake and extending as far
as Rhades.

No one was to be seen around Carthage, whether on the sea or in
the country. The slate-coloured waves plashed softly, and their
foam, tossed lightly by the wind, spotted them white. In spite of
all her veils, Salambo shivered in the freshness of the morning; the
motion and the open air dazed her. Then the sun rose: it beat upon
the back of her head, and made her doze a little in spite of herself.
The two animals ambled along, sinking their feet in the silent sand.

When they had passed the mountain of the Hot Springs, they
went more rapidly, as the ground was firmer.

Although it was the season for ploughing and sowing, the fields
were as empty as the desert as far as the eye could see. Here and
there were scattered heaps of corn; elsewhere the grain dropped
from the over-ripe barley. Villages stood out black against the clear

horizon, and the harmony of their lines was broken and mutilated.

At times they passed some half calcined piece of wall standing by the edge of the road. The roofs of the cottages were falling in, and in the interiors fragments of pottery might be seen, with rags of clothing, and all kinds of utensils, and things broken out of recognition. Often a creature clothed in tatters, with grimy face and flaming eyes, would emerge from these ruins: but it would very quickly begin to run, or vanish into some hole. Salambo and her guide did not stop at all.

They traversed one deserted plain after another. Over wide stretches of white earth spread irregular trails of charcoal dust which rose in clouds behind their horses' feet. Sometimes they came upon small peaceful dells, where a stream flowed through the long grasses; and as they mounted its further bank Salambo would pluck wet leaves to cool her hands. At the corner of an oleander clump her horse shied violently at the corpse of a man stretched upon the ground.

The slave settled her again upon the cushions. He was one of the servants of the Temple, a man whom Shahabarim was used to employ on perilous missions.

So as to omit no possible precaution he now went on foot beside her, between the horses; he would whip them with the end of a leather lash wound round his arm, or would perhaps take, from a scrip hanging against his breast, balls made of wheat, dates, and yolks of egg, and wrapped up in lotus leaves, and offer them to Salambo, without speaking, even as he ran along.

In the middle of the day three Barbarians clothed in beast skins crossed their path: and by degrees others appeared, wandering in bands of ten, twelve, or twenty-five men, many of them driving goats or a limping cow. Their heavy staves bristled with brass studs; cutlasses gleamed upon their uncouth, filthy clothing, and they opened eyes of menacing amazement. Some of them as they passed called out a conventional blessing, others an obscene jest; & Shahabarim's man answered each in his own idiom. He told them that this was a sick youth going to be cured at a distant temple.

Meanwhile the day was closing in. They heard a dog bark, and went towards the sound.

In the twilight they saw an enclosure of unmortared stones about a shapeless building. The slave threw pebbles at a dog which ran along the top of the wall, and they entered a high vaulted hall.

In the middle crouched a woman warming herself at a brushwood fire, the smoke of which escaped through holes in the roof. She was half hidden by the white hair which fell to her knees; she would pay no heed to any question, but in an idiot manner kept mumbling words of vengeance against the Barbarians and the Carthaginians.

After ferreting about from right to left, the guide came back to her and asked for something to eat. The old woman shook her head, and murmured with her eyes fixed upon the charcoal:

'I was the hand. The ten fingers are cut off. The mouth no longer eats.'

The slave showed her a handful of gold pieces. She threw herself upon them, but soon resumed her immobility.

At last he drew a dagger from his girdle and held it at her throat. Then she went tremblingly and raised a large stone, and brought back an amphora of wine and some fish from Hippo-Zaritus preserved in honey.

Salambo turned away from this unclean food, and fell asleep on the horses' caparisons which were spread in a corner of the hall.

The man woke her before daylight.

The dog was howling: and the slave went up to it quietly, and struck off its head with a single blow of his dagger. Then he rubbed the horses' nostrils with the blood to revive them. The old woman hurled a curse after him, and perceiving this, Salambo pressed the amulet which she wore upon her heart.

They resumed their journey.

From time to time she asked whether they would not soon reach their destination. The road undulated over little hills. Nothing was to be heard but the grating cry of the grasshoppers. The sun warmed the yellow grass; the ground was all broken up, as it were, into monstrous paving-stones. Sometimes a viper crossed their path, or eagles flew by; and the slave went on running. Salambo mused under her veils, and in spite of the heat did not put them aside, for fear of soiling her fine garments.

At regular intervals stood towers built by the Carthaginians for the purpose of keeping a watch on the tribes. They would go into these to get some shade, and then set forth again.

As a measure of prudence they had made a wide detour the day before; but now they met with no one, for this was a barren district, where the Barbarians had not been.

Gradually they entered a fresh region of devastation. Sometimes a piece of mosaic stood up in the middle of a field, the sole remnant of a vanished mansion; the leafless olive trees looked at a distance like great thorn bushes. They passed through a town in which the houses were burned to the ground: the walls were lined with the skeletons of men, dromedaries and mules, and the streets blocked with lumps of half-gnawed carrion.

Night fell. The sky hung low, and was filled with clouds.

For two hours more they climbed towards the west, until suddenly they perceived a number of little flames before them.

These shone at the bottom of an amphitheatre, and their light was caught and flung back by gold plates moving hither and thither: the cuirasses of the Clibanarii in the Punic camp. Then they made out other and more numerous lights on every side; for the armies of the Mercenaries, now that they were combined, spread over a vast area.

Salambo made a movement to advance, but Shahabarim's man led her further aside, and they passed along by the terrace which enclosed the Barbarians' camp. There they found an opening, and the slave vanished through it.

A sentry was walking upon the top of the entrenchment with a bow in his hand and a pike on his shoulder.

Salambo continued to approach; the Barbarian knelt and loosed a long arrow which pierced the hem of her cloak. Then as she stood still and cried out, he asked her what she wanted.

'To speak to Matho,' she answered. 'I am a fugitive from Carthage.'

He gave a whistle; and this was echoed again and again into the distance.

Salambo waited; and her frightened horse moved, snorting, round and round.

When Matho came, the moon was rising behind her; but she had a yellow veil with black flowers over her face, and so many draperies about her body that it was impossible to form any idea of her. From the top of the terrace he gazed upon this vague shape which stood like a ghost in the evening shadows.

At last she said to him: 'Lead me to your tent! I wish it!'

A memory which he could not identify flashed through his mind.
He felt his heart beat. Her air of command intimidated him.
'Follow me!' he said.

The barrier was lowered, & immediately she was in the Barbarians'
camp.

It was filled with a great tumult and a great throng. Bright fires
burned under hanging pots; and while the crimson reflections of
these lit up some places, they left others entirely in the dark. There
was a shouting and calling; long straight lines of hobbled horses
stood between the tents, which were round or square, of leather or
of canvas; also there were reed huts, and holes in the sand such as
dogs make. Soldiers were carting faggots, or resting on their elbows
upon the ground, or wrapping themselves in mats for sleep; and
Salambo's horse sometimes had to stretch forth one leg and jump
in order to pass over them.

She remembered having seen them before; but their beards were
longer now, their faces even darker, & their voices hoarser. Matho,
as he walked before her, waved them aside with a gesture that
raised his red mantle. Some kissed his hands; others bent themselves double as they came to learn his orders: for he was now the
Barbarians' true and only chief; Spendius, Autharitus, and Narr'-
Havas had become disheartened, and he had displayed such bold-
ness and determination that all obeyed him.

Salambo followed him through the entire camp. His tent was at
the end, three hundred paces from Hamilcar's entrenchments.

She noticed a wide ditch on the right, and it seemed to her that
there were faces resting upon its edge on a level with the ground,
just as if they had been struck from their bodies. But their eyes
moved, and their half-opened mouths were groaning in the Punic
tongue.

Two negroes holding resin torches stood on each side of the tent
door. Matho abruptly drew aside the canvas, and she followed
him in.

It was a deep tent with a pole standing upright in the middle. It
was lighted by a large sconce shaped like a lotus and filled with a
yellow oil having handfuls of burning tow floating upon it; it cast
a glitter upon the military accoutrements in the shadows. A naked
sword leant against a stool by the side of a shield; whips of hippo-

potamus hide, cymbals, bells and necklaces were piled pell-mell in baskets of esparto grass; there was a felt rug soiled with crumbs of black bread; some copper money was heaped carelessly upon a round stone in one corner, and through the rents in the canvas the wind brought dust from the outside, together with the smell of the elephants, which could be heard eating and rattling their chains.

'Who are you?' asked Matho.

She looked slowly around her without answering; then her glance was arrested by something blue and glittering at the back of the tent, upon a bed of palm branches.

She started quickly forward, uttering a cry. Behind her, Matho stamped his foot.

'Who brings you here? Why do you come?'

'To take it!' she answered, pointing to the zaimph.

And with her other hand she tore the veils from her head. He recoiled, drawing back his elbows, gaping, well nigh terrified.

She felt as if she leaned upon the strength of the gods; looking him in the face, she asked him for the zaimph. She demanded it, eloquently and proudly.

Matho did not hear: he was gazing at her, and his eyes made no distinction between her garments and her body. The sheen of her stuffs, like the splendour of her skin, was something apart and belonged to her alone. Her eyes and her diamonds both sparkled; the polish of her nails was of one lustre with the stones which loaded her fingers; the two clasps of her tunic raised her breasts a little and brought them closer together, and his thought lost itself in that narrow valley, down which there fell a thread supporting an emerald plaque, which showed through the violet gauzes lower down. She had as ear-rings two little sapphire balances, each bearing a hollow pearl filled with liquid perfume. From moment to moment a little drop would fall through the hole in the pearl and moisten her naked shoulder. Matho watched it fall.

He was gripped by an ungovernable curiosity; as shyly as a child laying his hand upon a strange fruit, he lightly touched the upper part of her bosom with the tip of his finger. Her flesh, which was a little cold, yielded but was firm and resilient.

This contact, though scarcely perceptible, shook Matho to his depths. Every instinct of his being was lifted and urged him to-wards her. He would have liked to enfold her, to absorb her, to drink her up. His breast heaved, and his teeth were chattering.

Taking her by the wrists, he drew her gently to him, and sat down upon a cuirass beside the palm-leaf couch, which was covered with a lion's skin. She stood before him, and he looked her up and down, holding her thus between his knees, and saying again and again:

'How beautiful you are! How beautiful you are!'

Salambo was embarrassed by this fixed gazing into her eyes, and her discomfort and repugnance grew so acute that it was an effort for her not to cry aloud. The thought of Shahabarim came to her; she resigned herself.

Matho still held her little hands in his own; and from time to time, in spite of the priest's command, she turned away her face and tried to thrust him off by shaking her arms. He opened his nostrils wide, the better to savour the scent of her body, so fresh and in-definable, yet as intoxicating as perfume smoke. There was honey in it, and pepper, and incense, and roses, and a something beside.

But how did she come to be with him in his tent, at his pleasure? Someone had surely forced her? She had not come for the zaimph? His arms fell, and he bent his head, suddenly overpowered with dreaming.

To soften him, Salambo said plaintively:

'What have I done to you that you should desire my death?'

'Your death!'

She continued:

'I saw you one evening by the light of my burning gardens among fuming cups and my slaughtered slaves, and so fierce was your rage that you bounded towards me & I had to flee away! Then a terror came to Carthage. It was noised about that towns were sacked, fields burned, and soldiers massacred; and you were the destroyer, you were the assassin! I hate you! Your very name is a gnawing remorse to me! You are more accursed than the plague, than the Roman war! The provinces shudder at your fury, the ditches are full of dead! I have followed the tracks of your fires, and I might have been walking in the wake of Moloch!'

Matho leaped up; his heart was swelled with a great pride; he felt equal to a god.

With quivering nostrils and clenched teeth, she went on:

'As if your sacrilege were not enough, you came to me in my sleep, clothed in the zaimph! Your words I did not understand; but I knew you wished to drag me towards something terrible, to the bottom of some abyss.'

Matho, wringing his hands, exclaimed:

'No! No! It was to give it to you! To restore it to you! It seemed to me that the Goddess had left her garment for you, and that it belonged to you! What does it matter whether it be in her temple or in your house? Are you not all-powerful, immaculate, radiant, and beautiful even as Tanit?'

And with a look of infinite adoration, he added:

'Unless, perhaps, you are Tanit?'

'I, Tanit!' said Salambo to herself.

They were silent for a while. The thunder rolled in the distance. Some sheep began bleating, frightened by the storm.

'Oh, come near to me!' he went on. 'Come near to me! There is nothing to fear! Once I was only a soldier, one of the ruck of the Mercenaries, and so meek that I used to carry wood on my back for the others. Do I trouble about Carthage? All her mighty populace are but whirling specks to me in the dust of your sandals, & all her treasures and provinces, fleets and islands, do not raise my appetence like the freshness of your lips and the turn of your shoulders. But I would have thrown down her walls to reach you and possess you! Besides, in the meantime, I took my revenge. Now I crush men like shells, & throw myself upon phalanxes; I turn aside the long pikes with my bare hands, I seize stallions by the nostrils and check them; no catapult could kill me! Oh, if you knew how, in the midst of war, I think of you! Sometimes the memory of a gesture, or of a fold in your garment, suddenly takes me and entangles me like a net! I see your eyes in the flames of fire-darts, in the gilding of shields! I hear your voice in the sounding of the cymbals. I turn round, but you are not there! And I hurl myself again into the battle!'

He raised his arms, with intercrossing veins like ivy on the branches of a tree. Sweat rolled down his breast between the squares of his muscles; and his quick breathing made his sides heave under his bronze girdle, fitted with many straps hanging down to knees firmer than marble. Salambo, who was accustomed to eunuchs, yielded to amazement at the strength of this man. This was the punishment of the Goddess or the influence of Moloch moving about her in the five armies. A feeling of lassitude overpowered her; and through her stupor she heard the intermittent shouting of the sentinels as they answered one another.

The flames of the lamp flickered in the gusts of hot air. There were occasional flashes of lightning, which left the darkness deeper; and she could see no more than Matho's eyes, like two coals in the night. All the time she felt that she was in the grip of some doom, that she had reached a supreme & irrevocable moment: making a vast effort, she went up again to the zaimph and raised her hands to seize it.

'What are you doing?' exclaimed Matho.

She answered calmly:

'I am going back to Carthage.'

He came towards her with folded arms and so terrible a look that she felt her feet fastened to the ground.

'Going back to Carthage!'

He stammered and, grinding his teeth, repeated:

'Going back to Carthage! Ah, you came to take the zaimph, to triumph over me and then disappear! No, no! You belong to me! No one now shall snatch you from here! Oh! I have not forgotten the insolence of your great calm eyes, and how you crushed me with the haughtiness of your beauty! It is my turn now! You are my captive, my slave, my servant! Call, if you will, on your father and his army, on the Elders, the Rich, and your whole accursed people! I am lord of three hundred thousand soldiers! I will bring more from Lusitania, from Gaul and from the depths of the desert, and I will overthrow your city and burn all her temples; her triremes shall float on waves of blood! I will not leave one house, one stone, one palm tree standing! And if I have not men enough, I will draw bears from the mountains and drive lions before me. Do not seek to escape, or I shall kill you!'

Pale and with clenched fists, he quivered like a harp whose strings are about to break. All at once he was choked with sobs, and sank down upon his hams:

'Ah! Forgive me! I am infamous, and viler than scorpions, than mud and dust! Just now while you were speaking, your breath passed over my face, and I was enraptured as a dying man lying flat on the edge of a stream to drink. Crush me, so I but feel your feet! Curse me, so I but hear your voice! Do not go! Have pity! I love you! I love you!'

He was on his knees on the ground before her; he twined his arms about her, his head thrown back, and his hands wandering; the golden discs hanging from his ears glittered upon his bronze neck; great tears like silver globes gathered in his eyes; he sighed caressingly, and murmured vague words, lighter than a breeze and sweet as a kiss.

Salambo was assailed by a weakness in which she lost all consciousness of herself. Some power within and at the same time above her, a command from the gods, forced her to yield to it; she was borne up as upon clouds, & fell back swooning upon the lion-skin couch. Matho caught her heels, her golden chainlet broke, and the two ends as they flew apart hit the canvas like vipers striking. The zaimph fell and enveloped her; she could see Matho's face bending over her breast.

'Your fires are burning me, O Moloch!'

And the soldier's kisses coursed over her, hungrier than flames; it was a hurricane sweeping her upward; she was caught in the might of the sun.

He kissed each of her fingers, her arms, her feet, and the long tresses of her hair from end to end.

'Take it,' he said. 'What is it to me? Take me with it! I abandon the army! I renounce everything! Beyond Gades, twenty days' journey into the sea, there is an island covered with dust of gold, with green, and full of birds. On the mountains great flowers filled with smoking perfume sway like everlasting censers; in citron trees higher than cedars, milk-coloured serpents cut the fruit with the diamonds of their jaws, so that it falls upon the turf; the air is so mild that there can be no death. Oh, I shall find it, you will see! We shall live in crystal grottoes cut out at the foot of the hills. Either there is no one yet living there, or I shall become its king.'

He brushed the dust from her boots; he tried to place a quarter of pomegranate between her lips; he made a cushion of garments behind her head. He went out of his way to serve her, to humble himself; he even spread the zaimph over her legs as if it were a simple rug.

'Have you still,' he said, 'those little gazelle horns upon which your necklaces are hung? You will give them to me? I love them!'

For he spoke as if the war were finished, and broke into joyous laughter. The Mercenaries, Hamilcar, each obstacle had already disappeared. The moon was gliding between two clouds. They could see it through an opening in the tent.

'Ah, what nights I have spent gazing upon her! It seemed to me that she was a veil hiding your face; you used to look at me through it; the memory of you blended with her beams, and I could no longer distinguish which was you!'

And, with his head between her breasts, he wept abundantly.

'And this,' she thought, 'is the man of dread, the man who makes Carthage tremble!'

He fell asleep. Then, disengaging herself from his arm, she put one foot to the ground, and saw that her chainlet was broken.

The maidens of the great families were taught to pay an almost religious honour to these shackles; and it was with a blush that Salambo wound the two ends of the golden chain about her legs.

Pictures of Carthage, of Megara, of her house, her room, and the country through which she had passed, whirled tumultuously yet clearly through her memory. But an abyss had opened between, and all these things were far, infinitely far from her.

The storm was passing; slow drops of water splashed down one by one and shook the tent roof.

Matho slept like a drunken man, stretched on his side with one arm hanging over the edge of the couch. His band of pearls had crept a little up upon his brow, leaving it bare; his teeth were parted in a smile, and gleamed through his black beard; and in his half-closed eyes there was a silent and almost indecent gaiety.

Motionless, Salambo looked at him, her head bent and her hands crossed.

On a table of cypress-wood at the head of the couch lay a dagger, and the sight of the gleaming blade kindled in her a lust for murder. Mournful voices drifted to her across the distant shadows, a spirit choir urging her on. She drew near and took the weapon by the haft. At the rustling of her dress Matho half opened his eyes, moving his lips to her hands; and the dagger fell.

There was a sudden outcry; a terrible light flashed behind the stuff of the tent. Matho raised it, and they saw the camp of the Libyans wrapped in vast flames.

Their reed huts were burning, and the stems twisted and snapped in the smoke and flew off like arrows; black shadows ran frantically across the red horizon. They could hear the shrieks of those in the huts; the elephants, oxen, and horses plunged in the midst of the crowd, trampling upon it and upon the stores and baggage which were being rescued from the fire. Trumpets sounded. There were calls of 'Matho! Matho!' There were men at the door trying to get in.

'Come! Hamilcar is burning the camp of Autharitus!'

He sprang up. She found herself quite alone.

Then she examined the zaimph; and when she had well considered it she was surprised to find that she did not experience that joy which she had once pictured to herself. Her dream was accomplished; yet she was melancholy.

The bottom of the tent was lifted, and a hideous form appeared. Salambo could at first distinguish only the two eyes, and a long white beard hanging down to the earth; for the rest of the body, which was cumbered with the rags of a tawny garment, dragged along the ground, & with every movement forward the two hands clawed up into the beard and then fell back. Crawling in this way, it reached her feet, and Salambo recognised the aged Gisco.

To prevent the captive Elders from escaping, the Mercenaries had broken their legs with bronze bars; and had bundled them pell-mell into a filthy ditch to rot. The strongest of them used to raise themselves and shout when they heard the noise of platters; and it was in this way that Gisco had seen Salambo. He had guessed that she was a Carthaginian by the little balls of sandastrum slapping against her boots; and, sensing some great mystery, he had succeeded, with the help of his companions, in scrambling out of the ditch; then he had dragged himself on his elbows for twenty paces, up to Matho's tent. There were two voices speaking in it. He had listened outside, and had heard everything.

'It is you!' she said at last in an extremity of horror.

He raised himself on his wrists and answered:

'Yes, it is I! They think that I am dead, do they not?'
She bent her head, and he continued:
'Ah, why have not the Baalim granted me that mercy!'
He came so near that he touched her:
'They would have spared me the pain of cursing you!'
Salambo sprang quickly back: she was terrified by this filthy creature, as hideous as a spectre, as terrible as a phantom.
'I shall soon be a hundred years old,' he said. 'I have seen Agathocles; I have seen Regulus and the Roman eagles march over the Punic fields in full harvest! I have seen all the horrors of battle, and the sea littered with the wrecks of our fleets! Barbarians whom I used to command have chained my four limbs, as if I had been a slave and a murderer. My companions are dying round me one after the other; the stench of their corpses wakes me in the night; I drive away the birds that come to peck out their eyes: and yet not for a single day have I despaired of Carthage! Though I had seen all the armies of the earth come up against her, and her flames soaring above the temples, still I should have believed in her eternity! But now all is over! All is lost! The gods are cursing her! A curse upon you, who have hastened her ruin by your shame!'
She opened her lips.
'Ah, I was there!' he cried. 'I heard you panting with whorish love. He pled his lust to you, and you let him kiss your hands! If you must needs bow to the force of a mad lubricity, you might at least have behaved as well as the wild beasts that couple in secret, instead of parading your shame under your father's eyes!'
'What?' she cried.
'Ah! You did not know that the two entrenchments are but sixty cubits from each other, and that your Matho in his overweening pride has posted himself exactly opposite Hamilcar. Your father is there behind you; and if I could climb the path up to the platform, I should call to him: "Come and see your daughter in the Barbarian's arms! She has put on the garment of the Goddess to please him; and in yielding her body she betrays the glory of your name, the majesty of the gods, the vengeance of her country, the very life of Carthage!" '
The motion of his toothless mouth made all his beard move up and down; his eyes were riveted upon her and devoured her: and,

panting in the dust, he went on saying:

'Ah, sacrilegious one! May you be accursed! Accursed! Accursed!'

Salambo had drawn back the canvas; she held it at arm's length and, without answering him, looked in the direction of Hamilcar.

'It is this way, is it not?' she asked.

'What matters that to you! Turn away from it! Begone! Rather crush your face against the earth! It is a holy spot, and your eyes would profane it!'

She threw the zaimph about her waist, swiftly picked up her veils, mantle and scarf, and cried:

'I run to him!'

And Salambo rushed forth and disappeared.

At first she walked through the darkness without meeting a soul, for everyone was rushing to the fire; the uproar increased, & great flames made the sky all purple behind her. A long terrace barred her way.

She searched blindly to right and left for a ladder, a rope, a stone, anything to help her. She was afraid of Gisco, and she felt that the shouting and the footsteps pursued her. Day was beginning to whiten. She discovered a path in the thick gloom of the entrenchment. As her robe hindered her, she took the hem of it in her teeth, and in three bounds was upon the platform.

From the shadows below her rang out a cry, the same which she had heard at the foot of the galley stairway; and leaning over, she recognised Shahabarim's man with his coupled horses.

He had wandered all night between the two entrenchments; then, uneasy concerning the fire, he had turned back, trying to see what was happening in Matho's camp; knowing that this spot was nearest to Matho's tent, he had obeyed the priest's command not to move far from it.

He stood up on one of the horses, Salambo let herself slide down to him, and they fled at full gallop, circling the Punic camp to find a gate.

Matho had re-entered his tent. The smoky lamp gave but little light, and he thought that Salambo slept. So he gently felt the lion's skin on the palm-tree couch. He called, but she did not answer; he quickly tore down a strip of canvas to let in light: the zaimph was gone.

The earth was shaken by a host of feet. Loud shouts, the neighing of horses, and a clash of armour rose in the air, and clarion calls sounded the charge. It was as if a hurricane were whirling about him. An uncontrollable frenzy made him leap to his arms, and he hurled himself outside.

The long files of the Barbarians were running down the mountain side, and the Punic squares were advancing against them, swaying to a heavy & regular rhythm. The mist, rent by the rays of the sun, made little hovering clouds which, as they rose, gradually disclosed standards, helmets and spear-points. Under the rapid evolutions, parts of the ground which were still in the shadow seemed to be moving bodily; or it was as torrents crossing one another, with massive thorn bushes standing motionless among them. Matho could distinguish the captains, soldiers, and heralds, and even the serving-men in the rear mounted upon asses. Narr'Havas, instead of maintaining his position so as to cover the foot soldiers, turned abruptly to the right, as if he meant to be crushed by Hamilcar.

His horsemen outstripped the elephants, which were slackening their speed; and all the horses, stretching out their unbridled necks, galloped so furiously that their bellies seemed to graze the earth. All at once Narr'Havas rode resolutely up to a sentry, threw down his sword and lance and javelins, and disappeared among the Carthaginians.

The king of the Numidians came to Hamilcar's tent and, pointing to his men, who had halted at a distance, said:

'Barca! I bring these to you. They are yours!'

Then he prostrated himself in token of subjection, and to prove his fidelity recalled his conduct since the beginning of the war.

In the first place, he had prevented the siege of Carthage and the massacre of the captives; in the second, he had taken no advantage of the victory over Hanno after the defeat at Utica. As to the Tyrian towns, they were on the frontiers of his kingdom. Finally, he had taken no part in the battle of the Makar; he had absented himself expressly in order to evade the obligation of fighting against the Suffete.

The truth was that Narr'Havas's intention had been to secure his own aggrandisement by encroaching upon the Punic provinces, and that he had alternately assisted and forsaken the Mercenaries according to the chances of victory at the moment. But seeing that Hamilcar would ultimately prove the stronger, he had now gone over to him; and his desertion may in some part have been due to resentment against Matho for having gained the supreme command, or to his old rivalry with him in love.

The Suffete listened without interrupting him. The man who thus presented himself before an army which justly owed him retribution was not to be despised as an ally; and Hamilcar at once realised the utility of such an alliance in his great projects. With the Numidian on his side he would get rid of the Libyans: then he could lead the western tribes to the conquest of Iberia. Without asking Narr'Havas why he had not come sooner, or taxing him with any of his lies, he kissed him, thrice clasping him breast to breast.

It was as a last despairing resort that he had fired the Libyan camp. This army came to him like help from the gods; and, dissembling his delight, he answered:

'May the Baalim look favourably upon you! I do not know what the Republic will do for you; but Hamilcar is not ungrateful.'

The tumult increased, and certain captains entered. He armed himself as he continued:

'Come, do you return! With your cavalry you shall cut down their infantry between your elephants and mine! Courage! Exterminate them!'

And Narr'Havas was rushing away, when Salambo appeared.

She leaped nimbly down from her horse, opened her wide cloak and, spreading out her arms, displayed the zaimph.

As the leather tent was looped up at the four corners, the entire circuit of the mountain, with its hosts of soldiers, lay within view; and since it was itself in the centre, Salambo could be seen from all sides. A mighty shout arose, a long cry of triumph and hope. Those who were moving halted in their stride; the dying leaned on their elbows and turned round to bless her. The Barbarians knew now that she had recovered the zaimph; some could see her from afar, and the rest thought they could see her; other cries, cries of rage and vengeance, could be heard in spite of the cheers of the Carthaginians. Thus did the five armies, spread out in tiers upon the mountain, stamp and shout around Salambo.

Hamilcar, who was unable to speak, nodded her his thanks. He looked from the zaimph to her, from her to the zaimph, and noticed that her chainlet was broken. Then he shivered, seized with a terrible suspicion. Soon recovering his imperturbability however, he looked sidelong at Narr'Havas without turning his head.

The Numidian king was standing discreetly apart; on his brow stayed a little of the dust which he had touched when prostrating himself. At length the Suffete advanced towards him with an air of great gravity.

'As a reward for the services you have rendered me, Narr'Havas, I give you my daughter.'

And he added:

'Be my son, and protect your father!'

Narr'Havas made a gesture of great surprise; then he threw himself upon Hamilcar's hands and covered them with kisses.

Salambo, calm as a statue, did not seem to understand. She blushed a little, and lowered her eyes; and her long curved lashes threw shadows upon her cheeks.

Hamilcar wished to unite them immediately in a betrothal that could never be broken. A lance was placed in Salambo's hand, and offered by her to Narr'Havas; their thumbs were tied together with a thong of oxhide & corn was poured upon their heads; the grains falling about them rang and rebounded like hail.

THE AQUEDUCT

CHAPTER XII

TWELVE HOURS LATER, THE MERCENARIES WERE BUT
a mountain of wounded, dead, and dying.

Hamilcar had suddenly broken from the bottom of the gorge, and
down the western slope facing toward Hippo-Zaritus; for the
ground broadened out at this spot, and he had taken care to draw
the Barbarians into it. Narr'Havas had surrounded them with his
cavalry, while the Suffete drove them back and crushed them.
They were already defeated by the loss of the zaimph; even those
who cared nothing for it were somehow distressed by a consciousness of weakened power. Hamilcar, whose pride did not disdain
to leave his ally in possession of the battle field, had drawn off a
little to the left to certain heights from which he dominated the
army.

The outlines of the camps were shown by their battered palisades. A long heap of black cinders burned on the site where the
Libyans had been; the soil was a sea as of churned waves, and the
tents with their tattered canvas looked like wandering ships held
lost in the breakers. Cuirasses, pitchforks, clarions, pieces of wood,
iron and brass, corn, straw, and garments lay scattered about among
the dead; here and there a fire-dart was burning out against a heap
of baggage; in some places the earth was completely hidden under
shields; the carcasses of horses made a long line of little hills; legs,
sandals, arms, and coats of mail were everywhere; and heads, held
in their helmets by the chin-straps, still rolled about like balls; the
thorn bushes were festooned with human hair; elephants with
their towers still on their backs lay gasping in pools of blood, their

guts trailing from out them. Slimy things were felt under the foot, and there were swamps of mud although no rain had fallen.

This jumble of dead bodies filled the whole mountain from top to bottom.

The survivors were just as still as the dead. They squatted in irregular groups looking at one another, dismayed and silent.

At the end of a long stretch of grassland the lake of Hippo-Zaritus glittered in the setting sun. To the right a group of white houses stood out above the encircling wall, and beyond lay the infinite expanse of the sea: the Barbarians, with their chins in their hands, sighed as they thought of their own lands. A cloud of grey dust was settling.

Each breast expanded to the evening breeze; and as it grew cooler the vermin could be seen leaving the chilling corpses and running over the warm sand. Crows perched motionless upon the big stones and watched the dying.

After night-fall yellow-haired dogs, those filthy beasts which followed the armies, came quite softly among the Barbarians. At first they licked the clots of blood on the still tepid stumps; then they began to eat, starting at the bellies.

The fugitives came back one by one like shadows; the women also ventured to return, for there were still some of these left, especially among the Libyans, in spite of the dreadful massacre of them by the Numidians.

Some lighted ropes' ends to serve as torches. Others, crossing their pikes, placed the dead upon them and bore them away.

The dead lay in long lines upon their backs, with their mouths open and their lances beside them, or else were piled up pell-mell so that it was often necessary to dig through a whole heap and pass a torch slowly over their faces to find the missing. They had been horribly mutilated by hideous weapons. Green strips of flesh hung from their foreheads; they were slashed to pieces, crushed to the marrow, blue from strangulation, widely gashed by the elephants' tusks. Although they had died almost simultaneously, they were in various different stages of decomposition. The men of the north were bloated and livid and swollen, while the more wiry Africans looked as if they had been smoked and were already drying. The

Mercenaries could be distinguished by the tattooing on their hands: in the case of the veterans of Antiochus this was a sparrow-hawk; those who had served in Egypt had the head of a cynoce-phalus; those who had served with the princes of Asia, a hatchet, a pomegranate, or a hammer; those who had served in the Greek republics, the side view of a citadel, or the name of an archon; and there were some whose arms were entirely covered with such de-signs, which blended with their old scars and recent wounds.

Four great funeral piles were built for the men of Latin race, the Samnites, the Etruscans, the Campanians and the Bruttians. The Greeks dug graves with their sword points. The Spartans took off their red cloaks & with them shrouded their dead; the Athenians laid them out with their faces toward the rising sun; the Cantabri-ans buried them under a heap of pebbles; the Nasamones trussed them double with ox-hide thongs, and the Garamantes went down and interred them on the shore, so that they might for ever be washed by the waves. The Latins mourned because they could not collect the ashes in urns; the Nomads sighed for the hot sands in which they mummified their dead, and the Celts for their three rough stones under a rainy sky at the end of some gulf of many islands.

At first there were loud cries, and then a long silence, to compel the dead spirits to return. Then the shouting was persistently re-sumed at regular intervals.

They asked pardon of the dead for their inability to honour them as the rites prescribed: for, owing to this deprivation, the dead would pass for infinite periods through every kind of chance and metamorphosis. They questioned them, asking what they desired; and others loaded them with abuse for having allowed themselves to be overcome.

Bloodless faces, upturned here and there on fragments of armour, showed paler in the light of the great pyres; tears provoked tears, the sobbings grew shriller, the recognitions & embracings yet more frantic. Women stretched themselves on the buried corpses, mouth to mouth and brow to brow with them; they had to be beaten off so that the earth could be thrown in. They blackened their cheeks; they cut off their hair; they slashed themselves about in imitation of the wounds that disfigured their dead. Howlings broke through the clash of the cymbals. Some snatched off their amulets and spat upon them. The dying rolled in the bloody mire, savagely biting their mutilated fists; & forty-three Samnites performed a veritable 'ver sacrum' by cutting one another's throats like gladiators. Soon there was no more wood for the pyres, the flames died out, and every spot of ground was occupied; weary with shouting, weakened, tottering, they fell asleep beside their dead brethren, some still clinging to a life of terror, and others wishing never to wake again. In the greyness of the dawn some soldiers appeared on the fringe of the Barbarian camp, and filed past with their helmets raised on the points of their pikes; they saluted the Mercenaries and asked whether they had no messages to send to their native lands. Others approached, and the Barbarians recognised some of their former companions.

The Suffete had offered all the captives service in his army. Several had fearlessly refused; and, being quite resolved neither to support them nor to abandon them to the Great Council, he had sent them away with orders to fight no more against Carthage. As to those who had been cowed by the fear of torture, they had been armed with weapons taken from the enemy; and these were now showing themselves off to the vanquished, not so much to win them over, but rather from an impulse of pride and curiosity.

They told how well the Suffete treated them; and the Barbarians listened to them enviously, although they despised them. At the first word of reproach the cowards flew into a passion; from a safe distance, they showed them their own swords and cuirasses and abusively invited them to come and take them. The Barbarians picked up stones, and they took to flight; nothing more could be seen on the summit of the mountain than the spear-points sticking up over the palisades.

The Barbarians were overwhelmed with a sorrow which was heavier than the humiliation of their defeat. They thought of the emptiness of their courage, and stood with fixed gaze, grinding their teeth.

The same thought came to all. They rushed tumultuously towards the Carthaginian prisoners. It chanced that the Suffete's soldiers had been unable to discover these, and as he had withdrawn from the field of battle, they were still in the deep pit.

They were set upon the ground in a level place. Sentries formed a ring about them, and the women were let in upon them thirty or forty at once. Wishing to make good use of the short time allowed them, they ran from one to the other, hesitating and panting; then, bending over the poor bodies, they pounded them with all their might like washerwomen beating linen; shrieking their husbands' names, they tore them with their nails and dug out their eyes with their hair pins. Next came the men, and tortured them from their feet, which they lopped off at the ankles, to their foreheads, from which they tore crowns of skin to put upon their own heads. The Eaters of Unclean Things were atrocious in their devisings: they poisoned their wounds by pouring in dust and vinegar, and broken potsherds. After them waited others; blood flowed, and they made merry like vintagers about the fuming vats.

Matho was seated on the ground in the same place where he had been when the battle ended, his elbows on his knees and his temples in his hands: he saw nothing, heard nothing, & had ceased to think. At the shrieks of joy uttered by the crowd he raised his head. Before him a strip of canvas caught on a pole and trailing along the ground partially covered a confusion of carpets and a lion's skin. He recognised his tent, & riveted his eyes upon the ground, as if Hamilcar's daughter, when she disappeared, had sunk into the earth there.

The torn canvas flapped in the wind, the long strips sometimes passing across his mouth; and he saw a red mark on it like the print of a hand. It was the hand of Narr'Havas, the token of their alliance. Matho rose, took a still smoking firebrand, and threw it disdainfully upon the wreckage of his tent. Then with the toe of his boot he pushed the things which fell out back into the flames, so that nothing might be left.

Suddenly, so that it was impossible to say from what point he had sprung up, Spendius appeared.

The former slave had bound two splints of a broken lance against his thigh, and was limping pitiably, gasping and groaning.

'Take them off,' said Matho. 'I know what a brave fellow you are!' For he was so crushed by the injustice of the gods that he had no spirit left to be indignant with men.

Spendius beckoned to him & led him to a mountain hollow where Zarxas and Autharitus were lying hidden.

These, like the slave, had fled; the one in spite of his cruelty, and the other in spite of his bravery. But who, they said, could have foreseen the treachery of Narr'Havas, the burning of the Libyans' camp, the loss of the zaimph, the sudden attack by Hamilcar and, above all, those manoeuvres of his which had forced them back to the bottom of the mountain under the direct attack of the Carthaginians? Spendius would not confess to his terror, and persisted in maintaining that his leg was broken.

At last the three chiefs & the shalishim consulted as to what course they should now adopt.

Hamilcar was blocking their road to Carthage; they were wedged between his soldiers and the provinces belonging to Narr'Havas; the Tyrian towns would join the victors; they would be driven to the sea coast, where all these united forces would crush them. This must infallibly happen.

There was no possible way of avoiding the war; therefore they must pursue it to the bitter end. But how were they to make the necessity for an interminable struggle understood by all these disheartened men, who still lay bleeding from their wounds?

'I will undertake that!' said Spendius.

Two hours later a man came from the direction of Hippo-Zaritus and climbed the mountain at a run. He was waving some tablets at arm's length, and as he was shouting very loudly the Barbarians gathered round him.

These were despatches from the Greek soldiers in Sardinia, recommending their African comrades to keep a careful watch over Gisco and the other captives. A merchant of Samos, one Hipponax, coming from Carthage, had told them that a plot was being hatched to effect their escape, and the Barbarians were urged to take every precaution, seeing that the Republic was powerful.

Spendius's stratagem did not meet with the success for which he had hoped. So far from rousing them to fury, this assurance of a new danger did but enhance their fears; and remembering the warning that Hamilcar had hurled amongst them before, they expected something unlooked for and terrible. The night was spent in great distress; several even threw away their weapons, so as to mollify the Suffete when he came.

On the morrow, at the third watch of the day, a second runner appeared, still more breathless and begrimed with dust. The Greek snatched from his hand a roll of papyrus covered with Phoenician writing. The Mercenaries were not to be disheartened: the brave men of Tunis were coming with large reinforcements.

Spendius first read the letter aloud three times in succession; then, held up by two Cappadocians who bore him seated on their shoulders, he had himself carried from place to place and re-read it. For seven hours he harangued them.

He reminded the Mercenaries of the promises made to them by the Great Council: to the Africans he recalled the cruelties of the stewards, and to all the Barbarians the injustice of Carthage. The Suffete's leniency was only a bait to entrap them. Those who surrendered would be sold as slaves; and the vanquished would die under torture. As to flight, what roads were open to them? No nation would willingly receive them. But by continuing their efforts they would win at once freedom, vengeance, and money! And they would not have long to wait, since the people of Tunis, the whole of Libya, was hurrying to relieve them. He showed them the unrolled papyrus:

'Look! Read! Here are their promises! I do not lie!'

Dogs were prowling about with their black muzzles plastered in red. The men's bare heads grew hot in the burning sun. A nauseous smell rose from the ill buried dead, some of whom even protruded from the ground as far as the waist. Spendius called upon the living to witness the truth of his words; then he raised his fists in the direction of Hamilcar.

All the time he was being watched by Matho; and to mask his cowardice he simulated anger until he was gradually carried away by it. Devoting himself to the gods, he heaped curses upon the Carthaginians. The torture of the captives was child's play. Why spare them, only to be cumbered for ever by such useless cattle?

'No! We must make an end of them! We know their plots! A single one of them could ruin us! Let there be no pity! Prove your worth by your fleetness of foot and the might of your blows.'

They turned again upon the captives. Several of these were still alive, though barely, and they finished them off by thrusting their heels into their mouths, or stabbing them with a javelin point.

Then they thought of Gisco. He was nowhere to be seen; and this made them very uneasy. They wished both to convince themselves of his death, & to bear a part in it. Three Samnite shepherds found him fifteen paces from the spot where Matho's tent had stood. They recognised him by his long beard, and called the others. Stretched as he was on his back, his arms against his hips and his knees pressed together, he looked like a dead man laid out for the sepulchre. Nevertheless his wasted sides rose and fell, and his eyes, set wide open in his white face, were fixed in an intolerable glare.

The Barbarians looked at him with utter astonishment. Since he had been living in the pit he had been almost forgotten and now, made uneasy by old memories, they held off, not daring to raise their hands against him.

But those behind were murmuring and pressing forward; and when a Garamantian passed through the crowd brandishing a sickle, all understood his thought: their faces crimsoned and, smitten with shame, they yelled: 'Yes! Yes!'

The man with the curved steel approached Gisco, took his head and, resting it upon his knee, sawed it off with rapid strokes. It fell, and two great jets of blood made holes in the dust. Next Zarxas had leapt upon it and, lighter than a leopard, was running towards the Carthaginians.

When he had covered two-thirds of the mountain he drew Gisco's head from his bosom, and holding it by the beard, whirled his arm round rapidly several times; finally he released it, so that it described a long parabola and disappeared behind the Punic entrenchments.

Soon at the edge of the palisades there rose two crossed standards, the recognised sign for the reclamation of the dead.

Then four heralds, chosen for their depth of chest, came out with great horns and, speaking through brass tubes, declared that henceforth between the Carthaginians and Barbarians there was neither faith, pity, nor gods; that they rejected in advance all overtures, and that all envoys would be sent back with their hands cut off.

Immediately afterwards Spendius was sent to Hippo-Zaritus to procure provisions; the Tyrian city sent some the same evening, and they ate greedily. Thus fortified, they hastily collected the remnants of their baggage & their broken arms; the women massed themselves in the centre; and, heedless of the wounded left weeping behind them, they set out along the river bank at a rapid pace, like a pack of departing wolves.

They were marching upon Hippo-Zaritus, determined to take it; for they had need of a town.

Watching them from a distance, Hamilcar was smitten with despair, in spite of his pride at seeing them flee before him. He ought to have attacked them at once with fresh troops. Another such day, and the war was over! If matters were protracted, they would come again in greater strength; the Tyrian towns would join them; his clemency to the vanquished had been of no avail. He resolved to be pitiless.

That same evening he sent the Great Council a dromedary laden with bracelets collected from the dead, and with terrible threats ordered another army to be despatched to him.

For a long time everyone had thought him lost; on learning of his victory their amazement was very near to terror. The vaguely reported return of the zaimph completed the miracle. The gods and the might of Carthage seemed now to belong to him.

None of his enemies ventured upon a single complaint or recrimination. Thanks to the enthusiasm of one party & the pusillanimity of the other, an army of five thousand men was ready before the prescribed interval had elapsed.

This army promptly made its way into Utica to support the Suffete's rear, while three thousand of the most notable citizens embarked in vessels which were to land them at Hippo-Zaritus, whence they were to drive back the Barbarians.

Hanno had accepted the command; but he entrusted the army to his lieutenant Magdassan, so as to reserve for himself the leadership of the troops for disembarkation; for he could no longer endure the jolting of his litter. His disease had eaten away his lips and nostrils, and had thus made a large hole in his face; the back of his throat could be seen from a distance of ten paces, and he knew himself to be so hideous that he wore a veil over his head like a woman.

Hippo-Zaritus paid no attention to his summonings. The pleas of the Barbarians were equally ignored; but every morning the inhabitants lowered provisions for them in baskets, & from the tops of the towers shouted their excuses, on the ground of the Republic's exigence, and conjured them to withdraw. They signalled the same protestations to the Carthaginians stationed on the sea.

Hanno contented himself with blockading the harbour, not risking an attack. But he persuaded the judges of Hippo-Zaritus to admit three hundred soldiers of his into the town. Then he sailed away to the Cape of Grapes, and made a long circuit so as to hem in the Barbarians: an ill-timed & even dangerous operation. His jealousy prevented him from relieving the Suffete, he arrested his spies, impeded him in all his plans, and compromised the success of his enterprise. Hamilcar wrote to the Great Council to rid him of Hanno, and the latter then returned to Carthage, furious at the baseness of the Elders and his colleague's madness. After such great hopes, the situation was now yet more deplorable than before: they tried not to think of it, and even not to talk about it.

As if there were not misfortune enough for the time, news came that the Sardinian Mercenaries had crucified their general, seized the strongholds, and everywhere massacred all men of Canaanite race. The Romans were threatening the Republic with immediate hostilities unless she gave them twelve hundred talents, together with the whole of the island of Sardinia: they had formed an alliance with the Barbarians, and sent them flat-bottomed boats laden with meal and dried meats. The Carthaginians chased these and captured five hundred men; but three days later a fleet coming from Byzacium, conveying provisions to Carthage, foundered in a storm. Evidently the gods were declaring against her.

Upon this the citizens of Hippo-Zaritus, under pretext of an alarm, caused Hanno's three hundred men to mount the walls; then they came up behind and took them by the legs, and suddenly threw them over the ramparts. Some, who were not killed, were harried into the sea and drowned.

Utica was burdened with the presence of soldiers; for Magdassan had acted like Hanno and, in accordance with the latter's orders and deaf to Hamilcar's prayers, was investing the town. His soldiers were given wine mixed with mandrake, and their throats were cut as they slept. At the same time as the Barbarians arrived, Magdassan fled and the gates were opened; and thenceforward the two Tyrian towns displayed an obstinate devotion to their new friends and an inconceivable hatred for their former allies.

This abandonment of the Punic cause served as both an example and a precedent. Hopes of deliverance were revived, and populations hitherto uncertain hesitated no longer. There was a general breaking up. The Suffete learned of this, and had no help to look for! He was now irrevocably lost.

He immediately dismissed Narr'Havas, who had to guard the frontiers of his kingdom. He himself resolved to re-enter Carthage in order to raise soldiers and begin the war anew.

The Barbarians posted at Hippo-Zaritus saw his army as it descended the mountain.

Where could the Carthaginians be going? Surely they were being driven on by hunger; distracted by their sufferings, they were coming to give battle in spite of their weakness. But they turned to the right: they were fleeing. They might be overtaken & completely crushed. The Barbarians dashed out in pursuit of them.

The Carthaginians were checked by the river, which was on this occasion wide: for the west wind had not been blowing. Some swam over, and the rest floated across on their shields; then they resumed their march. Night fell, & they could no longer be seen.

The Barbarians did not stop; they climbed higher to find a narrower place. The people of Tunis hurried to their help, bringing those of Utica with them. Their numbers grew, as it were, at every bush; and the Carthaginians, from where they lay on the ground, could hear the tramp of their feet in the darkness. From time to time Barca loosed back a volley of arrows at them to check them, and several were killed. When day broke they were in the Ariana Mountains, at the place where the road bends like an elbow.

Matho, who was marching at their head, thought that he could distinguish something green on the horizon at the top of an eminence. As they reached lower ground, obelisks, domes and houses came into view. It was Carthage!

He leaned against a tree to keep from falling, so hard did his heart beat.

He thought with infinite wonder and bewilderment of all that had come to his life since the last time he had passed that way! Then he was transported with joy at the thought of seeing Salambo again. He was reminded of the reasons which he had for execrating her, but he very swiftly rejected them. Quivering and with straining eyes he gazed at the lofty terrace of a palace above the palm trees beyond Eshmun; a smile of ecstasy lit up his face, as if some great light had reached him; he opened his arms, and sent kisses on the light wind, and murmured: 'Come! Come!' His breast heaved with a sigh, and two long tears like pearls fell upon his beard.

'What are you staying for?' cried Spendius. 'Make haste! Forward, forward! The Suffete will escape us! But your knees are shaking, and you look at me like a drunken man!'

He stamped with impatience and urged Matho on, and his eyes twinkled as at the approaching achievement of some long sought object:

'Ah, we have reached it! We are there! I have them!'

He had so assured and triumphant an air that Matho was surprised from his torpor, and found himself infected by his enthusiasm. These words, coming when his distress was at its deepest, goaded his despair to vengeance and gave food for his wrath to feed upon. He rushed up to one of the camels which were among the baggage, tore off its halter, and with this long rope beat the stragglers with all his might, running right and left alternately in the rear of the army, like a dog driving a flock.

At the thunder of his voice the men closed up their ranks and even the lame hurried their steps: half way over the isthmus they had narrowed the gap between the two armies, so that the foremost of the Barbarians were marching in the dust raised by the Cartha-ginians, and were almost in touch with them. But the gates of Malqua and Tagaste, and the great gate of Khamon threw wide their valves. The Punic square divided into three columns, and these were swallowed in a whirling stream under the porches. Soon the too tightly packed mass could advance no further; their pikes clashed above them, and the Barbarians' arrows came shiver-ing against the walls.

Hamilcar appeared on the threshold of Khamon, turned, & shouted to his men to scatter. He dismounted from his horse and, pricking it on the crupper with his sword, sent it against the Barbarians. It was an Orynx stallion, fed upon balls of white meal, and would bend its knees to allow its master to mount. Why, then, was he sending it away from him? Was it a sacrifice?

This noble horse galloped into the midst of the lances, knocking men over, and then, entangling its feet in its harnessing, fell down; but it rose again with furious leaps and, while the enemy were trying to stay it, or were looking upon it in surprise, the Carthaginians had closed again. They entered the ponderous gate and it shut echoing behind them.

It would not yield. The Barbarians came crashing against it; for some minutes a wave rippled over the entire army, then slowly subsided, and at last came utterly to rest.

The Carthaginians had placed soldiers on the aqueduct, and these began to hurl stones and balls and beams. Spendius declared that it was useless to persist; the Barbarians retired and posted themselves further off, fully resolved to lay siege to Carthage.

Meanwhile noise of the war had gone beyond the confines of the Punic empire, and from the Pillars of Hercules to the other side of Cyrene shepherds mused on it as they kept their flocks, and caravans talked of it at night under the stars. This great Carthage, this mistress of the seas, as splendid as the sun, and terrible as a god: there were men who dared to go up against her! Several times her fall had been reported, and all had believed it, for all wished it: the subject populations, the tributary villages, the allied provinces, the independent hordes, those who execrated her for her tyranny, or were jealous of her power, or coveted her wealth. The bravest had joined the Mercenaries very early; but the defeat at the Makar had checked the rest. Now they had recovered confidence, had advanced and were near at hand; now the men of the eastern regions were lying in the sandhills of Clypea on the other side of the gulf. As soon as they saw the Barbarians, they showed themselves.

These were not Libyans from the neighbourhood of Carthage, who had long composed the third army, but Nomads from the tableland of Barca, bandits from Cape Phiscus & the promontory of Dernah, from Phazzana and Marmarica. They had crossed the desert, drinking at brackish wells walled in with camel bones; the Zuaeces, with their covering of ostrich plumes, had come in quadrigae; the Garamantes, masked with black veils, riding well back on their painted mares; others were mounted on asses, onagers, zebras, and buffaloes;

and some dragged the roofs of their boat-shaped huts after them, and their families and their idols. There were Ammonians with limbs wrinkled by the hot water of the springs, and Atarantes, who curse the sun; Troglodytes, who bury their dead with laughter under the trees, and the hideous Auseans, who eat grasshoppers; the Achyrmachidae, who eat lice, and the vermilion-painted Gyssante, who eat apes.

They were all drawn up along the edge of the sea in a great straight line. Then they advanced like storms of sand raised by the wind. In the middle of the isthmus the horde halted, since the Mercenaries who were posted in front of them close to the walls were unwilling to move.

Then from the direction of Ariana appeared the men of the west, the people of the Numidians. For Narr'Havas actually ruled only over the Massylians: and moreover, they had a custom which permitted them to forsake their king after any defeat; therefore they had assembled on the Zainus, and had then crossed it at Hamilcar's first movement. First there came at a run all the hunters from Malethut-Baal and Garaphos, clad in lion skins, and driving with their pike staves little lean horses with long manes; then marched the Gaetulians in serpent-skin cuirasses; then the men of Pharus, wearing tall crowns of wax and resin; and the Caunians, Macarians, and Tillabarians, each holding two javelins and a round shield of hippopotamus hide. They stopped at the foot of the Catacombs, among the first pools of the Lagoon.

But when the Libyans had moved away, the place which they had occupied was seen to be filled by a multitude of Negroes, like a cloud on a level with the ground. These had come from the White Harush, the Black Harush, the desert of Augila, and even from the vast country of Agazymba which is four months' journey south of the Garamantes, and from regions further still! In spite of their red wooden ornaments, the filth on their black skins made them look like mulberries that had been long rolled in the dust. They had bark-fibre breeches, & tunics of dried grass; they wore the muzzles of wild beasts on their heads; they howled like wolves, and had rods furnished with rings which they shook, and cows' tails which they flourished.

Beyond the Numidians, Maurusians, and Gaetulians, pressed the

yellowish men who are scattered among the cedar forests beyond
Taggir. They had cat-skin quivers flapping against their shoulders,
and led enormous dogs in leash, which were as tall as asses, and
never barked.

Finally, as if Africa had not been sufficiently emptied, and it had
been necessary to recruit the very lowest races in search of further
savagery, behind all the rest could be seen men with bestial profiles,
grinning with idiot laughter, wretches ravaged by hideous disease,
deformed pigmies, mulattoes of doubtful sex, and albinos whose
red eyes blinked in the sunlight. They stammered unintelligible
sounds, and put a finger to their mouths to show that they were
hungry.

As great confusion of weapons reigned as of dress & peoples. There
was no single deadly device which was not present, from wooden
daggers, stone hatchets and ivory tridents, to long sabres with saw-
like teeth, slender & forged from pliant copper. These men wielded
cutlasses which were forked into several branches like antelopes'
horns, bills tied to the ends of ropes, iron triangles, clubs & stilettos.
The Ethiopians from the Bambotus had little poisoned darts hidden
in their hair. Many had brought bags of pebbles. Others came
empty handed, but opened and closed their teeth.

This multitude surged and swayed unceasingly. Dromedaries,
smeared all over with tar like ships, knocked down women carrying children on their haunches, as they moved about. Provisions
kept spilling from the baskets; pieces of salt, packages of gum, rotten dates, and guru-nuts kept crushing under foot; and sometimes
against a verminous breast could be seen a diamond that Satraps
had coveted, an almost fabulous stone of worth enough to purchase
an empire, hanging from a slender cord. For the most part they did
not even know what they wanted, but were impelled by fascination
or curiosity; and Nomads who had never before seen a town were
frightened by the shadow of the walls.

The isthmus was now completely covered with men; and this long
stretch of tents, looking like huts in a flood, reached to the first
lines of the other Barbarians, which were as a river of steel flowing
symmetrically upon both sides of the aqueduct.

The Carthaginians were still in their panic at the arrival of these
men, when they saw coming straight towards them like monsters,

like buildings, with their masts, their arms, their ropes, articulations, capitals and carapaces, the siege engines sent by the Tyrian towns: sixty carroballistas, eighty onagers, thirty scorpions, fifty tollenos, twelve rams, and three gigantic catapults which would hurl pieces of rock weighing fifteen talents. These were pushed forward by masses of men who clung to their bases; at every step they quivered and shook, and in this way they arrived in front of the walls.

Some days were yet needed to complete the preparations for the siege. The Mercenaries, who had learned from their defeats, would not imperil themselves in useless engagement; and on both sides there was no hurry, for each well knew that they were on the threshold of a terrible action, and that the outcome of it would be complete victory or utter extermination.

Carthage could hold out for a long time; her broad walls presented a series of re-entrant and projecting angles, which formed an advantageous arrangement for repelling assaults.

Part of the wall by the Catacombs had crumbled, & on dark nights it was possible to see through the disjointed blocks the lights in the hovels of Malqua, which in some places overlooked the top of the ramparts. It was here that the Mercenaries' women who had been driven away by Matho were living with their new husbands: but when they saw their men again, their hearts went out to them once more. At first they waved their scarves from afar; then they came in the darkness and chatted with the soldiers through the cleft in the wall, and one morning the Great Council learned that they had all fled. Some had passed through between the stones; others with greater daring had let themselves down by ropes.

At last Spendius resolved to put his design into execution.

The war, by keeping him at a distance, had withheld him from this hitherto; and since his people had returned before Carthage it had seemed to him that the inhabitants suspected his intention. But soon some of the sentries were taken away from the aqueduct; for there were not too many for the defence of the walls.

For some days the one time slave practised shooting arrows at the flamingoes on the lake. Then, one moonlit evening, he begged Matho to light a great fire of straw at midnight and bid all his men raise a shout at the same time; after this he took Zarxas with him and departed along the edge of the gulf in the direction of Tunis.

When they were on a level with the last arches, they returned straight towards the aqueduct; the place was unprotected: they crawled to the base of the pillars.

The sentries on the platform were walking tranquilly up & down.

Flames shot into the sky, clarion calls rang out; and the sentries, believing there to be an assault, rushed away towards Carthage.

One man remained, showing black against the sky. The moon was shining behind him, and his extravagantly long shadow looked in the distance like an obelisk striding across the plain.

Zarxas seized his sling: but whether from prudence or ferocity, Spendius stopped him.

'No, the whiz of the pellet would make a noise! Leave it to me!'

Then he bent his bow with all his strength, resting the lower end of it against the great toe of his left foot; he took aim, and the arrow flew.

The man did not fall, but disappeared from sight.

'If he were wounded, we should hear him!' said Spendius.

He mounted quickly from story to story with the help of a rope and a harpoon. When he had reached the top and was beside the corpse, he let the rope fall back. The Balearian fastened it to a pick which he drove in with a mallet, & then returned to the camp.

The trumpets no longer sounded, and all was now quiet. Spendius raised one of the flag-stones and, entering the water, replaced it above him.

Calculating the distance by the number of his steps, he came to the exact spot where he had noticed an oblique fissure; and for three hours until morning he worked unceasingly and furiously, breathing with difficulty through the interstices in the upper flag-stones, suffering violent pain, and twenty times thinking he was going to die. At last a crack was heard; a huge stone, ricocheting on the lower arches, rolled to the ground, and suddenly a cataract, a whole river, fell from the skies into the plain. The aqueduct, cut through in the centre, was emptying. It was death to Carthage and victory for the Barbarians.

In an instant the awakened Carthaginians showed upon the walls, the houses, and the temples. The Barbarians pressed forward with a shout, dancing deliriously round the great waterfall and, in their extravagance of joy, plunging their heads in it.

On the top of the aqueduct they saw a man in a torn brown tunic. He stood leaning over the very edge, with his hands on his hips, and looked down below him as if in amazement at his own work. Then he drew himself up and surveyed the horizon with a haughty air which seemed to say: 'All this is now mine!' The applause of the Barbarians burst forth anew; while the Carthaginians, realising their disaster at last, shrieked in despair. Then Spendius began to run along the platform from one end to the other: distraught with pride, like a charioteer triumphant at the Olympic Games, he raised his arms on high.

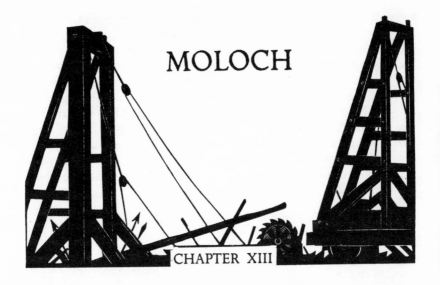

MOLOCH

CHAPTER XIII

THE BARBARIANS HAD NO NEED OF ANY EARTH-WORKS on the side facing Africa, for Africa was in their hands. To give themselves an easier approach to the walls, they threw down the entrenchments bordering the moat. Matho then divided the army into great semi-circles the better to surround Carthage: the Mercenaries' hoplites were stationed in the van, with the slingers and cavalry behind them; the baggage, the chariots and the horses were placed quite at the back; and in front of this throng bristled the war engines at a distance of three hundred paces from the towers.

These engines were known by an infinite variety of names, which changed several times in the course of the centuries; but they could all be classed under two systems: those which acted like slings, and those which acted like bows.

The former, the catapults, consisted of a square frame of two uprights and a cross bar. Wound round a drum at the back was a cable, which restrained a great beam hollowed into a spoon in which the projectiles were placed. The base of the beam was caught in a hank of twisted threads; and when the ropes were let go it sprang up and struck against the bar, multiplying its force by this sudden check. Engines of the second system had a more complicated mechanism.

A cross piece was fixed to a short upright so as form a T, and at right angles from the junction of these two ran a sort of channel. At the ends of the cross bar were two caps of twisted hair to which two small beams were fastened; and from these a cord stretched to the base of the channel, where it was fixed to a bronze tablet. This metal plate was released by a spring and, sliding along grooves, propelled the arrows.

The catapults were also called onagers, after the wild asses that fling up stones with their feet; and the ballistas were called scorpions, on account of the hook which stood on the tablet and which, when struck down by the fist, released the spring.

Their construction involved learned calculation: the hardest wood had to be selected for them, and all their gearing had to be of brass; levers, tackle-blocks, capstans or tympanums were used to bend them; their aim was adjusted by means of strong pivots; they were moved forward on rollers; and the most considerable of them were brought up piece by piece and assembled in front of the enemy.

Spendius arranged three catapults opposite the three principal angles; he placed a ram before every gate, a ballista before every tower; and carroballistas were to be wheeled about in the rear. But it was necessary to protect all these against fire thrown by the besieged, and first of all to fill up the trench which separated them from the walls.

They pushed forward galleries made of hurdles of green reeds and oaken ribs, like enormous shields on three wheels; the workers were sheltered in little huts covered with raw hide and padded with wrack; the catapults and ballistas were protected by rope curtains which had been steeped in vinegar to make them fire-proof. The women and children went to the beach for stones and gathered earth in their hands and brought it to the soldiers.

The Carthaginians, too, were making preparation.

Hamilcar had very soon reassured them by declaring that there was enough water in the cisterns for a hundred and twenty-three days; and this assertion, together with his presence and, above all, that of the zaimph, gave them good hope. Carthage recovered from her dejection; and those who were not themselves of Canaanitish origin were carried away by the passion of the rest.

The slaves were armed, the arsenals emptied, and every citizen had his allotted post & employment. There were still twelve hundred of the fugitives remaining, and the Suffete made them all captains: carpenters, armourers, blacksmiths and goldsmiths were put in charge of the engines, of which the Carthaginians had kept a few in spite of the conditions of the peace with Rome. These men understood such work, and the pieces were repaired.

The city was protected by the sea and the gulf upon the north and the east, and was therefore inaccessible. On to the wall fronting the Barbarians they carried up tree-trunks, mill-stones, jars of sulphur and vats of oil; and there built furnaces. They heaped up stones on the platforms of the towers, and the houses abutting on the rampart were crammed full with sand in order to strengthen it and add to its thickness.

The Barbarians grew angry at the sight of these preparations. They wanted to fight at once. They loaded the catapults with such unconscionably heavy missiles that the beams broke, and the attack was delayed.

At last on the thirteenth day of the month of Shebat, at sunrise, a great crash was heard at the gate of Khamon.

Seventy-five soldiers were hauling at the ropes at the base of a gigantic beam, horizontally suspended by chains from a gibbet, and terminating in a ram's head of pure brass. It had been wrapped in ox-hides, and had iron rings about it here and there; it was three times as thick as a man's body, a hundred and twenty cubits long, and under the mass of naked arms pushing it forward and drawing it back, swung regularly to and fro.

The other rams before the other gates were set in motion. Men could be seen treading from step to step in the hollow drum wheels. The pulleys and capitals creaked, the rope screens were lowered, & there was a simultaneous shower of stones and arrows. All the scattered slingers ran forward. Some of them approached the ramparts with pots of burning resin under their shields and hurled these with all their might. This hail of bullets, darts and flames passed in a curve over the front ranks and fell behind the walls. But long cranes, used for masting ships, were set up on the top of the ramparts; and from them were lowered huge pincers, in the form of two semi-circles toothed on the inside, and these bit on to the rams. The soldiers clung to the beam to drag it back; the Carthaginians heaved in order to raise it: and this struggle went on until the evening.

When the Mercenaries resumed their task on the following day, the tops of the walls were completely carpeted with bales of cotton, and with cloths and cushions; the crenellations were stopped up with mats; and a line of forks and blades, fastened upon sticks, showed between the cranes on the rampart. A furious resistance began.

Trunks of trees affixed to cables continuously fell and were hauled up again, crashing upon the rams; cramp-irons hurled by the ballistas tore away the roofs of the huts; and cataracts of flints and stones were poured from the platforms of the towers.

The rams broke the gates of Khamon and Tagaste. But the Carthaginians had piled up such an abundance of material on the inside that their valves did not open, and they remained standing.

Then the besiegers drove augers against the walls, applying them to the joints of the blocks so as to loosen them. The engines, too, were better managed; for their teams were now divided into squads, and they were worked from morning until evening without intermission and with the monotonous precision of a weaver's loom.

Spendius never wearied of supervising them. It was he in person who tautened the cordage of the ballistas. In order that there should be complete equality of tension on each side, it was the custom to strike the ropes on the right & the left as they tightened, until they both sounded the same note. Spendius mounted upon the frames and softly tapped the ropes with the end of his foot, straining his ears like a musician tuning a lyre. Then when the beam of the catapult rose, when the pillar of the ballista trembled to the shock of the spring, and rays and streams of stones and darts poured forth, he bent his whole body forward and flung his arms into the air, as if he would follow them.

The soldiers admired his skill and executed his orders. In the joy of their work they made jokes on the names of the machines. Thus the grapplers for seizing the rams were called 'wolves', and the covered galleries were 'vines'; they themselves were lambs, or they were going to gather grapes: and as they loaded their pieces they would say to the onagers: 'Be off, and have a good fling,' and to the scorpions: 'Sting them to the heart!' These jokes, which never varied, kept up their courage.

Nevertheless the machines did not demolish the rampart, for it was formed of a double wall completely filled with earth. They battered down the top parts, but each time the besieged would raise them again. Matho ordered the construction of wooden towers to reach as high as the towers of stone. His men threw turf, stakes, pebbles, and chariots with their wheels on, into the trench to fill it up the more quickly; even before this task was completed the immense throng of Barbarians came in one wave over the plain and beat against the foot of the walls like a swollen sea.

They brought up rope ladders, straight ladders, and 'sambucas', these last being formed of two poles from which a series of bamboos ending in a movable bridge were lowered by means of tackling. A great number of these were set up against the wall, and the Mercenaries began to mount them in file with their weapons in their hands. Not a Carthaginian showed himself. They had climbed two-thirds of the way up, when the battlements opened like the jaws of a dragon, vomiting flames and smoke. Scattered sand entered the joints of their armour, bitumen stuck to their clothes, molten lead splashed upon their helmets and made holes in their flesh; a shower of sparks spouted into their faces, and their empty eye-sockets seemed to be weeping tears as big as almonds. Men were yellow with oil, and their hair was in flames; they rushed about, setting fire to the rest. Some smothered the flames upon their comrades with mantles steeped in blood, thrown from a distance over their faces. Some who had not been wounded stood still, stiffer than stakes, with open mouths and outspread arms.

The assault was renewed on several successive days, the Mercenaries hoping that their unexampled energy and audacity would win them the victory.

Sometimes men would stand on the shoulders of others, drive in pins between the stones and, using these as steps to reach still higher, drive in a second and a third; protected by the overhanging ledge of the battlement, they would thus climb slowly upwards: but on reaching a certain height they always fell back again. The great trench grew full to overflowing; the wounded were heaped pell-mell with the dead and dying under the feet of the living. Charred bodies made black blots amidst a welter and confusion of entrails, brains, and blood; you would find half an arm or half a leg sticking straight up out of the heap, like a prop in a burned vineyard.

As the ladders failed in their purpose, the besiegers brought up the tollenos: instruments consisting of a long beam set transversely upon another, and bearing at its end a square basket which could hold thirty foot-soldiers and their weapons.

Matho wanted to go up in the first of these that was ready; but Spendius stopped him.

Men bent to the turning of a windlass; the great beam reached a horizontal position, rose till it was almost vertical, and, being overweighted at the end, bent like a huge reed. The soldiers were massed together and hidden up to their chins; only their helmet plumes were visible. At last, when it was fifty cubits in the air, it swayed many times to the right and left, and was then lowered; like a giant arm holding a cohort of pigmies in its hand, it set down the basketful of men upon the edge of the wall. They leaped into the crowd, and never returned.

All the other tollenos were quickly made ready; but it would have needed a hundred times as many to capture the town. They were used murderously: Ethiopian archers were placed in the baskets; then the cables were made fast, and they remained suspended in the air and shot poisoned arrows.

The fifty tollenos overtopped the battlements and thus surrounded Carthage like monstrous vultures; and the Negroes laughed to see the guards on the rampart dying in horrible convulsions.

Hamilcar sent hoplites to these posts; and every morning made them drink the juice of certain herbs which rendered them immune from the poison.

One evening when it was dark, he embarked the best of his soldiers on lighters and rafts and, turning to the right of the harbour, landed them on the Taenia. They advanced to the first Barbarian lines and, taking them in flank, made terrible slaughter of them. Also men were let down at night by ropes from the top of the wall with torches in their hands; they burned the Mercenaries' works, and were hauled up again.

Matho was exasperated; each obstacle added to a fury which led him into terrible extravagances. Mentally, he summoned Salambo to an interview, and awaited her arrival. She did not come; and this seemed to him a fresh piece of treachery; thenceforth he execrated her. If he could have seen her dead body, it is possible that he would have been content to raise the siege. He doubled the outposts, planted forks at the foot of the rampart, drove caltrops into the ground, and commanded the Libyans to bring him a whole forest that he might set it on fire and burn Carthage like a den of foxes.

Spendius obstinately continued the siege, trying to devise new and terrible machines.

The other Barbarians, encamped at a distance on the isthmus, were astounded at these delays; and since they complained, they were unleashed.

Then they charged with their cutlasses and javelins, and beat against the gates with them. Their nakedness made them easy to wound, and the Carthaginians slaughtered them freely; the Mercenaries rejoiced at this, through greed, no doubt, for the coming plunder. Hence there arose quarrels and fights among them. The country had been ravaged, and provisions soon grew scarce. They became disheartened and numerous hordes of them went away; but the multitude was so great that their loss was not apparent.

The best of them tried to dig mines; but the soil was badly propped, and fell in. They began them again in other places, but Hamilcar always detected the direction they were taking by holding his ear against a bronze shield: he bored counter-mines under the path along which the wooden towers were to move, and when these were pushed forward they sank into the holes.

At last all realised that the town was impregnable unless a long terrace could be raised to the height of the walls, so that they could fight on the same level. The top of it would have to be paved so that the machines might be rolled along it. Then it would be quite impossible for Carthage to hold out.

The town was beginning to suffer from thirst. Water, which was worth two kesitahs the bath at the beginning of the siege, was now sold for a shekel of silver: the supplies of meat and corn were also giving out. The people began to fear a famine, and some, to the consternation of all, began talking about useless mouths.

From the Square of Khamon to the temple of Melkarth the streets were cumbered with dead; and as it was the end of the summer, the combatants were harassed by great black flies. Old men carried off the wounded, and the devout continued to perform fictitious funeral rites for their relatives and friends who had died far away during the war. Wax figures, clothed and with hair upon them, were laid out across the house doors. They melted in the heat of the candles burning beside them, the paint trickled down upon their shoulders, and tears streamed over the faces of the living as they chanted mournful dirges at their side.

And all the time the crowds were running to and fro, the captains were shouting orders, and all could hear the incessant crashing of the rams.

The heat grew so oppressive that the dead bodies swelled & would no longer fit into their coffins; therefore they were burned in the middle of the courts. But in such confined spaces the fires spread to the neighbouring walls, and long flames leaped from the houses like blood spurting from an artery. Thus did Moloch possess Carthage; he embraced the ramparts, he rolled through the streets, he devoured the dead themselves.

Men wearing cloaks of chance-found rags in token of despair, stationed themselves at the corners of the cross-ways, and declaimed against the Elders & against Hamilcar, prophesying utter ruin to the people, and inciting them to general destruction and license. The most dangerous of these were the henbane drinkers who, in their crises, believed themselves to be wild beasts, and leaped upon the passers by, and rent them. Mobs collected about them, and the defence of Carthage was forgotten. The Suffete devised a scheme to pay others of their kind to support his policy.

To keep the Spirits of the Deities within the town, their images had been covered with chains. Black veils were placed over the Pataec Gods, & hair-cloth round the altars. Men tried to stir up the pride and jealousy of the Baalim by singing in their ears: 'You will let yourself be vanquished! Surely the others are more powerful! Show yourself! Help us, lest the nations say: "Where are now their Gods?"'

The colleges of the pontiffs were in a state of perpetual anxiety. Those of the Rabbet were especially afraid, since the restoration of the zaimph had been of no avail. They kept themselves shut up in the third enclosure, which was as impregnable as a fortress. Only one of them, the high priest Shahabarim, dared to go out.

He used to visit Salambo. But he would always either remain perfectly silent, gazing fixedly upon her, or else he would be prodigal of words, and his reproaches more bitter than ever.

With inconceivable inconsistency he could not forgive the girl for having obeyed his orders. Shahabarim had guessed all, and the obsession of this thought had revived the jealousy of his impotence. He accused her of being the cause of the war. Matho, he maintained, was besieging Carthage solely to recover the zaimph; and he poured out curses and bitter irony upon this Barbarian who pretended to the possession of holy things. Yet it was not this that the priest wished to say.

Salambo had no fear of him. The anguish from which she had formerly suffered had left her, and a strange calm possessed her. Her eyes were not so restless, and shone with limpid fire.

The python had sickened again, and as Salambo, on the contrary, appeared to be recovering, old Taanach rejoiced in the belief that her mistress's languor had passed to the serpent.

One morning she found it coiled up behind the ox-hide bed, colder than marble, and with its head buried under a mass of worms. Her cries brought Salambo, who turned it over for a while with the toe of her sandal: the slave was amazed at her indifference.

Hamilcar's daughter did not keep such long or such rigid fasts now. She spent whole days on the top of her terrace, leaning her elbows against the balustrade, and amusing herself by gazing forth. The summit of the walls at the end of the town zigzagged unevenly against the sky, and the sentries' lances were like a fringe of spikes along them. Looking farther between the towers, she could see each manoeuvre of the Barbarians; and on days when there was a pause in the siege, she could even discern their occupations. They mended their weapons, greased their hair, and washed their bloody arms in the sea; the tents were closed, the beasts of burden feeding; and in the distance the scythes of the chariots, drawn up in a semi-circle, looked like a silver scimitar laid at the base of the mountains. Shahabarim's words came back to her. She was waiting for Narr' Havas, her betrothed. In spite of her hatred of him, she would have liked to see Matho again. Of all the Carthaginians she was, perhaps, the only one who would have spoken to him without fear.

Her father often came into her room. He would sit down on the cushions and gaze at her with an almost tender look, as if he found rest from his fatigues in the sight of her. He sometimes asked her about her journey to the Mercenaries' camp, & enquired whether anyone had urged her to undertake it. She shook her head in denial: so proud was Salambo of having saved the zaimph.

But, under pretext of seeking military information, the Suffete always came back to Matho. He could not understand how she had spent those hours in his tent. Salambo said nothing of Gisco; for words have a potency in themselves, & curses may turn against those to whom they are reported: also she was silent concerning her impulse to murder Matho, lest she should be blamed for not having yielded to it. She said that the shalishim appeared furious, that he had shouted a good deal, and that he had then fallen asleep. Salambo told no more, perhaps through shame, or else because in her extreme ingenuousness she attached but little importance to the soldier's kisses. For the rest, it was all a melancholy and misty memory floating in her mind like the recollection of a depressing dream; she would not have known how or in what words to express it.

One evening, when they were thus face to face with each other, Taanach entered in a state of confusion. There was an old man with a child out in the courts, and he wished to see the Suffete. Hamilcar turned pale, and then quickly answered:

'Let him come up!'

Iddibal entered without prostrating himself. He was leading by the hand a young boy clothed in a goat's hair cloak, and at once raised the hood which screened his face.

'Here he is, Master! Take him!'

The Suffete and the slave withdrew into a corner.

The child remained in the middle of the room and looked about him, attentively rather than with astonishment, at the ceiling, the furniture, the pearl necklaces hung upon the purple draperies, and at this majestic girl who leaned towards him.

He was perhaps ten years old, and no taller than a Roman sword. His curly hair shaded his prominent brow. You would have said that his eyes were searching through space. His delicate nostrils flared widely, & there was about his whole person the indefinable splendour of those who are destined to great enterprise. When he had thrown off his heavy cloak, he remained clad in a lynx skin, which was fastened about his waist, and he planted his little naked feet, all white with dust, resolutely upon the flooring. No doubt he guessed that important matters were being discussed, for he stood still, with one hand behind his back, his chin lowered, and a finger in his mouth.

Hamilcar beckoned to Salambo, and said in a low voice:

'You will keep him with you, you understand! No one, not even of the household, must know of his existence!'

Then, returning behind the door, he again asked Iddibal whether he were quite sure that they had not been noticed.

'No!' said the slave. 'The streets were empty.'

Since the war had engulfed all the provinces, he had feared for his master's son. Not knowing where to hide him, he had come along the coasts in a sloop: and for three days Iddibal had been tacking about in the gulf, watching the ramparts. That evening, as the environs of Khamon seemed to be deserted, he had darted through the channel and landed near the arsenal, since there was still free entry to the harbour.

But soon the Barbarians anchored a huge raft in front of it in order to prevent the Carthaginians from emerging. They were now building their wooden towers, and the terrace rose at the same time.

Outside communications were cut off, and an intolerable famine began.

They killed all the dogs, all the mules, all the asses, and then the fifteen elephants which the Suffete had brought back with him. The lions of the temple of Moloch had become ferocious, and the temple servants no longer dared to go near them. At first they fed them with wounded Barbarians: then they threw them corpses that were still warm; but they would not eat these, and so they died. People wandered in the twilight along the old enclosures, and gathered grasses and flowers among the stones to boil them in wine; for wine was cheaper than water. Others crept as far as the enemy's outposts and entered their tents to steal food; and the astounded Barbarians sometimes allowed them to return. A day came when the Elders privately resolved to slaughter the horses of Eshmun. These were sacred animals whose manes were plaited by the pontiffs with gold ribbons, and whose existence symbolised the motion of the sun, the concept of fire in its noblest form. Their flesh was cut into equal portions & buried behind the altar. Then every evening the Elders, under pretence of some act of devotion, would go up to the temple and regale themselves in secret; also they would take away a piece under their tunics for their children. The inhabitants of the deserted quarters remote from the walls, whose sufferings were not so acute, had barricaded themselves through fear of the rest.

The stones from the catapults and the demolitions ordered for purposes of defence, had accumulated heaps of ruins in the middle of the streets. At the quietest of times, crowds would suddenly rush forth screaming; from the top of the Acropolis leaped flames like crimson rags blown and twisted about the terraces by the wind.

The three great catapults were never idle, and their ravages were phenomenal. In one instance a man's head came bounding from the pediment of the Syssitia; also in the Street of Kinisdo a woman in confinement was crushed by a block of marble, and her child was hurled with her bed as far as the crossways of Cinasyn, where the coverlet was found.

The slingers' balls caused the greatest exacerbation of all. They fell upon the roofs, & in the gardens, and in the middle of courts where folk sat at table before some slim repast, their hearts surcharged with sighs. These cruel missiles were embossed with letters which stamped themselves upon the flesh they hit; on the bodies of the dead could be read such insults as 'pig', 'jackal', or 'vermin', & sometimes such pleasantries as 'catch!' or 'I have thoroughly earned it!'

All the rampart, from the corner of the harbours to the level of the cisterns, was battered down.

Then the people of Malqua found themselves caught between the old enclosure of Byrsa behind, and the Barbarians in front. But there was enough to do to strengthen the wall and make it as high as possible, without troubling about them: they were abandoned, and all perished, and although they were universally hated, this aroused a mighty horror against Hamilcar.

On the next day he opened his store pits of corn, and his stewards gave it to the people. For three days they gorged themselves.

This only served to aggravate their thirst the more, and the long cascade of the clear falling water of the aqueduct gleamed ever before their eyes.

Hamilcar did not weaken. He was counting upon some decisive and prodigious happening.

His own slaves tore off the silver plates from the temple of Melkarth; four long boats were drawn out of the harbour and brought by means of capstans to the foot of the Mappales quarter, the wall facing the shore was bored through, and men set out for the Gallic countries to buy Mercenaries at no matter what price. Nevertheless Hamilcar was distressed at his inability to communicate with the king of the Numidians, whom he knew to be behind the Barbarians, ready to fall upon them. But Narr'Havas felt himself too weak to risk anything by himself. The Suffete caused the rampart to be raised twelve palms higher, had all the material in the arsenals piled up in the Acropolis, and once more repaired the machines.

Sinews from bulls' necks or stags' legs were commonly used for the twists of the catapults, and there were no stags or bulls in Carthage. Hamilcar asked the Elders for their wives' hair, and they all made this sacrifice; but it did not furnish enough material. In the buildings of the Syssitia were twelve hundred marriageable slaves destined for the brothels of Greece and Italy; the hair of these, which had become elastic through the use of unguents, was admirably suited for engines of war: but the consequent loss, it was thought, would be too considerable. Accordingly it was decided to choose the finest heads of hair among the plebeians' wives, and these, with no thought at all for their country's needs, shrieked in despair when the slaves of the Hundred came with scissors to lay hands upon them.

The Barbarians were fired with redoubled fury. They could be seen from afar taking fat from the dead to grease their machines, while others pulled out their nails and stitched them together to make cuirasses. They conceived the idea of putting vessels filled with snakes, brought by the Negroes, into the catapults; the clay pots broke on the flag-stones, and the snakes crawled about in swarms so numerous that they appeared to issue naturally from the walls. Dissatisfied with this scheme, the Barbarians improved upon it; they hurled all kinds of filth, human excrement, pieces of carrion, and whole corpses. The plague broke out again. The teeth of the Carthaginians fell from their mouths, & their gums became discoloured like those of a camel which has been travelled too far.

The machines were set up on the terrace, although this did not as yet reach to the height of the rampart. Before the twenty-three towers on the fortifications stood twenty-three others of wood. All the tollenos were mounted again, and in the centre, further back, appeared the formidable 'helepolis' of Demetrius Poliorcetes, which Spendius had at last reconstructed. It was in the form of a pyramid, like the pharos of Alexandria, and was a hundred and thirty cubits high and twenty-three wide, with nine stories diminishing in size as they approached the top, and protected by plates of brass; these were pierced with numerous doors and were filled with soldiers, and on the topmost platform stood a catapult flanked by two ballistas.

Hamilcar set up crosses in readiness for any who spoke of surrender, and even the women were formed into brigades. The people lay in the streets, waiting and filled with anguish.

Then one morning a little before sunrise (it was the seventh day of the month Nisan) they heard the Barbarians raise a great shout; the leaden-tubed trumpets pealed, & the great Paphlagonian horns bellowed like bulls. All rose and ran to the rampart.

A forest of lances, pikes and swords bristled at its base and leaped against the walls. The ladders grappled, and Barbarian heads appeared in the openings of the battlement.

Beams lifted by long files of men were battering at the gates; and, to demolish the wall at the places where the terrace was wanting, the Mercenaries came up in serried cohorts, the front rank crouch-

ing, the second bending their hams, and the others rising in succession to the last rank, which stood upright. Elsewhere the tallest
advanced in the front to the escalade and the shortest in the rear.
All held their shields over their helmets with their left arms, pressing them edge to edge together so tightly that they might have
been taken for a company of great tortoises. The projectiles glanced
over these slanting masses.

The Carthaginians hurled down mill-stones, pestles, vats, casks,
beds, and everything that was heavy enough to crush a man. Some
watched in the embrasures with fishermen's nets, and when a Barbarian ascended he found himself caught in the meshes, & struggled
like a fish. They demolished their own battlements, so that portions of wall crumbled downwards, raising a great dust. And as the
catapults on each side were shooting directly against one another,
their stones would sometimes strike together and shiver into a
thousand pieces, which fell in great showers upon the combatants.

Soon the two hosts formed but a single great chain of human
bodies; this overflowed into the gaps of the terrace, and, being
somewhat looser at the two ends, swayed perpetually without advancing. They clasped one another, lying flat on the ground like
wrestlers. They crushed each other. The women leaned over the
battlements and shrieked, and were dragged down by their veils,
and the whiteness of their suddenly uncovered sides shone in the
arms of the Negroes, as they buried their daggers in them. The
crowd so pressed about some of the corpses that these did not fall,
but, being upheld by their companions' shoulders, went on for
some minutes, upright and with staring eyes. Some were pierced
through both temples by a javelin, and swayed their heads about
like bears. Mouths which had been opened to shout remained
gaping, and severed hands flew far through the air. Mighty blows
were dealt, and these were long talked of by the survivors.

Arrows flew from the wooden and the stone towers, and the long
yards of the tollenos were ever in rapid motion. The Barbarians
had sacked the old cemetery of the aborigines under the Catacombs, & now hurled the tombstones against Carthage. Sometimes
the cables broke under too heavily laden baskets, & masses of men
would fall from mid-air, throwing up their arms as they fell.

Up to mid-day the veteran hoplites had made a fierce attack upon the Taenia in order to break through into the harbour and destroy the fleet; but Hamilcar had a fire of damp straw lit upon the roof of Khamon, and as the smoke blinded the attackers they fell back to the left, & came to swell the horrible rout which was pressing forward in Malqua. Syntagmata, composed of very strong men chosen for the purpose, had broken in three gates, but were checked by lofty barriers of nail-studded planks: a fourth gate yielded easily; they dashed over it at a run, and rolled into a pit of hidden snares. At the south-west angle, Autharitus and his men broke down the rampart where the fissure had been stopped with bricks. The ground behind sloped upward, and they climbed it nimbly; but at the top they found a second wall built of stones and long beams laid flat and alternating like the squares of a chessboard. This was a Gallic fashion which the Suffete had adapted to the requirement of his situation, and the Gauls imagined themselves before one of their own native towns. They attacked feebly, and were repulsed.

All the circuit from the Street of Khamon as far as the Herb Market was now in the Barbarians' hands, and the Samnites were killing off the dying with their pikes. Or, with one foot on the wall, they gazed down at the smoking ruins beneath them, and at the battle recommencing far away.

The slingers at the rear kept up an incessant fire. But from long use the springs of the Acarnanian slings had broken, and many were now throwing stones with their hands like shepherds; others hurled leaden bullets in the handle of a whip. Zarxas, whose long black hair covered his shoulders, leaped in every direction and hounded the slingers on. Two pouches hung at his hips, and he thrust his left hand continually into them, while his right arm whirled and whirled like a chariot wheel.

Matho had at first refrained from fighting, the better to command the Barbarians as a whole. He had been seen along the gulf with the Mercenaries, by the lagoon with the Numidians, and on the shores of the lake among the Negroes. Also, from the back of the plain, he had urged forward the unending masses of soldiers as they came up against the line of fortifications. Little by little he had come nearer; the smell of blood, the sight of carnage, and the blare of clarions had at last set his heart to dancing. He had gone back into his tent, and, throwing off his cuirass, had put on his lion's skin, as being more convenient for battle. The muzzle fitted over his head, fringeing his face with fangs; the two fore-paws were crossed upon his breast, and the claws of the hind-paws fell below his knees.

He had kept on his stout belt, in which glittered a two-edged axe, and with his great sword in both hands had dashed impetuously through the breach. Like a pruner lopping willow branches and trying to cut down as many as possible so as to earn more money, he went forward, mowing down the Carthaginians about him. Those who tried to take him in flank he knocked down with the pommel of his sword, when any attacked him in front he ran them through, and if they fled he cut them down. Two men jumped together upon his shoulders; but he leaped backwards against a gate and crushed them. His sword fell, and rose, and at last shivered against the angle of a wall. Then he took his heavy axe; and both before and behind, he disembowelled the Carthaginians like a flock of sheep. The farther he advanced the more widely they scattered, and he reached the second enclosure at the foot of the Acropolis. The steps were cumbered with material flung from the summit, and were thus heaped higher than the wall. Matho turned back amid the ruins to summon his followers.

He saw their crests scattered among the multitude; they were failing and about to perish. He dashed towards them, and the vast ring of red plumes closed in, & soon they rejoined and surrounded him. A mighty crowd was discharging from the side streets. He was caught by the hips, and lifted up and carried away outside the rampart, to a spot where the terrace was high.

Matho shouted a command; every shield was lowered to the helmet; he leaped upon them that he might take hold of something which would help him to re-enter Carthage. Brandishing his terrible axe, he ran like some sea god over the brazen waves of the shields.

Meanwhile, a man robed in white was walking along the edge of the rampart, impassible and indifferent to the death surrounding him. Now and again he would shield his eyes with his right hand as if looking for someone. Matho passed beneath him. Suddenly his eyes flamed, his livid face was contorted, and, raising his thin arms, he shouted abuse at him.

Matho did not hear, but he felt so cruel and furious a look enter his heart that he uttered a great bellow and hurled his long axe at him. Certain folk threw themselves upon Shahabarim, and Matho, seeing him no more, fell back exhausted.

A terrible creaking now drew near, mingled with the rhythm of hoarse voices singing in cadence.

It was the great 'helepolis', surrounded by a crowd of soldiers who were dragging it with both hands, and hauling it with ropes, and pushing it with their shoulders; for the slope rising from the plain to the terrace, though extremely gentle, had been found impracticable for a machine of such prodigious weight. It had eight wheels banded with iron, and had been advancing slowly in this way since the morning, like a mountain climbing a mountain. Suddenly an immense ram was projected from its base, & its doors were lowered, disclosing cuirassed soldiers within, like pillars of iron. Some were climbing up and down the two flights of stairs which led from story to story, and some waited to rush forth as soon as the cramps of the doors should grip the walls. In the midmost of the upper platform the skeins of the ballistas were twisting, and the great beam of the catapult was being lowered.

Hamilcar was standing at that moment on the roof of Melkarth. He had judged that it would come straight towards him, where the wall was least vulnerable & had been, for that very reason, denuded of sentries. For a long time his slaves had been fetching water-skins to the circular road, where they had built two transverse clay partitions to form a sort of basin. The water now flowed over the terrace, and, strangely enough, this seemed to cause Hamilcar no anxiety.

When the 'helepolis' was about thirty paces off, he commanded planks to be placed over the streets between the houses from the cisterns to the rampart; and a file of the people passed helmets and amphoras from hand to hand and continually emptied them. The Carthaginians cried out in indignation at this waste of water. The ram was proceeding to demolish the wall, when suddenly a fountain spurted from the disjointed stones. Then the lofty brazen mass, nine stories high, which contained and gave work for more than three thousand soldiers, began to rock gently like a ship. The water had penetrated the terrace and broken up the path; and the wheels stuck in the mire. Between the leather curtains on the first story Spendius showed his head, distending his cheeks as he blew an ivory horn. The great machine heaved up convulsively and advanced perhaps ten paces; but the ground grew softer and softer, the mud reached to the axles, and the 'helepolis' stopped dead, leaning over perilously to one side. The catapult rolled to the edge of the platform and, carried away by the weight of its beam, fell over, shattering the lower stories beneath it. Those soldiers who were standing on the doors slipped into the abyss, or else clung on to the ends of the long beams, and by their weight increased the inclination of the whole edifice. The 'helepolis' was falling to pieces, and cracked in all its joints.

The other Barbarians rushed in a dense throng to help their fellows. The Carthaginians came down from the rampart and, taking them in rear, killed them at leisure: but scythe-armed chariots hastened forward and galloped about them, forcing them to climb up the wall again. Night came on, and the Barbarians gradually retired.

Nothing could now be seen on the plain but a sort of black and swarming mass, stretching from the blue gulf to the dead white lagoon; and the lake itself, into which blood had flowed, lay further off like a great crimson pool.

The terrace was now so laden with corpses that it had the appearance of being built of them. In the centre stood the armoured 'helepolis', and from time to time huge fragments fell from it, like stones from a crumbling pyramid. The walls were marked with broad tracks made by the streams of molten lead. Here and there a foundered wooden tower was burning, & the houses showed dimly like the tiers of a ruined amphitheatre. Heavy columns of smoke rose up with sparks which whirled and were lost in the black sky. Meanwhile the thirst-parched Carthaginians had rushed to the cisterns and broken open the gates, only to find the bottoms covered with a muddy swamp.

What was to be done now? The Barbarians were without number, and when they had recovered from their fatigue would surely begin again.

The people discussed the situation all night in groups at the street corners. Some said that they must send away the women, the sick, and the old men; others proposed to abandon the town and found a colony elsewhere far away. But they lacked ships; and when the sun rose they had come to no decision.

There was no fighting that day, for all were far too exhausted. The sleepers looked like corpses.

The Carthaginians, while trying to find the cause of their disasters, remembered that they had neglected to send to Phoenicia the annual offering due to the Tyrian Melkarth; and a great terror came upon them. The Gods were angry with the Republic, and would prosecute their vengeance to the end.

They were considered as cruel masters, who could be appeased with supplication and who allowed themselves to be bribed with gifts. They were all feeble in comparison with Moloch, the Devourer. The existence, the very flesh of man belonged to Him. Therefore, in order to preserve it, the Carthaginians used to offer up a portion of it to him, to allay his fury. Children were burned on the forehead, or on the nape of the neck, with woollen wicks; and as this mode of satisfying the Baal brought much money to the priests, they did not fail to recommend it as being the easier and more pleasant method.

This time, however, the Republic herself was at stake. As every profit must be purchased by some loss, and as every transaction had to be regulated according to the needs of the weaker and the demands of the stronger, there was no suffering great enough for the God, since he delighted in the most horrible torment, and they were now at his mercy. He must therefore be fully satisfied. Precedents showed that in this way the scourge might be averted. Also it was believed that an immolation by fire would purify Carthage. The ferocity of the populace was attracted in advance by this idea. The choice, too, must fall exclusively upon the families of the great.

The Elders sat long in deliberation. Hanno had come to the assembly and, as he was now unable to sit, remained reclining near the door, half hidden among the fringes of the lofty tapestry. When the pontiff of Moloch asked them whether they would consent to surrender their children, his voice suddenly broke forth from the shadow like the roar of a spirit in the depths of a cavern. He regretted, he said, that he had none of his own blood to give; and he gazed at Hamilcar, who faced him at the other end of the hall. The Suffete was so much disconcerted by his look that he dropped his eyes. All bent their heads in turn in token of approval. In accordance with the rites he had to reply: 'Yes; be it so,' to the high priest. Then the Elders decreed the sacrifice in traditional circumlocution: for there are things more irksome to speak of than to perform.

This decision was made known in Carthage, and there was loud lamentation. The cries of the women could be heard on all sides; their husbands consoled them, or remonstrated with them and cursed them.

Three hours later even stranger news began to spread abroad: the Suffete had discovered springs at the foot of the cliff. There was a rush to the place. Water could be seen at the bottom of holes dug in the sand, and some were already lying flat on the ground and drinking.

Hamilcar did not himself know whether it was advice from the gods, or a dim recollection of a revelation made to him by his father, which had impelled him, on leaving the Elders, to go down to the shore and dig in the gravel with his slaves.

He made gifts of clothing, boots, and wine. He gave all the rest of the corn that he was keeping. He even let the crowd enter his palace, and opened up his kitchens and stores to it, and all the other rooms except Salambo's. He announced that six thousand Gallic Mercenaries were coming soon, and that the king of Macedonia was sending soldiers.

But on the second day the springs had already sunk very low, and on the evening of the third day they were dried up. Then the decree of the Elders was again on every lip, and the priests of Moloch began their task.

Men in black robes presented themselves at the houses. In many cases the owners had already deserted their children under pretence of some business, or of some dainty that they were going to buy; & the servants of Moloch came and took them away. Others dazedly surrendered them in person. Then they were brought to the temple of Tanit, where the priestesses were charged to amuse and feed them until the solemn day.

They visited Hamilcar suddenly, and found him in his gardens.

'Barca! We come for that you know of ... your son!'
They added that some people had seen the boy one evening during the previous moon in the middle of the Mappales district being led by an old man.

He felt at first that he must suffocate. Then, since he understood that all denial would be vain, he bowed, and led them into the counting house. Some slaves, who had run up at a sign from him, kept watch about it.

He entered Salambo's room in a state of distraction. He seized Hannibal with one hand, and with the other snatched up the braiding of a trailing garment, and tied his feet and hands with it. Then he thrust the end into his mouth to form a gag, and hid him under the bed of ox-hides, letting an ample drapery fall to the ground about it.

Next he walked about from right to left, throwing up his arms, and wheeling round, and biting his lips. And next he stood with staring eyes, gasping as if he were about to die.

Finally, however, he clapped his hands three times: and Giddenem appeared.

'Listen!' he said. 'Go and take from among the slaves a male child from eight to nine years of age, with black hair and prominent brows! Bring him here! Hurry!'

Giddenem soon returned, leading a young boy by the hand.

He was a miserable child, thin and at the same time bloated; his skin looked greyish, like the noisome rag that hung to his sides; his head was sunk between his shoulders, & with the back of his hand he kept rubbing his eyes, which were filled with flies.

How could he ever be mistaken for Hannibal! And there was no time to choose another. Hamilcar looked at Giddenem, and felt ready to strangle him.

'Begone!' he cried.

And the master of the slaves fled.

So the misfortune he had so long dreaded had come upon him. He made frenzied efforts to discover whether there were not some manner or means of escaping it.

Abdalonim suddenly spoke from behind the door. The Suffete was being asked for. The servants of Moloch were growing impatient.

Hamilcar repressed a cry, as if a red hot iron had burned him, and again began to pace the room like a madman. Then he sank down beside the balustrade and, with his elbows on his knees, pressed his forehead against his clenched fists.

The porphyry basin still held a little clear water for Salambo's ablutions. In spite of his repugnance & his pride, the Suffete dipped the child in this and began, like a slave merchant, to wash him and rub him with strigils and red earth. Then he took two squares of purple from the receptacles round the wall, placed one on his breast and the other on his back, and joined them together over the collar bones with two diamond clasps. He poured perfume upon his head, passed an amber necklace about his neck, and put pearl-heeled sandals upon his feet: his own daughter's sandals! He stamped with shame and vexation, and Salambo, who busied herself in helping him, was as pale as he. The child, dazzled by such splendour, smiled and, growing bold, was even beginning to clap his hands and leap about, when Hamilcar took him away.

He held him firmly by the arm as if he were afraid of losing him, and the child, whom he was hurting, cried a little as he ran beside him.

Abreast of the slave prison, under a palm tree, he heard a voice, a mournful and supplicant voice, murmuring:

'Master! Oh, Master!'

Hamilcar turned and saw by his side a man of abject appearance, one of the wretches who led a haphazard existence about the household.

'What do you want?' asked the Suffete.

Trembling horribly, the slave stammered:

'I am his father!'

Hamilcar walked on, and the other followed him with stooping loins, bent hams, and head thrust forward. His face was convulsed with unspeakable anguish, and he choked with suppressed sobs, so eager was he at once to question him, and to cry: 'Mercy!'

At last he dared to touch the other's elbow lightly with one finger.

'Are you taking him to ... ?'

He had not strength to finish: and Hamilcar stopped, being quite amazed at such grief.

So immense was the gulf separating them from each other that he had never thought there could be anything in common between them. It even seemed to him a sort of outrage, an encroachment upon his own privilege. He replied with a look colder and heavier than an executioner's axe; the slave swooned and fell in the dust at his feet. And Hamilcar stepped over him.

The three black-robed men were waiting in the great hall, standing against the stone disc. As soon as he was in their presence he tore his garments and rolled upon the pavement, uttering shrill cries.

'Ah, poor little Hannibal! Oh, my son! My consolation! My hope! My life! Kill me also! Take me away! Woe! Oh, Woe!'

He ploughed his face with his nails, tore out his hair, and shrieked like a woman who mourns at a funeral.

'Take him, then! I suffer too much! Away! Ah, kill me with him!'

The servants of Moloch were astonished that the great Hamilcar should be so faint-hearted. They were almost moved.

A noise of naked feet was heard, and a spasmodic panting, like the breathing of a fierce beast as it charges: a man, pale, terrible, and with outspread arms, appeared on the threshold of the third gallery between the ivory posts, crying:

'My child!'

With a bound Hamilcar threw himself upon the slave and, covering the man's mouth with his hand, shouted yet more loudly:

'It is the old man who reared him! He calls him "my child!" It will make him mad! Enough! Enough!'

And thrusting the three priests and their victim by the shoulders, he went out with them, and with a great kick shut to the door behind him.

Hamilcar strained his ears for some minutes in a constant fear of seeing them return. He then considered getting rid of the slave so as to be quite certain that he would not talk: but the danger had not entirely passed, and if the gods were angered by the man's death their anger might be turned against his son. So, changing his intention, he sent Taanach to him with the best viands from his kitchens: a quarter of a goat, beans, & preserved pomegranates. The slave, who had eaten nothing for a long time, rushed upon these things; and his tears fell into the dishes.

At last Hamilcar returned to Salambo and unfastened Hannibal's cords. The raging child bit his hand and drew blood, but he pushed him off with a caress.

To keep him quiet, Salambo tried to frighten him with Lamia, a Cyrenian ogress.

'But where is she?' he asked.

He was told that brigands were coming to put him into prison, and he rejoined: 'Let them! I will kill them!'

Hamilcar told him the terrible truth. But he fell into a passion with his father, declaring that he was quite able to destroy the whole people, since he was master of Carthage.

At last, exhausted by his exertions and his anger, he fell into a troubled sleep. He spoke in his dreams as he lay against a scarlet cushion; his head was thrown back a little, and his little arm was flung straight out from his body in a gesture of command.

When the night was dark Hamilcar gently lifted him and, without a torch, bore him down the galley stairway. As he passed through the counting house he took up a basket of grapes and a flagon of pure water. The child woke before the statue of Aletes in the vault of gems, and smiled on his father's arm, as the other child had smiled, at the glittering lights around him.

Hamilcar felt quite sure now that his son could not be taken from him. This was an impenetrable spot communicating with the beach by an underground passage known only to himself. He drank in a great draught of air as he glanced about him. Then he set the child down upon a stool beside some golden shields.

No one could see him now, and there was no longer need for vigilance; therefore he gave way to his feelings. Like a mother finding her first-born who had been lost, he threw himself upon his son and clasped him to his breast, laughing and weeping at the same time, calling him by the fondest names and covering him with kisses. Little Hannibal was frightened by such terrible tenderness, and fell silent.

Hamilcar stole noiselessly back, groping along the walls, and came into the great hall where the moonlight entered by one of the openings in the dome. The glutted slave lay sleeping full length upon the marble floor in the middle of it. He looked at him, and was touched by a sort of pity. With the tip of his boot he pushed a rug under his head. Then he raised his eyes and gazed at Tanit, whose slender crescent shone in the sky, and felt himself stronger than the Baalim, and full of contempt for them.

The arrangements for the sacrifice had already begun.

A section of the wall in the temple of Moloch was knocked down so that the brazen god could be dragged forth without disturbing the ashes on the altar. Then, as soon as the sun appeared, the temple servants pushed him towards the Square of Khamon.

He moved backwards, sliding upon rollers, and his shoulders over-topped the walls. The Carthaginians fled precipitately from the sight of him; for one might not look with impunity upon the Baal except when he was exercising his wrath.

An odour of aromatics wafted through the streets. All the temples had been simultaneously thrown open, and from these there issued tabernacles borne upon chariots, or upon litters carried by the pontiffs. Great plumes nodded at the corners of them, and rays flashed from their slender pinnacles, topped by balls of crystal or gold, silver or copper.

These were the Canaanitish Baalim, offshoots of the supreme Baal, who were returning to their first Cause in order to humble themselves before his might and lose themselves in his splendour.

Melkarth's canopy, which was of fine purple, sheltered a flame of bitumen oil: on Khamon's, which was of hyacinth colour, stood an ivory phallus ringed about with gems: between Eshmun's curtains of ether blue a python slept in a circle, with its tail in its mouth: and the Pataec Gods, held up in the arms of their priests, looked like huge babes in swaddling clothes with their heels touching the ground.

Then came all the inferior forms of the Divinity: Baal-Samin, god of celestial space; Baal-Peor, god of the sacred mountains; Baal-Zebub, god of corruption; and those of neighbouring countries & kindred races: the Iarbal of Libya, the Adrammelech of Chaldaea, the Kijun of the Syrians; Derceto with a maiden's face, crawling upon her fins; and the dead Tammuz drawn along on a catafalque among torches and heads of hair. To subject the kings of the firmament to the Sun, and to prevent their individual influences from impeding his, stars of variously coloured metal were brandished at the end of long poles. All were there, from black Nebo, the spirit of Mercury, to the hideous Rahab, which is the constellation of the Crocodile. The Abaddirs, stones fallen from the moon, were whirled in slings of silver thread; little loaves made in the form of a woman's sex were carried in baskets by the priests of Ceres. Others bore fetishes and amulets; forgotten idols were brought to light; and the mystic symbols had even been taken from the ships, as if Carthage meant to give herself up wholly to a single thought of death & desolation. Before each tabernacle a man balanced on his head a large vase of smoking incense. The hangings, pendants, and embroideries of the sacred pavilions could just be distinguished among the hovering clouds and the thick vapours of it. The gods moved slowly because of their enormous weight. Sometimes their axles stuck fast in the streets; then the pious profited by the opportunity to touch the Baalim with their garments, which they afterwards kept as holy things.

The brazen statue continued to advance towards the Square of Khamon. The Rich, bearing sceptres with emerald balls, set out from the bottom of Megara; the Elders, crowned with diadems, had assembled in Kinisdo; and the masters of finance, governors of provinces, merchants, soldiers, sailors, and the numerous horde customary at funerals, all with the insignia of their offices or the tools of their trade, were making toward the tabernacles, as these descended from the Acropolis between the colleges of the pontiffs.

Out of deference to Moloch the priests had adorned themselves with their most splendid jewels. Diamonds sparkled on their black garments, but their rings were too large for their wasted hands, and dropped off; nothing could have been more mournful than this silent crowd, where ear-rings tapped against pale faces, and golden tiaras encircled brows contracted with stern despair.

At last the Baal arrived exactly in the centre of the Square. His pontiffs arranged an enclosure of trellis work to keep off the crowd, and stood about him at his feet.

The priests of Khamon, in tawny woollen robes, were drawn up in line before their temple under the columns of the portico; those of Eshmun, in linen mantles with necklaces of hoopoes' heads and pointed tiaras, posted themselves on the steps of the Acropolis; the priests of Melkarth, in violet tunics, took the western side; the priests of the Abaddirs, swathed in bands of Phrygian stuffs, placed themselves on the east; and ranged on the southern side, with the tattooed necromancers, were the howlers in patched cloaks, the ministers of the Pataec Gods, and the Yidonim who divined the future by placing a dead man's bone in their mouths. The priests of Ceres, who were dressed in blue, had prudently halted in the street of Satheb, and in low tones were chanting a thesmophorion in the Megarian dialect.

From time to time came files of stark naked men with arms outstretched, each one holding another by the shoulders. From the depths of their chests they intoned hoarsely and cavernously; their eyes, which were fastened upon the colossus, shone through the dust, and they swayed their bodies together at regular intervals, as if all were shaken by a single movement. They were so frenzied that the temple servants struck them with their staves to preserve order, and made them lie flat upon the ground, with their faces resting against the brazen trellis work.

At this moment a man in a white robe came forward from the back of the Square. He made his way slowly through the crowd, and the people recognised him as a priest of Tanit, the high priest Shahabarim. The crowd hooted, for the tyranny of the male element was uppermost that day in every heart, and the Goddess so completely forgotten that the absence of her priests had not been noticed. But their amazement was redoubled when he was seen to open one of the doors in the trellis work reserved for those who would go in to offer victims. The priests of Moloch thought that he was come to insult their God, and they sought with violent gestures to turn him back. Fed on the meat of the holocausts, clad in purple like kings, and wearing triple crowns, they despised this pale eunuch, weakened with his macerations. Angry laughter shook the black beards which flowed over their breasts in the sun.

Shahabarim walked on, giving no reply to them, and, crossing the whole enclosure step by step, stood under the legs of the colossus. Then, spreading out his arms, he touched it on both sides. This was a solemn act of adoration. For a long time Rabbet had tortured him, and now in despair, or perhaps for lack of a God who completely satisfied his idea, he had decided to turn to this one.

The crowd, stunned by this act of apostasy, gave a long murmur. They felt that this was the breaking of the last tie which bound their souls to a merciful divinity.

But, owing to his mutilation, Shahabarim could take no part in the worship of the Baal. The men in the red cloaks expelled him from the enclosure: when he was outside, he went round all the colleges in succession, and finally this priest without a god disappeared in the crowd. It scattered before him.

Meanwhile a fire of aloes, cedar, and laurel was burning between the legs of the colossus. The tips of his long wings dipped into the flame; the unguents with which he had been anointed flowed like sweat over his brazen limbs. About the circular flag-stone on which his feet rested, the children, wrapped in black veils, stood in a motionless ring; and his long, monstrous arms reached down their palms to them as if to seize this crown and carry it to the sky.

The Rich, the Elders, the women, the whole multitude thronged up behind the priests and on to the terraces of the houses. The great painted stars no longer revolved, the tabernacles were set upon the ground, and the fumes from the censers rose perpendicularly now, like giant trees spreading blue branches into the clear sky.

Many fainted, and others were frozen to still stone in their ecstasy. An infinite agony weighed upon them. The last shouts died away one by one, and the people of Carthage stood breathless, absorbed in the longing of their terror.

At last the high priest of Moloch passed his left hand under the childrens' veils, plucked a lock of hair from their foreheads, & threw it upon the flames. Then the men in the red cloaks chanted their sacred hymn: 'Homage to thee, O Sun! O King of the two zones, and Creator self-begotten: Father and Mother, Father and Son, God and Goddess, Goddess and God!'

Their voices were lost in the crash of instruments sounding together to drown the victims' cries. Eight-stringed sheminiths, ten-stringed kinnors, twelve-stringed nables, twanged and whistled and thundered. Huge leather bags, bristling with pipes, made a shrill rolling noise; timbrels, beaten with all the player's might, resounded heavily & rapidly; and not the furious blare of the clarions could drown the salsalim, which snapped like locusts' wings.

The temple servants, with a long hook, opened the seven compartments which were disposed one above the other in the body of the Baal. They put meal into the highest, two turtle doves into the second, an ape into the third, a ram into the fourth, a sheep into the fifth; &, as they had no ox for the sixth, a tanned hide from the sanctuary was thrown within it. The seventh compartment still yawned.

As a preliminary precaution it was well to test the God's arms. Slender little chains stretched from his fingers to his shoulders and fell down behind him, where men pulled them to make the two open hands rise level with the elbows and meet together against the belly. The priests worked them up & down several times with little abrupt jerks. Then the instruments of music were hushed, and the fire roared.

The pontiffs of Moloch walked about on the great flag-stone, scanning the multitude.

An individual sacrifice was necessary, a voluntary oblation to carry the others along with it. No one had as yet come forward; and the seven passages leading from the barriers to the colossus were completely empty. Then the priests, to encourage the people, drew bodkins from their girdles and gashed their faces. The Devotees lying on the ground outside were brought within the enclosure: a bundle of horrible irons was thrown to them, and each chose his own torture. They drove spits into their breasts; they split their cheeks; they put crowns of thorns upon their heads; then they linked arms together & surrounded the children in a second great circle, which kept expanding and contracting. They reached the balustrade, and threw themselves back again, and then began once more, drawing the multitude to them by the dizziness of their movements and the blood and shrieks that accompanied them.

By degrees people came into the end of the alleys, and flung pearls and gold vases, and cups and torches, and all their wealth into the flames. The offerings grew more and more splendid, more and more numerous. At last a man pale and hideous with terror staggered up, and thrust forward a child: a little mass of black was seen for a moment between the hands of the colossus, and then it sank into the dark opening. The priests leaned over the edge of the great flag-stone, and there burst forth a new song celebrating the joys of death and the fresh birth of eternity.

The children rose up slowly, and, as the smoke whirled about them in lofty eddies, they seemed, from a distance, to vanish into a cloud. Not one of them stirred. Their wrists and ankles were tied, and the dark drapery prevented them from seeing, and from being recognised.

Hamilcar, cloaked in red like the priests of Moloch, was standing by the great toe of the Baal's right foot. When the fourteenth child was brought up, all men could see his violent gesture of horror. But he soon resumed his former attitude, with folded arms, and looking upon the ground. The high priest stood on the other side of the statue as motionless as he: his head was bowed under its Assyrian mitre, & he watched the gold plate covered with prophetic stones upon his breast. The flames were reflected in it with an iridescent light; and he grew pale and dismayed. Hamilcar bowed his forehead. They were both so near the pyre that the hems of their cloaks, in rising a little, brushed it from time to time.

The brazen arms were working more quickly now, and paused no more. Each time that a child was placed in them the priests of Moloch spread out their hands over him, to lay upon him the crimes of the people, crying: 'They are not men, but oxen!' And the multitude about them repeated: 'Oxen! Oxen!' The Devotees exclaimed: 'Eat, Lord!' And the priests of Proserpine, conforming in terror to the need of Carthage, muttered the Eleusinian formula; 'Pour rain! Give birth!'

The victims hardly reached the edge of the opening before they disappeared like a drop of water on a red hot plate; white smoke rose through the wide crimson glow.

But the God's appetite was not appeased. He wanted yet more. To feed him the more abundantly, the victims were now piled up on his hands with a big chain over them to keep them in place. Some devout persons tried at first to count them, to see whether their number tallied with the days of the solar year; but when others were added, it became impossible to distinguish them in the dizzy motion of those horrible arms. So the thing continued indefinitely until evening. Then the inner partitions took on a more sombre glow, and burning flesh could be seen. Some even thought they could distinguish hair, and limbs, and whole bodies.

Night fell, and clouds gathered above the Baal. The pyre, now flameless, made a pyramid of embers up to his knees, so that he showed completely red, like a giant covered with blood. His head was thrown back, and he looked as if he were staggering under the great weight of his drunkenness.

The greater the haste of the priests, the greater grew the people's frenzy. As the numbers of the victims decreased, some cried out to spare them, and others that still more were needed. It seemed as if the over-crowded walls must give way under that howling of terror and mystic voluptuousness. The faithful came into the alleys dragging their children, who clung to them; they beat them to make them let go, and handed them over to the men in red. The musicians sometimes paused from exhaustion; then could be heard the cries of the mothers, and the frizzling of the fat upon the hot embers. The henbane drinkers crawled on all fours about the colossus, roaring like tigers; the Yidonim prophesied, & the Devotees sang through their cloven lips. The trellis work had been broken through, for each one wished to share in the sacrifice: and fathers whose children had died before that day now cast their effigies, their playthings, even their preserved bones into the fire. Some who had knives rushed upon their fellows. They cut each other's throats. The temple servants took the fallen ashes at the edge of the flag-stone with bronze winnowing fans, and cast them into the air that the sacrifice might be scattered over the town and even to the region of the stars.

The stupendous noise and the great light had attracted the Barbarians to the foot of the wall; they clung to the wreck of the 'helepolis' to have a better view, & gazed in open-mouthed horror upon what they saw.

THE PASS
OF THE HATCHET

CHAPTER XIV

THE CARTHAGINIANS HAD NOT GONE BACK INTO THEIR
houses before the clouds gathered; those who raised their faces towards the colossus felt great drops on their foreheads, and the rain
fell.

It rained all night in a profuse torrent, and the thunder growled; it
was the voice of Moloch, triumphant over Tanit. She was pregnant
now & opened out her vast bosom from high heaven. At times she
could be seen in a region of clear light resting upon cloud cushions:
then the darkness would close in again as if she were still too weary
and wished to sleep again. The Carthaginians, who believed that
water is generated by the moon, shouted to ease her labour.

The rain beat upon the terraces and flooded them, forming lakes in
the courtyards, cascades on the stairways, and eddies at the street
corners. It poured down in warm heavy masses and spouting
streams; great foaming jets leaped from the corners of the buildings; the rain was like a white sheet hung dimly upon the walls,
and the washed temple roofs shone black in the gleam of the lightning. Torrents foamed down from the Acropolis by a thousand
paths; houses suddenly crumbled, and small beams, plaster-work,
and pieces of furniture went racing down the streams as they ran
impetuously over the pavements.

Amphoras, flagons, and canvas buckets had been set in the open;
but the torches were extinguished, & brands to replace them were
taken from the pyre of the Baal. The Carthaginians bent back their

necks and opened their mouths to drink. Some plunged their arms up to the shoulders in the muddy pools, and sated themselves so plenteously with water that they vomited it out again like buffaloes. A freshness gradually pervaded the atmosphere; they breathed in the moist air and felt a joyous freedom of limb, and the happiness of their intoxication soon gave rise to a mighty hope. All their miseries were forgotten. Their country lived again.

They felt the need, as it were, to expend upon others the excess of the fury which they had been unable to wreak upon themselves. Such a sacrifice could not be vain, & although they felt no remorse, they found themselves carried away by a frenzy born of complicity in irreparable crimes.

The storm had fallen upon the Barbarians in their poorly closed tents, and next day, while they were still numbed, they had to wade through the mud in search of their stores & weapons, which were spoiled and lost.

Hamilcar went to see Hanno of his own accord, and, by virtue of his plenary powers, entrusted the command to him. The aged Suffete hesitated for a few minutes between his hatred and his appetite for authority; but finally he accepted.

Hamilcar then took out a galley armed with a catapult at each end, and anchored it in the gulf opposite the raft; then he embarked his stoutest troops on such vessels as he could get together. He seemed to be fleeing as he sailed northwards and disappeared in the mist.

But three days later, when the attack was about to begin again, there came up a tumultuous throng of people from the Libyan coast. Barca had come among them, had levied provisions on every side, and his troops were spreading over the country.

The Barbarians were indignant, as if he had betrayed them. Those who were most weary of the siege, and especially the Gauls, did not hesitate to leave the walls in order to try to rejoin him. Spendius wished to reconstruct the 'helepolis'; Matho had traced an imaginary line from his tent to Megara, and had sworn to himself to follow it: and not a man of theirs stirred. But the rest, under the command of Autharitus, departed, abandoning the western part of the rampart, & in the deep general apathy no one thought of replacing them.

Narr'Havas saw them going from far off in the mountains, and during the night led all his men along the outer side of the lagoon, and entered Carthage.

His appearance there was that of a saviour, for he brought six thousand men all carrying meal under their cloaks, and forty elephants laden with forage & dried meat. The people quickly flocked around the elephants, giving them names: the sight of these mighty animals, which were sacred to Baal, gave the Carthaginians even more joy than the arrival of the relief itself; it was a sign of the God's compassion, a proof that he was at last about to intervene in the war and protect his people.

Narr'Havas received the compliments of the Elders, and then went up to Salambo's palace.

He had not seen her since the time when, in Hamilcar's tent amid the five armies, he had felt her little cold, soft hand bound to his own; for she had returned to Carthage after the betrothal. His love, which had been thrust aside by other ambitions, had now come back to him, and he expected to enjoy his rights, to marry and possess her.

Salambo did not understand how this young man could ever become her master! Although she prayed to Tanit every day for Matho's death, her horror of the Libyan was growing less. She was confusedly aware that there was something almost of religion in the hatred with which he had persecuted her; and she would have liked to see in Narr'Havas a reflection, as it were, of a violence which still bemused her. She wished to know him better, and yet his presence would have embarrassed her, so she sent him word that she could not receive him.

Hamilcar, also, who hoped to retain his loyalty by putting off his reward until the end of the war, had forbidden his servants to admit the King of the Numidians to see her. In his fear of the Suffete, Narr'Havas withdrew.

But he bore himself haughtily towards the Hundred. He altered their plans; he demanded privileges for his men, & placed them at important posts. The Barbarians stared when they saw Numidians on the towers.

The surprise of the Carthaginians was greater still when four hundred of their own people, who had been taken prisoners during the Sicilian war, arrived on an old Punic trireme. Hamilcar had secretly sent back to the Quirites the crews of the Latin vessels taken before the defection of the Tyrian towns; and, to reciprocate this act of courtesy, Rome was now sending him back her captives. She had scorned the overtures of the Mercenaries in Sardinia, and would not recognise the inhabitants of Utica as subjects.

Hieron, king of Syracuse, was led to follow this example. For the safety of his own State it was necessary for a balance of power between the two nations to be maintained. He had therefore an interest in the welfare of the Canaanites, declared himself their friend, and sent them twelve hundred oxen, with fifty nebels of pure wheat.

He had a deeper motive still for helping Carthage. It was quite apparent that if the Mercenaries triumphed, every man, from soldier to dish-washer, would rise in revolt, and that no government and no house could resist them.

All this time Hamilcar continued to subdue the eastern districts. He drove back the Gauls, & the Barbarians found themselves more or less in a state of siege.

Afterwards he set himself to harass them. He would march forward, and then retire; and by constantly repeating this manoeuvre he gradually drew them forth from their encampments. Spendius was obliged to follow them, & in the end Matho yielded to his example. He did not pass beyond Tunis, but shut himself up within its walls. His wisdom in persisting in this course was soon made obvious when Narr'Havas was seen to issue from the gate of Khamon with his elephants and soldiers. Hamilcar had recalled him: but the other Barbarians were already wandering about the provinces in pursuit of the Suffete.

He had been reinforced by three thousand Gauls from Clypea, and had had horses brought to him from Cyrenaica, and armour from Brutium. He began the war again.

Never had his genius been so impetuous and fertile. For five moons he lured his enemies after him, and there was a goal to which he was guiding them.

The Barbarians had at first tried to hem him in with small detachments, but he always escaped these, so now they no longer divided.

Their army was about forty thousand strong, and they often had the pleasure of seeing the Carthaginians in retreat.

What worried them most was Narr'Havas's cavalry. Often, at the most oppressive time of day, when they were marching over the plains and dozing under the weight of their arms, a great line of dust would rise suddenly on the horizon and come galloping towards them. A rain of darts would pour from the bosom of a cloud surcharged with flaming eyes. The Numidians in their white cloaks would utter loud cries, and raise their arms, and press their rearing stallions with their knees. Then, wheeling them abruptly, they would disappear. They had dromedaries at a distance with fresh supplies of javelins, and would return more terrible than before, howling like wolves, and wheeling like vultures on the wing. The Barbarians posted on the flanks of the files fell one by one; and so things went on until evening, when they tried to break for the mountains.

Although this was dangerous for the elephants, Hamilcar made his way into the mountain country, following the long chain which extends from the promontory of Hermaeum to the top of Zaguan. The Barbarians thought this to be a ruse to hide the insufficiency of his troops; but the continual suspense in which he kept them ended by exasperating them more than any defeat. Still they did not lose heart, and continued to march after him.

At last one evening they surprised a body of light infantry among some great boulders at the entrance of a pass between the Silver Mountain and the Lead Mountain; also the entire army was surely in front of them, for they could hear the tramp of feet & the sound of clarions. The Carthaginians fled precipitately through the gorge, which sloped down into a plain shaped like an iron hatchet and surrounded by high cliffs. The Barbarians charged into the gorge after the velites; at the far end were oxen galloping, and among these they could see other Carthaginians running in a tumult to and fro. They saw a man in a red cloak . . . the Suffete. The sight of him redoubled their fury and their joy. Several of the lazy or timid had remained on the threshold of the pass; but now cavalry debouched from a wood and drove them with pikes and sabres down upon the rest. Very soon all the Barbarians were below in the plain.

This great mass of men swayed to and fro for some moments and then stood still; for they could discover no outlet.

Those who were nearest to the pass retired, but the passage of it had entirely disappeared. They shouted to those in front to advance, as they were being crushed against the mountain, and those in front hurled back abuse at their companions, because they could not find the way again.

No sooner, in fact, had the Barbarians descended than men who had been crouching behind the rocks levered them up with beams and overthrew them; as the slope was steep the huge blocks had rolled down pell-mell and completely choked the narrow opening.

At the other end of the plain lay a long passage, split here and there by fissures, and leading to a ravine which rose to the upper plateau, where the Punic army was stationed. Ladders had been placed in readiness against the cliff-side in this passage; and, being protected by the windings of the fissures, the velites were able to seize and mount them before they were overtaken. Several even made their way to the bottom of the ravine, and were pulled up on cables; for the ground at this spot was a moving sand, and so steep that it was impossible to climb it even on hands and knees. The Barbarians reached this place almost immediately; but a portcullis, forty cubits high and made to the exact measurement of the intervening space, suddenly dropped in front of them like a rampart fallen from heaven.

The Suffete's combination had therefore succeeded. None of the Mercenaries knew the mountain, and, as they marched at the head of their columns, they had led the rest into a trap. The rocks were rather narrower at their bases and had been easily thrown down; and Hamilcar's whole army had raised shouts as of distress from afar as it ran. It is true that he might have lost his velites, and had in fact lost half of them; but he would have sacrificed twenty times as many for the success of such an enterprise.

Until morning the Barbarians marched in compact files from end to end of the plain. They felt the mountain with their hands, trying to find a passage through it.

At last day broke; and they saw a great white wall rising sheer about them on every side. There was no means of escape, no hope! The

two natural outlets from this cul-de-sac were closed by the portcullis and the heap of rocks.

They all looked at one another without speaking, and then sank
down in collapse, feeling an icy coldness in their loins, and an overwhelming weight upon their eyelids.

Some rose up, and leaped at the rocks. But those at the bottom
were pressed down by the weight of the rest, and were thus immovable. They tried to scale the rocks and gain the summit, but the
great masses of stone bellied outwards, making it impossible to obtain any hold at all. They tried to hack through the ground on each
side of the gorge, but their tools broke. They made a great fire with
the tent poles; but the fire could not burn the mountain.

They returned to the portcullis, and found it studded with long
nails as thick as stakes, as sharp as the quills of a porcupine, and
closer than the hairs of a brush. But such was their fury that they
hurled themselves against it. The foremost were pierced to the
backbone, those that followed were shocked back upon themselves;
all fell away, leaving those horrible branches laden with fragments
of flesh and bloody hair.

When they had recovered a little from their despair, they took
stock of their provisions. The Mercenaries, whose baggage was lost,
had barely enough for two days; and all the rest found themselves
destitute, for they had been awaiting a convoy promised by the
villages of the South.

But there were cattle roaming hither and thither, which the Carthaginians had loosed into the gorge to lure the Barbarians on. These
they killed with their lances and ate, and with the filling of their
stomachs their thoughts grew less mournful.

Next day they slaughtered the mules, some forty in all; they scraped
the hides, boiled the entrails, pounded the bones, and did not yet
despair: no doubt the army from Tunis had been apprised of their
fate, and was even now moving to their rescue.

But on the evening of the fifth day their hunger became acute; they
gnawed their sword belts, and also the little sponges which lined
the bottom of their helmets.

These forty thousand men were massed in a sort of amphitheatre
formed round them by the mountain. Some stayed before the

portcullis, or at the foot of the rocks; the rest spread confusedly over the plain. The strong shunned one another; and the timid clung to those who were brave and yet could not save them.

To avoid infection the bodies of the velites had been quickly buried, and it was no longer possible to see where the pits had been dug.

All the Barbarians lay on the ground exhausted. Here and there a veteran would pass between their lines. They howled curses against the Carthaginians and Hamilcar, and against Matho, although he was not to blame for their plight; but it seemed to them that they would not suffer so much if he were sharing their agony. They groaned, and some sobbed quietly like little children.

They approached their captains, begging for something to help their sufferings. But these either did not answer or, in a fit of fury, would pick up stones and fling them in their faces.

Not a few carefully kept a reserve of food in a hole in the ground, a few handfuls of dates, or a little meal; they ate of this at night, hiding their heads in their cloaks. Those who had swords kept them naked in their hands, & the most suspicious remained standing with their backs to the mountain side.

They blamed and threatened their chiefs. But Autharitus was not afraid of showing himself: with a typical Barbaric obstinacy which nothing could break down, he would go twenty times a day up to the rocks, hoping each time to find that some chance had displaced them. With his heavy fur-covered shoulders, he looked to his companions like a bear coming out of its cave in the spring time to see whether the snows have melted.

Spendius, with his Greeks, hid in one of the fissures and, being afraid for his life, caused a report of his death to be circulated. They were all now hideously emaciated; their skin was mottled with bluish marblings, and on the evening of the ninth day three Iberians died. Their frightened companions left the spot. The dead were stripped, and the white, naked bodies lay on the sand in the sunshine.

Then the Garamantes began to prowl slowly round about the three. They were men accustomed to desert life, and reverenced no God. At last the oldest of the band made a sign. They bent over the corpses and cut strips from them with their knives, then squatted upon their heels and ate. The others looked on from a distance, uttering cries of horror; but many, at the bottom of their hearts, envied the courage of the Garamantes.

In the middle of the night some of these last approached, and, dissembling their eagerness, asked for a small mouthful: just to taste, they said. Then bolder ones came forward; their number grew, and there was soon a crowd there. But nearly all of them dropped their hands when they felt the cold flesh against their lips; yet others devoured it with relish.

That they might have an example to encourage them, they urged one another. Such as had at first refused went to see the Garamantes, & did not come back. They cooked pieces over hot embers on their sword points, and seasoned them with dust, and quarrelled for the best bits. When nothing was left of the three corpses, their eyes searched the length of the plain for others.

But had there not been twenty Carthaginian prisoners taken in the last encounter, whom none had noticed up to the present? These went; it was but an act of vengeance. Then, since they must live, and since they had developed a taste for food and were starving, they cut the throats of the water-carriers, and the grooms, and all the serving men belonging to the Mercenaries. They killed some every day, and certain of them, who ate heartily, recovered their strength and were no longer sad.

Soon this resource failed, and then they turned gluttonous eyes upon the sick and wounded. Since these could not recover, it was as well to release them from their suffering; as soon as a man began to stagger, they all cried out that he was now lost and ought to be used for the benefit of the rest. They practised tricks upon them to hasten their death; the last remnant of their filthy portion was stolen from them; they were trodden on as if by accident. Those who were at the point of death tried to prove their strength by stretching out their arms, and rising and laughing. Men who had swooned came to themselves at the touch of a notched blade beginning to saw at a limb. Also they still killed, ferociously and needlessly, to appease their fury.

On the fourteenth day a warm and heavy fog, such as is common in those regions at the end of winter, settled down upon the army. This change of temperature caused many deaths, and corruption

set in with frightful rapidity in the moist warmth which was retained by the mountain walls. The small rain that fell upon the
corpses softened them, and the plain soon became one wide mass
of putrescence. Whitish mists hovered over the ground, and stung
the nostrils, penetrated the skin, and troubled the eyes; in these
the Barbarians thought they could see the spent breath, the souls of
their companions. An immeasurable disgust overpowered them.
They did not wish for anything any more: they would rather die.

After two days the weather cleared again, and their hunger came
back to them. Sometimes they felt as if their stomachs were being
clawed out with hooks; they rolled about in convulsions, flung
handfuls of earth into their mouths, and bit their arms, and burst
into frantic laughter.

Their thirst caused them an even worse torture; for they had not
one drop of water; their leather bottles had been dry since the ninth
day. To cheat their need, they put their tongues to the metal plates
of their belts, & their ivory pommels, and the steel of their swords.
Some old caravan leaders tightened their waists with cords, and
others sucked a pebble. They drank urine cooled in their brass
helmets.

And they were always waiting for the army from Tunis! Allowing
for the time it would take to come, they reckoned that it must be
with them very soon. Besides, Matho was a fine fellow, and would
not desert them. 'It will be to-morrow!' they told one another:
and then to-morrow passed.

At first they had offered up prayers and vows, and had practised
all kinds of incantation. Just now they felt nought but hatred for
their gods, and tried to avenge themselves upon them by believing
in them no more.

The men of violent humour died first, and the Africans held out
better than the Gauls. Zarxas lay inert at full length among the
Balearic Islanders, his hair tossed over his arm. Spendius found a
plant with broad leaves abundantly filled with juice, and, after
declaring that it was poisonous, so as to keep others from it, fed
himself well.

They were too weak to knock down the flying crows with stones.
Sometimes when a bearded vulture perched on a corpse & had been

mangling it for some time, a man would begin to crawl towards it with a javelin between his teeth; he would lean on one hand, and after a careful aim, would throw his weapon. The white-feathered beast, disturbed by the noise, would pause and look calmly about, like a cormorant on a reef. Then it would thrust in its hideous yellow beak again, and the man, in despair, would fall flat on his face in the dust. Some managed to find chameleons and snakes, but it was the love of life which kept them alive: they concentrated their minds exclusively upon this thought, clinging to existence by an effort of will that, of itself, prolonged it.

The most stoical kept close to one another, sitting in circles here and there among the dead in the midst of the plain; they wrapped themselves in their cloaks and gave themselves up silently to their misery.

Those who had been born in towns thought of the noisy streets, and the taverns, and theatres, and baths, and the barbers' shops where tales are to be heard. Others had visions of a country-side at sunset with waving yellow corn, and great oxen climbing back over the hills with ploughshares about their necks. Travellers dreamed of certain water cisterns, and hunters of their forests, and veterans of their battles; in their sleepy state of stupor their thoughts jostled one another with all the precipitate precision of dreams. Hallucinations came suddenly upon them; they looked for a door in the mountain to escape by, and would pass there through. Others thought they were sailing in a storm, and gave orders for the handling of a ship; some fell back in terror, seeing Punic battalions in the clouds. There were those who thought themselves at a feast, and sang songs.

Many were afflicted with a strange mania which caused them to repeat the same word, or continually to make the same gesture. When they chanced to raise their heads and look at one another, they were choked with sobbing at the sight of the fearful ravages shown on the faces of their fellows. Some had ceased to suffer, & to while away the hours, told stories of the dangers they had escaped.

Death was certain and imminent for them all. How many times had they not tried to open up a way through! As for begging terms from their conqueror, what means had they for doing so? They did not even know where Hamilcar was.

The wind was blowing from the direction of the ravine. It sent the sand flowing in perpetual cascades over the portcullis; the cloaks and the hair of the Barbarians were covered with it, as if the earth were rising to bury them. All was still, and the everlasting mountain seemed yet higher to them each morning.

Sometimes flocks of birds flew swiftly through the blue sky in the freedom of the air, and the men closed their eyes that they might not see them.

At first they felt a buzzing in their ears, then their nails grew black, and a coldness gripped their breasts; they lay upon their sides, and gave one groan, and died.

On the nineteenth day two thousand Asiatics were dead, fifteen hundred from the Archipelago, eight thousand from Libya, the youngest of the Mercenaries, and whole tribes beside; in all twenty thousand soldiers—half the army.

Autharitus, who had only fifty Gauls left to him, was about to kill himself and make an end of things, when he thought he saw a man on the top of the mountain in front of him.

At such a height the man seemed no taller than a dwarf, but Autharitus recognised a shield shaped like a trefoil on his left arm, and exclaimed:

'A Carthaginian!'

Immediately each rose to his feet, before the portcullis and beneath the rocks, throughout the plain. The soldier walked along the edge of the precipice, and the Barbarians gazed up at him.

Spendius lifted the skull of an ox, and made a diadem with two belts which he tied to the horns of it; this he lifted on the end of a pole in token of peaceful intention. The Carthaginian disappeared, and the Barbarians waited.

At last at evening, a sword baldric fell from above, like a stone loosened from the cliff; it was made of embroidered red leather, with three diamond stars, and it bore, stamped in the centre, the mark of the Great Council: a horse beneath a palm tree. This was Hamilcar's reply; he sent a safe-conduct to them.

They had nothing to fear, for any change in their fortunes meant an end of their misery. They were moved to ungovernable joy, and embraced one another, and wept. Spendius, Autharitus, and Zarxas, with four Italiotes, a Negro & two Spartans, offered themselves as envoys, and were accepted. But they did not know by what means they could get away.

A crash sounded from the direction of the rocks, and the topmost crag, after swaying to and fro for a while, bounded to the bottom of the ravine. For though the rocks were immovable on the side of the Barbarians (since they would have had to be forced up an inclined plane & were, moreover, heaped together by the narrowness of the gorge), it only needed a violent push on the other side to send them tumbling. The Carthaginians pushed at them, and at daybreak they led out into the plain like the steps of a great ruined stairway. The Barbarians were still unable to climb, and so ladders were let down for them. They all rushed upon these, but a catapult shot drove the rest back, and only the ten were allowed to depart.

They walked between the Clibanarii, leaning their hands on the horses' buttocks for support.

Now that their first joy had passed, they began to feel uneasy. Hamilcar's demands would be cruel. But Spendius reassured them:

'I will do the talking!'

He boasted that he knew what best to say for the safety of the army.

Behind each bush were ambushed sentries, who prostrated themselves before the baldric which Spendius had placed over his shoulder.

When they reached the Punic camp, the multitude flocked round them, and they could hear a sort of whispering and laughter. The flap of a tent was opened.

At the back of this tent sat Hamilcar on a stool by a table on which gleamed a naked sword. He was surrounded by captains, and they were standing.

He started back on seeing these men, and then bent forward to look at them.

Their pupils were strangely dilated, and they had great black rings round their eyes, reaching to the lower parts of their ears; their noses were blue, and stood out between hollow cheeks, furrowed by deeply cut wrinkles; their skins were too large for their muscles, and were covered by a slate-coloured dust; their lips were glued to their yellow teeth, and they exhaled a pestilent odour; they might have been partially opened tombs, or living sepulchres.

In the middle of the tent, on a mat where the captains were about to sit, stood a steaming dish of gourds. The Barbarians fastened their gaze upon it, trembling in all their limbs, and tears came to their eyes. But they restrained themselves.

Hamilcar turned to speak to someone, and then they all flung themselves flat on the ground before the food. Their faces were steeped in the fat, and the noise of their deglutition mingled with their sobs of joy. Through astonishment, doubtless, rather than pity, they were allowed to finish the mess. When they had risen again, Hamilcar made a sign for the man who bore the baldric to speak. Spendius was afraid, and stammered.

As he listened to him, Hamilcar kept turning a large gold ring round his finger, the same with which he had stamped the seal of Carthage upon the baldric. He let it fall to the ground, and Spendius immediately picked it up: his servile habits came back to him in the presence of a master. The others quivered with indignation at such baseness.

But the Greek raised his voice &, setting forth the crimes of Hanno, whom he knew to be Barca's enemy, he tried to arouse his pity by detailing the miseries of his own people & recalling their devotion. He spoke for a long time rapidly, insidiously, and even vehemently, and in the end lost himself in the heat of his eloquence.

Hamilcar answered that he accepted their excuses, therefore peace was to be concluded, & this time it would be final! But he required that ten Mercenaries, of his own choosing, should be delivered up to him without weapons or tunics.

They were not expecting such clemency, and Spendius exclaimed: 'Oh, twenty if you wish, Master!'

'No! Ten are enough,' replied Hamilcar quietly.

They were dismissed from the tent to deliberate, and as soon as they were alone Autharitus protested against such a sacrifice of their companions, and Zarxas said to Spendius:

'Why did you not kill him? His sword was there quite close to you!'

'Him!' ejaculated Spendius.

And he repeated: 'Him! Him!' several times, as if the thing were impossible, and Hamilcar an immortal.

They were so overcome with fatigue that they lay upon their backs on the ground, not knowing what to decide.

Spendius pressed them to consent; and at last they yielded, and went back into the tent.

Then the Suffete put his hands into the hands of each of the ten Barbarians, and pressed their thumbs. Afterwards he wiped his hands on his clothes, for their clammy skin was both rough and soft to the touch, with an oily tingling which made his hair bristle. Then he said to them:

'You are all, in very truth, chiefs of the Barbarians, and have sworn on their behalf?'

'Yes!' they answered.

'Freely, from the depth of your hearts, and with the intention of fulfilling your promise?'

They assured him that they were about to return to the rest in order to fulfil it.

'Very well!' said the Suffete. 'In accordance with the terms agreed upon between myself, Barca, & the ambassadors of the Mercenaries, I choose you, and it is you I shall keep!'

Spendius fell swooning upon the mat. The other Barbarians, as if forsaking him, pressed close together; not a word came from any of them, not a murmur.

When their companions, who awaited them, did not see them return, they thought themselves betrayed. The envoys had doubtless given themselves to the Suffete.

They waited for two days longer, and then, on the morning of the third, their resolution was taken. With ropes, picks, and arrows fitted like rungs between strips of canvas, they succeeded in scaling the rocks, and, leaving some three thousand of the weakest behind them, they began their march to rejoin the army at Tunis.

At the top of the gorge lay a stretch of grassland sparsely sown with shrubs, and the Barbarians devoured the buds of them. Afterwards they found a field of beans, & these vanished as if a cloud of locusts had passed by. Three hours later they reached a second plateau bordered by a belt of green hills.

At intervals, among the undulations of these, silvery sheaves glittered, and the Barbarians, who were dazzled by the sun, could confusedly descry great black masses beneath them. Then these rose up, and were seen to be lances in towers, upon elephants terribly armed.

In addition to the spears on their breasts and the pointed caps of their tusks, the brass plates which covered their sides and the daggers fastened to their knee-caps, these beasts had a leather band at the end of their trunks, into which the hilt of a broad cutlass was inserted. They started forward all together from the back of the plain, and advanced on both sides of their foe in parallel lines.

The Barbarians were frozen with a nameless terror. They did not even try to flee. They were already surrounded.

Into this mass of men the elephants entered, and the spurs on their breasts divided it, the ferrules on their tusks turned it over like ploughshares. They cut and hewed and hacked with the scythes on their trunks. The towers had been filled with fire-darts, and now showed like moving volcanoes; nothing could be distinguished but a great mass pitted with white spots of human flesh, grey patches of bronze, and red spashes of blood. The terrible brutes ploughed black furrows as they passed through the midst of it.

The fiercest was ridden by a Numidian, crowned with a diadem of plumes. He hurled javelins with terrifying rapidity, uttering at intervals a long shrill whistle. And the great beasts, which were as docile as dogs, kept one eye upon him during the carnage.

Their circle slowly closed in; the enfeebled Barbarians offered no resistance, and the elephants were soon in the middle of the plain. There was not room enough for them, and they reared half up as they crowded together, and their tusks clashed against one another. Narr'Havas quietened them, and they wheeled round and trotted back to the hills.

Two syntagmata had taken refuge in a hollow on the right. They had thrown away their weapons, and were all kneeling with their faces toward the Punic tents, lifting up their arms and begging for mercy.

These were bound hand and foot, & when they had been stretched side by side on the ground, the elephants were brought back.

The breasts of the victims cracked like breaking boxes; at each step of the elephants two were crushed. The great feet sank into their bodies with a motion of the haunches which made the beasts seem to limp. They went on until they came to the end.

The surface of the plain was once more still, and the night fell. Hamilcar was already exulting at the sight of his vengeance, when suddenly he started.

He saw, and all saw, six hundred paces away to the left on a pap

of the hills, more Barbarians still! Four hundred of the stoutest
Mercenaries, Etruscans, Libyans and Spartans had scaled the heights
at the very first, and had there remained in uncertainty until this
moment. After the massacre of their companions they resolved to
cut their way through the Carthaginians, and now they descended
in serried columns, in a strangely menacing manner.

A herald was immediately despatched to them. The Suffete needed
soldiers, and admired their bravery so much that he would take
them unconditionally. They could even, added the Carthaginian
emissary, come a little nearer, to a place which he pointed out to
them, where they would find provisions.

The Barbarians ran thither and spent the night eating, and upon
this the Carthaginians broke into a murmur against the Suffete's
partiality for the Mercenaries.

Was he cowed by these outbursts of insatiable hatred, or was he
actuated by a refinement of treachery? The next day he came
himself, without a sword and bare-headed, but with an escort of
Clibanarii, and announced to the four hundred that, as he had too
many to feed, he did not intend to keep them. But since he needed
men, and did not know how to select the best, he bade them fight
one another to the death, promising to admit the victors into his
own bodyguard. This death, he said, was quite as good as another.
Then, moving his soldiers to one side (for the Punic standards hid
the sky line from the Mercenaries), he showed them the hundred
and ninety-two elephants of Narr'Havas drawn up in one straight
line, their trunks brandishing broad steel blades so that each looked
like a giant arm poising an axe above the head.

The Barbarians looked at one another in silence. It was not death
that made them turn pale, but the terrible constraint under which
they found themselves.

These men had lived together for so long that they had formed
deep friendships for one another. For most of them, the camp
stood for their country, and, because they lived without a family,
all their natural tenderness was centred upon some companion.
They would sleep side by side in the starlight under the same cloak.
In their endless wanderings through every sort of land, & through
murder and adventure, they had formed strange loves, obscene
alliances with all the seriousness of marriage. The stronger pro-

tected the younger in battle, helped him to cross chasms, sponged the sweat of fever from his brow, and stole food for him. And the other, a child picked up by the roadside and become a Mercenary, repaid this devotion by a thousand delicate attentions and married complaisances.

They exchanged necklaces and ear pendants, presents which they had made to one another in former days in hours of drunkenness after some great danger. All asked to die, and none would strike. Here and there a youth said to a man with a grey beard: 'No, no! You are the stronger! You will avenge us. Kill me!' And the man would reply: 'I have fewer years to live! Strike to the heart, and think no more of it!' Brothers gazed on each other with locked hands, and lover bade eternal farewell to lover, standing and weeping upon his shoulder.

They drew off their cuirasses to give easier entry to the sword points and this brought to light the scars of the heavy blows which they had received for Carthage: inscriptions, as it were, upon columns.

They formed up in four equal ranks, after the manner of gladiators, and engaged one another timidly at first. Some had bandaged their eyes, and the swords of these waved feebly in the air like a blind man's stick. The Carthaginians hooted at them and shouted that they were cowards; at last the Barbarians were roused, and the fighting became general, headlong and terrible.

Sometimes two men covered with blood would cease, and fall into each other's arms, and die kissing. Not one of them flinched; all hurled themselves upon the extended blades. They were worked to such a delirious frenzy that the Carthaginians, standing at a distance, became afraid.

At last they stopped, and sent forth a great rasping sound from their breasts. Their eyes showed through their long hair, which hung down as if it had been dipped in a purple bath. Several spun quickly round, like panthers wounded in the forehead. Others stood motionless, looking at the corpse at their feet; then they suddenly tore their faces with their nails, & took their swords in both hands and plunged them into their bellies.

There were still sixty left, and these asked for drink. The Carthaginians cried to them to throw away their swords; and when they had done so, water was brought to them.

While they were drinking, with their faces buried in the cups, sixty Carthaginians leaped upon them and slew them, stabbing them in the back with daggers.

Hamilcar had brought this about to gratify the instincts of his army and, by such treachery, to grapple them to him.

And so the war was over, or at least he believed it to be. Matho would not resist. In his impatience the Suffete ordered an immediate departure.

His scouts came to tell him that a convoy had been seen making towards the Lead Mountain; but Hamilcar did not concern himself for it. Once the Mercenaries were annihilated, the Nomads would give him no further trouble. The important thing was to take Tunis, and he advanced by forced marches upon it.

He sent Narr'Havas to Carthage with news of his victory; and the Numidian King, in the pride of his success, presented himself at Salambo's palace.

She received him in her gardens under a great sycamore tree, among cushions of yellow leather, and with Taanach beside her. Her face was covered with a white scarf which passed over her mouth and forehead, and allowed only her eyes to be seen. But her lips shone through the gauzy stuff as the gems on her fingers did; for Salambo kept her hands wrapped away, and did not make a gesture all the time they spoke.

Narr'Havas told her of the defeat of the Barbarians; & she thanked and blessed him for the service he had rendered her father. Then he began to tell of the whole campaign.

The doves in the palm trees about them cooed softly, & other birds fluttered in the plants: ring-necked pratincoles, Tartessus quails, and Punic guinea-fowl. The garden, which had been long uncultivated, was overgrown with greenery; colocynths reached up into the cassia trees, asclepias lay scattered over the rose fields, and every kind of vegetation laced into tangled bowers; and here and there the sun's rays slanted down and outlined the shadow of a leaf upon the ground, as in the woods. Domestic animals, now grown wild again, fled at the slightest noise. At times a gazelle passed, trailing scattered peacock feathers after its little black hoofs. The clamour of the distant city was lost in the waves' murmuring, the sky was pure blue, and not a sail was to be seen upon the sea.

Narr'Havas ceased speaking: Salambo looked at him without answering. He wore a flower-painted robe, fringed with gold at the hem; his braided hair was caught up at his ears by two arrows of silver; his right hand rested on a pike adorned with bands of amber and tufts of hair.

As she watched him she was wrapped about with a host of vague thoughts. This young man, with his gentle voice and woman's figure, charmed her eyes by the grace of his person, and seemed like an elder sister sent by the Baalim to protect her. The thought of Matho came to her, and she could not resist a desire to learn what had become of him.

Narr'Havas answered that the Carthaginians were advancing upon Tunis to take it. As he explained their chances of success & Matho's weakness, she seemed to exult in an extraordinary hope. Her lips trembled, her bosom heaved; and when he finally promised that he would himself kill Matho, she cried:

'Yes! Kill him! That needs must be!'

The Numidian answered that he ardently desired the man's death, since he himself would be Salambo's husband when the war was over.

She started, and bent her head.

Narr'Havas went on to compare his longings with flowers languishing for rain, with lost travellers waiting for the day. He told her, not for the first time, that she was more beautiful than the moon, more welcome than the morning breeze or than the face of a guest. He would bring for her from the country of the Blacks such things as there were not in Carthage; the apartments of their house should be sanded with gold dust.

Evening fell, and the air became filled with the odours of balm. For a long time they looked at each other in silence, and Salambo's eyes, far back in her long draperies, were like two stars in the rift of a cloud. Narr'Havas withdrew before sunset.

The Elders felt themselves rid of a great anxiety when he left the city. The people had received him with even more enthusiastic acclamation than on the first occasion, and if Hamilcar and the King of the Numidians triumphed unaided over the Mercenaries, there would be no holding them. To weaken Barca, therefore, they resolved to make the aged Hanno, whom they loved, share in the deliverance of Carthage.

Hanno proceeded at once toward the western provinces, to stage his revenge on the very places that had witnessed his shame. But the inhabitants and the Barbarians were dead or hidden or fled, and he vented his rage upon the country. He burned the ruins of the ruins, he left not a tree standing, nor a blade of grass. If he met with any children or infirm persons, he had them tortured; he gave the women to his soldiers to be violated before they were butchered. The most beautiful of these were thrown into his litter, for his atrocious disease had filled him with a hot, impetuous desire, which he gratified with all the fury of a desperate man.

Often, on the crests of the hills before him, black tents would be struck as if overturned by the wind, and wide discs with shining rims, which he knew for chariot wheels, were rolled along with a plaintive murmuring and gradually disappeared into the valleys. Those tribes which had abandoned the siege of Carthage were now wandering thus through the provinces, waiting for some opportunity, or for the Mercenaries to win a victory, before they returned. Whether from terror or famine, they all took the roads to their native lands at last, and vanished utterly.

Hamilcar did not grudge Hanno his successes; but he was in a hurry to end matters, and therefore ordered him to fall back upon Tunis. Hanno was under the walls of the town on the appointed day.

It had its population of aborigines, and twelve thousand Mercenaries for its defence, and all the Eaters of Unclean Things as well; for these, like Matho, stayed, as it were, riveted to the sky line of Carthage, upon whose lofty walls the people & the shalishim gazed from afar, dreaming of unlimited delights behind them. With such unison of hatred, resistance was quickly organised. They took wine skins and fashioned them into helmets, the palm trees in the gardens were cut down to make lances, and they dug cisterns; for provisions they caught great white fish, fed on dead bodies and filth, along the shores of the Lake. Their ramparts, kept in a state of ruin by the jealousy of Carthage, were so weak that they could have been pushed over by a man's shoulder. Matho stopped up the holes in them with the stones of the houses. It was the last effort; he hoped for nothing at all, and yet told himself that fortune was fickle.

As the Carthaginians drew near, they saw a man on the rampart who overtopped the battlements from his belt upwards. The arrows that flew about him seemed to frighten him no more than a flight of swallows and, miraculously, not one touched him.

Hamilcar pitched his camp on the southern side. Narr'Havas, to his right, occupied the plain of Rhades. And Hanno held the shore of the Lake. The three generals were to maintain their respective positions, so that they might attack the walls together.

Hamilcar wished first to show the Mercenaries that he could punish them like slaves. He had the ten envoys crucified side by side on a hillock facing the town.

At this sight, the besieged abandoned their rampart.

Matho had told himself that, if he could pass between the walls and Narr'Havas's tents so quickly that the Numidians had no time to come forth, he could fall upon the rear of the Carthaginian infantry, who would thus be caught between his division and those inside the town. He dashed out with his veterans.

Narr'Havas saw him, and crossed the lake shore to warn Hanno to send men to Hamilcar's assistance. Did he think that Barca was not strong enough to resist the Mercenaries? Was this treachery, or merely folly? No one could ever know.

Hanno, in his desire to humiliate his rival, did not hesitate. He shouted an order for the trumpets to be sounded, and his whole army rushed upon the Barbarians. The latter turned about against the Carthaginians, and hurled them over and crushed them under their feet. Driving them back in this way, they reached the tent of Hanno, who was now surrounded by thirty Carthaginians, the most illustrious of the Elders.

He appeared stupefied by their audacity, and called for his captains. The Barbarians shook their fists in his face and shouted abuse. They jostled one another, and those who had their hands on him found much difficulty to keep their hold. Meanwhile he tried to whisper in their ears:'I will give you anything you want! I am rich! Save me!'

They dragged him away and, heavy as he was, his feet did not touch the ground. The Elders had already been carried off, and his terror redoubled.

'You have beaten me! I am your prisoner! I will ransom myself! Listen to me, my friends!'

And, as he was borne along by all those shoulders pressed against his sides, he went on saying:

'What are you going to do with me? What do you want? I am not resisting; you can see that! I was always a generous fellow!'

A gigantic cross stood at the gate, and the Barbarians yelled: 'Here! Here!'

But he raised his voice still more loudly, and in the names of their gods called upon them to lead him to the shalishim, because he had something to confide to him upon which their safety depended.

They paused, some declaring that it would be prudent to summon Matho, and the latter was sent for.

Hanno sank down on the grass, and saw around him still other crosses, as if the torture by which he was about to perish had been multiplied beforehand. He made an effort to convince himself that he was deceived, that there was only one; and even to believe that there was none at all. At last he was lifted up.

'Speak!' said Matho.

He offered to deliver Hamilcar into his hands; they would enter Carthage and both reign as kings.

Thinking this a mere ruse to gain time, Matho signed to the others to make haste, and himself withdrew.

The Barbarian was mistaken. Hanno was in one of those desperate predicaments when a man does not stop to consider. Also he so detested Hamilcar that he would have sacrificed him and all his soldiers for the slenderest hope of safety.

On the ground at the foot of the thirty crosses languished the Elders, with ropes already passed beneath their armpits. So the aged Suffete understood that he must die, and wept.

They tore off what clothes were still left to him, and the horror of his person was revealed. This unspeakable mass of flesh was covered with ulcers, and his toe-nails were buried under the fat of his legs. A sort of greenish strips hung from his fingers. The tears trickling between the tubercles on his cheeks gave him an air of appalling sadness, for they seemed to take up more room than upon another face. His royal fillet, which was half unfastened, trailed with his white hair in the dust.

Thinking they had no ropes strong enough to hoist him up to the top of the cross, they nailed him upon it, after the Punic fashion, before it was erected. But his agony stirred his pride to life, and he began to load them with abuse. He foamed and twisted like a sea-monster that is slaughtered on the shore; he predicted that they would come to a still more horrible end, and that he would be avenged.

And so he was. On the other side of the town, whence jets of flame and columns of smoke were now escaping, the envoys of the Mercenaries were in their last agony.

Some of them, who had at first fainted, had now revived in the freshness of the wind; but their chins still hung upon their breasts, and their bodies drooped a little forward, although their arms were nailed above their heads. From their heels and hands the blood was falling in great drops, slowly, as ripe fruit falls from the branches of a tree: and Carthage, the gulf, the mountains, and the plains seemed to them to be spinning like a gigantic wheel. Sometimes a cloud of dust rose from the ground and enveloped them in its eddies; they burned with intolerable thirst, and their tongues were curled up in their mouths. They knew an icy sweat flowing over them with their parting souls.

Yet, at an infinite depth below them, they were still aware of streets, and marching soldiers, and the swinging of swords; the tumult of battle came to them dimly, like the noise of the sea to a shipwrecked man dying in a ship's rigging. The Italiotes, being hardier than the rest, were still shrieking. The Lacedaemonians were silent, with closed eyes. Zarxas, who had been once so vigorous, hung like a broken rush. The Ethiopian beside him had his head thrown back over the arm of the cross. Autharitus stayed motionless, rolling his eyes, and his great head of hair, caught in a cleft of the wood, stood straight up from his forehead. His death rattle was more like a roar of anger. As for Spendius, a strange courage had come to him; he despised life now in his certainty of an almost immediate and an eternal emancipation; he waited death with indifference.

They sometimes started awake, in their swooning, at the brushing of feathers across their lips. Great wings made swaying shadows around them, and croakings sounded in the air. As the cross of Spendius was the highest, it was upon his that the first vulture alighted. Then he turned his face toward Autharitus, and said to him slowly, with an indescribable smile:

'Do you remember the lions on the road to Sicca?'

'They were our brothers!' answered the Gaul in dying.

The Suffete, meanwhile, had broken through the walls of Tunis and reached the citadel. The smoke was suddenly dispersed by a gust of wind, discovering the horizon as far as the walls of Carthage; he even thought that he could distinguish folk watching on the platform of Eshmun. Then, turning his eyes, he saw thirty immense crosses to his left on the shore of the lake.

To make them the more terrible, the Barbarians had built them of tent poles fastened end to end, so that the thirty corpses of the Elders showed high in the sky. They had what seemed to be white butterflies on their breasts; but these were the feathers of arrows which had been shot at them from below.

At the top of the highest cross glittered a broad fillet of gold; it hung down over the shoulder, since there was no arm on that side, & Hamilcar had some difficulty in recognising Hanno. His spongy bones had given under the iron nails, pieces of his limbs had dropped away, and nothing was left on the cross but a shapeless remains, like the fragments of beasts hung at a huntsman's door.

The Suffete could not have known anything of this; for the town in front of him masked all that was beyond and behind it; and not one of the captains who had been sent to the generals had come back. Fugitives arrived with the tale of the rout, and the Punic army halted. This catastrophe, falling in the midst of their victory, rather stupefied them, and they no longer heeded Hamilcar's commands.

Matho took advantage of this situation to continue his ravages among the Numidians.

He had turned round at them, after having overthrown Hanno's camp. The elephants came out against him; but the Mercenaries deployed over the plain, flourishing lighted firebrands which they had snatched from the walls. And the great beasts, in their fright, ran headlong into the gulf, where they killed one another in their struggles, and were weighed down by their cuirasses and drowned. Then Narr'Havas had launched his cavalry. But Matho's men threw themselves face downwards upon the ground, and, when the horses were within three paces of them, sprang up under their bellies and ripped them open with daggers. Half the Numidians had already perished when Barca advanced.

The exhausted Mercenaries could not hold out against his troops. They retired in good order to the mountain of the Hot Springs, whither the Suffete was prudent enough not to pursue them. He made his way instead to the mouths of the Makar.

Tunis was in his hands; but it was nothing but a heap of smoking rubbish. The ruins fell through the breaches in the walls into the middle of the plain, and in the background, between the shores of the gulf, the bodies of the elephants drifted before the wind and bumped into one another: an archipelago of black rocks floating on the sea.

In order to sustain the war, Narr'Havas had drained his forests of these animals, taking young and old, and male and female. And the military force of his kingdom could not recover from this loss. The people, who had seen the beasts perish from a distance, were in despair. Folk lamented in the streets, calling them by their names, as if they had been dead friends:

'Ah, Invincible! Victory! Ah, Thunderer! Oh, Swallow!'

On the first day folk spoke even more of them than of their dead citizens.

On the next day the Mercenaries' tents were seen on the mountain of the Hot Springs. Then so deep was their despair that many, and especially women, flung themselves headlong from the top of the Acropolis.

Hamilcar's intentions were not known. He lived alone in his tent with no one near him save a young boy, and no one ever ate with them, not even Narr'Havas. To this man he paid unusual attention since Hanno's defeat; but the king of the Numidians had too great an interest in becoming his son to harbour any suspicion against him.

A careful plan lay behind this inaction. By all kinds of ruses Hamilcar won over the village chiefs, and the Mercenaries were hunted, and driven back and hemmed in like wild beasts. No sooner had they entered a wood than the trees burst into flame about them.

When they drank from a spring, it was poisoned. If they hid in a cave to sleep, this was walled up on them. The tribes which had hitherto protected them, and been their old allies, now pursued them. And they often recognised Carthaginian arms among these bands.

The faces of many were eaten up with a red tetter, & they thought they had contracted this through touching Hanno. Others imagined that it had come because they had eaten Salambo's fishes; far from repenting, they dreamed of more abominable sacrilege still, that they might heap even greater humiliation upon the Punic Gods. They would have liked to blot them out utterly.

For three months they dragged along the eastern coast in this fashion, and then behind the mountain of Sellum, and as far as the first sands of the desert, seeking some place of refuge, no matter where. Utica and Hippo-Zaritus alone had not betrayed them; but Hamilcar now surrounded these two towns. Then they turned northwards at haphazard, without even knowing the ways; for, by dint of suffering, their minds were unbalanced.

They no longer felt aught but an ever increasing sense of exasperation; one day they found themselves back again in the gorges of Cobus, once more before Carthage!

Then followed innumerable engagements in which Fortune favoured neither side; and both were so wearied that they longed for a great battle instead of all these skirmishes, provided it were really decisive.

Matho wished to carry this proposal in person to the Suffete, but one of his Libyans devoted himself to the mission. All were convinced, as they saw him depart, that he would not come back.

He returned the same evening.

Hamilcar accepted their challenge. They would meet on the following day at sunrise, in the plain of Rhades.

The Mercenaries asked whether he had not said anything else, and the Libyan added:

'As I remained in his presence, he asked me for what I waited. "To be killed!" I answered, and then he said: "No! Begone! That will be for to-morrow, with the rest."'

Such generosity astonished the Barbarians: some were terrified by it, and Matho regretted that the envoy had not been killed.

He still had three thousand Africans, twelve hundred Greeks, fifteen hundred Campanians, two hundred Iberians, four hundred Etruscans, five hundred Samnites, forty Gauls, and a troop of Naffur, nomad bandits met with in the date region: in all, seven thousand two hundred and nineteen soldiers; not one complete syntagma. They had stopped up the holes in their cuirasses with the shoulder blades of animals, & had replaced their bronze buskins with ragged sandals. Their garments were weighted with copper or steel plates; their coats of mail hung in tatters about them, and scars showed like purple cords through the hair on their arms and faces.

The wrath of their dead companions visited their souls & redoubled their vigour; they felt, in a confused fashion, that they were the ministers of a god whose temple was in the hearts of all the oppressed, and that they were, so to speak, the high priests of universal vengeance! Also the misery of an ineffable injustice filled them with a rage which was but the more enflamed by the sight of Carthage on the horizon. They swore to fight for one another to the death.

They killed the beasts of burden and ate as much as they could of them, so as to gain strength; and then they slept. Some of them prayed, turning towards different stars.

The Carthaginians were first in the plain. They had rubbed the surface of their shields with oil to make the arrows glance off from them; the foot soldiers, who usually wore their hair long, had taken the precaution of cutting it short over the forehead. Hamilcar had ordered all food bowls to be turned upside down from the fifth hour, knowing the disadvantage of fighting on a too full stomach. His army amounted to fourteen thousand men, about double the number of the Barbarians. Yet he had never felt so much anxiety. If he were beaten, it would mean the annihilation of the Republic, and he himself would perish on the cross. If he triumphed, he could reach Italy by way of the Pyrenees, the Gauls, and the Alps, and the empire of the Barcas would become eternal. Twenty times during the night he rose to make a personal inspection of all things, down to the most minute detail. As for the Carthaginians, they were exacerbated by their long drawn terror.

Narr'Havas suspected the loyalty of his Numidians, and also considered it possible that the Barbarians might beat them. A strange weakness had come upon him, and every moment he drank great cups of water.

But a man whom he did not know opened his tent and laid on the ground a crown of rock-salt, adorned with hieratic designs in sulphur and lozenges of mother-of-pearl. Such a marriage crown was sometimes sent to a betrothed husband as a proof of love, a sort of invitation.

Yet Hamilcar's daughter had no affection for Narr'Havas.

She was intolerably troubled by the memory of Matho, & it seemed to her that the death of this man might rid her of her thoughts, as people cure themselves of the bite of a viper by crushing it against the wound. The king of the Numidians was dependent upon her bidding. He was impatient for the wedding, and, as that was to follow the victory, Salambo made him this present to stimulate his courage. His anxieties thereupon disappeared, & he thought only of the happiness of possessing so fair a woman.

The same vision had assailed Matho; but he cast it off immediately. And the love which he thus thrust back within himself was poured out upon his companions in arms. He cherished them as if they were parts of his own person and of his hatred: his spirit felt the nobler for it, and his arm the stronger. He had a clear picture of all that he must do. If a sigh escaped him at times, it was because he was thinking of Spendius.

He drew up the Barbarians in six equal ranks. He posted the Etruscans in the centre and linked them together with a bronze chain; the archers were kept in the rear, and on the wings he distributed the Naffur, who were mounted on short-haired camels, & covered with ostrich plumes.

The Suffete arranged the Carthaginians in similar formation. He placed the Clibanarii outside the infantry, next to the velites, and the Numidians beyond these. When morning came, the two armies stood thus in line face to face, and looked at one another from a distance with great wild eyes. There was at first some hesitation; but at last both armies moved.

The Barbarians came on slowly, so as not to get out of breath, and stamped upon the ground: the Punic centre bellied out in a convex curve. Then came a stupendous shock, like the crash of two fleets in collision. The first rank of the Barbarians had swiftly opened out, and the marksmen hidden behind them now discharged their bullets and arrows and javelins. Meanwhile the Carthaginian curve slowly flattened, became quite straight, and then bent inwards; the two sections of the velites converged in unison, like the arms of a compass closing. The Barbarians, who were furiously attacking the phalanx, entered the gap between these two lines, and were in imminent danger. But Matho checked them and, while the Carthaginian wings continued to advance, extended the three inner ranks of his line so that they covered his flanks, and his army had trebled the length of its frontage.

But the Barbarians at the two ends of this line were the weakest, especially those on the left, who had emptied their quivers. Therefore the troop of velites, which had at last made contact with them, slaughtered them freely.

Matho bade them fall back. On his right were certain Campanians armed with axes, and these he hurled against the Carthaginian left. His centre was already attacking, and those on the other wing, who were out of immediate danger, kept the velites at a distance.

Then Hamilcar divided his horsemen into squadrons, which he alternated with hoplites, and sent them against the Mercenaries.

These conical masses presented a front of horse, and their broader sides were packed with bristling lances. It was impossible for the Barbarians to stand against them, for only the Greek foot-soldiers had brazen armour, and all the rest had but cutlasses fixed on poles, scythes taken from the farms, or swords improvised from the fellies of wheels. Such blades were too soft, and a blow could bend them. While they were straightening them under their heels, the Carthaginians massacred them right and left at leisure.

But the Etruscans, riveted in their chain, did not give back; those who were killed were prevented from falling, and formed a barrier with their corpses; the great bronze line expanded and contracted, supple as a serpent and unshakable as a wall. The Barbarians would shelter behind it to re-form their ranks and recover their breath for a while, and then make forward again with their splintered weapons in their hands.

Many were already weaponless, and these leaped upon the Carthaginians, biting their faces like dogs. The Gauls stripped themselves of the 'sagum' in their pride, displaying their splendid white bodies from afar, & making their wounds gape to terrify the enemy. The voice of the crier of orders was heard no longer in the Punic syntagmata; their signals were passed by standards raised above the dust. Every man of them was swept off his feet in the seething of the mass around him.

Hamilcar commanded the Numidians to advance: but the Naffur rushed to meet them.

These men were clad in vast black robes, wore a tuft of hair on the top of their heads, and carried a shield of rhinoceros hide. They swung a blade with no handle at a rope's end; and their camels, which bristled all over with feathers, uttered long, hoarse chuckling sounds. Their blades fell precisely on the right spot, and then rose again with a sharp pull, carrying off a limb. Their enraged beasts galloped through the syntagmata, and some, whose legs were broken, went hopping like wounded ostriches.

The entire Punic infantry turned in a concerted attack upon the Barbarians, and broke through them. Their maniples wheeled at intervals from one another. The brighter Carthaginian armour formed rings of gold about the Mercenaries; there was a swirling at their centre, and the sun, striking down upon them, tipped their sword-points with flickering white fire. There were whole files of Clibanarii lying stretched upon the plain; some of the Mercenaries tore off the armour from these and clothed themselves in it, and then returned to the fray. The Carthaginians were frequently deceived by this and found themselves cut off among them. Then they would stand stupidly still, or else surge backwards in retreat. The triumphant shouting from afar seemed to drive them along like wrecks in a storm. Hamilcar was growing desperate; all his hopes were foundering upon Matho's genius and the indomitable courage of the Mercenaries!

Suddenly a great noise of drums was heard from the horizon. A crowd of old men, sick persons, fifteen-year-old children, and even women, had been unable to endure their suspense any longer, and had therefore set out from Carthage. To have the protection of something formidable, they had taken from Hamilcar's palace the only elephant the Republic now possessed, the one whose trunk had been cut off.

It seemed to the Carthaginians that their Country had forsaken her walls to come and bid them die for her. They were seized with a double fury, & the Numidians fired the rest with their enthusiasm.

The Barbarians had set themselves with their backs to a hillock in the middle of the plain. They had no chance of victory, or even of survival; but here were the best of them, the bravest and the strongest.

The people of Carthage began to throw spits, larding-pins and hammers over the heads of the Numidians, and these men, who had struck fear into the hearts of consuls, now died under the sticks of women. The Punic populace was killing out the Mercenaries.

The Barbarians had taken refuge on the top of the hill. Their circle closed up after every fresh breach in it; twice they charged down, to be driven back violently. The disorderly mob of the Carthaginians stretched out their arms, thrusting their pikes between their companions' legs, and probing at random before them. They slipped in the blood, and the steep slope of the ground sent their dead bodies rolling to the bottom: the elephant, as it tried to climb the hill, was up to its belly in corpses. It seemed to sprawl over them with delight, and the broad end of its mutilated trunk rose from time to time like an enormous leech.

There was a general pause. The Carthaginians ground their teeth as they gazed up at the hill, for the Barbarians were still on their feet there.

At last they made a sudden charge, and the fight began again. The Mercenaries often let them come near, shouting to them that they wished to surrender, and then, with a terrifying sneer, would kill themselves at a single blow. As the dead fell, the rest mounted upon them to defend themselves. It was like a slowly rising pyramid.

Soon there were only fifty, then only twenty, only three, and, finally, only two: a Samnite armed with an axe, and Matho who still had his sword.

The Samnite crouched upon his hams and swept his axe to right and left, warning Matho of the blows that were aimed at him: 'This way, Master! Over there! Stoop down!'

Matho had lost his shoulder-pieces, his helmet, and his cuirass; he was completely naked, and paler than the dead. His hair was perfectly ordered, and two patches of foam stood at the corners of his mouth. His quick sword made an aureole about him. It was broken near the guard by a stone, the Samnite died, & the flood of Carthaginians closed in upon Matho and touched him. Then he raised his empty arms towards heaven, closed his eyes, and, opening out his hands like a man throwing himself from the top of a cliff into the sea, hurled himself upon the pikes.

They scattered before him. Again and again he ran at the Carthaginians: but they always drew back and turned their weapons aside from him.

His foot struck against a sword, and he tried to grasp it. Then he felt himself snared at the wrists and knees, and fell.

Narr'Havas had been following him for some time, step by step, with one of those great nets used for trapping wild beasts. Taking advantage of the moment when he stooped down, he had cast it over him.

He was bound upon the elephant with his four limbs in a cross, and all who were not wounded escorted him in a great tumultuous rush towards Carthage.

The news of the victory had, in some inexplicable way, reached the city at the third hour of the night. The clepsydra of Khamon had just marked the fifth hour as they arrived at Malqua. Then Matho opened his eyes. There were so many lights in the houses that the whole city seemed to be on fire.

He was dimly aware of a great clamour; lying upon his back, he looked at the stars.

A door closed, and he was plunged in darkness.

Next day, at the same hour, died the last of the men in the Pass of the Hatchet.

On the day on which their companions had set forth, some Zuaeces who were returning home had tumbled the rocks down for them, and for some time had provided them with food.

The Barbarians were always expecting Matho, & through dejection or languor, and the obstinacy of sick men who hate to be moved, refused to leave the mountain. At last the food was exhausted, and the Zuaeces went away. It was known that the survivors scarcely numbered more than thirteen hundred men, and there was no need for soldiers to put an end to them.

Wild beasts, and especially lions, had multiplied during the three years of the war. Narr'Havas had beaten the bushes over a wide area and, after tethering goats at intervals to mark their way, had closed in upon the brutes and driven them towards the Pass of the Hatchet. They were all living in that place when the man arrived who had been sent by the Elders to learn what was left of the Barbarians.

Lions and dead bodies lay over the whole tract of the plain, and with the dead were inextricably mingled clothing and pieces of armour. Nearly all had the face or an arm missing, though a few appeared to be still intact. Some had completely dried up, and the skulls in their helmets were crumbled to powder. Fleshless feet stuck forth from the greaves; some of the skeletons still wore their cloaks; sun-whitened bones made shining patterns on the sand.

The lions lay with their breasts against the ground and both paws stretched out, blinking in the glare which beat back intensified from the white rocks. Some sat on their hind quarters and stared before them, and others slept, rolled in a ball and half hidden by their great manes. They all looked well fed, weary & listless. They were as still as the mountain, or as the dead. Night fell, the western sky was streaked with broad red bands.

In one of those heaps, which formed irregular bosses upon the plain, arose something that was vaguer than a ghost. Then one of the lions started to move, his monstrous form cutting a black shadow on the purple sky; when he was quite close to the man, he felled him with a blow of his paw.

Then, stretching himself flat upon his victim, he slowly drew out the entrails with his teeth.

Afterwards he opened his jaws, and for whole minutes sent forth a roar which was repeated by the mountain echoes, until it was finally lost in the waste place.

Some small gravel rolled from above, and there came a pattering of rapid feet. From the direction of the portcullis and the gorge came pointed muzzles and straight ears, and bright yellow eyes. The jackals were coming to eat what was left.

The Carthaginian, after leaning over the top of the precipice to look at these things, returned home.

MATHO

THERE WAS JOY IN CARTHAGE, A DEEP, UNIVERSAL, unbridled and frantic joy. The breaches of the ruins had been stopped, the statues of the gods repainted; the streets were strewn with myrtle, incense smoked at the street corners, and the crowds on the terraces looked like masses of flowers blossoming in air, because of the many colours of their garments.

The cries of the carriers watering the pavement rose above the continuous yelping of voices; Hamilcar's slaves were distributing roasted barley & pieces of raw meat in his name; people greeted one another and embraced with tears; the Tyrian towns were taken, the Nomads dispersed, & all the Barbarians annihilated. The Acropolis was hidden under coloured canopies; the beaks of the triremes, drawn up outside the mole, shone like a bank of diamonds; everywhere was a feeling of restored order, of the beginning of a new life, of a vast and wide-spread happiness. It was the day of Salambo's marriage to the king of the Numidians.

On the terrace of the temple of Khamon were three long tables laden with gigantic gold plate, at which the Priests, the Elders, and the Rich were going to sit; and there was a fourth and higher one for Hamilcar, Narr'Havas, and for her: since Salambo had saved her country by the recovery of the zaimph, the people made her wedding an occasion of national rejoicing, and were waiting in the Square below for her to appear.

Another and a keener desire whetted their impatience: Matho's death had been promised them for this ceremony.

It had at first been proposed to flay him alive, to pour molten lead into his bowels, to starve him to death; he should be tied to a tree, and there should be an ape behind him to beat him on the head with a stone; he had offended Tanit, and Tanit's baboons should avenge her. Others were of the opinion that he should be led about on a dromedary after linen wicks, steeped in oil, had been inserted in various parts of his body; they delighted to picture the great animal wandering through the streets, with this man upon it writhing under the flames, like a candelabrum blown in the wind.

But which of the citizens should be charged with his torture, and why should the rest have their desires frustrated? They would have liked some kind of death in which the whole city could take part, and that every hand, every weapon, everything Carthaginian at all to the very paving-stones of the streets and the waves of the gulf, should share in the rending, the crushing & the annihilating of him. Therefore the Elders decided that he should go from his prison to the Square of Khamon without any escort and with his arms bound behind his back: so that he might live the longer, it was forbidden to strike him to the heart; or to put out his eyes, so that he might see his torture to the end; or to hurl anything against his person, or to lay more than three fingers upon him at a time.

Although he was not to appear until the end of the day, they sometimes fancied they could see him, & the crowd would surge toward the Acropolis, leaving the streets empty, and then return with much murmuring. Some had stood in the same place since the evening before, and these would call to one another from a distance and show their nails, which they had allowed to grow long so as to bury them the deeper in his flesh. Others walked restlessly about, & some were as pale as if they had been waiting their own execution.

Suddenly, over the people's heads, tall feather fans could be seen behind the Mappales. It was Salambo leaving her palace; and there was a general sigh of relief.

But the procession was long in coming: it moved only step by step. First the priests of the Pataec Gods filed past, then those of Eshmun, those of Melkarth, and all the other colleges in succession, with the same insignia and in the same order as had been observed at the time of the sacrifice. The priests of Moloch passed with lowered heads, and the crowds shrank back from them in a kind of remorse. But the priests of Rabbet advanced with a proud step, holding lyres in their hands: the priestesses followed in transparent robes of yellow or black, uttering cries like birds and writhing like vipers; or else they whirled round to flute music in imitation of the dance of the stars, & their light vestments wafted puffs of soft odour through the streets. Among these women, and sharing in their applause, were the Kedeshim, with their painted eyelids, who symbolised the hermaphroditism of the Divinity; they resembled the priestesses in spite of their flat breasts and narrower hips, for they were perfumed and dressed like them. The female principle dominated and permeated all things on this day; a mystic lasciviousness lay upon the heavy air; the torches were already lighted in the depth of the sacred woods; there was to be a great prostitution there during the night; three vessels had brought courtesans from Sicily, and others had come from the desert.

As the colleges arrived they ranged themselves in the courts of the temples, on the outer galleries, & along the double stairways which rose against the walls and converged at the top. Rows of white robes showed between the colonnades, and the buildings were peopled with human statues, motionless as stone.

Next came the masters of the treasury, the governors of provinces, and all the Rich. A vast tumult rose below. From the neighbouring streets the crowd kept pouring forth, and the temple servants drove them back with staves. Salambo appeared, surrounded by the Elders in their golden crowns, in a litter surmounted by a purple canopy.

At this a tremendous shouting arose; the cymbals and clappers crashed more loudly, the drums thundered, and the great purple canopy disappeared between the two pylons.

It came into sight again on the first landing. Under it Salambo was walking slowly; she crossed the terrace to take her seat at the back on a kind of throne cut out of a tortoise-shell. An ivory stool with three steps was placed under her feet; two negro children knelt on the edge of the first step, and sometimes she would rest both her arms, which were too heavily laden with bracelets, upon their heads.

From her ankles to her hips she was enveloped in a network of tiny links in imitation of the scales of a fish, and these shone like mother-of-pearl; her waist was clasped in a blue zone, which let her breasts be seen through crescent slashes; carbuncle pendants hid their nipples. She had a headdress of peacocks' feathers starred with gems, & a wide cloak, as white as snow, fell down behind her. With her elbows close to her sides, her knees pressed together, and circles of diamonds on the higher part of her arms, she sat straight upright in a hieratic attitude.

Her father and her husband sat on two lower seats. Narr'Havas was dressed in a yellow simar, and wore his crown of rock-salt, from which escaped two tresses of hair twisted like the horns of Ammon; Hamilcar sat in a violet tunic brocaded with golden vine leaves, and had a battle-sword by his side.

In the space enclosed by the tables the python of the temple of Eshmun, with its tail in its mouth, lay upon the ground in pools of rose-pink oil, making a great black circle from the midst of which mounted a copper column supporting a crystal egg. Rays flashed from every part of it, as the sun shone down upon it.

Behind Salambo were ranged the priests of Tanit in linen robes; on her right the Elders, in their tiaras, made a great line of gold, and on the other side the Rich, with their emerald sceptres, a great line of green; right at the back stood the priests of Moloch, forming a wall of purple with their cloaks. The other colleges occupied the lower terraces.

The crowd overflowed the streets, climbed up to the house-tops, and stretched in long rows to the summit of the Acropolis. Having thus the people at her feet, the firmament above her head, & about her the immensity of the sea and the gulf, the mountains and the distant provinces, Salambo became one with Tanit in her splendour, and seemed the very Spirit of Carthage, its embodied soul.

The feast was to last all night, & lamps with several branches were planted like trees on the painted woollen cloths which covered the low tables. Great amber flagons, blue glass amphoras, tortoise-shell spoons, and little round loaves were crowded between the double row of pearl-bordered plates; clusters of grapes in their leaves had been twined about ivory vine-stocks in the manner of the thyrsus;

blocks of snow were melting on ebony salvers; and lemons, pomegranates, gourds, and water-melons were piled in little hills under
the tall argentry; boars with wide open mouths wallowed in spice
dust; hares, still with their fur on them, seemed to bound among
the flowers; there were shells filled with forcemeat, the pastry was
made in symbolic shapes, and when the dish-covers were removed,
doves flew from under them.

Meanwhile the slaves, with tucked-up tunics, went about on tiptoe;
from time to time a hymn sounded upon the lyres, or a chorus of
voices rose. The hum of the people, incessant as the noise of the sea,
floated vaguely about the feast, soothing it like some vaster harmony. Some recalled the banquet of the Mercenaries. The people
gave themselves up to dreams of happiness. The sun began to sink,
and the crescent moon was rising in another quarter of the sky.

But Salambo turned her head, as if someone had called her; and the
people, who were watching her, followed the direction of her eyes.

At the top of the Acropolis the door of the dungeon hewn in
the rock at the base of the temple had just opened; and on the
threshold of this black hole a man was standing.

He came out crouching and doubled, with the frightened air of a
wild beast that is suddenly set free.

The light dazzled him, and he stood still for a while. Each one had
recognised him, and held his breath.

They regarded the body of this victim as something peculiarly their
own, and imbued with an almost religious splendour. They craned
forward to see him; especially the women, who burned to gaze upon
the man who had caused the death of their husbands and children;
from the bottom of their souls sprang up, in spite of themselves, an
infamous curiosity, a desire to know him utterly, a longing mingled
with remorse, which turned to an aggravation of hatred.

At last he came forward, & the spell of numb surprise was broken.
Many arms were raised, and he was hidden from sight.

The stairway of the Acropolis had sixty steps. He descended them
as if he had been rolled down in a torrent from the top of a mountain; he was seen to give three leaps, and then he alighted at the
bottom on his feet.

His shoulders were bleeding, his chest heaved with great tearing
gasps; and he made such efforts to burst his bonds that his arms,

crossed upon his naked loins, swelled like the coils of a serpent.

Several streets led off from the spot where he stood. In each of them a triple row of bronze chains, fastened to the navels of the Pataec Gods, extended in parallel lines from one end to the other; the people were packed against the houses, and some of the Elders' slaves walked up and down between them, brandishing whips.

One of the latter drove him forward with a great blow; and Matho began to move.

They thrust their arms over the chains, shouting out that he had been left too wide a road; and as he passed along, he was felt and scratched and rent by all those fingers. When he reached the end of one street, another lay before him; several times he flung himself to one side and tried to bite them, but they scattered swiftly, the chains held him back, and the crowd burst out laughing.

A child tore his ear, and a young girl, who had the point of a spindle hidden in her sleeve, split his cheek. They tore out handfuls of hair from him, and strips of flesh; some had sponges soaked in filth on the end of sticks, & rammed these into his face. A stream of blood spurted from the right side of his neck, and at that frenzy was loose. This last Barbarian represented the whole of the Barbarians, the entire army; they were avenging themselves on him for their disasters, their terrors, and their shame. The rage of the mob was fed by its gratification; the over-strained chains bellied out and were on the point of snapping; the people did not feel the slaves strike at them to drive them back; some clung to the projections of the houses, and every opening in the walls was full of heads; they shrieked at him the hurts they could not do him.

Atrocious, filthy abuse mingled with ironical encouragement and with imprecations; as if his present torture were not enough for them, they foretold others still more terrible for his eternity.

This vast baying went on & on with a stupid monotony throughout Carthage. Frequently some single syllable, one hoarse, deep and frantic sound, would be repeated for several minutes by the entire people. The walls would vibrate with it from top to bottom, and the two sides of the street would seem to Matho to be coming against him and lifting him off the ground, like two huge arms that choked him in the air.

Yet he remembered that he had once before experienced something not unlike this. The same crowd was upon the terraces, with the same looks and the same fury; but then he had walked free, and all had scattered, for a god protected him. This memory, growing slowly clearer, brought a crushing sadness upon him. Shadows passed before his eyes; the city swam in his head, his blood poured from a wound in his hip, and he felt that he was dying. His legs gave under him, and he sank quite gently upon the pavement.

Someone fetched from the peristyle of the temple of Melkarth the bar of a tripod heated red hot in the coals, and, sliding it under the first chain, pressed it against his wound. The flesh was seen to smoke; the hooting of the people drowned his cries; and he was on his feet again.

Six more paces, and he fell a third and again a fourth time; but some new torture always goaded him up. They squirted little drops of boiling oil at him through tubes; they strewed broken glass under his feet; still he walked on. At the corner of the street of Satheb he leaned his back against the wall under the pent-house of a shop, and went no further.

The slaves of the Council struck him with whips of hippopotamus hide, so furiously and long that the fringes of their tunics were drenched in sweat. Matho seemed insensible: then suddenly he started up and began to run at random, making a blubbering noise with his lips like one who shivers under intense cold. He passed from the Street of Budes, and the Street of Soepo, and crossed the Herb Market and reached the Square of Khamon.

He belonged to the priests now; the slaves had dispersed the crowd and there was more room. Matho gazed round him, and his eyes fell upon Salambo.

She had risen at the first step he took; then, as he approached nearer, she had advanced involuntarily and by degrees to the edge of the terrace; soon every external was blotted out, & she saw only Matho. A silence had fallen upon her soul, one of those gulfs wherein the whole world vanishes under the pressure of a single thought, of a single memory, a look. This man allured her as he walked towards her. Nothing but his eyes retained a semblance of humanity. He was just a tall mass of red; his broken bonds hung down his thighs, but were indistinguishable from the tendons of his wrists, for these were quite bare of flesh. His mouth remained wide open & from his eye-sockets darted two flames which seemed to mount to his hair: and still the wretch walked on!

He reached the foot of the terrace. Salambo was leaning over the balustrade; those terrible eyes fixed themselves upon her, and there rose within her a knowledge of all he had suffered for her sake. Although he was in his death agony, she could once more see him kneeling in his tent, clasping his arms about her waist, stammering gentle words. She thirsted to feel and hear these things again, and was on the point of screaming aloud. Matho fell backward, and moved no more.

Salambo was borne back swooning to her throne by the priests who flocked about her. They congratulated her, saying that this was her work. All clapped their hands and stamped their feet, bawling her name.

A man sprang upon the corpse. Although he had no beard, he wore the cloak of a priest of Moloch on his shoulder, and in his belt that kind of knife which was used for cutting up the sacred meat and had a golden spattle at the end of the handle. He cleft Matho's breast with a single blow, snatched out his heart and laid it upon the spoon. Shahabarim raised his arms and offered it to the Sun.

The sun was sinking behind the sea; & its rays fell like long arrows upon the red heart. It dipped slowly into the waters as the heart's pulsation died away, and at the last throb it disappeared.

Then, from the gulf to the lagoon, and from the isthmus to the pharos, from all the streets, from all the houses, and from all the temples, rose a single shout. Sometimes it checked, only to break forth again; and the buildings shook with it. Carthage was convulsed in a spasm of Titanic joy and boundless hope.

Narr'Havas, drunken with pride, passed his left arm about Salambo's waist in token of possession, &, taking a gold cup in his right hand, drank to the Spirit of Carthage.

Salambo rose like her husband, with a cup in her hand, to drink also. She fell back with her head lying over the board of the throne, pale and stiff and with parted lips, and her loosened hair hung down upon the ground.

So died Hamilcar's daughter because she had touched the mantle of Tanit.